The Generation Starship
in Science Fiction

The Generation Starship in Science Fiction

A Critical History, 1934–2001

SIMONE CAROTI

McFarland & Company, Inc., Publishers
Jefferson, North Carolina, and London

LIBRARY OF CONGRESS CATALOGUING-IN-PUBLICATION DATA

Caroti, Simone, 1972–
　　The generation starship in science fiction : a critical history, 1934–2001 / Simone Caroti.
　　　　p.　　cm.
　　Includes bibliographical references and index.

　　ISBN 978-0-7864-6067-0
　　softcover : 50# alkaline paper ∞

　　1. Science fiction, American — History and criticism.
2. Star Trek fiction — History and criticism.　I. Title.
PS374.S35C37　2011
809.3'8762 — dc22
　　　　　　　　　　　　　　　　　　2011003412

BRITISH LIBRARY CATALOGUING DATA ARE AVAILABLE

© 2011 Simone Caroti. All rights reserved

No part of this book may be reproduced or transmitted in any form or by any means, electronic or mechanical, including photocopying or recording, or by any information storage and retrieval system, without permission in writing from the publisher.

Cover art: Bill Knapp, *Arrival*, oil on board, 16" × 11", 2011

Manufactured in the United States of America

McFarland & Company, Inc., Publishers
　Box 611, Jefferson, North Carolina 28640
　　www.mcfarlandpub.com

To my wife,
Gioia Donna Massa,
with love

Table of Contents

Preface 1
Introduction: Death and Rebirth of a Dream 5

1. Fathers 19
2. The Gernsback Era, 1926–1940 39
3. The Campbell Era, 1937–1949 80
4. The Birth of the Space Age, 1946–1957 120
5. The New Wave and Beyond, 1957–1979 143
6. The Information Age, 1980–2001 192

Conclusion. Trip's End? 239
Appendix. The Generation Starship: A Chronological Bibliography ... 249
Chapter Notes 253
Bibliography 261
Index 265

Preface

I have always loved stories, and I have always preferred to see them dressed in the garb of the fantastic. There is something about the displacement of real-life situations into a nonmimetic world that stimulates my desire to reflect on the here and now. I read Vernor Vinge's *A Fire Upon the Deep* (1992) and spent the following weeks thinking about communications-based technologies and the information revolution. I finished Iain M. Banks' *Excession* (1996) and got to pondering utopia, hope for the future, and posthuman societies. On the nonfiction side, after reading Carl Sagan's *Pale Blue Dot* (1995) I bought every book of Hubble Space Telescope pictures I could lay my hands on, studied all the universal atlases out of which I could extract some meaning (I'm very bad at visualizing orbital mechanics and celestial coordinates), and generally speaking tried pretty hard to turn myself into a space-age Renaissance man. The effort largely failed, but I carry with me some useful lessons from those early years.

Thus, science fiction and the idea of spaceflight have become, in the course of my personal growth, guiding principles and salves for the soul. I have utilized my readings as engines of hope, interpretive lenses through which I could make sense of a world whose unfolding often seemed opaque to my understanding, and this expansion of my intellectual horizons shaped my thinking on a great many issues, as well as getting me through some of the darker days in my personal life. Thus, when the time came to pack my belongings and leave Italy for graduate school at Purdue University, Indiana, I embarked upon the enterprise with the idea of turning a lifelong passion into an academic job through the auspices of a Master's and a Ph.D. (I used to suffer from a chronic, recursive form of hallucination in which serious people in three-piece suits give me tenure for talking about warp drives.) I conducted my graduate studies in the Comparative Literature program at Purdue, and I began thinking about writing a book of science fiction criticism, and what it might focus upon.

It turns out I had just the thing.

By the time I began researching the generation starship concept, I had read only a smattering of narratives in the subgenre — Brian Aldiss's *Non-Stop* (1958), J. G. Ballard's "Thirteen to Centaurus" (1962), Frank M. Robinson's *The Dark Beyond the Stars* (1991), Richard Paul Russo's *Ship of Fools* (2001), and Ken MacLeod's *Learning the World* (2005). They were not numerous enough to give me a fully triangulated picture of the subgenre as a whole, but they possessed enough critical mass to spark my interest — the idea of entire cultures or nations living out their lifespans on board gigantic worldships, often not even remembering that they *were* on a ship and having to learn the world all over again, pleased my sense of aesthetics and stimulated my thinking on society, civilization, and the often difficult relationships between generations. This intellectual curiosity was soon joined by a rather amazed sense of happiness at my great good fortune when, as soon as I started doing research on the subject, I realized that nobody had yet written a book-length history of the generation starship in science fiction. There were articles in journals, yes, and a few books on generational space travel as a scientific and technological possibility (which did use science fiction narratives as a jumping-off point for their arguments), but no book on the science fictional treatments of the concept.

I liked generation starship stories; they spurred me to think hard about issues that mattered to me, and from a purely academic point of view I could see a gap in science fiction criticism, a void I thought I could partly fill with the first book on the subject. I began my research with an article on generation starships in John Clute and Peter Nicholls' *Encyclopedia of Science Fiction* (1993), and from there I gathered a rough sense of the basic steps in the development of the concept and its use by science fiction writers: Konstantin Tsiolkovsky's first formulation of the idea in 1928; Laurence Manning's and Don Wilcox's SF narratives (1934 and 1940 respectively), the first in SF history to feature generation starships; Robert Heinlein's "Universe" and "Common Sense" (1941); Aldiss's *Non-Stop*; and so on.

After the *Encyclopedia*, I hit every database and directory I could find in my search for generation-starship stories and scholarly articles, trying to develop as complete a chronology as I could and then match it with concomitant developments in science fiction as a whole. A narrative started emerging, an overarching story of stories that traced the birth and growth of the subgenre as an active participant in the life of its parent field. The changes affecting science fiction throughout the decades found a resonance chamber in generation starship narratives, which often acted as an engine of further developments, both within the subgenre and in SF at large.

The present work is divided into six chapters, plus the introduction and a conclusion. Chapters 2 through 6 contain the history of the generation starship in science fiction from 1934, when Laurence Manning published "The Living Galaxy," to 2001, when *Return to the Whorl*, the last book in Gene Wolfe's *New/Long/Short Sun* sequence, appeared. Following the thread that had become apparent during research, I have organized these five chapters in terms of the two great narratives whose interlocking paths they trace: the story of science fiction through its various incarnations, and the story of the generation starship as the microcosmic environment within which those incarnations reflected themselves. Thus, Chapter 2 presents the history of the generation starship during the Gernsback period (1926–1940), and focuses on "The Living Galaxy" and Don Wilcox's "The Voyage That Lasted 600 Years." Chapter 3 introduces the early years of the Campbell era (1937–1949), and concentrates on Robert Heinlein's "Universe" and "Common Sense" (1941). Chapter 4 continues the narrative of the Campbell years until *Sputnik* and the end of SF's first great age (1946–1957), highlighting Arthur C. Clarke's "Rescue Party" (1946), Leslie R. Shepherd's non-fiction article "Interstellar Flight" and Clifford D. Simak's "Spacebred Generations" (both 1953), and Frank M. Robinson's "The Oceans Are Wide" (1954). Chapter 5 addresses the twenty or so years separating the beginning of the end of Campbellian SF from the onset of the information age, and analyzes John Brunner's "Lungfish," Chad Oliver's "The Wind Blows Free" (both 1957), Aldiss's *Non-Stop*, J. G. Ballard's "Thirteen to Centaurus" and Samuel R. Delany's *The Ballad of Beta-2* (both 1962), Poul Anderson's *Tau Zero* (1970), Arthur C. Clarke's *Rendezvous with Rama* (1974), and two non-literary generation-starship stories: Harlan Ellison's largely failed TV series *The Starlost* (1973–75) and James M. Ward's *Metamorphosis Alpha* (1976), at once the first science fiction role-playing game and the first generation-starship role-playing game (unfortunately, it has so far remained the only one). Finally, Chapter 6 narrates the story of the generation starship from the beginning of the information age to the end of the twentieth century (1980–2001), focusing on Frank M. Robinson's *The Dark Beyond the Stars*, Gene Wolfe's *Book of the Long Sun* (1993–96), and Bruce Sterling's *Taklamakan* (1998).

Sandwiching the five main chapters are the Introduction, Chapter 1, and the Conclusion. The Introduction is devoted to defining the matter under discussion — what is a generation starship, and why did we come up with the idea? How would one work, either in a SF story or in actuality? What are the advantages of generational space flight, and what are its problems? What are the basic premises of the subgenre within a science-fictional environment? Why and how did I include certain story patterns, while at the same time excluding others?

Chapter 1 traces the history of the generation starship's birth in the minds of its fathers — Robert Goddard, Konstantin Tsiolkovsky, and J. D. Bernal — and tries to map out as precisely as possible the moments in which scientific thinking gave way to science-fictional thinking in the course of their brainchild's conception. The Conclusion, on the other hand, attempts to trace the end of this book's envelope, looking at the twin histories of SF and generation starship narratives during the ten or so years between 2001 and today, focusing briefly on Ken MacLeod's *Learning the World*.

Many people lent a hand (and often far more than that), either to this book or to its author. Without them, there would be no book at all. My thanks to the following:

Professor Leonardo Buonomo, Professor William Boelhower, Doctor Nicholas Carter, and Professor Clyde Snelling of the University of Trieste. They educated me, almost literally growing me from a bean, and a difficult task it must have been indeed. I owe them more than I can express.

Professors William Palmer, Cary Mitchell, Charles Ross, Shaun Hughes, and Kip Robisch of Purdue University. After I had exhausted the resources, both mental and physical, of the gentlemen in Italy, I happened to *them*— for almost nine years, during which they had to turn me into a Ph.D. and then help with this book (one of them retired immediately thereafter, although the existence of any connections between the two events remains purely conjectural). Again, I owe them a profound debt of gratitude.

My special friends, all-purpose morale boosters, victims of mood swings, and professional readers Martin Whitehead, Gioia Massa, and Adam Toering. Lady and gentlemen, your voices are in here. Thank you from the grateful, slightly worn bottom of my heart.

My friends on both sides of the Atlantic, and my adoptive family in the United States.

My father, Mauro Caroti, my mother, Anna Marina Caroti (née Scabbia), and my brothers Niccolò and Marco. You are in here too.

The readers, writers, and scholars of science fiction. You gave my intellect everything, and this is not enough to repay you. But it's a beginning.

Introduction: Death and Rebirth of a Dream

On February 15, 2002, the American Association for the Advancement of Science (AAAS) hosted the symposium *Interstellar Travel and Multi-Generation Space Ships* in Boston, Massachusetts. Among those attending were Yoji Kondo, former head of the NASA astrophysics laboratory at Johnson Space Center for the Apollo and Skylab missions, who writes science fiction (SF) under the pseudonym of Eric Kotani; Charles Sheffield, mathematician, engineer, and SF writer; Freeman Dyson, famous among other things for his concept of the Dyson sphere; Joe Haldeman, award-winning science-fiction writer, part-time professor at Massachusetts Institute of Technology (MIT), and member of the Board of Advisors for the National Space Society. The aims of the symposium were to present an overview of the research thus far accomplished on the concept that also constitutes the subject of this work: the generation starship, a solution to the problem of negotiating interstellar distances using vessels traveling at sub-light speeds. The book that resulted from the symposium's proceedings collects contributions from several disciplines in an effort to establish "a meeting of the two fields that have been considered separately":

> We shall discuss (I) scientific and engineering (what is often known as hard technical) issues related to interstellar travel, and (II) anthropological, genetic, and linguistic (usually thought of as humanity-related) issues — together. We would be most pleased if the readers find that the twain have met on this fascinating subject [Kondo et al. 6].

In support of this goal, the topics treated by the articles collected in the book range from highly technical discussions of propulsion systems, fuel requirements, and manufacturing problems to inquiries into the sociological aspects of generational space travel: optimal crew composition, the potential for linguistic drift over a period of decades or centuries, and the need for genetic variation. More importantly for the purposes of this work, the articles also addressed the somewhat more intangible aspects of the generation-starship concept, those dealing with human motivations and psychological reactions, such as reasons that would prompt people to take part in such an endeavor, effects on the human psyche of prolonged exposure to the environment of deep space, and the potential for cultural change in such conditions.

Of particular interest is Charles Sheffield's article, which presents a historical overview of the development of the generation-starship concept in literature and science. Sheffield establishes three main periods of speculation on space travel: an early period, ranging from 1600, when Giordano Bruno was burned at the stake for his belief in the plurality of worlds, to 1838, the year in which the distance between our planet and another star was first measured; a middle period from 1838 to 1905, the year Einstein published his first paper on relativity; and a contemporary period, from 1905 to the present day (20). His choice of 1905 as the cutoff point for the most recent phase of intellectual work on the subject highlights the discovery of the limitations which, in the course of the two decades following it, would generate the first conceptualizations of generational space travel:

> An imaginative writer such as Jules Verne might reasonably have presumed in the 1860's through 1890's that a spacecraft equipped with some unspecified propulsion system would accelerate to higher and higher speeds, without limit.... After 1905, such assumptions were unacceptable [24].

In that year, Albert Einstein wrote "On the Electrodynamics of Moving Bodies," the paper in which he outlined what we know today as the special theory of relativity. One of the laws postulated by special relativity establishes the absolute speed limit for any object with any rest mass at c, the speed of light (186,000 miles/sec). It could be an elephant, a whole planet, or a grain of sand; as long as its mass exceeds zero, no matter how tiny it might be, this mass will increase exponentially the closer it approaches the speed of light, until, upon reaching 186,000 miles per second, the value reaches infinity. In more specific terms, a starship trying to breach the light-speed barrier would find the efficiency of its engines' fuel requirements decreasing exponentially with every inch per second gained on the speedometer, because the more massive an object, the greater the amount of energy needed to make it reach a certain speed. At c, the mass of this hypothetical starship would be infinite, which means that the vessel would require infinite energy just to reach light speed, and to go beyond that it would need more than infinite energy. Both these scenarios describe a set of conditions that we will never be able to meet, irrespective of how advanced our science and technology will become in the future.

For us on Earth, from the viewpoint of the aggregate of human experience across the ages, the light-speed limit has, until recently, meant little. The Earth's equator is about 25,000 miles in circumference (Asimov 1); the transfer of electromagnetic waves across our planet is for all intents and purposes instantaneous, and our means of transportation (planes, cars, trains) do not need to reach even a tenth of a percent of that speed to make travel times throughout the world easily negotiable within a timeframe compatible with the exigencies of the average human being's life. As soon as we leave our planet, however, distances escalate to the point where even light is not fast enough to quickly reach every location in our solar system, let alone in other parts of the universe. The farther away we get, the greater our time-lag becomes. In the years following Einstein's discovery, as more precise telescopes and spectrometers revealed to the human eye a bewilderingly large universe, the magnitude of the dilemma kept increasing. It reached a culmination point in 1929, when Edwin Hubble discovered that the indistinct objects that we had hitherto believed were nebulas within our galaxy were, in fact, other galaxies, resting in space a long way away from here, and that these galaxies were actually not resting at all; they were moving away from us at considerable speed, and getting faster the further away they got. Today, we know that we exist in a universe populated by about a hundred billion galaxies, each one comprising anywhere between a few thousand and a few trillion stars. Earth is situated in the outlying region of one of the spiral arms comprising one of these galaxies, the Milky Way, roughly 27,000 light-years from its center. The size of the cosmos is estimated at 13.7 billion light-years (Dickinson 12–13, 99–110), and it is increasing all the time as the galaxies keep speeding away from each other. These figures are so enormous that, once we pass the threshold of our human experience of time over distance, they stop making sense. In his introduction to the anthology *Starships* (1983), Isaac Asimov puts cosmic distances in some sort of human-functional perspective:

> Suppose you want to take a trip across the country from Portland, Maine, to Portland, Oregon. That's roughly 3,000 miles. A trip around the world along the equator is a little over eight times that, 25,000 miles. To go from the Earth to the moon is only about nine times the equatorial jaunt, about 240,000 miles. Beyond that? Well, Venus at its closest is just over a hundred times the distance to the moon; it is about 25,000,000 miles away. And right now, Pluto is just about as near to Earth as it ever gets, but it is over a hundred times the distance of Venus. It is about 2,800,000,000 miles away. So far we've stayed in our solar system, but beyond that are the stars. Even the nearest star is nearly 9,000 times as far away as Pluto is right now. The nearest star is Alpha Centauri and it is 25,000,000,000,000 miles away…. The distance across the Milky Way galaxy is 23,000 times the distance from Earth to Alpha Centauri. The distance from here to the Andromeda galaxy, the nearest large galaxy to our own, is about

twenty-three times the diameter of the Milky Way galaxy. And distance from here to the farthest quasar is about 4,000 times that from here to Andromeda [1–2].

The magnitude of the distances revealed by Asimov's calculations also constitutes an index of how inadequate our earth-centered units of measurement are in helping us comprehend these distances. It was for this reason that we devised the light-year: we needed a unit of measurement that could reduce our quantification of cosmic space to more manageable figures, and at the same time provide us with a sense, not just of distance, but also of time over distance.[1] In our current Einsteinian understanding of the nature of the universe, a place where space and time are the two constituent features of the fabric of reality, there is no other choice but to think about time and distance as one and the same. For human beings, this means that once we start traveling into deep space, the problem becomes one of making it to our destination not by dinner or by Christmas, but by the end of our life. Even if we could reach 99 percent of the speed of light, the time it would take us to reach the center of the Milky Way would exceed the entire lifespan of human civilization by several orders of magnitude. And that is just within town limits, so to speak. What about the rest of our 13.7 billion-light-year-across universe? More to the point, what speeds can we reach now, and what speeds do we expect to reach with the next generation of propulsion systems?

Following are a few examples of our achievements thus far: launched in 1977, the *Voyager 1* and *Voyager 2* probes respectively reached Pluto and Neptune, the two outermost planets of the solar system, in 1989. Now, traveling at about 40,000 miles per hour, largely thanks to gravity assists[2] received from Earth and Venus, they have entered the Oort cloud, the trillion-strong halo of cometary and asteroidal bodies whose outer boundary marks the edge of the Sun's gravity well. It will take both probes something like 20,000 years to clear the edge of the Oort cloud (Sagan 1995).

Launched in 1989, the *Galileo* probe reached its intended destination, Jupiter, in 1995 (Matloff et al. 176). More recently, the *Cassini* probe arrived at its rendezvous point with Saturn in 2004, seven years after launch (Prantzos 82; Dickinson 64), while the NASA New Horizons mission, which left for Pluto in 2006, will reach it no earlier than 2015 (Dickinson 65; Matloff et al. 164). Again, the time to target achieved by each of these probes would not have been possible without gravity assists; the engines we can design and build right now would take relevantly longer to get to the same destination without those maneuvers.

Using propulsion technologies not far removed from those that powered the *Saturn V* booster, the same that took the *Apollo* crews to the moon, the future manned mission to Mars will take six months to reach our second closest planetary neighbor. According to Robert Zubrin, whose plan for the exploration and colonization of Mars has become the blueprint for current NASA efforts, the estimated turnaround time for the initial phase will be between eighteen and twenty-four months, surface to surface (1–18).

These are only the distances we can quantify, and they do not even reach out to the nearest star. To go all the way to the edge of the local Oort cloud is, in cosmic terms, equivalent to paying a visit to our next-door neighbors. The gulfs of space separating our solar system from the rest of creation remain essentially incomprehensible to us, and it is easy to see what H. P. Lovecraft meant when, in his 1926 story "The Call of Cthulhu," he wrote that mankind

> live[s] on a placid island of ignorance, and it was not meant that we should voyage far. The sciences, each straining in its own direction, have hitherto harmed us little; but some day the piecing together of dissociated knowledge will open up such terrifying vistas of reality, and of our frightful position therein, that we shall either go mad from the revelation or flee from the deadly light into the peace and safety of a new dark age [125].

We are insects stuck in amber. Of all the mythological figures that populate the lattice of our culture's history, of all the demigods and heroes that provide the basic human templates through which storytellers help us make sense of the world, the dream of interstellar flight after Einstein has existed under the star of Sisyphus. Perhaps we were too cunning and scheming, too daring in our conceit of power, and something stopped us. Now we push and push, brutes heaving blindly against the unmovable wall of the real, and the strength of our engines diminishes with increasing speed the closer we get to that unreachable cusp in space-time — until they fail altogether, and the wall repulses us. The dream of flying to the stars within the lifetime, not of any one human being, but conceivably of our entire civilization, died in 1905. Between 1905 and 1930, it was reborn as something else, a different set of solutions with different parameters. Science fiction, in its constant striving to balance the two worlds encapsulated in its name — to create, in John Clute's expression, "a set of arguable untruths about the turning of the world" (*Scores* 236) — started providing speculative alternatives, loopholes, and special cases to reopen the door of imagination that relativity seemed to have closed in actuality, and came up, Janus-faced, with two solutions to the problem: the faster-than-light (FTL) drive and the generation starship. Of the two proposed solutions to overcoming the light-speed limit, the FTL option is by far the most fanciful and problematic. In his historical introduction to generational travel, Charles Sheffield reflects on the various devices and pseudo-physical principles that animate the majority of spacefaring SF stories, and this is how he treats the idea of FTL propulsion as a fictional solution to Einstein's discoveries:

> Many writers chafe at the imposition of reality. They dismiss or ignore Einstein's results, invoke an unexplained faster-than-light drive, and go anywhere they choose, as fast as they choose. By popping into an ansible, a Bose node, a portal, a star gate, or some other invented term, travelers arrive where they want to be in nothing flat. The assumption, implicit or explicit, is that there is some way to get around the relativistic limitation imposed by Einstein's work.... All these are convenient devices for storytelling. However, in terms of real physics, they are just one step removed from sprinkling the top of your head with fairy dust and wishing you were somewhere else [25].

Lest the reader believe Sheffield is attacking what is essentially the whole community of SF writers from the beginning to the present day, we should mention that his tongue is in his cheek here; in the series of novels begun with *Summertide* (1990), he indulged in more than a bit of fairy-dust sprinkling himself, postulating a spacefaring human polity linked by a network of "Bose portals"—essentially, wormhole-like stargates through which a starship can instantaneously travel to a distant star system. His mention of "Bose nodes" in the article referenced here seems to indicate that, rather than constituting a blanket condemnation of the concept itself, his criticism of fictional FTL drives may have more to do with the purpose of the article: in this instance, Sheffield's role of mathematician and engineer is probably required to trump his career as writer of science fiction. But even so, his point is fairly clearly laid out. To employ warp drives and quantum entanglement devices in a story brings the SF writer dangerously close to the kind of treatment that the genre is classically supposed to steer well clear of—fantasy. Such a borderline science fiction tale would become a narrative enabled by the use of essentially magical artifacts, no more plausible than Aladdin's carpet or the seven-league boots. The only difference in such a case would be the pseudo-scientific trappings purporting to plausibly "explain" the workings of the warp drive, so as to provide a rather thin justification for placing the resulting work of fiction in the SF shelf at the bookstore.

Ultimately, it becomes a question of what "plausible" means. If we decided to adopt an interpretation of the term that refuses any speculation beyond what we know to be true and doable today, then most science fiction would be on very shaky ground. If, on the other hand, we accept that the general incredulity concerning such exotica as warp drives, wormholes, AIs, and the like closely resembles the incredulity with which most of the scientific world of the time met Einstein's theories, then science fiction becomes the literary genre that dramatizes the impact of possible — indeed, plausible — discoveries, and in the process of doing so stimulates thinking about *making* these discoveries. And more importantly, we do not really need to go as far as exotic particles today, because even the fundamentals of interstellar flight escape us. We have done a lot more dreaming and speculating about space flight than actual flying, so that a "realistic" treatment of the possibility of manned interstellar missions very quickly becomes speculative in nature — as soon as we start talking about leaving the Earth-Moon system, in fact. Any discussion involving a human voyage beyond our satellite, at any speed, immediately becomes the subject of science fictional thinking, which may be one of the reasons why many space scientists and engineers are also SF writers.

It is with science fiction in mind that Sheffield describes the second solution to the relativity problem, one that would not involve the invention of FTL travel. This solution is a small man-made world, a microcosm, a self-contained living space fully provided with the necessities of a long voyage through space:

> By the 1940s, certain writers with more respect for science looked for non-magical solutions to the problem of interstellar travel. At the time, there was one obvious answer. If travel to the stars implied travel times of hundreds or thousands of years, and if the average human lifetime remained less than a century, one must build flying worlds. These would be self-contained biospheres, able to provide their own power, grow their own food, and recycle their own wastes over many centuries. Within them would exist human societies in microcosm, people living their whole lives aboard the ship and finding nothing unnatural in this — any more than we find it unnatural to spend our whole life moving through space within the particular biosphere of the Earth [25].

While our planet travels in space in a fixed orbit determined by non-sentient gravitational forces, this vessel, called a generation starship, would negotiate a route established by human agents; there would be a specific purpose to the trip — a mission, a set of goals. Engines imply intentions. The ship Sheffield describes in his article is also known as a "slow boat to the stars," and the description itself rather closely follows the one given by Konstantin Eduardovich Tsiolkovsky, the Russian pioneer of space flight and SF writer who first developed the idea. In his 1928 paper, "The Future of Earth and Mankind," Tsiolkovsky imagined the construction of what he described as "Noah's Arks" (Clute & Nicholls 480), enormous vessels possessed of advanced life-support systems that could take us to the stars over a period of centuries or millennia. In Tsiolkovsky's mind, such an adventure would be part of the process by which mankind could leave its ancestral cradle, and find its true sense of purpose among the stars. His idea was echoed a year later by John Desmond Bernal in his book *The World, the Flesh, and the Devil*, which we can describe as the actual first formulation of the idea. It was only five years after the publication of Bernal's book that the concept — or at least the beginnings of it — appeared in a science-fiction story, Laurence Manning's "The Living Galaxy" (1934). The first true generation starship story is usually considered (Clute & Nicholls 480) to be Don Wilcox's "The Voyage That Lasted 600 Years" (1940), whereas the first novel-length treatment appeared in 1941, in the form of two stories by Robert Heinlein, "Universe" and "Common Sense," which were later published as a single novel with the title *Orphans of the Sky* (1963).

The same basic characteristics that make the concept of the generation starship a very relevant scientific and human challenge also ensure its validity as science fiction. Quite apart from the technical problems involved in manufacturing a self-sustaining, self-renewing biosphere, and quite besides the logistical hurdles attending the sending of such an artifact into deep space, utterly out of the reach of any kind of support infrastructure, who would want to go on such a mission? In his book *Spacefaring: The Human Dimension* (2001), Albert A. Harrison writes:

> Except for the final generation, there would be no sense of completion, and generations would die not knowing if the mission would succeed. There would be no latitude for people who have a change of heart, and no chance to return to Earth alive.... Voyagers would lose touch with their past. This is not simply a question of prolonged distance with family and friends: it is a question of losing touch with them completely. Cousins and siblings on Earth would die, but twenty-five light-years out the starfarers would never hear about it. During the early years of migration personal communications would be possible, but these would become slower and less frequent, not just because of increased distances but because tardy responses would discourage people from communicating [248].

Further down the road, the ship's population would inevitably experience even more pronounced alterations, first of all in their perspective towards Earth, and secondly in their priorities concerning the vessel's mission. Human beings born on the ship from the third or fourth generation onwards, and who had therefore never had any direct access to anybody who was actually born on Earth, would not possess any natural sense of allegiance or duty towards their planet of origin, and neither would they feel any particularly strong drive to keep putting the original goals of their mission, those that mattered only to the initial crew and to the people left back home, before any other consideration.

It is likely that a completely new lifestyle, exclusive to shipboard existence, would eventually shape a succession of human generations more at home within the enclosed space of their vessel than out in the open sky of a planet, something they have never seen and therefore cannot miss — and possibly not even conceptualize. How does one explain a breeze to someone who has never experienced, or needed, one? Unforeseeable events in space — encountering a singularity, the explosion of a supernova, the entrance into an intensely active star-forming region — and onboard the ship — political and cultural developments, revolutions, epidemics, environment-related genetic and behavioral changes — would conspire to create a culture unique to the vessel, devoid of any point of contact with planet-bound life. For these reasons, generational space travel could, at some point in its unfolding, usher a new strain of the human race onto the galactic stage.

Another relevant problem in the generation starship concept concerns the economic aspects of the venture. In the early '80s, Frank Drake estimated that the energy costs necessary to send a colony of 100 people on a 100-year, 3-parsec^3 voyage would equal "the total energy necessary to meet all the energy requirements of a major country, such as the United States, for a period of time of hundreds of years" (Finney & Jones 250). Even allowing for the development of more efficient, more cost-effective solutions to the energy problem, who would want to finance such an initiative? By the time the ship reached whatever destination was appointed for it, enough time would have passed on earth to make any prospect of financial or political returns highly speculative at best. Also, what if the cultural and genetic changes mentioned above were fundamentally to alter the priorities onboard the ship and the crew decided that, after three or four hundred years of constant traveling, the destination they are supposed to reach was not that important after all? There would be no way for a very distant planet Earth to influence their decision. Those who financed and began the trip would be long dead, and the original mission, along with the sense of purpose that supported it, would be subject to the same kind of shifts that propel fundamental social changes over centuries on earth.

The essential dramatic irony at the heart of every generation starship story consists of this tension, that a collective possessing the characteristics of an entire planet-bound society receives the kind of mission that is usually given to an isolated ship, an artificial entity manufactured, equipped, and manned by human elements of that society — a tendril of that society's policy, intentions, values, and goals, expressive of them by proxy but also independent of them. Initially bound (like an aircraft or a submarine) to the collective that built it, made it into its own world, and then gave it a specific mission, the generation starship will one day find itself too far away from this collective for its original mission to retain its full meaning. On the other hand, enough time will have elapsed to not just allow, but actually require, the birth of a shipboard society with its own values and goals. At that point, time and distance will inevitably bring the people onboard to a crisis point, a moment of decision where the different values of two societies will clash for control, and the distant descendants of those for whom no such clash was in sight will have to make a choice. The collective of science fiction stories and scientific theories that constitute the subject of this book represent a speculative look at the various ways in which the potential problems of this basic scenario, as well as their solutions, are played out to a certain conclusion.

By their very nature, generation starship stories represent an exercise in the retention of memory, or in the regaining of it once it is lost — or again, in the decision to let memory *stay* lost, superseded by newer goals and values, they in turn connected to their own set of remembrances. Across the gulf of time that separates 1905 from today, across generations of readers, writers, and thinkers, the generation starship has traced its course, changing its mode of representation and focus of attention — its mission, one might say — from one set of interpretive models to another, following the change in morals, goals, values, and policies that parsed the passage of the years in this long century of SF writing. The story of the generation starship concept, begun with Konstantin Tsiolkovsky two years after Hugo Gernsback created the first science fiction magazine, along with the genre itself, closely follows the various generational shifts in the field: from the early SF of the forties and fifties, the science fiction of Robert Heinlein, Isaac Asimov, and John W. Campbell, to the New Wave of the sixties; from the consolidation of the seventies and the information explosion of the eighties to the post-cyberpunk nineties and early 21st century, when science fiction finally looked at the future and found that it was the present, and that its job was now to tell the present to a new generation of information-stricken readers. There are generation starship stories everywhere and in every period since the formulation of the concept, and it is only proper that it should be so. Its voyage, begun in a time now distant from this side of the data frontier, has only just begun, and the original plan for its destination, however detailed it might have been in the minds of those who established it, has now changed to the point where today's writers have entirely new goals in mind — to be superseded, it would not be shocking to imagine, by the aims of the writers, readers, and thinkers to come.

In an article written for the fall 2003 issue of the SF journal *Extrapolation*, Christopher Palmer developed an interesting thought experiment: besides mapping out and examining the premises of the generation starship template, with special attention paid to Heinlein's "Universe" and "Common Sense" as well as Brian Aldiss's *Non-Stop* (1958), he also linked it to four other stories, not generation starship tales at all, through a process of thematic expansion aimed at identifying several common points between the two groups:

> By that stage ... the discussion will have taken a step beyond the narrative framework Heinlein laid down, so that by then we have to ask the reader of this essay to accept that the stories adduced in evidence are still in fact relevant although they are no longer Generation Starship stories, because, so it may be inferred, after a certain point radical variation of the details of the pattern becomes subversion of the pattern itself [312].

The "narrative framework" Palmer mentions, which Heinlein did perfect but did not develop anew (this distinction goes to Wilcox in "The Voyage

That Lasted 600 Years"), represents the leitmotif of the generation starship sub-genre. We might call it the "forgetfulness pattern." As developed in "Universe" and "Common Sense," this pattern runs something like this: at some point during the voyage, far away from Earth or any other external source of help, a disaster of some kind strikes the ship, be it a mutiny, a plague, an error in planning, or an unforeseen event out in space. Books are lost, computers crash and fail, fundamental equipment is destroyed, and crewmembers of critical importance for the success of the mission die (teachers, technicians, leaders). In the aftermath of this disaster, the survivors' ability to pass on knowledge is impaired to the point where they enter a phase of seemingly irreversible social and cultural decay. In deadly progression, the loss of scientific and technological understanding causes them to gradually lose every relevant recollection they have, including their world view. The crew forgets how to maintain the ship, repair or replace broken machinery, navigate, and then even comprehend what they see outside the viewing ports. At the end of this long descent into night, they have forgotten everything, including that they are on a ship in the first place. They believe they are the sum total of mankind's heritage, and that they have always lived where they are; there is no ship anymore, and no outside through which the vessel should be traveling. The universe stops at the bulkheads. Whatever automated processes still run onboard the ship are explained in religious or mythical terms, and any remaining memory of the crew's original mission is interpreted allegorically as a representation of the voyage of life, from its origin in the womb to its destination at death.

The focus of all the stories in the "forgetfulness pattern" is on the struggle to retrieve lost memories and, in an interesting inversion of the Garden of Eden myth, to return to an original state not of innocence, but of knowledge. The process of retrieval is usually triggered by one Galilean character—Galilean, that is, in the sense that this character shares with their real-life predecessor characteristics of uncommon curiosity and rationality, characteristics which (1) prompt them to ask questions that end up exposing the inconsistencies in the quasi-religious world-view embraced by their generation, and (2) set them at odds with their society, which censors and punishes them for holding heretical views. Once the conflict between the far-seeing individuals and their collective has been established, the narrative proceeds to chart the series of events at the end of which the visionaries are proven right, in the eyes of the readers if not necessarily in those of their contemporaries. As Palmer points out, the quest for knowledge in which the Galilean characters are engaged is sandwiched between the inferior level of awareness of their society and the superior level of awareness in the readers. The protagonists painstakingly, dangerously re-acquire knowledge we already possess, thus casting us in the role of intellectual foster parents watching a bright child go through the pains of growing up — and then, as children do in real life, surpassing us, because they contextualize the newly regained knowledge within an environment the readers do not understand. Such stories are useful for speculating on the future of space travel, life in the universe, exotic technology, and variant social realities.

Palmer's point in transferring the forgetfulness pattern to the four nongeneration ship texts he discusses — J. G. Ballard's *Concrete Island* (1973) and "The Concentration City" (1978); Philip K. Dick's *A Maze of Death* (1970) and *Lies, Inc.* (1985) — is that these stories share a number of common points with the sub-genre they engage in dialogue: they portray individuals living in closed-off, isolated enclaves within which the transfer of knowledge has been blocked by an external force (the government, their physical surroundings). Their quest for knowledge does not involve a generational voyage through space, but it does repeat part of the forgetfulness pattern, at least up until the point where the stories configure their trip as allegorical rather than actual. The thematic link connecting the four tales above to the body of work comprising the generation starship subgenre consists, in Palmer's formulation, "[in] each author's wide-ranging dismissal of the whole notion of the voyage of exploration or adventure through a knowable, impersonally existing universe" (318). In other words, Palmer views these two groups of stories through the lens of a transformational perspective: in them, the objective trip through outer space of the generation starship becomes a subjective voyage into the psyche of the characters. The protagonists' process of cognitive discovery of the world outside, so fundamental in science fiction, essentially loops back in towards them, and leads them to realize that "the revelation as to the nature of the journey [they] have been sent on is in effect a revelation that there has been no journey" (320).

Palmer's perspective is a very interesting one, and if his line of reasoning becomes difficult to follow at times, it should also be said that he is fully aware of it. As evidenced by the passage quoted above, he is openly asking the reader to follow him in the performance of a thought experiment that uses the tropes of a subset of space-faring science fiction to illuminate the quest for knowledge of characters trapped in "stagnation, blockage, and perversity ... the anti-journey or the journey that loses any constructive purpose, or never had one" (318). And, to the extent that the context within which the article operates has been carefully limited by the author, the thought experiment does indeed work very well — at the necessary price of sidelining the two characteristics that, more than any other, define the subgenre: (1) the process of mnemonic and cultural transmission between generations of inhabitants on an actual ship, and (2) the presence of the element of spaceflight, not so much as a metaphor, but first and foremost as an objective reality, an external set of conditions that inform and define the shape of internal life, both social and personal, onboard the vessel. There is plenty of inner searching in generation starship stories, and this work will certainly touch on the utilization of objective space flight as generator of subjective voyages of personal discovery, but it should be clear that personal discovery cannot exist without the vehicle. This work of literary criticism requires space flight no less fundamentally than the stories which constitute its subject matter.

As for mnemonic and cultural transmission between shipboard generations, it informs the choices made as to which narratives should be included in the present study, and which should remain outside its scope. In his article for the AAAS conference, Joe Haldeman writes:

> It's not absurd to think that [in the near future] we may have learned a lot about learning — that it might be possible to teach anybody anything, whether they are initially interested in it or not. It could be that we would also know a lot more about creating people to order, and instead of hoping to educate a few generations of living breathing sanitary engineers, say, we might just ship the proper egg and sperm (or blastocyst-in-waiting) along with a sanitary engineer expert system, to wait until a few years before landing, create a properly motivated girl or boy, and teach it exactly what it hungers to learn about being a sanitary engineer [66].

This solution to the light-speed problem would certainly be feasible, and true to form, science fiction has had something to say about the idea in stories such as Kurt Vonnegut's "The Big Space Fuck" (1972). Also, another solution would be to put the crew in suspended animation and let the ship fly itself all the way to its destination (or use a skeleton or robotic crew to handle it while everyone else sleeps), at which point everybody would be revived and colonization would begin. Again, there are examples of this story pattern, such as Cordwainer Smith's "The Lady Who Sailed *The Soul*" (1960), James White's *The Watch Below* (1966), or Robert J. Sawyer's "On the Shoulders of Giants" (2000). While these two narrative types are valuable contributions to the debate on interstellar space flight, they are not included in this study because they are not generational trips at all — the cryo-sleep or geneseed carrier premise changes the story pattern by eliminating the social and generational aspect of the trip. By contrast, the generation starship stories examined here have been selected because, in their varied interpretations and readings, they share a set of premises. They are answers to the same question, each one differing from the others in many fundamental particulars, but all of them unified by the choice their authors made to tackle the issue of generational space flight carried out by living, interacting humanity. Moreover, because this is science fiction after all, this purely literary choice is supported by practical considerations informing the planning of real-life space missions. While the cryo-sleep or gene-seed options would simplify the human aspect of the mission by doing away with the socio-historical problems altogether, there are relevant dangers inherent in leaving several centuries' worth of traveling exclusively to automated processes, without any human supervision at all. Human beings have never traveled beyond the moon, and we do not really have any idea as to what may or may not lie out there: singularities, chemical compounds in unexplored planetary nurseries, violently active areas of star formation, unforeseen radiation emitted by as yet undiscovered physical phenomena, and so on. It would probably be very difficult to design software and hardware capable of flexibly and effectively dealing with all these unknown variables over a period of centuries. Whatever our technological capabilities in the future, the most flexible system we know of remains the individual human being, working in concert with machines and other human beings to assess, evaluate, and react to new contingencies.

Finally there is one other group of narratives that did not make the final selection, for reasons similar to the ones that informed the rejection of the cryo-ship and gene-carrier premises. In the case of each member in this group of stories, the reason is that the deep space voyage lasts only a few years, typically less than ten, so that the offspring of the original colonists are either born on the planet after arrival or, if they were born during the trip, reach their destination long before they are adult enough to experience a shipboard existence. Either way, the generational aspect never comes into play. Examples of this story type include Murray Leinster's "Proxima Centauri" (1935), Leigh Brackett's *Alpha Centauri — or Die!* (1963), and Paul Levinson's *Borrowed Tides* (2001).

CHAPTER 1

Fathers

At the beginning of his book *The World, the Flesh and the Devil* (1929), at once a work of scientific prophecy and one of the first treatises to formulate the concept of the generation starship, J. D. Bernal writes:

> There are two futures, the future of desire and the future of fate, and man's reason has never learnt to separate them. Desire, the strongest thing in the world, is itself all future, and it is not for nothing that in all the religions the motive is always forwards to an endless futurity of bliss or annihilation. Now that religion gives place to science the paradisiacal future of the soul fades before the Utopian future of the species, and still the future rules. But always there is, on the other side, destiny, that which inevitably will happen, a future here concerned not as the other was with man and his desires, but blindly and inexorably with the whole universe of space and time [3].

Bernal did not set out to explicitly develop the generation starship idea in his book. In much the same way as Konstantin Tsiolkovsky and Robert Goddard, the other two members of the triad that fathered the concept, he saw the generation starship as a vehicle for our survival and evolution, a physical platform humans would need to progress from their present state of awareness to another, larger state, cognizant of the vastness of the cosmos and the interplay of the forces comprising it. Before it became an engine of story, before the vastness of its hull started carrying the constituent elements of the human drama in the science fiction of the time, the generation starship began life as the enabling device of a certain vision for a utopian human future, and for the scientific outlook that, in Bernal's opinion, was necessary to ensure the advent of that future. The future Bernal fleshes out in *The World, the Flesh and the Devil* exists in dynamic equilibrium between the selective blindness of human advocacy and the objectivity of scientific prediction.

Science fiction operates within the same environment, in the energy field generated by the tension between the future we want and the future we get.

As the latter transmogrifies into the present, it becomes fuel for further desire, which directs speculation from present trends to future possibilities. Thus the wheel turns, as we keep trying to fit the preferred outcome of our wishes into the shape of the world to be. The objective, one might imagine, is to fuse wish and actuality into one single entity.

It was this kind of desire that pushed the great theoreticians of the first space age to focus their energies on solving the problem of human spaceflight — a yearning to transform the visionary power of early works of science fiction into reality, so as to bring about a quantum leap in human affairs. Hermann Oberth in Germany, Konstantin Tsiolkovsky in Russia, and Robert Goddard in the United States directed their efforts towards the task of propelling a rocket out of our atmosphere because the science fiction of their time, from the more famous works by Verne and Wells to lesser known stories such as Edward Everett Hale's *The Brick Moon* (1869) and Percy Greg's *Across the Zodiac* (1888), stimulated their analytical thinking at the same time as it fired up their imagination. At a time when many people on Earth had difficulty believing that any man-made object heavier than air could fly, or that a horseless carriage could function in place of a coach, these men were bending their intellect to the task of reaching the stars. In the course of their endeavors, Goddard and Tsiolkovsky, together with Bernal himself, became the fathers of the generation starship.

Robert Goddard (1882–1945)

The intellectual foundation for the birth of the space age lies at the heart of the industrial revolution. The unprecedented onslaught of scientific and technological discoveries triggered the beginning of a synergistic relationship between scientific and science fictional thought:

> As the nineteenth century progressed, it began to seem to the average person and to scientists and engineers as well that there might quite literally be nothing that was beyond the abilities of science and engineering. Between 1800 and 1865, an astounded public saw the introduction of ... literally thousands of other inventions and discoveries in technology and science.... At this same time, explorers were opening the hitherto unknown territories of Africa and the poles. For the first time, engineers, explorers, and scientists were considered public heroes; they were held in an esteem previously reserved for generals and admirals [Miller 28–29].

It was this combination of industrial might, technological prowess, and curiosity for the opening of new frontiers that stimulated nineteenth-century writers in Europe and America to dramatize the conquest of the ultimate frontier, space, in scientifically plausible terms. Gone were the fanciful expedients through which authors of previous epochs had been able to send their characters on their individual star treks. In 1609, Johannes Kepler could easily enough suspend his audience's disbelief by having the protagonist of his *Somnium* fly to the moon on the back of a demon, and Domingo Gonsales, hero of Francis Godwin's 1638 story *Man in the Moone*, was capable of plausibly voyaging to the same orb by training forty *gansas* (a kind of goose) and then harnessing them together. But by the second half of the 19th century the physical reality of the environmental conditions prevailing in outer space was already too well understood to allow such enabling devices to operate unquestioned. The general public of the time knew that space was nothing but airless vacuum, crisscrossed by potentially dangerous asteroids and meteors, subject to extremes of heat and cold, and devoid of any possibility of sustenance. Moreover, the extraordinary surge in technological inventions and scientific discoveries of those years had created a cultural climate in which plausibility and exactitude in fiction were not simply advisable, but rather necessary — if there was nothing science and technology could not accomplish, then fiction needed to hold up a mirror to the new world they were creating.

And so it did. The publication in 1865 of Jules Verne's seminal space novel, *De la terre à la lune* (*From the Earth to the Moon*), inaugurated the first great era of science fictional speculation on space travel. Between plays, short stories, and novels, at least forty-six works of spacefaring SF were published between 1865 and the end of the century, whereas at least seventy-four works of the same kind were published in various genres between 1900 and 1926, the year Hugo Gernsback began publishing *Amazing Stories* and inaugurated the golden age of science fiction pulps — at which point the sheer number of spacefaring tales published makes keeping count irrelevant (Miller 46–144). The aggregate of speculation and imaginative extrapolation contained in these works served two purposes: first, it dramatized the impact on human beings of environmental conditions in outer space by bringing home to the reading public the sense of wonder inherent in such an endeavor. Secondly, it inspired the fathers of the first space age. In an April 1932 fan letter to H. G. Wells, written at the age of 50, the American pioneer of rocket flight, Robert H. Goddard, explained:

> In 1898, I read your *War of the Worlds*. I was sixteen years old, and the new viewpoints of scientific applications, as well as the compelling realism of the thing, made a deep impression. The spell was complete about a year afterward, and I decided that what might conservatively be called "high altitude research," was the most fascinating problem in existence ... "aiming at the stars," both literally and figuratively, is a problem to occupy generations, so that no matter how much progress one makes, there is always the thrill of just beginning [qtd. in Crouch 20].

Goddard was a dreamer — literally. Every year after 1899 he would annotate in his diary the date of October 19, his "anniversary day." On that day, he climbed a cherry tree to trim the dead limbs from its top, and, possibly under the influence of his Wellsian daydreams, he had what Tony Osman describes as a "near-mystical experience" (22), and "imagined how wonderful it would be to make some device which had even the *possibility* of ascending to Mars, and how it would look on a small scale, if sent up from the meadow at my feet.... I was a different boy when I descended the tree from when I ascended, for existence at last seemed very purposive" (qtd. in Clary 13). Goddard's daytime vision of breaking free from the bonds of gravity — a Newtonian yearning soon to find itself cast out in an Einsteinian universe — was amply supplemented throughout his life by nighttime dreams of extreme vividness, like the one he had on August 8, 1915, when he dreamed of flying to the moon and, upon awakening the next morning, remembered enough of the spaceship he had used to draw a sketch of it (Crouch 31). These imaginative experiences bore fruit first in 1919, the year the Smithsonian Institution published his seminal work *A Method of Reaching Extreme Altitudes*, and later in 1926, when Goddard launched the first liquid-fueled rocket in the history of mankind from his aunt's farm in Worcester, Massachusetts. By then, he had already written "The Last Migration" (1918), the very first attempt to formulate the possibility of generational space travel. In this four-page manuscript, Goddard postulated a far-future solar system in which a dull, dim Sun has exhausted its store of nuclear fuel, and is now incapable of keeping the Earth warm enough to sustain life. In order to ensure the survival of the human race, "great interstellar 'arks,' powered by 'intra-atomic energy' and filled with people and libraries containing the sum of all human knowledge, are dispatched to the far corners of the Milky Way. Once such a craft is well on its way, it will be allowed to cool 'to the temperature of space.' The contents of the ship would 'remain motionless and inanimate throughout.... After long intervals of time,' a special device, perhaps a 'radioactive alarm clock,' would begin to warm and reanimate the crew" (Crouch 313). In an age when most researchers and thinkers interested in space were setting the limit of their ambition to reaching the moon or, at most, Mars, Goddard was one of the few who aimed for wider perspectives, both in time and space. His vision of human migration owes the rationale underpinning it not only to his imagination, but also to more carefully considered opinions concerning human evolutionary goals. In September 1913, he had started an essay entitled "Outline of Article on 'The Navigation of Interplanetary Space'" with these words:

> From an economic point of view, the navigation of interplanetary space must be effected to insure the continuance of the race; and if we feel that evolution has, through the ages, reached its highest point in man, the continuance of life and

progress must be the highest end and aim of humanity, and its cessation the greatest possible calamity [qtd. in Clary 47].

Deep space travel as the best — and possibly last — hope for mankind's future; a fleet of giant ships carrying the living memory of the human experience to the stars, seeding them with our genetic blueprint as well as our culture; the built-in biblical reference to a Noah's Ark writ large, the vessel we construct to survive the ultimate flood; the vast sweeps of time spent in transit, sleeping through dark, cold centuries until we reach a new home. All the elements that would later animate the thematic of the generation starship concept are present in those four pages, with one glaring exception: instead of reflecting on the possibility of having his arks manned by living, breathing humanity, thus making the ships themselves into homes for generations of spacefaring Homo sapiens, Goddard chose to have his future travelers face the centuries asleep, and to have them awaken only by the light of a new star. The choice itself is neither evil nor cowardly; there are reasons to believe that, if cryo-sleep could be perfected, thus sparing people the psychological strain of living under utterly alien conditions for a period of generations, it might be the best thing to do for them — maybe the only thing to do. However, Goddard's recipe for long-term space travel is closer to the idea of the sleeper ship than to that of the generation ship. The full expression of the latter would have to wait another ten years, when another dreamer in another country wrote another essay on deep space travel not only as a guarantee for the survival of the human race, but also as an instrument of transcendence.

Konstantin Tsiolkovsky (1857–1935)

There is the mark of genius about the person and the life story of Konstantin Eduardovich Tsiolkovsky. Born in 1857 in Izhevskoye, a village located 600 miles east of Moscow, he was the son of an impoverished inventor who scraped up a meager income first as a forester, and then as a clerk. A bout with scarlet fever, contracted at the age of nine, left him deaf and "estranged me from others and compelled me, out of boredom, to read, concentrate, and daydream. Because of my deafness, every minute of my life that I spent with other people was torture. I felt I was isolated, humiliated — an outcast. This caused me to withdraw deep within myself, to pursue great goals so as to deserve the approval of others and not be despised" (qtd. in Burrows 36). Tsiolkovsky's pursuits combined with his handicap to push him into a life of study and contemplation. He read every book on mathematics, physics, and astronomy he could find until, at the age of sixteen, he had exhausted the resources available in the local library. At that point, his family gathered enough money to send him to Moscow, where "he rented a corner of a room from a laundress and virtually camped in the public library, where he taught himself differential and integral calculus and trigonometry. He also attended lectures on science and mathematics and used most of his allowance to buy chemicals for experiments" (Burrows 36). Tsiolkovsky was the first among the fathers of the space age. At the time of his Moscow studies, neither Goddard nor Oberth had been born yet. Working alone, virtually ignored in his own country and secluded from the wider European intellectual milieu by the nature of life in Tsarist Russia, he taught himself everything his century knew about science and technology, and then used it to create a new discipline — today we call that discipline astronautics. In 1903, two years before Einstein wrote his paper on special relativity, Tsiolkovsky published his seminal study "The Exploration of Space with Reaction Propelled Devices" in a nearly unknown scientific journal. From that time onward, he dedicated himself to perfecting his spaceship concepts, elaborating solutions for propellants, life-support systems, steering mechanisms, and designing multi-stage launch vehicles and spacecraft (Crouch 28–30). His designs rested on a solid foundation of scientific rigor and careful methodological application, sustained and motivated by a survivalist, transcendental philosophy that construed space as the ultimate dwelling place of humankind.

Two main influences shaped Tsiolkovsky's philosophical views, and they both date back to his Moscow years. The first was his discovery of Jules Verne's work, which clothed his childhood daydreams in the garb of speculative fiction:

> I think the first seeds were sown by the imaginative tales of Jules Verne, which stimulated my mind. I was assailed by a sense of longing, and this set me to thinking in a specific way ... the basic drive to reach out for the sun, to shed the bonds of gravity, has been with me ever since my childhood. Anyway, I distinctly recall that my favorite dream in very early childhood, before I ever read books, was a dim consciousness of a realm devoid of gravity where one could move unhampered anywhere, freer than a bird in flight.... I dimly perceived and longed after such a place unfettered by gravitation [qtd. in Rynin 29].

Verne's influence stayed with Tsiolkovsky for the whole of the latter's life and prompted him to create his own science fictional imaginings. Of the eighty-four major works Tsiolkovsky wrote during his career, a fairly large number of them are science fiction novels and short stories like *A Dream of Earth and Sky* (1895) and *Beyond the Earth* (1920)[1] — works of the imagination in which the rockets he was designing in his scientific treatises became vehicles for his vision of humankind freed from the bonds of gravity. "Speculation, fantasy, and invention inevitably precede scientific calculations," he wrote in the introduction to his 1926 work "Exploration of the Universe with Reaction Machines," and then he concluded that "execution follows reflection, and exact calculations follow flights of the imagination" (qtd. in Rynin 213). Unfortunately for Tsiolkovsky, both the Tsarist regime and the Greek Orthodox Church found his dreams of freedom from gravity—and therefore from government—unappealing; censors held up publication of *A Dream of Earth and Sky* for several years (Burrows 39).

The second great philosophical influence on Tsiolkovsky's work is represented by his encounter with Nikolai Fyodorov. Fyodorov was the illegitimate son of Prince Pyotr Gagarin, and in the course of his life he served as chief cataloger at the Moscow library, while pursuing his interests in Christian theory and mysticism. Tsiolkovsky was one among a number of young students whom Fyodorov took under his wing,[2] giving them books he bought with his own salary and providing them with room in the library, where they could study and receive his teachings (Burrows 37). In retrospect, and in the light of Tsiolkovsky's career, it is easy to see what he found in Fyodorov's theories:

> Fyodorov believed that Earth is not humanity's natural home; rather, human beings are organisms who are more properly at home in the entire cosmos. He also taught that everything in the firmament, from gigantic suns in other galaxies to the tiniest pebbles on Earth, was alive in some state and had a degree of consciousness. But as creatures of the highest consciousness, he told his disciples, humans had the special task of bringing design and purpose to the chaos of life on Earth and throughout the cosmos. In other words, he was convinced that it was mankind's task to "regulate nature" [Burrows 37].

This is the crucial difference between Tsiolkovsky's outlook and Goddard's. For all the sense of wonder and mystery that Goddard felt in the idea of overcoming the Earth's gravitational field, there was an eminently practical streak in his vision of the motives that would eventually push mankind into outer space—the survival of the species, as we have seen, was one of its key components. Unlike Tsiolkovsky, Goddard was a practical experimenter as well as a theorist, the only one in the triad and the first to ever give his theories an actual shape, and this practicality tempered his flights of fancy at the same time as it gave them a rocket engine. Tsiolkovsky, on the other hand, was a purer visionary than his younger American counterpart. Fired up by Verne's stories and fueled by Fyodorov's philosophy of an immanent cosmic overmind, he saw his rockets as a means to an end, the necessary technological buffer between the human body and the harshness of outer space that would enable us to reach the full potential of our species.[3] His rocket ship designs were certainly a source of wonder in themselves, and Tsiolkovsky lavished plenty of working hours on them, but in the end their true purpose was to be served by allowing human beings to survive in an inhospitable future, and by facilitating a transcendent relationship between hitherto separated elements of that cosmic super-consciousness in which he believed.

This vision of mankind's future vividly animated Tsiolkovsky's writings during the last decade or so of his life. By the mid–1920s, he was no longer the eccentric recluse he had been during the Tsarist regime. The Bolshevik revolution of 1917 had ushered in a government that, often for the wrong reasons, was very interested in the potential of technology as an instrument for world control — in both senses of control over other nations and over nature. Within two years of the collapse of the Tsarist state, Tsiolkovsky found himself a fresh member of the Soviet Academy of Sciences, and the recipient of a pension that enabled him to quit his job as a teacher and concentrate on his research and his writing. Ironically, Tsiolkovsky's work after 1919 was largely devoted to expanding Fyodorov's philosophical influence into an intellectual framework for the human venture in space, and for that the Stalinist regime had little or no use at all. The Soviet government was quick to exalt Tsiolkovsky as one of those intellectuals who expounded a vision of technology's domination over nature, but they also rejected what they saw as the manifest absurdities in his thinking — living rocks, life outside the Earth, the cosmic principle (Burrows 42–43).[4]

Tsiolkovsky paid little heed to this process of lionization, and kept elaborating his cosmic philosophy in a series of writings that even today are virtually unknown outside very specialized circles. Among them, two are of particular relevance for the purposes of this work: the first, written in 1930, was his fourteen-stage plan for the human colonization of space. The first six stages are essentially a distillation of Tsiolkovsky's designs into a timeline for their practical application — developing a rocket plane of increasing complexity and capability, propelled by increasingly more powerful rocket engines, until the final version is capable of sustained space flight. The remaining eight stages are worth quoting in their entirety:

7. Develop regenerative life support systems.
8. Develop a space suit.
9. Breed plants to aid #7.
10. Develop space stations and colonies.
11. Develop solar energy for propulsion, as well as a source of energy.
12. Build asteroid colonies as well as colonies on other small bodies.
13. Develop asteroid colonies further.
14. "Human society and its individual members become perfect" [qtd. in Miller 198].

Tsiolkovsky had been thinking about life-support systems for his entire career, and had discussed their potential characteristics and application in "Exploration of the Universe with Reaction Machines." Now he inserted their development into his timeline for the birth of mankind's cosmic consciousness as the first, necessary step towards allowing unmodified humans to survive in the vacuum of space. Later on, the harnessing of solar energy and the establishment of permanent colonies outside Earth would complete the process of man's emancipation from the shackles of gravity, setting us on our path to stage 14, the transcendental moment of achieved perfection. Tsiolkovsky was no mere apologist of technology for its own sake, however. On the contrary, "[he] believed in the power of man to overcome the boundaries imposed by time and space and to settle freely throughout all the solar systems in the universe, but he did not consider man ready to test his capabilities. Man must first adapt to the environment of the future by reaching a state of perfection. Nature, too, must be perfected before all the possibilities of the universe can be realized" (Goldstein 137). Here again is Fyodorov's concept of the duty of man to "regulate nature," recontextualized by Tsiolkovsky within the framework of the practice of spaceflight and space colonization. It is with a vision of man's accomplishment of this duty that he begins "The Future of Earth and Mankind" ("Budushchee Zemli i Chelovechestvo," 1928), the 28-page essay in which he formulated the first fully-fledged concept of the generation starship. As part of the overall process,

> Marine animals would be killed to save them from suffering the predations of other beasts. On land, harmful snakes, insects, and other horrors would be exterminated, and there would be no weather left to speak of. The blandness of this new world did not trouble Tsiolkovsky, for it would be maximally energy-efficient. Man would dominate an earth where both buildings and plants were structured to capture the sun's energy and use it to their greatest advantage. Once his environment was perfected, man would be ready to perfect his race [Goldstein 139].

To contemporary eyes, Tsiolkovsky's recipe for perfection reads like a profiteer's guide to environmental irresponsibility, and there is indeed a contradiction in his attitude towards the species he considers harmful, despite his long-held belief, derived from Fyodorov's teachings, that all matter is alive and capable of feeling, from the largest star to the tiniest atom. However, although Tsiolkovsky shared Fyodorov's belief that the path to perfection involved "eradicating evil from the universe," he differed from his mentor in one fundamental respect: "If evil for Fyodorov was exemplified by death, for Tsiolkovsky it represented anything that stood in the way of ultimate happiness for all atoms. Anything that hindered man's gaining dominance over the earth — which Tsiolkovsky believed would render all atoms happy — was an evil in his eyes" (Goldstein 139). And so snakes and other horrors must go, and other non-harmful species must be reengineered to make them more energy efficient, all in the name of pushing the universe's hive-consciousness — of which mankind is a constituent part — towards perfection and happiness.

It is at this point that human beings, now happy and fully in control of their environment (what is left of it), can take to the stars onboard generation starships. Tsiolkovsky called them "Noah's Arks," unwittingly echoing Goddard's biblically derived description of his seeder vessels, and envisioned for them travel times in the order of thousands of years (Clute & Nicholls 480). These ships would essentially represent the logical next step in the direction taken in stages 12 and 13 of Tsiolkovsky's timeline — hitherto stationary space colonies that would now be provided with engines and sent out into space, sustained throughout their peregrinations by advanced life-support systems capable of turning them into mobile worlds, traveling homes for the inheritors of mankind's legacy. In its definitive form, at least in the shape and for the purpose Tsiolkovsky envisioned, the generation starship stops being a ship in the sense earthbound humans would give the term, and its wanderings stop being a voyage in the sense we mean when we use the word today. The generational vessel becomes a fully functioning, self-sustaining technosphere, a bio-technological entity — alive insofar as all its atoms are possessed of consciousness — whose purpose and direction cannot be determined by any power other than the entity itself. In Tsiolkovsky's philosophical framework, the reasons that would prompt human beings to decide to spend their lives onboard their generation starship are the same that would prompt them to choose to live on Earth or any other suitable planetary body. There is no specific sense of mission for his space arks, or at least no other mission than the one we give ourselves when we make the existential decision to further our individual and collective growth as human beings. Tsiolkovsky's generational travelers spread throughout the universe, using their ships to colonize planets or to simply exist, one with the immanent cosmic principle.

Tsiolkovsky died a few years after writing "The Future of Earth and Mankind," on September 19, 1935. Goddard, his junior by twenty-five years, only survived him for ten more; he died on August 10, 1945, four days after the atomic explosion that ushered in the atomic era, the Cold War, and the first space age. Ironically, the visions of freedom and human growth that had animated both men's work only became reality as a function of the nuclear standoff between their two countries, itself an offshoot of the German V-2 rocket program that, drawing on the work of Hermann Oberth and his pupil Wernher von Braun, forged the practical application of the dream of space in the furnace of war. Also, while Tsiolkovsky and Goddard were well known in their respective countries, the world at large did not hear of them until after their discoveries had been replicated by others on the public stage:

> As incredibly prescient as [Tsiolkovsky's] discoveries were, no one outside of Russia knew about them. Every one of them, and many more that came after, had to be rediscovered decades later by either Oberth, Goddard or both....
> Of course, by mid century, some twenty years after his death, with the space

age just getting under way, the Soviet propaganda machine wasted no effort in trumpeting these discoveries [Hagerty and Rogers 2].

The September 1957 celebration of the centenary of Tsiolkovsky's birth, for which occasion Sergei Korolyov, then head of the Soviet space program, gave a speech exalting his pioneering work in astronautics (Hagerty and Rogers 2–3), was the first the world had heard of him. Tsiolkovsky's technical treatises have since been translated into several languages, and have now taken their rightful place in the history of astronautics; his science fiction has likewise enjoyed translation and publication in several countries. His philosophical writings, however, are almost unknown. Works like "The Future of Earth and Mankind" did not interest NASA planners and DoD strategists, and the three volumes of NASA technical translations dedicated to Tsiolkovsky's opus have never been followed by a fourth collecting his philosophical theories. To this day, they have never been translated into English.

As for Goddard, the largely negative attitude the American press displayed towards *A Method of Reaching Extreme Altitudes* in the early 1920s increased his natural shyness to the point of turning it into outright seclusion from the outside world. From that moment onwards, "although Goddard's work was widely recognized within U.S. scientific circles, his refusal to participate in even the most rudimentary promotional efforts assured that his influence on the popular conception of space in the United States would be nearly as slight as Tsiolkovskii's" (McCurdy 17–18). In the particular case of "The Last Migration," this tendency went even further; Goddard enclosed his four-page manuscript in an envelope, and wrote on the front of the envelope that it was "to be given to the Smithsonian Institution, after the owner has finished with it, there to be preserved on file, and used at the discretion of the Institution. The notes should be read thoroughly only by an optimist" (qtd. in Crouch 312–13). As it turned out, the manuscript was not published until November 1972 (Miller 120).

In the then burgeoning field of astronautics and rocket propulsion, the comparative obscurity both Tsiolkovsky and Goddard suffered during their lifetimes meant that it was Hermann Oberth (1894–1989), the third member of the triad, who ended up influencing the efforts that would eventually lead to the early U.S. space program and its crowning achievement, the *Apollo* missions. Oberth, himself a fan of Jules Verne and a technical consultant for one of the earliest SF motion pictures, Fritz Lang's *Frau im Mond* ("Woman in the Moon," 1929), had discovered both Goddard and Tsiolkovsky during his studies in rocketry, and had written to them both, expressing praise to Tsiolkovsky and requesting data from Goddard (from the first he received a warm acknowledgement; from the second a guarded, suspicious cooperation). A theorist like his Russian counterpart, Oberth expressed his influence chiefly through his followers — men like Wernher von Braun (1912–1977), who came to the United States after helping the German war machine develop the V-2 rocket missile, and Willy Ley (1906–1969), who expatriated in 1935 and later became involved, along with von Braun himself, in the promotional efforts designed to get the American public interested in funding the space program. Along the way, Ley and von Braun associated themselves with science fiction writers and artists.

As far as the subject of this work is concerned, the generation starship had so far been traveling alone and in obscurity. The two works that could have placed the idea out in the open were themselves invisible, their authors' profiles dim in the spotlight, and the rest of the early space-age pioneers had their sight set on shorter-term goals — reaching low Earth orbit, the Moon, or Mars within the twentieth century, for example. It fell to the third intellectual father of the concept to finally give the generation starship a degree of public exposure.

J. D. Bernal (1901–1971)

John Desmond Bernal did not have the space bug. He was no Tsiolkovsky, dreaming of the realm of the sun in a vision of freedom from gravity, and no Goddard, imagining a trip to Mars from the top branches of a tree. He did, however, develop an early fascination with science and its processes, and went about making his discovery in a way that would probably have pleased Victor Frankenstein — or scared him stiff. At the age of seven, after reading Faraday's *Chemistry of the Candle*, he decided to make oxygen and hydrogen at home, and got his mother to write to the local chemist, asking him to provide her son with the necessary materials. "My mother," Bernal later wrote, "who knew even less science than I did ... obediently wrote it all down and the chemist handed the stuff over, which of course if he had had any sense, he would not have done, because what he gave me in fact was a small bottle of concentrated sulphuric acid — oil of vitriol — with which I could have done myself and the house very much damage" (qtd. in Freeman 126).

And so he did — almost. He decided to stage his experiment just outside the house, which was a good thing because the enterprise ended in a great explosion. The accident did not give Bernal much reason for pause, however. As he himself wrote years later to his friend, the Russian writer Boris Polevoi, "I was absolutely convinced of the truth of science" (in Freeman 126), a truth powerful enough to remain with him throughout the upheavals that marked his intellectual development. The most relevant of these upheavals occurred in 1919, when Bernal, then aged eighteen, left his native Ireland to go to

Emmanuel College, Cambridge. There, on November 7, the second anniversary of the Russian revolution, Bernal and his friend Henry Dickinson spent the entire night discussing politics. At the end of their conversation, he had developed the strong Marxist outlook which would inform his future work on the social relevance of science:

> This socialism was a marvelous thing. Why had no one told me about it before? ... The theory of Marxism, the great Russian experiment, what we could do here and now, it was all so clear, so compelling, so universal. How narrow my Irish patriotism seemed, how absurdly reactionary my military schemes. All power to the Soviets. It was the people themselves that would sweep away all the things that I hated, smash the arrogance of the public schoolboy gentleman. It would bring the Scientific World State [qtd. in Synge 11].

Bernal does not explain what he means by "Scientific World State," and the term does not seem to occur again in his correspondence. It is likely that, in the rush of enthusiasm following his conversation with Dickinson, he coined a label that, for him, indicated the preferred shape of the future for human society. This future seems to be characterized by a centralized, world-encompassing government — structured, we can assume, around a socialist blueprint of some kind. Scientists would comprise the main governing body of this political system, but again, Bernal does not elaborate on the point at this stage. However, the germs that would later shape his social, economic, and scientific thinking are already contained in that grab-bag term, and it is somewhat startling for a contemporary reader to realize just how close this inchoate formulation for a future world government comes to the one presented in the various incarnations of the *Star Trek* universe. Bernal dubbed it the Scientific World State, while Gene Roddenberry called it the United Federation of Planets, but the key traits are all there: a unified Earth under one government espousing a faint, fuzzily defined socialist credo,[5] supported and motivated by a set of democratic beliefs strongly influenced by the application of the error-correcting machinery of the scientific method to human affairs. As Gene Roddenberry himself explained, it is the marriage of scientific rationalism and human compassion that will give us utopia and the stars in one single stroke. Bernal's utopian vision of the "Scientific World Government" is certainly juvenile in its lack of detail, and it also owes a lot to an equally juvenile enthusiasm for a newfound call in life, but it did not stay that way. At the age of eighteen, Bernal may have been the incarnation of the typical recent convert, but he eventually grew up — and so did his thinking. During the '20s, he experimented with political commitment and found it wanting. After joining the Communist Party of Great Britain in 1923, he quickly became disillusioned by the way local politicians and reformists put into practice the ideals he had started espousing in 1919. Around 1927, "[Bernal's] growing detachment from active socialist politics was accompanied by an increasingly favourable disposition towards scientists acting as a political force" (Steward 57). His belief in the values expressed by the socialist world view had not changed; what had was his perception of which force could finally develop the critical mass necessary to trigger a socialist "Scientific World State." Starting at the end of the decade, Bernal expressed his plan for the role of the enlightened scientist in the world in a series of writings whose titles are in themselves revealing of their agenda: *The Social Function of Science* (1939); *Marx and Science* (1952); *Science and Society* (1953); *Science in History* (1954); and, most importantly, *The World, the Flesh and the Devil* (1929), the forerunner to them all, the first book Bernal wrote and published, and the work in which he set down the generation starship concept (all Bernal quotes, unless otherwise indicated, are from this seminal work).

Subtitled *An Enquiry into the Future of the Three Enemies of the Rational Soul,* Bernal's work identifies these three enemies as "the massive, unintelligent forces of nature" (the world), "the things closer to [man], animals and plants, his own body, its health and disease" (the flesh), "and lastly ... his desires and fears, his imaginations and stupidities" (the devil) (10). In the three chapters following the introduction, each dedicated to one of rationality's enemies, Bernal establishes a template for an attempt at predicting how future humans might divest themselves of their influence, and finally progress towards maturity. "Bernal's own desire," writes Fred Steward, "was for social change, to enable people to 'find the capacity to live at the same time more fully human and fully intellectual lives.' At core, his social outlook strove to integrate social, intellectual and emotional themes" (59). The single group that in Bernal's mind could foster this development was constituted by what he calls "the aristocracy of scientific intelligence." This aristocracy was an increasingly integrated group of scientists who, initially confined to an advisory role within the administrations of the various governments of the world, would eventually see this role expand and increase in power, chiefly owing to "advance[s] in the direction of more rational psychology" and "the broadening of private interests to include ... some consideration of humanity." In the end, such advisory bodies would become the de facto rulers of planet Earth, with the twin function of "keep[ing] the world going as an efficient food and comfort machine, and to worry out the secrets of nature for themselves" (73–74). Bernal's attention to the political and social developments of his time far exceeds both Goddard's, who was too secretive and wary of negative public exposure, and Tsiolkovsky's, who simply did not much care about the contingent geopolitical situation in which he lived, preferring instead to concentrate on transcendental concerns too far removed in our future to make any difference to the here and now.

Bernal's two predecessors were space dreamers in the strictest sense of the word, intellectuals and scientists for whom the human venture into space represented a self-sustaining, self-justifying endeavor, the ultimate reason for our efforts here on Earth. Bernal, on the other hand, spent his life keeping his gaze firmly fixed on current affairs, constantly trying to formulate a set of parameters for triggering the socialist-scientific revolution that could bring about his Scientific World State. He saw the colonization of space more as another battlefield in the struggle against the "enemies of the rational soul" than as the ultimate reason for mankind's existence. And yet, there is a whiff of Robert Goddard in the reasons Bernal gives for going out:

> All these developments [in science, technology, industry, and world government] would lead to a world incomparably more efficient and richer than the present ... but still a world limited in space to the surface of the globe and in time to the caprices of geological epochs. Already ambition is stirring in men to conquer space as they conquered the air, and this ambition ... becomes more and more reinforced by necessity. Ultimately it would seem impossible that it should not be solved [14–15].

The perspective on space Bernal displays in this passage has less to do with the siren call of the wonderful than with an eminently pragmatic attitude towards the inevitable. Venturing out into space is not so much advisable as necessary, and for the same reason that prompted Goddard to imagine his sleeper ships in "The Last Migration"—survival. However, there are Tsiolkovskian overtones as well, chiefly the idea that the conquest of space should happen after humanity has reached a certain plateau of maturity, once again as a function of the necessity of reaching utter independence from the dangers of the world. Moreover, Tsiolkovsky himself would probably have found resonance in Bernal's notion that the key factor in our emancipation from want and danger lies in tapping the Sun's energy directly from space, as opposed to staying on Earth, where atmospheric dispersal only enables us to utilize a tiny percentage of this energy. This idea represents a strong insurance policy against the kind of planet-wide disasters—asteroid impacts, biospheric collapse—which, were we to remain on Earth, would wipe out the entire human race.

Nor would human beings exist solely on planets. Like Tsiolkovsky before him, Bernal is thinking specifically about the construction of man-made habitats, technospheres built using the lightest, most resistant synthetic materials available and provided with all the features necessary to ensure their survival in a dangerous universe—hard and flexible enough to withstand meteoric impact, and multi-layered so as to preserve in their ideal conditions atmosphere, temperature, pressure, chemical composition of the air, gas exchanges, waste processing, and so forth. Also, these habitats would primarily draw the raw materials necessary for their construction from asteroids and comets, not from Earth. Together with the harnessing of solar energy, the plentiful supply of resources would enable space-inhabiting humans to lead lives far more free of want than anything we have so far known on this planet (18–21).

Interestingly, Bernal keeps referring to the whole habitat as a body, and to its functions as "metabolism" (21), so that the life-support and environmental control systems that ensure its existence can be thought of as metabolic processes rather than simple mechanical support. This desire to make the inner processes of the habitat mirror the workings of the human body represents, in Bernal's view, a necessary step for making it into a fully functioning substitute to planetary life (24). Bernal's spacefaring humanity goes out to stay. There are no temporary space stations and shuttle missions in his conception of our future outside the Earth, nor is there any sense of a sharp separation between the biological and the technological. In his future, they imitate one another, mirror each other's shapes until the distinction between natural and artificial largely loses its point. Also, the development of a fulfilling intellectual and emotional life for those living in the habitat goes hand in hand with the techno-biological development of the habitat itself. For his "globes," Bernal imagines a pattern of constant cultural renewal not too dissimilar from the one practiced by the Greek city-states in classical times, where the intense exchange of information between political and social entities ensured that the administrative cohesiveness of each *polis* did not translate into cultural stagnation (25–26).

The final evolutionary development that brought Bernal to formulate the idea of generational space travel was, in his opinion, an inevitable consequence of the improved living conditions onboard his "globes" and the resulting boom in human population. The eventual proliferation of habitats in the solar system, along with the eventual exhaustion of our supply of solar energy at the end of the sun's life span, would one day bring our distant descendants back to an economy of scarcity. The plethora of habitats around our star, with their teeming billions of human beings, would inevitably start competing with one another for the dwindling supply of energy and raw materials. At this point, Bernal writes, the changed conditions "would force some more adventurous colony to set out beyond the bounds of the solar system" (27), a long endeavor, fraught with dangers both from outside the habitats and from inside their shells:

> Interstellar distances are so large that high velocities, approaching those of light, would be necessary.... Even with such velocities journeys would have to last for hundreds and thousands of years, and it would be necessary — if man remains as he is — for colonies of ancestors to start out who might expect the arrival of remote descendants ... once acclimatized to space living, it is unlikely that man

will stop until he has roamed over and colonized most of the sidereal universe, or that even this will be the end [27–28].

And there it is. No fuss, no fanfare, and very little sense on Bernal's part that this prediction is any more fantastic or momentous than the many others he presents in *The World, the Flesh and the Devil*. As organically as the growth of a new skin layer on one of his space habitats, the idea of the generation starship emerges out of his discourse as the natural consequence of mankind's desire to improve its chances of survival and the quality of its collective life. Like Tsiolkovsky, Bernal was less interested in the idea of the generation starship in and of itself than he was in its potential for enabling humanity's transcendence. The two men did not know one another (and they both were just as ignorant of Goddard's work), but their vision of a distant human future is similar in several aspects. Tsiolkovsky, born in Russia during the Tsarist regime and essentially ignored by it, saluted the advent of the Revolution and the increased respect the new turn of events brought him, even at the cost of being largely misunderstood by a government that had little interest in the philosophical aspects of his thinking; Bernal, an Irishman dissatisfied with British rule during the early years of the 20th century, saw in socialism a powerful agent of change that, once allied with scientific thought, could bring about the paradigm shift in human affairs he thought was necessary to create a better world.

Along the way, and in the course of their forecasting, Tsiolkovsky and Bernal envisioned the generation starship as the vehicle to the stars. No whizbang solutions to the light-speed problem inform their conception of space travel, and no exotic materials or physical principles are at work in the future of their desire. The warp drive is not so much impossible as beside the point. There are only the slow-moving worldships, the natural offspring of the static, man-made habitat, itself a function of mankind's desire for perfection within a larger context—the environment of cosmic space. Tsiolkovsky, in similar fashion to Goddard, called his generation starships "Noah's Arks," certainly remembering the first worldship in the history of Western culture, whereas Bernal did not even bother to give them a name beyond the very generic one of "globes," possibly because he realized that the very concept of traveling tends to lose its meaning when one's vessel and one's country are the same entity. Everything travels in the universe — planets in orbit around their parent star, solar systems in orbit around their local star cluster, star clusters following the local galactic arm, the arm itself orbiting the centre of its galaxy in a million-year circle, galaxies clustered in mutually attracting groups, and on and on until there is nothing bigger than the universe itself, locked into a Newtonian waltz with its constituent parts. The difference between the man-made worldships of Konstantin Tsiolkovsky and John Desmond Bernal's imagination and the naturally occurring bodies peppering the cosmos is in agency, not in movement. The planets of our solar system cannot choose the direction of their wandering; the starships can, and in that they are indeed ships. As for their mission, something Earth-based vessels must constitutionally be given, there is no such thing for the generation starships in their original conception, because there is nowhere to come back to once the trip is accomplished. In the wanderings of the worldship, everywhere is exactly here, right at home, something that must have pleased Tsiolkovsky and Bernal in their utopian thinking.

The future of desire started this chapter. It will also end it. In the introduction to *The World, the Flesh and the Devil*, Bernal warns the reader against attempting to forecast future trends in human affairs without a solid scientific grounding, because in his mind only the scientific method could offer any hope of forestalling the intrusion of desire into our predictions. The future we want and the future we fear — for fear is, after all, a form of desire — have always guided us in our choices, and the yearning for one over the other has shaped our responses, both collective and personal, to the actual turn of contingent events in our present, soon to become the past. Bernal recognized this conundrum when he wrote that "Though the future according to our desires, is an illusion, our desires are, paradoxically, already tending to be the chief agent of change in the universe; it is only that the actual change is so rarely the desired change" (6). Thus Bernal married the knowledge of our desires with history and the physical sciences to form the scientific, objective triad through whose agency one could carry out the most accurate of future forecasts available to contemporary humanity. He knew that he was no less a subject of desire than the next man, and therefore applied himself to making his book of predictions as bias-free as he could and, whether proven right or wrong by the future of fate in the normal course of events, he largely succeeded.

Still, desire and fear creep in. Tiresias, the mythological father figure for all Western prophets, is blind. He wanted to see the gods, and they punished him by replacing his physical vision with the ability to see the consequences of the yearnings of other men. Before, exclusively aware of his immediate circumstances, Tiresias had no vision of future outcomes. Now, deprived of peripheral vision, such outcomes are all he can see. He can perceive the nebulous twists of the distant future as if they were drenched in light, but the immediate surroundings of his present are dark and remote to him, a direct result of the unintended consequences of his desires. Built into the representation of the blind prophet of Zeus is the awareness of a paradox — that the forecasting of large-scale human events lost in the far future is often more factually accurate than the prediction of the next five months of our life. Isaac

Asimov took this paradox to heart when he created the discipline of psychohistory in his *Foundation* stories. In the heat of the moment, blurred and warped by the shifting shape of present circumstances, the world we want superimposes itself on the world that should or should not be, and we confuse one with the other. From such blindness springs tragedy — and triumph.

The outcome of our collective fate has, in the short term, proven to be very different from the future desired and predicted by Konstantin Tsiolkovsky, Robert Goddard, and J. D. Bernal. The Communist experiment in Russia, once applied to flesh and bone, caused far more suffering than it alleviated before collapsing at the end of the 20th century. The space program, often touted by its advocates as a transforming experience on humanity's way to transcendence, was originally born as a function of war — World War Two first, and the Cold War later. The involvement of scientists in politics and government — Edward Teller and Trofim Lysenko immediately come to mind[6] — has not revealed any greater tendency towards benevolence and infallibility than that displayed by other categories of human endeavor. Tsiolkovsky's blindness towards the real nature of the Stalinist regime was more than matched by Bernal's when the latter continued advocating his idea of a socialist technocracy past the point at which the Western world's scientific community had rejected it. In particular, Bernal's lifelong support of Lysenko's theories cost him his reputation in the second half of his life. Blindness and vision, together inside all of us.

Other consequences, more felicitous ones, took place as well. The Soviet experience was not successful, but socialism as a political theory, when applied to government systems established along different parameters than that of the Soviet Union, has proven effective in tempering the excesses of otherwise unfettered capitalist doctrines. The space program may have been originated by the old human taste for destruction, but it did open up vistas of reality we had not imagined could be possible before, and it did provide human beings with a certain fundamental awareness of a larger context.[7] Scientists across the world have repeatedly espoused worthy causes: in countries ruled by a dictatorial government, their investment in the idea that knowledge, curiosity, and discovery are a fundamental human right has put them at the forefront of reform movements, political dissidence, and advocacy for freedom, while the scientific process has unlocked wonders beyond our wildest expectations, and still continues to do so today.

Since the days of Tsiolkovsky, Goddard, and Bernal, fate has merged with desire and transformed their near future into our present. Some of its features they had predicted, and would have been gratified to see realized; others would probably have shocked them, either happily or unhappily depending on their circumstances. In their mixture of foresight and blindness, they saw possible worlds they wanted and possible worlds they feared, and applied their considerable mental faculties to influence the shape of things to come. They desired, and spoke their desire. In the short term, the world did the rest.

We do not know today whether Robert Goddard, Konstantin Tsiolkovsky, and J. D. Bernal will ever be proven right in the predictions they aimed at deep time. Their conception of generational travel might yet become a dominant factor in shaping human destiny, or it may eventually be superseded by unforeseen developments. Maybe one day we will all inhabit one or more generation starships headed for a distant galaxy, carrying with them the aggregate of our hopes and fears. Or maybe we will invent the warp drive, the United Federation of Planets, and the starship Enterprise, and drink *raktajino* from our replicators while we take a one-day trip through the local spiral arm. We do not know.

But we can guess, and we have. The next chapters of this work will start looking at what happened when the writers of the 1930s, '40s and '50s decided to retrofit space habitats with the engine of story, thereby creating the generation starship concept in the world of literature. And literature, of course, is nothing less than another shape to fit the future of desire — a deferred and shifty one, no doubt, because it displaces its yearnings by presenting them as honest lies.

It's just a story.

But stories, like desire itself, creep in. We want the world they give us to become true, or fear it might come to pass. Had Bernal read *Brave New World* or *1984*, he might have found his desires mirrored in Huxley's or Orwell's fears. Would he have understood? Or maybe he did read them, and then decided that their authors' opinions were misplaced; again, blindness and vision, together within each one of us in the shaping of our future. In its stately progress, the generation starship has now reached the next stage in its long voyage, from philosophy and scientific forecast to science fiction.

CHAPTER 2

The Gernsback Era, 1926–1940

In later years, well into the twilight of the twentieth century and fully on this side of the data frontier, those of us who worked with science fiction, in science fiction, or simply waited at the bookstore for science fiction's newest utterance on the world we would all soon inhabit, looked back at the previous four decades or so of genre history and wondered how we could have failed so utterly. Where were the flying cars, portable jetpacks, and full-meal pills we had believed were just around the next bend in history? What had happened to the fin-rocket future of space exploration advocated, both visually and rhetorically, by Chesley Bonestell, Willy Ley, and Wernher von Braun in *The Conquest of Space* (1949) and in the 1952 *Collier's* magazine series? Hugo Gernsback, John W. Campbell, Robert Heinlein, Isaac Asimov and all their contemporaries, people who had dedicated the thirty years between the birth of genre SF and *Sputnik*'s first flight to giving us the American grand narrative of the first science fiction century, were not simply presenting their vision of a desirable world to come. They were telling us what that world looked like, and what we would all do once we were in it. They had seen it, polished and gleaming in crisp sunlight, and were simply reporting back to tell us how we could all get there.

"Nothing acquires quite as rapid or peculiar a patina of age as an imaginary future," wrote William Gibson in the 2003 introduction to his first short-story collection, *Burning Chrome* (originally published in 1986). Born in 1948, Gibson started reading SF during the sixties, and much of that had been written in the '40s and '50s by the Asimovs and Heinleins of those times, "Confident men, [who] knew exactly where we were coming from, exactly where we were, and exactly where they thought we were going. And they were largely wrong on all three counts, at least as seen from this much farther up the tracks" (xv). The fact that American science fiction, quite self-consciously the most prophetic of all literary modes (at least during the first three flashpoint decades of its assertive golden age), should have failed to foresee the advent of the information era was the exact index of how much these confident men had confused the future of their desire with the future of our fate, until in their minds the first appeared indivisible from the second.

Today, the world they advocated rings in the ear like nostalgia, the shape that yesterday thought tomorrow would take. The science fiction of the 1980s and onwards has often revisited it, either to lay to rest its more myopic assumptions in such stories as William Gibson's own "The Gernsback Continuum" (1981), or to look back at its more charming traits in postmodern pastiches like *Sky Captain and the World of Tomorrow* (2005), with its piston-engine whiz-bangs and quaint giant robots striding through a New York painted in soft pastels. Whatever the tenor of our criticism when we look back, however, that kind of advocacy for the future is gone. That world never happened, and its most fervent prophets were left stranded in a land alien to their wishes.

Like the previous installments in this work's retelling of the peregrinations of the generation starship, this chapter looks out on the panorama of a zeitgeist. In much the same way as J. D. Bernal and Konstantin Tsiolkovsky had envisioned generational space travel as one of the many, interconnected strands in the web of the future, so the SF writers of the '30s, '40s, and '50s looked at it as a stage in the evolutionary process that would lead to their promised tomorrows:

> Donald A. Wollheim has argued that by the 1950s sf writers had managed unconsciously to create a consensus future history or cosmogony, with a pattern of premises which enabled experienced readers to situate themselves in the context of any new story very rapidly. There is the initial exploration and colonization of the solar system, and perhaps the meeting with new alien races; the first flights to the stars, by generation ship or by some faster-than-light gimmick, further meetings with aliens and the colonization of planets; there is the rise of the Galactic Empire ... the whole story emerges only after reading the work of many authors [James 88–89].

Back then, dedicated SF readers would probably not have been conversant with the term "meta-text," but this is essentially what anyone reading generation starship stories like Heinlein's "Universe" (1941) or Frank M. Robinson's "The Oceans Are Wide" (1954) would have recognized. Readers familiar with the consensus history of the future presented in the American SF magazines of the '30s, '40s, and '50s would have contextualized those stories as part of a network of interlocking narratives, written by several different authors across a span of time comprising decades and constantly reiterated in their basic assumptions through the repeated presentation of contingent variations on the same basic theme. In the history of the genre, these narratives represented the most pervasive, sustained attempt ever seen to storytell the future into being. Belief shapes human circumstance, and if the belief in a certain form of advocacy for tomorrow develops enough gravitational pull, it may just convince enough people that the aesthetic of the world to come needs to have that particular shape, foster that specific set of morals, and channel its development through that exact network of social, technological, political, and industrial agents. Thus could the dream-shape of the world become solid practice, hard reality out of smoke and mirrors.

In eminently appropriate fashion for a literary mode so invested in representing the Other, the first citizen of the American future was an alien. Born in Luxembourg in 1894, Hugo Gernsback emigrated to the United States in 1904, started selling a radio set of his own design in 1906, and published his first pulp magazine in 1908. It was named *Modern Electrics*, later transformed into *Electrical Experimenter*, and Gernsback immediately showed his passion for tales of speculative science by making his publication the venue for his own experiments in the field: the novel *Ralph 124C 41+*,[1] serialized in *EE* between 1911 and 1912, and a series of short stories of scientific adventure featuring the Baron Munchausen (1915–1917). In 1920, he followed *EE* with another magazine, *Science and Invention*, which regularly featured tales of scientific speculation. The August 1923 issue of *S&I*, entirely dedicated to what Gernsback termed "scientific fiction," proved to be a one-issue trial run for the first SF pulp in the English language, *Amazing Stories*, which Gernsback inaugurated in April 1926 (Clute & Nicholls 490). In the editorial at the beginning of that first issue, he unveiled his definition of "scientifiction," the literary genre he had set about creating, and "By [which] I mean the Jules Verne, H.G. Wells, and Edgar Allan Poe type of story — a charming romance intermingled with scientific fact and prophetic vision (qtd. in Landon 50). Gernsback used the first few issues of *Amazing Stories* to reprint a number of tales by Verne, Wells, and Poe, a calculated operation through which, as Brian Attebery pointed out, "Gernsback made them sf writers after the fact, inventing a tradition to support his ambitions" (33). These ambitions consisted in making his newly concocted genre the chief scientific educator for the public at large, essentially through the judicious sugaring of hard scientific fact with a generous layer of "charming romance," for which he provided exact figures when he wrote that "[the] ideal proportion of a scientifiction story should be 75 percent literature interwoven with 25 percent science" (qtd. in Landon 51).

Gernsback's mention of "prophetic vision" also hints at where all this educational romance was meant to take us — the future, or rather the version of the future he thought should change the face of the world. Writing in an editorial in the June 1927 issue of *Amazing Stories*, Gernsback formulated a more precise function for the genre, which he now called by a modified version of the original name:

> Not only is science fiction an idea of tremendous import, but it is an important factor in making the world a better place to live in, through educating the public to the possibilities of science and the influence of science on life which, even today, are not appreciated by the man on the street.... If every man, woman, boy and girl, could be induced to read science fiction right along, there would certainly be a great resulting benefit to the community, in that the educational standards of its people would be raised tremendously. Science fiction would make people happier, give them a broader understanding of the world, make them more tolerant [qtd. in Landon 52].

Science fiction is here presented as education and edification, and only tangentially as entertainment. Whether Gernsback realized it or not, his assessment of the importance of SF for his contemporaries was not very dissimilar from the set of justifications that, at the beginning of the 18th century in England, comprised the cornerstone for the defense of prose writing against its detractors. Back then the novel, the short story, the editorial tract, and the magazine were under attack for their perceived lowbrow tendencies and production values, and found a political raison d'être as the intellectual teaching tools of the rising middle class. Two centuries later, science fiction, the bastard stepchild of the Industrial Revolution, explained its own existence in the United States, itself the unintended offspring of British Imperialism, through the same strategy. It may not have been sophisticated, the production standards of the magazines in which it appeared may have been as low as the necessity of turning their pages without instantly ripping them permitted, and the artwork on the covers may have been lurid and improbable, but SF, so Gernsback's argument went, was a necessity in the modern world. The citizen of a pervasively urbanized, highly mechanized and industrialized America at the beginning of the 20th century needed it to make sense of the present and indicate the path to the future—and Hugo Gernsback knew the way.

Gernsback's figure, as well as the role he played in shaping SF as a genre and determining the agenda through which it should express itself, have always been controversial. On the one hand, it is true that he gave a previously unconnected body of work identity, focus, and awareness of itself. "Whatever the prevailing literary opinion of Gernsback," writes Brooks Landon, "it seems clear that he advanced prescriptive guidelines for the writing of science fiction, helped organize clubs of fans to discuss its reception, helped foster the popular tradition of science fiction criticism in which readers and writers critiqued the genre, and, in short, marked the formal emergence of the genre" (53). James Gunn, one of those who became critics thanks in part to the very venues for SF literary analysis Gernsback created and then made available, answered the charge of low literary content in the early science fiction pulps when he commented: "Looking back on the place, it may have been a ghetto, but it was a golden ghetto, a place of brotherhood and opportunity and wonder. Before Gernsback there were science fiction stories. After Gernsback, there was a science fiction genre" (128).

On the other hand, while Gernsback can probably be safely indicated as the Father of Science Fiction, he also ended up stultifying and delaying the growth of his brainchild. Gernsback had lofty dreams for the genre, and his recipe for its role in shaping American popular culture into a tool for storytelling the future has merit—in fact, SF stories have always exercised, and still exercise today, an important function in raising public awareness of the social implications of scientific and technological advancements. However, the monthly schedule of Gernsback's pulps, combined with his miserly pay rates and therefore limited talent pool, conspired to erode the principles upon which his brand of science fiction was supposed to base its appeal, boiling them down to formulaic choices in terms of plot, characterization, and themes. In *Trillion Year Spree* (1996), Brian Aldiss describes Gernsback as "one of the worst disasters ever to hit the science fiction field" (217). Aldiss, author of a key generation starship text, is one of the British writers who rose to prominence at the end of the 1950s, when the influence of the American SF dream was beginning to wane, and whose work largely represented a reaction against the ultimately mechanistic world view writers and editors like Gernsback had fostered. Questioning the weight of Gernsback's role in creating science fiction as a genre, Aldiss highlights his "segregation of what he liked to call 'scientifiction' into magazines designed to contain nothing else, ghetto-fashion, [which] guaranteed the setting up of various narrow orthodoxies inimical to any thriving literature. A cultural chauvinism prevailed, with unfortunate consequences of which the field has yet to rid itself" (217). In his article on Gernsback in the *Encyclopedia of Science Fiction* (1993), Malcolm J. Edwards reinforces Aldiss's opinion, writing that "HG gave the genre a local habitation and a name; but he bestowed upon his creation a provincial dogmatism and an illiteracy that bedeviled U.S. sf for years" (491).

It is difficult to refute such arguments. Even the most fervent among the fans of golden-age science fiction would be hard-pressed to justify the plethora of unchallenged cultural assumptions that plagued the writing contained in SF pulps—not that science fiction was the only genre to suffer from them. Essentially every literary mode featured in the pulp magazine scene was guaranteed its fair share. It may be argued, however, that Gernsback had the chance to shape magazine SF into a more sophisticated form of cultural expression and failed.

Ultimately, the rift generated by the opposition between Gernsback's merits and his faults is irreconcilable. While SF writers and critics who dislike the genre's embarrassments during its early decades can lay such embarrassments at Gernsback's door, we also have to acknowledge the undeniable reality that, thanks to his work, we have a genre from inside which we can safely be angry at him. Moreover, as Brian Attebery points out, the sameness reigning in those magazines may well have been the result of purposeful editorial decisions rather than chance, failure, or simple philistinism:

> In a sense, the artwork, the scientific articles, the almost interchangeable stories and even the advertising in the pulp magazines represented a single continuous flow of information about the technological future. Reading one of those magazines from cover to cover is like watching an evening of television on one of the more focused cable networks. Nothing stands out; nothing is supposed to. Characters from one story reappear in another like guest stars in a situation comedy. Sometimes they have new names: Professor Brown instead of Professor Stone. Other times, they have the same name, for writers were encouraged to repeat popular scenarios as series [36].

If one is to give an entire country a vision of the future powerful enough to propel the collective imagination of its people towards making this vision real, one could do far worse than present it as a constantly reiterated metatext, hammering away at the aggregate of this society's desires until, through sheer force of repetition, the vision becomes something more. Thus Gernsback may have been trying to shape the technophilia of his time into the carrier wave of the future. The vision contained in the pulps he and his followers published was less sophisticated and comprehensive than the possible futures J. D. Bernal, Konstantin Tsiolkovsky, and Robert Goddard had imagined mankind would reach onboard a generation starship, but it was there and it was loud, and it struck the eyes of the reading public through a sequence of images, stories, scientific and pseudo-scientific articles, editorials, and letters, all designed to create a community of thinkers working in concert to shape tomorrow according to a certain form of desire. What is more, the SF editors of the pulps era were far from the only ones who supported a technology and science-driven agenda for future advocacy:

> [Andrew] Ross points out that Gernsback's "naïve" faith in the power of science was shared by a wide range of professionals of his time, including ... Herbert Hoover, Theodore Roosevelt, Thorstein Vleben, and Lewis Mumford, as well as by the European left. "To see this widely shared social fantasy as a naïve example of blind faith in technological progress is not good enough," claims Ross ... and he argues instead that "we are obliged to substitute for the given

wisdom about SF's 'uncritical technophilia' a more historically nuanced account of its place in a context better described as *critical technocracy*" [Landon 53].

Ross's point of view also indicates that Gunn's golden ghetto was in fact substantially more connected to the world at large than most observers have thus far been prepared to recognize. If the technocratic, future-shocked zeitgeist of the SF pulps was in fact only a comparatively small component within a much more comprehensive spirit of the times, shared by many more social aggregates than SF fandom alone, then the traditional perception of the genre's early American years becomes harder to sustain. Despite the undeniable roughness of its beginnings, pulp SF played a relevant role in nurturing a widespread form of desire for a heavily technologized future. That this role went largely unrecognized for years, and that the upper echelons of contemporary American letters treated science fiction with mild neglect at best, does not invalidate its importance. If anything, Ross's adoption of a popular culture perspective makes SF's relevance in shaping the aesthetics of the time all the more pronounced for going mostly unnoticed. People got up in the morning, had breakfast, and on the way to work picked up cigarettes, the newspaper, and once a month one of the pulps Gernsback and other editors in the field published. The aesthetic of the future was thus becoming something like a fact of life.

Nor was the transmission of this aesthetic only practiced by science fiction writers and editors. The term Ross employs at the end of the passage above, critical technocracy, can just as functionally be made to describe the philosophy of future prediction employed by Bernal, Tsiolkovsky, and Goddard — Bernal in particular, with his Scientific World State and his oligarchy of competence, a world run by a few intellectuals exercising power through the application of the error-correcting machinery of science and its ability to direct science's militant tendrils, technology and industry, to change the world. As for Tsiolkovsky and Goddard, they both understood the long reach of technology, and together with Bernal tried to factor its influence into a predictive system for anticipating and guiding socio-historical change.

And the system failed. For all its meaningful participation in the world of its time, for all its carefully built safeguards against confusing wish and actuality, the complex network of advocacies furthered by the technocratic elements of Western society, especially the science fiction of the pulps, could not manage to give us the future it had promised. Ironically, this failure was not rooted in the system's capacity to foresee scientific, technological, and industrial change in itself. In fact, we could meaningfully argue that the American science fiction of the early years did a reasonably good job in predicting it; the actual shape of a given invention might have differed from that portrayed on the covers of a magazine like *Amazing Stories*, but the essence was often there. However, Gernsback had not limited himself to assuring the public that science fiction could predict material change. He had also guaranteed his readers that, if only everybody read his magazines, "Science fiction would make people happier, give them a broader understanding of the world, make them more tolerant." His promise, which in the unfolding of the material circumstances of SF publishing at the time became the promise of everyone working in the field, was ultimately moral and emotional in nature. Learning science and technology, praising their power, and working to use this power to make their attending visions real would make us all happy and contented — delight through hardware, one might say.

Later in the twentieth century, the great global war of our times, capped by the shadow of the mushroom cloud and tainted by the knowledge that Nazi Germany, one of the most advanced techno-industrial powers of the time, had engaged in practices that re-defined the concept of evil for the foreseeable future, gave us all a very clear idea that technology and industry are not, in fact, moral values in and of themselves. The great failure of golden-age science fiction was built in from the very beginning, part of the failure of a larger socio-historical yearning. But maybe SF, like most children of a single, rather neglectful father, needed to live through an idealistic, unexamined adolescence, so that the eventual onset of reality could teach it what its parent did not — that telling the world there was only one way tomorrow could possibly happen represented an endeavor doomed from the outset. The science fiction that emerged on the other side of this form of advocacy was wiser than its predecessor had been. The tales that follow are tales of the days of future past, and it may be just as well that the world they advocated was never born.

In 1929, the same year *The World, the Flesh and the Devil* was published, Gernsback lost control of *Amazing Stories* to bankruptcy; he immediately returned to publishing pulp SF with two new magazines, *Air Wonder Stories* and *Science Wonder Stories*. In 1930, barely a year after *AWS* and *SWS* had begun publication, the economic depression forced Gernsback to merge them into one pulp, simply entitled *Wonder Stories*. It was in the September 1934 issue of this magazine that Laurence Manning's "The Living Galaxy," the first fully-fledged generation starship narrative, appeared.

"Here is an utterly different story," Gernsback's brief introductive paragraph proclaimed, "truly a tale at the limits of fantasy." Gernsback praised Manning's use of his imagination, and his desire to let it "have full reign — wander unlimited throughout the cosmos," something to which science fiction readers were bound to respond, because "Everyone has an imagination — some have more powerful ones than others, and it is well-known that science-fiction fans have the most vivid of all" (437). Apart from mentioning that in the course of the narrative "we come across light years, universes, galaxies, and curved space as we never have before" (437), this rather self-congratulatory passage did not give a clear idea of the contents of Manning's story.

It took sixteen years before Groff Conklin, editor of a small collection of SF stories entitled *The Science Fiction Galaxy* (1950), provided a more comprehensive introductory note. At this point, the subject matter of Conklin's paragraph carries a familiar ring:

> How long the human race will exist on the surface of the planet is a subject of frequent debate.... Perhaps ... the time may come when our descendants spread out among the stars of the universe, and this planet itself will be but a cold pinhead endlessly rolling around an equally cold orange which will be all that is left of the sun. Laurence Manning takes us ... out beyond the years and the light-years, to give us a glimpse of possibilities so far beyond tomorrow that the human mind can hardly conceive of the distance and the day. The very memory of the home planet has completely disappeared, but the human ideal continues, untarnished and unweakened by time [227].

"The Living Galaxy" is a Tsiolkovskian romp through space and time: millions of centuries, incalculable light years, and the thrust of human evolution, all compressed into eight pithy *Wonder Stories* pages. Like Tsiolkovsky and Bernal, Manning presents generational space flight not as a story unto itself, but rather as a participant in the story of a future worldview and as this story's facilitating device. Indeed, the human polity postulated in "The Living Galaxy" utilizes it to connect the numerous provinces comprising the expanse of human-inhabited space. The generation starships in this tale incorporate two fundamental representations: space travel as the thread of human intercourse uniting a multi-planetary civilization and as the dictate of literary creation — plot, the thread of authorial agency uniting the work of fiction. It is with an open address from the author himself that the thread of plot begins the story. In a foreword to the main body of the tale, Manning directly addresses the audience:

> It is impossible for me, as author, to write this story so that it is complete in itself; I must ask you, as reader, to lend a hand to the work. This is what must be done: Close your eyes and picture to yourself a classroom of children about six years of age. *You are one of these children*.... The date is very far in the future — more than 500,000,000 years, and the sun, Earth, Mars, Venus, and other ancient things have long since died and become as forgotten and legendary as the Garden of Eden [437].

In later decades, new generations of SF writers who had learned from the authors of the Gernsback era would develop strategies for narrating the history of the very distant future without needing to breach the fourth wall, but this is still 1934 and Manning is playing a brand new game. By appealing to our imagination in helping him lift the weight of disbelief, and by asking that we let our inner child take over for the duration, he makes us willing participants to the narrative, and therefore contributors to the future. Now we too have to believe.

So there is a classroom, a group of pupils, and a teacher named History Zeta Nine, who is over 100,000,000 years old and, true to his name, about to give us our first lesson in the eons-hence deeds of spacefaring humanity (437). "The Living Galaxy" is a lesson about the history of the future now past, seen from a point located, from our perspective as readers of *Wonder Stories*, even further down the track. History, by default the narrative of years now dead, doubles back on us to tell the tale of the dead years we have not seen yet. Hugo Gernsback had said from the beginning that science fiction stories, not unlike classroom lectures, are meant to entertain *and* instruct. The act of telescoping our view of ourselves in the here and now through a funnel of great gulfs of time and distance serves a didactic as well as an esthetic purpose. On the one hand, it increases our sense of wonder, delivering a frisson of cognitively overloaded pleasure at the contemplation, as Brian Aldiss once put it, of "galaxies like grains of sand."[2] On the other hand, it sets up the necessary conditions for a long-term perspective on what our customary short-term vision usually classifies as current events, a position from which the author of a science fiction story can dramatize the potential outcomes of choices whose import we do not necessarily see from the present.

Manning's choice of the classroom lecture scenario as an introduction to his narrative serves another purpose. Every SF story requires at least a default amount of infodump — one or more expository passages, strategically placed at key points in the narrative, whose function consists in giving readers the information they need to understand the basic premises of the alternate reality they are visiting. A *conditio sine qua non* for the existence of SF is the imaginative altering of our world into something else, and without understanding the world there is no understanding the story. Hence the practice of infodump, through which the readers of a science fiction narrative can gradually become conversant with the laws, both man-made and natural, underlying the reality postulated by the author. By the time Manning wrote "The Living Galaxy," the practice of delivering infodump through a lecture was already fairly old — indeed, Gernsback himself had used this device in *Ralph 124C 41+*, where a group of scientists discussing a new subway system between France and the United States inform one another of its characteristics. The characters talk, the readers overhear, and suddenly the world shifts into focus. The problem with this kind of infodump strategy is its crudeness, the awkwardness with which this sort of blunt force trauma approach to the delivery of information fits inside Gernsback's "charming romance" setup. It would not be long before John W. Campbell and his stable of writers started developing more sophisticated infodump strategies, but in 1934 such strategies had not been devised yet, so Manning fell back on a technique not overly dissimilar from those employed by early 18th-century novelists to entice their readers. His narrative persona fully opens himself up to the audience, presenting himself as a sort of clumsy historian or scribe in need of our help to make his world seem real in the mind's eye. Perhaps ironically, it is his very lack of guile that contrives to provide a more agile infodump experience than the transparently cumbersome lecture-within-the-story device employed by Gernsback and others, essentially because the good-natured exhortation to imagine ourselves into the role of ignorant children makes perfect sense. That's exactly who we are. In much the same way a six-year-old does not really know the world into which they were born, we have no idea of what the universe of five hundred million years from now looks like. Manning steps out of his narrator persona to invite us into a straight game of lying to ourselves so he can lie to us, because it is fun and instructive, and when he abandons the foreword with his last sentence—"Now, if you are ready, we will commence the history lesson" (437)—the juxtaposition of our twin roles as twentieth-century readers and far-future children exactly matches the juxtaposition of his twin roles as twentieth-century SF writer Laurence Manning and far-future history teacher History Zeta Nine. We are now ready to know the future.

And, so our guide tells us, what a future it is. In three flighty pages, History Zeta Nine's voice weaves the thread of a world of wonders. The harnessing of atomic power, with its attendant explosion of material wealth, ushers in a post-scarcity utopia possessing the nearly inexhaustible resources necessary to terraform planets, build habitats, and send out ships manned by countless settlers who colonize the rest of the solar system. Still the great gulfs of interstellar space elude us, because the sublight speeds to which the laws of physics confine our engines, together with the limited duration of the human lifespan, conspire to make sure that our expansion beyond humanity's cradle happens in slow, halting steps (438). We are fully within a generational pattern here, the stumbling block that constitutes the basic premise for every generation starship story: our best speeds are not sufficient to take us to another star within a human-functional framework. We die too soon, and the gates of the universe seal shut before our eyes. The solution each generation starship narrative presents to overcome this problem, irrespective of when the narrative in question was written, will determine the premises around which the fundamental dramatic tension of the story discharges its energies. We are in an SF world, where technological solutions stimulate psychological responses, and the starting conditions established by the engine of story dictate what is possible and what is not, both in the physical world and in the universe of the mind.

In "The Living Galaxy," neither the idea of a seeder ship nor that of cryogenic suspension à la Robert Goddard are even considered, so Manning solves the impasse through the postulation of another great invention: an anti-aging procedure, to be undergone once every hundred years in an individual's life, that frees us from Chronos's clasp and allows us to undertake multi-million-year trips without trouble. Along with granting virtual immortality to every man and woman alive at the time, this rejuvenating operation ensures the utter defeat of disease, pain, discomfort, and death, so that now the pupils gathered in the classroom in front of their history teacher have a full hundred years of academic training ahead of them, at the end of which they will take the anti-aging treatment. Once rejuvenated, they can finally choose their calling and spend the rest of their future-shocked eternity as members of the universal human polity their race's ingenuity has bequeathed them (437–438).

From a dramatic standpoint, another advantage of the infinitely protracted lifespan of the average human being is that the crew of a starship will never have to face the task of transmitting knowledge, purpose, and cultural values from one generation to the next until the end of the trip, thereby defeating the key problem inherent in generational space travel and freeing the author from the necessity of dealing with it. Moreover, everybody in this brave new world, History Zeta Nine tells us, is almost pathologically curious, intellectually vigorous, inventive, and happy with their circumstances, so that spending long centuries in transit between star systems does not really present any psychological problems. The crew of one of those ships simply dedicate themselves to inventing things and advancing human knowledge in every conceivable field, and after that they are happy — because they are the children of a Gernsbackian universe, the citizens of science fiction, and as Gernsback himself had pointed out a few years before Manning wrote his story, reading SF right along will make people happy. In his world, knowledge and invention are enough to fill the mind and the heart with their light, drowning out every other possible darkness within.

There is, however, darkness without. Sometime during the first few million years of our expansion through space, "astronomers reported in alarm a violent "shift to the red" in one area of the sky.... A great black empty area thrust its way towards the First Universe which then contained all the human race ... and in it there appeared to be nothing — absolutely nothing" (439). In 1929, Edwin Hubble had discovered that the light emitted by objects moving away from a stationary observer, when measured on a spectroscope, displayed a shift towards the red end of the spectrum (by the same token, the light emanated by objects approaching said observer displayed a shift towards the blue end of the spectrum). Once he discovered this law, which today we call redshift, Hubble used it to measure the speeds and distances of the numerous small nebulas peppering the night sky as seen through his telescope, and found out that they were not, as we had thought until then, nebulas existing inside what we called our universe; they were other universes, constantly moving away from us at a speed that kept increasing with their distance. Today we call those pocket universes, including our own, galaxies, while the term "universe" is now used exclusively to describe the cosmos at large — the ultimate fabric of reality, in other words, containing every galaxy, star, planet, and iota of dark matter in creation.

Always attentive to advances in science and technology, especially in the genre's early years, SF writers were quick to incorporate Hubble's discoveries into their works. Suddenly, the universe was revealed to be several orders of magnitude larger than hitherto believed, and science fiction authors found themselves with a substantially inflated playground for their stories, a functionally infinite and constantly expanding frontier. It really could not have gotten better than this: instruction and drama delivered in one single scientific discovery for the edification and pleasure of the reading public. "The Living Galaxy" itself represents a transitional story from the point of view of scientific terminology. Manning uses the term "shift to the red" instead of "redshift," and employs the words "galaxy" and "universe" as synonyms. Thus, the "First Universe" comprising mankind's known space at the time of the discovery of the "space cone" is what we know today as our galaxy, the Milky Way.

The cone of nothingness bearing down on human-inhabited space is the "living galaxy" of the title, an aggregate of dozens of individual galaxies spanning a properly staggering number of light-years and writhing in a tentacled mass like an Elder God out of a Lovecraft pastiche. If the mention of a tentacle in the description of a deep-space astronomical phenomenon seems extravagant even by the standards of pulp SF, the parenthetical suggestion is (barely) sustained by "the idea of one theory of its origin, which is that the protuberance was a creature of life in some form which utilized solar systems after the fashion of atoms" (441). There are no small numbers here; the universe is being threatened by a beast measuring a million light years by half a million, made up of a lot of galaxies, and hungry for all remaining matter in the cosmos — the only kind of measurements available if we are going to find anything that can pose any kind of danger to a pan-galactic polity of technologically advanced, immortal geniuses.

Of all these human beings, however, only thirteen actually rise up to meet the threat. They are twelve scientists and their leader, another scientist by the name of Bzonn.[3] When the living galaxy is detected Bzonn gathers his cohorts, and together they pick a small, uninhabited asteroid. Then they set about building their own generation starship to go chase down the beast:

Atomic motors of huge size were constructed and the entire core of the planet scooped out and its stone transformed into metal. From the center, great rocket tubes flared out to the surface — fifty miles away — and the entire planet was in a few centuries made into a rocket ship. A mile below the surface they made themselves living quarters and were ready to start [439].

The only small quantity in "The Living Galaxy" is the length of the story itself. Everything else, from the human lifespan to the duration of a voyage on a generation starship, is inflated to extremes. In fact, the voyage of the *Humanity*—so Bzonn and his people have named their worldship — lasts for about four million years, during which, besides dedicating themselves to the task of finding the living galaxy, the crew breed several generations of children who, in time, become scientists themselves and turn the *Humanity* into a gigantic lab (440). Because the people onboard Bzonn's generation starship are children of the Gernsback age to the last man and woman, the problems that might conceivably face less driven immortals on a four-million-year voyage to the end of the universe — loneliness and the strangeness of outer space preying on the mind; alienation and psychoses; political rivalries; romantic jealousies; depression and loss of purpose; despair; aimlessness — do not exist for them. Scientific inquiry and technological discovery are all they need and just to underscore the point, History Zeta Nine's voice assures us that "Progress was made in every phase of art and science" (440). And that is enough. The narrator's use of the passive clause gives his account the impersonal touch it needs to escape further probing on the part of inquisitive readers, because there really is no one to ask.

In a plot twist that neatly solves the issue of population control in a worldship where nobody is likely to ever die and conforms precisely to the colonization pattern established by both Bernal and Tsiolkovsky, Bzonn and the original crew of the *Humanity* set up a regular planetary drop-off schedule for their offspring, thereby triggering the birth of human expansion throughout the universe. During their multi-million-year trip, their generation starship stops multiple times in multiple galaxies, drops a population of colonists on a planet, and then leaves them there to proliferate and continue the seeding program. Therefore, they are the forefathers of every human being born outside the Milky Way. The pan-galactic commonwealth, of which the six-year-olds in History Zeta Nine's classroom are but a small part (and so are we *Wonder Stories* readers, after a fashion), owes them and their multi-million-year trek everything twice over: its birth and its continued existence. It is doubtful that Manning read Bernal before writing this story, and it is certain he never read Tsiolkovsky, yet it seems as though he wrote "The Living Galaxy" following almost exactly the blueprints provided in the others' writing. In the decade following the publication of the story, specifically towards the end of

2. The Gernsback Era, 1926–1940

World War II, Enrico Fermi would postulate that, were humanity to undertake a similar expansion pattern at similar speeds, it would indeed fill the known universe within a few million years.[4]

In the end, Bzonn and his companions destroy the living galaxy, and return to human-inhabited space. To pacify those in the Commonwealth who think he has unnecessarily killed a unique life-form he postulates the existence of a second beast — the living galaxy's mate, perhaps — and immediately sets off into space again to look for it. In the present of the story, he has been missing for twenty million years (444). In a brief afterword at the end of the story, Manning abandons his History Zeta Nine persona, and once again writes to us simply as himself. If, in the course of the story, he had camouflaged his representation of the future of his desire as pseudo-history, he now drops the pretense altogether. His narrative voice is a pure distillation of hundred-proof yearning: "There is the book before you. You are one of those who cannot wait for the next day to bring what it will — you must peer into the next chapter, driven by curiosity. For long hours you sit there over the book and I would give anything to know what you read there!" (444). Stories continue, with or without their writer. The ending of "The Living Galaxy" leaves the tale open for further adventures, and it does not really matter that it is now difficult to imagine how a story of such hyperdense material might develop from here. There is little doubt that it will in any event, if only in the form of a reader's inchoate musings about what lies beyond the edge of curved space.

Like every other writer in the SF pulps of his time, Manning knew that his tale was only one of the many elements in Attebery's "single continuous flow of information about the technological future," so that even if he himself did not write the next chapter in the book of days of the year A.D. 500,000,000, someone else would — and there is a certain joy in that, at least from a reader's perspective. The existence of a SF story in a pulp magazine, subsumed as it was within a collective endeavor established by editorial fiat, may have been more anonymous than that of, say, a novel or a short story in one of the slicks, but it also acquired a multifarious, collective existence as part of a multiplicity of narrative voices. Endlessly echoed and refracted in the fictional mirrors presented by other, similar examples of the same basic blueprint, a tale like "The Living Galaxy" became magnified in a sort of genre-specific resonance chamber — one of the many contrapuntal notes in the symphony of the far future — until sheer force of repetition made this symphony sound a little like a newscast or a History Channel documentary, its advocacy transmogrified from wish fulfillment to plausible forecast.

As far as plausibility goes, Manning's choice to shape his story as a chapter from a history book helps. First of all, presenting information about the future as if it were long-established fact gives the narrative a more authoritative voice and prevents most of the awkwardness usually associated with a forward-thrusting approach to prediction. One of the difficulties inherent in reading the kind of advocacy Tsiolkovsky and Bernal presented in "The Future of Earth and Mankind" and *The World, the Flesh and the Devil* consists in the growing sense of absurdity that develops as one delves further into the work. Constrained by the format of nonfictional prediction, neither author had any choice but to frame their future forecasts as a view looking forward into the unknown, so that the further these forecasts moved from the here and now, and therefore from plausible extrapolation out of established trends, the more difficult it became for the reader to take them seriously. How many repetitions of the future tense can one take in a single paragraph before their tone, heavy with scientific certainty while engaging the unimagined (and, some might think, the unimaginable), starts sounding shrill and pretentious? Tsiolkovsky and Bernal had no choice, and both were engaging writers. But even so, the advantage rests with the author of fiction, who can set up the house rules from the beginning.

Manning does indeed take advantage of his format, compressing the tale of eons into eight pages of upside-down history, thereby presenting the universe of the far future not as advocacy and desire (not until the very end, at any rate), but as a lopsided kind of hard fact. And it all works, because this is exactly how we receive historical fact today. If one were to pick up a primary or secondary school history textbook, roughly equivalent to what the children in History Zeta Nine's class are reading, and look at the section on the industrial revolution, one would read about the socio-political consequences of its onslaught, but there would be little information on the technical features of the actual machinery that started it. Historians usually do not know that much about technology itself, certainly not as much as an engineer would, and they do not have to. They only need to know enough to make their historical argument comprehensible. This is exactly what Manning does: he frames his explanations of the scientific and technological side of his distant future as historical analysis, thus neatly side-stepping the otherwise pressing need to make those explanations plausible by going into detail about how his wonderful machinery actually works — an attempt that would probably have pushed the narrative into absurdity. Moreover, the exiguous length of the story also becomes easily justifiable in the same terms, for the same reason that reading a ten-page chapter on the crusades is: if we forgive our historians for compressing whole centuries and millions of lives that actually took place into a few pages, it becomes harder to justify giving Laurence Manning a hard time for almost doing the same for the sake of a charming romance with a few instructive bits thrown in.

2. The Gernsback Era, 1926–1940

The presence of the generation starship in "The Living Galaxy" made the concept a fundamental participant in the world of the narrative. Without generational space flight there would have been no story. But even so, the planet-ship itself had not yet had a story of its own. Every narrative and form of advocacy presented about it had given it no more than the role of co-participant in a larger endeavor, without addressing the specific issues inherent in its makeup; Manning's narrative had merely hinted at the various elements that would influence the lives of its inhabitants, and then only from a multimillion-year historical distance as one of the many threads in a tale traveling in a different direction. That the concept was a part of Gernsback's vision of future advocacy was all well and good, but was there no way to maintain that advocacy in a story that could also afford SF readers a more intimate perspective on the worldship's long, slow voyage? At the end of the 1930s, twenty-two years since Goddard had written "The Ultimate Migration" and fourteen years after the birth of genre SF, no story had yet appeared that presented a view of the generation starship from inside its hull.

In the aftermath of the bankruptcy that had cost Gernsback his editorship—and ownership—of *Amazing Stories*, the magazine passed into the hands of T. O'Conor Sloane. Nine years later, in 1938, Sloane himself was replaced by Raymond A. Palmer. Palmer, a science-fiction writer with a passion for space opera, followed Sloane in his decision to keep the tone of the magazine essentially unaltered from its beginnings. Gernsback had left, taking his chief illustrator, Frank R. Paul, away with him to work on *Wonder Stories*, but the same kind of cultural thrust towards the technological future reigned unmolested in the magazine they had vacated. The second generation starship tale, the first to focus its entire attention on telling a story about the vessel itself, appeared in the October 1940 issue. As with "The Living Galaxy," the editor did not reveal much about the actual contents of the narrative. The tone of his introduction, however, is very reminiscent of Gernsback's:

> Once in a great while a writer sits down and does a yarn that he doesn't intend to sell, but which turns out to be a rare piece of science fiction, packed with real significance.... Thus, in this issue, you will find the most unusual story Don Wilcox has written to date. It is "The Voyage That Lasted 600 Years," and we believe it to be the most significant piece we've had in months [7].

The year is A.D. 2066. Gregory Grimstone, professor of history, has been chosen as the "Keeper of Traditions" aboard the S.S. *Flashaway*, mankind's ironically named first generation starship about to blast off on its 600-year voyage of planetary colonization. On the day of departure, as the crew is embarking on the vessel, the first captain of the expedition declares to the cheering throng of well-wishers that "'our *children's children*, born in space and reared in the light of our vision, will carry on our great purpose. And in centuries to come, *your children's children* may set forth for the Robinello planets, knowing that you will find an American colony already planted there'" (84). The thirty-two members of the generation starship's crew will never see Earth — or the United States — again, nor will they see their final destination. Even by the standards of the medical science of 2066, so the premises of Wilcox's story postulate, the human lifespan is no greater than that of a 1940 reader of *Amazing*—which is why the ship needs a Keeper of Traditions. Grimstone is the thirty-third member of the crew, the odd man out of the sixteen-couple arrangement, and his function onboard the *Flashaway* consists in maintaining the memory and practice of civilized life in the minds of the crew across the centuries (84). To accomplish this task, he will go into hibernation as soon as the ship leaves Earth orbit. The internal clock of the hibernation chamber is set to wake him at regular intervals of a hundred years each, so that he can walk again among the new generations of the *Flashaway*'s crew, telling them about the history and the values of the United States, monitoring — and where necessary reviving — their sense of purpose and dedication to the mission of colonizing the Robinello system in the name of American civilization. He is the thread of continuity that will keep the people aboard the generation starship rooted in the values and cultural assumptions that prompted the construction of the ship and the establishment of its function. Without him, it would not be too long before distant shipboard generations, born in space and deprived of contact with anyone who had any actual memory of Earth, ended up developing new, self-serving values, contingent to the local situation and at variance with the goals according to whose dictates the motherland had sent them out to colonize deep space.

But the nature of the colonists' journey is such that keeping their minds and those of their children firmly focused on completing the mission is not enough to ensure its success. The *Flashaway* is a generation starship, and this means that it will travel through uncharted, uninhabited space. There will be no chance to stop for provisions or repairs, and no home base to radio back in case of trouble — by the time the answer from Earth reached the ship, enough years would have elapsed to make it useless. The ship is essentially a closed ecological, technological, and social system. Everything must have a use and, when spent or worn out, an efficient disposal. Oxygen, food, and water are finite quantities, and therefore their consumption must be as close to 100 percent efficiency as possible — a set of conditions demanding population control. The original plan for the thirty-two crewmembers, the Clerk of the Council reads in his report to the captain during a public meeting, established an average of two children per couple, resulting in an offspring of thirty-two new crewmembers per iteration. Those, assuming they are evenly spread as to gender, will once again form sixteen families, a repeating pattern that would give the ship a steady population of about a hundred people at any given time, fairly equally distributed between children, parents, and grandparents. The voyage's planners, erring on the side of caution, have also foreseen a degree of tolerance in these numbers, establishing an acceptable maximum of 150 and an acceptable minimum of 75. Were the population of the *Flashaway* to drop to fifty or below, or rise to two hundred or above, the mission would find itself in serious trouble (89).

In a pulpish plot twist that does much to erode the plausibility of Wilcox's narrative, it only takes a hundred years for the mission to indeed find itself in serious trouble. In 2066, two stowaways had managed to get onboard the ship, exactly at the moment of departure: Bill Broscoe, an overeager journalist and former student of Grimstone's, and Louise, Grimstone's former fiancée. Louise had dumped Grimstone when a faulty alarm clock had caused him to miss their wedding, but now she had changed her mind and, as oblivious as Broscoe was of stepping inside a generation starship about to depart, she had followed her beloved. Looking out through the window of his hibernation chamber, Grimstone sees her in the ships' ballroom, but he only has time to make the decision to get out of the chamber and go to her before the machine knocks him out cold (85).

In the mid–21st century, security around a launch site at the moment of the actual launch is someone else's problem; so are locking mechanisms on starship hatches. Grooms experience no wedding-day nervousness to keep them alert enough not to miss the entire day, and seem to have no friends or best men to wake them up in case even the nervousness is not enough. Their brides have no initiative, common sense, or forgiveness, and their parents and relatives do not really care. Also, the grooms are majestically unlucky, because they only find out that they would not have needed to enlist in SF's equivalent of the French Foreign Legion an instant before their hibernation chamber puts them to sleep for one hundred years. To add insult to injury, when they wake up they find out that the now long-dead love of their life did the only thing she could under her unforgiving circumstances: marry the other stowaway aboard the ship. Broscoe and Louise's presence onboard the vessel, unchallenged and unconsidered by the rest of the crew (nobody bothered to abort the launch and escort them out of the ship), inserted an unforeseen alteration in the carefully arranged machinery of the mission. The great plan had become void the instant the *Flashaway* had left Earth orbit.

And worse news is on the way. Upon revivification in 2166, a now griefstricken Grimstone (whose last name, already unpromising at the beginning, now acquires a particularly painful sad-sack resonance) finds out that every window, porthole, and transparent surface on the *Flashaway* has been painted over for some reason. The pilot of the ship, now-aging William Broscoe II, is the first crewmember to greet the Keeper of Traditions on his return to the land of the living. Broscoe informs Grimstone that, as if the additional offspring resulting from the presence of the seventeenth, unplanned-for couple were not enough of a problem, an additional factor contributed to triggering an explosion in shipboard population: the so-called "romantic malady," an unforeseen psychological affliction that started influencing the crew when, during the early decades of the trip, the path of the *Flashaway* took it through a particularly luminous section of the heavens. On Earth, lovers usually find that one moon and a smattering of distant pinpricks are more than enough to trigger their mating instincts. In space, surrounded by glories previously undreamt of, the romantic malady has pushed the population past the two-hundred mark which the original plan considered the watershed separating safety from crisis. Moreover, the already difficult state of affairs is worsened by a series of rivalries, petty jealousies, and psychological problems affecting the crew, and particularly Dickinson, this generation's brutish, unimaginative captain. Dickinson, resentful at once of the disapproval his tenure has received from most of the crew and of Grimstone's influence as Keeper of Traditions, represents the quintessential third-generation inhabitant of the *Flashaway*. The oldest members of the crew, the children of those who had started the trip, surprise Grimstone for "how deeply imbued these greybeards were with *Flashaway* determination and patriotism. They had missed life in America by only one generation, and were unquestionably the staunchest of flag wavers on board" (88). Their parents had missed their country and their planet, and had therefore informed their children's life with a powerful yearning for it. The third generation, however, is essentially made up of people who received the tales of Earth at a substantially greater remove than their parents had—second-hand, unreliable memories of things their elders had never actually seen. The result was a far greater emotional investment in their families and children than in the motivations underlying the mission itself. They have the books, the tapes, and the memories of their elders to remind them of earth, but those are not enough to generate more than a passing intellectual investment in furthering the *Flashaway*'s mission (88–89).

And so Grimstone sets about fulfilling his function as Keeper. He talks, explains, storytells the past, and emplots the future of the trip in the minds of his listeners, all in the attempt to save what he can of the Great Plan from the onslaught of improbable coincidence and unforeseen psychological reactions to radically different environmental conditions. "I tried to impress upon them that they were a chosen group," he explains at one point, "but this had little effect. It stuck in their minds that *they* had had no choice in the matter" (89). Six years before Wilcox wrote "The Voyage That Lasted 600 Years,"

Laurence Manning had been able to blithely sidestep the necessity to address generational drift in "The Living Galaxy" by postulating an essentially endless lifespan for his characters. That lifespan was coupled with an unprecedented level of dedication to a single task over any conceivable length of time. Bzonn and his companions did not, could not suffer from generational drift. Their individual stories, drowned as they were in the wave of eons sweeping through the narrative, were seen from too great a vantage point to have anything but the minutest resonance within the weaving threads of the plot. Gregory Grimstone and his people are not so fortunate; their lives play out over a period no longer than that of an average human being, and the tale they inhabit has trapped them inside the hull of their vessel, unable to stop or do anything except continue on their path towards a destination that no longer matters very much, because it was chosen by people they have never met for reasons they cannot call their own. Environment dictates priorities; to third-generation crewmembers of the *Flashaway*, reality is not the Earth, the United States, or American values. It is the ship, the aggregate of girders, struts and bulkheads delimiting their universe (91). Five centuries from 2166, a timespan difficult to conceptualize for people who can expect to last no longer than eighty or ninety years at the most, their distant descendants will step outside the ship into a new life on a new planet. But the trip of everyone who comes before is essentially an unwavering death march.

Ultimately, despite his best efforts, Grimstone only achieves partial success. Captain Dickinson meets his suggestions for alternative activities to skywatching with scorn and despondency — they have all been tried a thousand times. When Grimstone presses him to come up with other endeavors, the captain simply tunes him out until a doctor walks in to congratulate him on his newborn children, at which point he simply walks away. Somber and worried, Grimstone "wrote out my recommendations and gave them all the weight of my dictatorial authority. I stressed the need for more birth control forums, and recommended that the heavens be made visible for further studies in astronomy and mathematics" (91). Then, his time of active intercourse in the affairs of the *Flashaway* all but expired for this iteration of his cycle, he returns to his hibernation chamber to wait out another century.

From that moment onwards, Grimstone's pattern of sleep and reawakening becomes the refrain of a losing battle. The intervals between live appearances are too great for his activities as Keeper of Traditions to have more than a superficial effect, and the developments in shipboard life while he sleeps have far too much inertia to be susceptible to permanent change over a period of a mere year. Gradually, inexorably, the population of the generation starship falls into a spiraling trend of devolution, forgetting the values of 21st-century America and rediscovering progressively more primitive forms of government and social interaction. When he awakes in 2266, Grimstone finds that the ship's population has now increased to a staggering 800, three quarters of whom are kept in a state of near-starvation by a dictatorial, self-elected oligarchy of quasi-feudal aristocrats at whose apex stand the current Captain Dickinson and his family, tyrants where their single ancestor had merely been dull and listless (92–95). The year 2366[5] brings worse news and further degradation: an epidemic has decimated the crew, who now teeter on the brink of the disaster-level minimum of 50, and shipboard power structures have further devolved into an arrangement of warring tribal clans — once again, the multiple heirs to the Dickinson name are at the forefront of all the trouble (96–99).

As the centuries wear on, social decay is also accompanied by a commensurate loss in technological know-how and scientific erudition, which the various movies and books onboard only end up magnifying by cementing in the crew's minds a perception of machinery as something magical and incomprehensible. The inhabitants of the generation starship have become sluggish in their intellect as well as barbaric in their humanity, two variables which Grimstone regards as the Janus face of the same basic loss of values. In the narrative economy of the story, the American cultural assumptions both Grimstone and Wilcox celebrate are not divisible from the techno-industrial society that gave its citizens the prosperity necessary to develop them in the first place. That the relative merits of these values are never discussed, only worshiped, is a problem pertaining to the basic premises around which Wilcox built his narrative. There is, however, a scarcely acknowledged irony inherent in Grimstone's position onboard the *Flashaway*. When he writes his first set of recommendations at the end of his 2166 iteration, he mentions giving them "all the weight of my dictatorial authority," an offhand comment that, while not giving Grimstone many reasons for self-examination, is nevertheless perfectly true — and destined to become truer the further the *Flashaway* travels towards its destination. The authority that gave him absolute control over everyone onboard is now long dead and far away. Already in 2166, most members of the crew did not really feel particularly beholden to American values, and by the time the Keeper of Traditions wakes up in post-epidemic 2366, nobody even knows what they are. If they had had the American way of life still firmly in their minds and hearts, there would be no crisis. As a result of this loss of institutional memory, the legitimacy of Grimstone's claim to absolute agency over the lives of the people onboard the generation starship has faded almost completely. Only two factors contribute to keep him in a position of power: the vague residue of an idea in the minds of the new generations that he is supposed to be fundamental for their welfare, and far more importantly, superior firepower. In a further ironic twist, it is precisely that lack of technological proficiency Grimstone bemoans so much that gives him the only real edge over the crew of the *Flashaway*: they have forgotten how to make and repair even comparatively simple machinery, so that their guns are now long gone, while his hibernation chamber carries a set of functioning pistols. By the time 2366 rolls around, Grimstone has become the textbook example of Jared Diamond's triptych of colonial domination[6]—he has the guns and the steel, while his now nearly aboriginal subjects, socially decayed and intellectually backward according to his first-world perspective, got the germs and died of them. Both semantically and practically, he is now the quintessential dictator.

It is as a dictator that Grimstone tries to solve the encroaching crises he discovers every time he awakens. In 2266, all he has to do is expose the weapons used by the Dickinsons to keep the vast majority of their shipmates subjugated as the hoaxes they are, at which point sheer force of numbers does the rest. Once their regime has been toppled, Grimstone embarks upon a radical program of sterilization for 700 members of the *Flashaway*'s crew, leaving only 100 capable of bearing children (94). The situation now settled after nearly a year of planning and study, the Keeper is ready to return to his chamber, but not before finding out that a young couple he cares a lot about has fallen outside the quota. The woman is a distant descendant and namesake of his beloved Louise, looking, as the dictates of pulp fiction would have it, very much like her, and this resemblance is enough to break Grimstone's resolve. He instructs the doctors to include her and her husband as an extra couple, under his own responsibility (95). So the man who had toppled a regime by judging it tyrannical replaces it with another that, from the point of view of those who will remain alive to face the effects of his decisions, also constitutes a tyranny of sorts, complete with special privileges for those the dictator deems indispensable for personal reasons.

The *Flashaway* is not Earth; there is no self-renewing biosphere on which one can count to make a small exception unimportant in affecting a trend in population control. Grimstone's choice has serious consequences for shipboard life, as he finds out when he awakes in the plague-stricken, underpopulated environment of 2366. During the century he spent sleeping, as the effects of his favoritism became increasingly magnified, a deep resentment festered among the crew, aimed not just at him, but also at the objects of his preference. Louise's entire clan is despised by the other tribal entities around which the remaining members of the crew have clustered, prominent among whom are the Dickinsons. Once again, the realities of formulaic fiction in the pulp era dictate that the small clan comprising the direct offspring of now-dead Louise Broscoe should embody all that is still good and decent among the ship's population, thereby providing a spurious metafictional justification for having

Grimstone alter things to satisfy his desires. They control all the remaining instruments of learning and science onboard, and hold essentially all the key positions — ship's pilots, doctors, scientists. It is a privileged state of affairs that only exacerbates their status as objects of resentment. In this iteration of the 100-year cycle, however, the Sperrys (the last name of 2266 Louise Broscoe's husband) are in danger: the Dickinsons and the other clans have the numerical advantage, and while they do not like one another, they are certainly united in their hatred of the Sperrys. Therefore, when a riot starts over who should marry Lora-Louise Sperry, who true to form is the most beautiful and fertile girl on the *Flashaway* and looks so much like that first Louise of three hundred years before, the only way for Grimstone to prevent the destruction of everything he holds dear is to act violently. He shoots a couple of rioters and, when the rest cower in fear of his gun and abandon any attempt at further trouble, he once again establishes a government of one, legitimized by nothing more than their fear of his thundering sticks. He now has to decide who will marry Lora-Louise, but his opinion of the contenders is not flattering. Neither is a Sperry, and both are nothing more than barbarians (Grimstone himself describes them in these terms). Now they are at once glaring at each other and leering at Lora-Louise, whom one of them is poised to marry, predator-fashion, dragging her into the mud with the rest of his benighted clan.

There is this to be said for a society's slide into darkness: if you think you occupy an intrinsically more exalted station on your scale of moral righteousness than those among its members you happen to despise, you will probably find your ethical choices a lot simpler to make. The Sperrys are now the *Flashaway*'s Eloi, the Dickinsons and Smiths its Morlocks, albeit without the moral and social complexities Wells had been capable of weaving into the narrative fabric of that part of his traveler's peregrinations in *The Time Machine*. The former are unconditionally worthy, the latter irredeemably warped, and there is no doubt in Grimstone's mind that the decayed members of the crew only have themselves to blame for their descent into the Dark Ages. The Sperrys are strong and healthy in mind, body, and ethics, beautiful and kind where everyone else is ape-like, brutish, and self-serving. Their lineage received a new lease in life because their matriarch happened to remind the Keeper of Traditions of his long-lost love, but they used this chance to make themselves into what any scale of shipboard accomplishment would describe as a true success story. By uplifting themselves out of the compost of local life into a higher state, they have in fact unknowingly upheld one of the defining characteristics of the American ethos. On the other hand, the rest of the clans squandered their intellectual and cultural resources with a carelessness comparable in magnitude to the dedication with which the Sperrys nurtured theirs, and now, in front of Grimstone's agonized eyes, two of them are vying for the right to take Lora-Louise not so much as their bride, but rather as their prey.

The thinly veiled fantasy of the civilized damsel in distress sexually threatened by slavering barbarians, giant apes, insectoid aliens, or evil robots was a staple of SF pulp covers of the time. In later years, from his editorial perch at the heart of *Astounding Science Fiction*, John W. Campbell would comment on the absurdity of such images, focusing especially on the scientifically ludicrous idea that creatures of such different biological makeup as insects could find a human female sexually appetizing just because human males do. And yet, many covers were painted and published for years that featured several permutations on the same basic pattern: a giant bug-eyed monster/giant robot/giant caveman running away with a beautiful, revealingly attired woman in its feelers/pincers/fur-clad arms, chased by a group of belligerent men brandishing a plethora of graphically useless weapons. The issue of *Amazing Stories* in which "The Voyage That Lasted 600 Years" appeared featured just such a cover, ironically illustrating a scene not from Wilcox's story, but from Robert Moore Williams's "Raiders out of Space": a giant metal robot is depicted exiting a spherical starship and attacking two men who are shooting at it with a glaring lack of success, while a beautiful woman in a pleasingly form-fitting evening dress dangles from under its right arm.

While it is true that most of those images were used more as titillation than as actual visual representations of scenes from the stories contained in the pulps, it must also be said that they did reveal a widespread, free-floating chauvinism affecting not just gender issues, but also power relations between cultural, national, and religious communities. One of the most evident failures of Gernsback-era science fiction in the United States was that the pulps' famously low pay rates conspired with their often hectic publishing schedule to generate crude, benighted narratives that boiled their ethical conundrums down to their most basic form — it's us versus them; they are all barbarians and it's their fault; they want our women; and so on. Often, these stereotypes existed together within the same tale. Even today, stories are often mistaken for soapboxes, fictional constructs specifically designed to reward their writers' viewpoint and punish those at variance with it, and stories published in the SF pulps of the early to mid-twentieth century were particularly susceptible to being used as such.

Seen through this interpretive lens, the predicament of the inhabitants of the *Flashaway* involves something more than Grimstone's simple dichotomy between barbarian and enlightened clans. At this point in the voyage, the path he took — or rather, the path he told everyone they were going to take once he was back in his freezer — appears to have been vindicated by the way events actually turned out: he was right in letting the Sperrys live because without them there would be no enlightened heirs to American values left onboard the ship. This line of reasoning, however, only raises the question of why those American values have been made into inarguable dogma. When Grimstone exclaims "Barbarians!" and then proceeds to rail at the Dickinsons and Smiths for letting themselves slip into social decay, he is essentially charging them with treason against his motherland, which in his mind is theirs as well. They have the movies, books, spools of instructional tape, and instruments; they also have their Keeper. Why did they not act like the Sperrys and retain their civilized identity? Why did they not follow the program? Another equally meaningful question, however, would be this: why should they have done so? America is gone forever, and so are those whose values the crew of the *Flashaway* are meant to replicate. With the exception of Grimstone himself, none of those onboard the ship in 2366 have ever seen Earth, and none of them will ever see it. Earth itself has no power over them, because there is no chance to even communicate. In these circumstances, why should anyone feel compelled to follow a now dead, artificially imposed ethos?

The automatic answer, the one that the story itself smoothly presents in front of the reader's eyes, is that those who went with the program stayed civilized, and those who did not became scarcely better than beasts. The Sperrys were rewarded and the others punished. For Grimstone, betraying the American values cannot but lead to barbarism because those values are the only ones standing between us and that. Since there is no other way to do things, and since this binary response scenario establishes a causal relationship between moral attitudes and practical outcomes, the Keeper is now free to influence the lives of those he does not like with a clear conscience — he does not like them because they are bad. If they weren't, they would not have become uncivilized. It is not his fault that things turned out the way they did; he tried, but the Dickinsons and the Smiths were just not good enough, and as for his special concession in 2266, thank God he did it! If he had not, he would now be left without any civilized crewmembers. So it is without any qualms that Grimstone lets himself be proposed to by a very forward Lora-Louise, who, in a forgiving twist of fate that only reinforces the goodness of his decisions in Grimstone's eyes, happens to hate the barbarians at least as much as he does. They get married and have a son, who in their intentions is scheduled to become the captain of the *Flashaway* upon reaching adulthood. A year and a half after his birth, they both say goodbye to the child and go into hibernation, leaving him in the care of the remaining members of the Sperry clan.[7]

If the aim of SF is to instruct as well as to please, and if the application of the scientific method is an endeavor to be praised in theory and honored in practice, then the flow of events onboard the *Flashaway* should act as the springboard for a reflection on the values we transmit to our children, how we ourselves need to be objective embodiments of those values, and how those values can sometimes become obsolete. The transfer of identity, goals, ethics, and morals from one generation to the next represents the defining characteristic of every narrative in the generation starship subgenre, and the deciding factor in determining how the plot of every such narrative should develop. Since it is difficult to regard Grimstone's fulfillment of his duties as wise, impartial, or even plausible (what kind of civilized couple brings a newborn into that kind of world and then leaves him immediately thereafter?), the crucial questions concerning the establishment of a proper system of values onboard the *Flashaway* are: should the many failures of the Keeper of Traditions be laid at his door, or should they be laid at the door of his creator, the writer himself? Is Grimstone at fault because he is a flawed character, or is he at fault because he is a good character operating within a flawed, unfairly rigged narrative?

Frustratingly, the story does not fully answer either question. It turns out that there is more than one demiurge at work in the weaving of the plot of "The Voyage That Lasted 600 Years," and his agency suddenly shifts into focus at the beginning of the narrative detailing the events of Grimstone's fourth iteration. Upon waking up in 2466, the Keeper of Traditions finds himself in a world next to which the situation of 2366 was comparatively hopeful. The captain tells him that the crew has destroyed all the tools of learning onboard the ship, and then proceeds to give him a long list of occurrences of destructive behavior, culminating in a riot in which Grimstone's own son is killed. This event is the final trigger for the utter degradation of everyone onboard the ship, irrespective of their 2366 family affiliation. Not even the memory of the Keeper of Traditions has endured undamaged, because following the loss of every tool of knowledge and learning, the crew's cultural decay spirals out of control until all they have left to make sense of the past and transfer knowledge to future generations are a network of baroque legends through whose lens the destruction of those years has become Grimstone's fault alone:

> I was the one who had started all the killing! *I, the ogre*, who slept in a cave somewhere in the rear of the ship, came out once upon a time and started all the trouble.... I was the Traditions Man; or rather, the "Traddy Man." ... And the Traddy Man, as every grownup knew, could storm out of his cave without warning.... When the bravest, strongest men would cross his path, he would hurl instant death at them. Then he would seize the most beautiful woman and marry her [100].

In his grief and anger, Grimstone gazes at the irreparable degradation of everything he had sworn to protect on the voyage to Robinello. Yet for all his outrage, he does not acknowledge that, however twisted the legend of which he is protagonist, there is more than a kernel of accuracy surviving in it. Seen from the point of view of the *Flashaway*'s crew between 2366 and 2466, the legend does tell the truth in a roundabout, perverse fashion. Grimstone had indeed come storming out of his hideaway with powerful weapons blazing, and then stolen from them the woman that rightly belonged to life onboard the ship, not to the Keeper's stuttering intervals of papier-mâché immortality. In yet another of the many ironies of this strange, awkward, beautiful story, Grimstone has become the giant kidnapping robot on the cover of that issue of *Amazing Stories*, all artificial life, powerful weapons, and alien intent, and the woman in his arms truly is beautiful and defenseless, in physical if not psychological terms. That even the Sperrys would decay, and that even the presence of his proxy on the ship could not avert the disaster, is something Grimstone has a lot of trouble accepting, until the captain of the ship in the 2466 iteration, probably the only friend he has aboard at the time, is finally forced to blurt it out to him: "You want us to be like your friends in the twenty-first century. *We can't be*" (101). In the end, the captain understands the nature of generational space flight better than his Keeper.

In science fiction, demiurges are fairly common. Even without invoking metafictional approaches to its interpretation, it is often in the nature of a SF story that there should be an unfolding hierarchy of progressively higher-powered players within the plot itself— Asimov's *Foundation* series and Frank Herbert's *Dune* constituting two particularly clear examples of this trend. Gregory Grimstone had been trained as the demiurge of the *Flashaway* by those who had organized the trip, and in the eyes of the crew as well as in his own he truly is that. However, Grimstone has a demiurge of his own—the laws, customs and values of the United States of America, circa 2066. Throughout the trip, he had found constant sustenance in his belief that he could always influence the outcome of the trip by applying these values to the problems he encountered, just like a good professor of history would. Now, with everything in shambles around him, his son dead before he could give birth to a Grimstone lineage, and not a single spark of civilized life onboard (with the possible exception of the unnamed captain), he has lost everything. By its very nature, the function of Keeper of Traditions requires utter certainty in the permanence and infallibility of 21st-century American values; if they are indeed infallible and something goes wrong in their application, then it must necessarily follow that the Keeper is not. At the end, it truly is Grimstone's fault, even in his own eyes. He has failed his mission, his country, and his family, and the only thing he has left is to bemoan the decay of his charges and the shattering of their collective dream (101).

It is at this point that a ray of mercy shines upon him; he cannot see it, but the reader can. At the end of the sentence quoted immediately above, a small asterisk directs our eyes to the bottom of the page, where we find an editorial interpolation from Raymond Palmer:

> Professor Grimstone is obviously astounded that his charges, with all the necessities of life onboard their space ship, should have degenerated so completely. It must be remembered, however, that no other outside influence ever entered the *Flashaway* in all its long voyage through space. In the space of centuries, the colonists progressed not one whit. On a very much reduced scale, the *Flashaway* colonists are a more or less accurate mirror of a nation in transition. Sad but true it is that nations, like human beings, are born, wax into bright maturity, grow into comfortable middle age and ofttimes linger on until old age has impaired their usefulness. In the relatively short time that man has been a thinking, building animal, many great empires — many great nations — have sprung from humble beginnings to grow powerful and then wane into oblivion, sometimes slowly, sometimes with tragic suddenness. Grimstone, however, has failed to take the lessons of history into account through the mistaken conception that because the colonists' physical wants were taken care of, that was all they required to keep them healthy and contented.— Ed [101].

With this editorial reflection on the causes for the tribulations onboard the *Flashaway*, we are squarely within the Gernsbackian pattern of entertainment and instruction, aesthetics and science, advocacy and forecast. In fact, we have unknowingly been within it from the very beginning of "The Voyage That Lasted 600 Years." We can now trace our way back through the influences at the heart of this story's conception to identify all the layers of agency that shaped its vicissitudes, and find at their apex not just a person or a committee, but ultimately a cultural attitude. The *Flashaway* truly is a rat's puzzle-box, a lab experiment conducted on the characters in a narrative in order to instruct the reading public on the parameters along which the future is to take shape. In his commentary, Palmer is not talking to the generation starship's crew, to Grimstone, or to Don Wilcox. He is addressing his constituency directly, showing us what the Keeper's miscalculations were, and how they played out their role in shaping his responses to the crises with which he found himself confronted. Running through the existence of every character in the tale is a thread of agency that connects its lowest rung — the crew of the *Flashaway* in their transient, butterfly lives spent as the human capital of the enterprise of planetary colonization — to its highest — the editor of *Amazing Stories*. Palmer is the final demiurge who regiments the economy of this narrative through the implementation of the overarching goal of integrated advocacy, something as alien to the envelope of a single story as the Great Plan of 2066 is incomprehensible to the decayed humans of 2466.

The time is today, the pupils are us, and the goal is to learn the future so we can make it real. It is an operation akin to influencing the trends of the present through the analysis of events in the past—history, in short, only the history of events that have not happened yet, and since there is no historical evidence for the future we have to make some. It is not Raymond Palmer or Don Wilcox's fault, and certainly not Gregory Grimstone's, if the future is so uncooperative as to refuse us a map to help us reach it. In the absence of such a guide, fiction will have to do. From this perspective, science fiction is literally the history of the future. There is nothing else available, and since history only comes into play once the future has become the past, there might never be. If this idea sounds ludicrous, we should remember that, as Hayden White has shown, the process of historical reasoning is closer to an exercise in storytelling than to a scientific approach to the study of the past. Back in the 1940s, White's theories were still a few decades away, and if expressed in their embryonic form they may well have attracted little more than scorn. The largely modernist conception of history prevailing in those times considered it a scientific experiment in search of the truth, not a storytelling exercise in search of a worldview. The various contributors to "The Voyage That Lasted 600 Years," from Wilcox and his editor to their reading public, shared that perception, which is why the job of keeping the *Flashaway* grounded in the ethos of the heartland went to a historian.

Again, there is irony in this choice. With all those layers of agency, with such a comprehensive cross-checking system for teaching the ways of the future, nobody—not even Wilcox himself—realized that Grimstone's practical implementation of his duties as Keeper of Traditions is essentially performative in nature. When the members of the generation starship's crew ask him for information on the planet they left behind, they do not frame it in terms of a request for historical analysis; they invite him to numerous gatherings and literally ask him to tell them stories of distant earth (88–89). Grimstone's own response, moreover, is not that of a historian in today's sense of the term. One of the solutions to the romantic malady he suggests to Dickinson is the development of a shipborne tradition in the performing arts, to which the captain replies that earth had all the drama. Life onboard the ship carries no story worth performing (90).

Nobody onboard the *Flashaway* has ever experienced anything of Earth, other than through a number of two-hundred-year-old movies and phonograph records. How do they know that there is no drama in their world? At the same time as they try to tell Grimstone what the reality of their circumstances is like, they are themselves engaging in a representation of it, culled from fictional works coming from and talking about a place they have never seen. Drama happens where people are; there is no reason for Dickinson to answer Grimstone in that way, except for lack of imagination. Part of the predicament in which the inhabitants of the generation ship have found themselves consists in the fact that they do not know how to write stories of their own.

Grimstone responds to his charge's conditions by engaging in further emplotments of this mythical place. Later on, he rationalizes his actions as the result of objective, rational requirements, but in the heat of the moment he acts like an itinerant minstrel, a storyteller who stopped by on his way to somewhere else to unspool a few yarns about exotic lands no one but him has ever seen — a really rather accurate description of who he actually is. Grimstone is not a poor historian, and far from a poor storyteller; he is just facing a difficult crowd. But he does win them over in the end, and it is a shame that the real reason for whatever successes his enterprise enjoyed in 2266 escapes him. If he had kept in mind that his job had less to do with providing the people onboard the *Flashaway* with evidence of the Earth's existence (something they already had anyway) than it did with giving them the thread of story uniting those disjointed pieces into the narrative of a world, maybe he could have set up a learning pattern to keep the grand narrative of American values alive throughout the trip. Saying that the past can help illuminate the path to a better future is one thing; both storytellers and historians know this to be a valid view. Saying that the past is itself the documentary evidence for the future, however, is quite another. In the first case we exist within the realm of open, direct advocacy; in the second, where advocacy masquerades as newscast in a ruse to justify forcing the future to regurgitate the past, we are in a realm of revenants, a place of ghosts in which the future cannot endure.

Unfortunately, such was the situation when "The Voyage That Lasted 600 Years" appeared. The worldview fostered in Raymond Palmer's magazine gave history the status of science, not of fancy.[8] Historians were scientists engaged in a precise endeavor, and so were SF writers — a tough break for their characters, who found themselves having to perform according to a script established around hard facts rather than charming romances. History needs to be taught, so once we have had our fun with our simulation and seen the Keeper of Traditions bumble through its set-piece experiments, it is time for us to sit up and listen to editor Ray Palmer's lesson on the future. In fact, a substantial amount of commentary in that editorial interpolation makes a lot of sense, starting with his analysis of the peculiar social and cultural situation of the inhabitants of a generation starship. The idea that the transmission of values from generation to generation is fundamental for this sub-genre is true, but it is also true for every other kind of narrative addressing the issue — in fact, such a story would not even have to be science fiction. Dickens's *Hard Times*, Shakespeare's *Romeo and Juliet*, and Toni Morrison's *Beloved* are only three among the numerous examples one could cite of fictional works addressing the transmission of values from parents to children, and what happens when this process is neglected or perverted.

What makes it particularly important in a generation starship narrative is implied in Palmer's comment about the ship's human collective being the rough equivalent of a nation undergoing change. This comparison, sound as it is, breaks down when we consider that a nation on Earth represents only one among many such entities, all of them linked to one another through a web of social, political, and cultural relations. Sometimes these relations may be strained or break down altogether, but the fact remains that nations on Earth are never truly alone.[9] On the contrary, there is only one collective onboard a generation starship, and it does not have any chance of refreshing the cultural assumptions underlying the life of its inhabitants through intercourse with other, similar entities. The ship is a finite, isolated social nexus, too far away from home to conduct any communication with it, dead to outside influences because it is traversing a region of space utterly devoid of human habitation, and paralyzed in its cultural, ethical, and techno-scientific progress — unless it comes from inside, which becomes more difficult without external influences from other communities. If, for whatever reason, the process of generational transfer breaks down in a nation on Earth, the environment surrounding it is usually able to alleviate at least some of the damage through the various communication channels open between it and other countries: shows, movies, books, and music from their artists; news from their agencies; tourists from their populations; political and diplomatic missions from their governments; internet-based communication channels between individuals on all sides. All these influences constantly provide a default transfer of knowledge and values, thereby ensuring that, if nothing else, the collective in the throes of a generational crisis can endure and repair the damage in the fullness of time. The same goes for scientific and technological know-how; in the aftermath of World War II, for example, many of the belligerent nations received material help of one kind or another to bring their technological and industrial base up from the ashes, and one of the major endeavors facing all of us today consists in doing the same for those so-called Third World nations that have not been able to emerge from the era of colonialism with the necessary know-how to build a modern industrial infrastructure.[10]

Onboard a generation starship, however, there is no help from outside, and no communication with other societies; no osmosis between different kinds of cultural and artistic output, and no chance to travel to see other places; no genetic diversity, and no variation in the ethos informing the life of the collective. To survive in these conditions, the society onboard a generation starship needs to become literally self-sufficient, self-renewing, self-motivating, and self-assessing, lest it face the same fate of the people onboard the *Flashaway*, who, Palmer acknowledges, ended up spiraling into degradation because they spent centuries in space without social growth of any kind. Every skill and ability, every achievement and discovery, every intellectual trend and philosophical school of thought has to be not just preserved and recorded against forgetfulness, but also improved upon using only the creative energies available within the population of the worldship, so that at the moment in which an older generation starts passing its skills and ethos on to a new one, the process reverberates on every meaningful level of social interaction, enriching itself through endless refractions and echoing in the cultural milieu of a new, raw worldview. The price of not doing so, as Palmer indicates and Gregory Grimstone probably knows, is a matter of historical record. It can be seen in the ruins of all the empires and civilizations that succeeded one another at the top of the human adventure on Earth, only to fall and be replaced by their successors. If a civilization can die on Earth, where both the social and natural environment are at their most forgiving, it is all the more likely that it should happen to a careless crew consisting of comparatively few people onboard a steel coffin on its way to the stars. Within a Gernsbackian worldview, we cannot let such a disaster happen when the time comes for us to actually embark on a generational journey; the success of our attempt to construct Wollheim's "consensus future history" depends on our capacity to successfully execute every one of its stages. So we train, and every training exercise has its simulators. In Ray Palmer and Don Wilcox's mind, we could argue, "The Voyage That Lasted 600 Years" is one of the simulators of the generation starship stage, and this time the simulation is designed to end in failure, complete with what we can learn from it by using Palmer's editorial interpolation as a guide.

Ultimately, however, the guide fails. In the last paragraph of his analysis, Palmer's assessment of Grimstone's failures as Keeper of Traditions indicates that the most glaring of them is his inability to distinguish between lack of physical want and lack of moral want. Because the Keeper treated the former as automatically ensuring the latter, he became blind to the psychological predicament of his subjects. However, even a casual reading would reveal the contradictions in Palmer's argument: if anything, Grimstone worries too much about the psychological welfare of his wards. He is a historian charged with a role specifically designed to impact the moral life of the *Flashaway*'s crew, and he knows it. Every decision he makes must perforce involve an initial act of material influence—sterilization in 2166, food distribution in 2266, riot control in 2366. That, however, only happens because every time he wakes up from hibernation he is confronted with a crisis whose urgency leaves him no other choice but to take immediate action against some overwhelming material want. Once the immediate danger is past, Grimstone immediately returns to his role of teacher, historian, and custodian of American culture.

Flawed and emotional he may be, and his actions may well have amounted to disaster in the end, but he is all about morals and values — a frustrating thought to say the least, since he treats these morals as if they were scientific laws. Indeed, one might easily argue that it was precisely his lack of coldness that prompted him to make the mistake of favoring Louise's lineage in 2266, or again marrying her distant descendants in 2366 and precipitating the destruction with which he is confronted upon awakening in 2466.

Bad demiurge, indeed, but not for the reasons Palmer gives. Grimstone failed because he assumed that, since the colonists' distant ancestors had shared the American ethos at the time of launch, their descendants would find the same inspiration in the constant reiteration of this ethos without allowing it to change with time and circumstance. Palmer does utter this thought at the beginning of his interpolation, but at its end he refuses to face its logical consequences. Ultimately, it would appear that the final demiurge in the development of "The Voyage That Lasted 600 Years" is not the editor of *Amazing Stories*, because the editor himself obeys another entity: the laws, customs, and values of the United States of America, circa 1940. For him, these values are as incorruptible and impermeable to challenge as the American values of 2066 are for Grimstone, and Palmer's ultimate failure consists in his inability to see that the two are one and the same. There was no 2066 in 1940. That time was just an extrapolation of current trends into the kind of future which 1940 thought was going to take shape. However, if some of those trends were not susceptible to change (almost as if they had been scientific principles in their own right), then it was inevitable that they should not just survive unaltered all the way to our tomorrows, but actually shape those tomorrows according to a dogmatic, inflexible cultural blueprint. In the final analysis, the failure of the Keeper of Traditions does consist in the application of the wrong set of values, and part of the blame does lie with him for that, but even the larger metafictional perspective provided by the editor cannot penetrate the last layer of emplotment in the story — the grand narrative of a Platonic American ethos enduring forever in a heaven of unimpeachable first principles.

In later decades, the unexamined chauvinisms in the American mindset of those years came into sharp focus: violent racism and xenophobic greed in the treatment of racial and cultural Others; sexism in the treatment of women; homophobia in the treatment of alternate sexualities. While the United States was certainly not the only country on the planet to display those chauvinisms, and certainly not the worst in their implementation, it was also true that it was the only country whose ethos had been elevated to godhood by the local branch of the single literary genre wholly dedicated to advocating the future. The analysis of a generation starship narrative like "The Voyage

That Lasted 600 Years," with its emphasis on transmission of societal values over a long period of years in a closed environment, will point our attention in the direction of the choices made by SF writers and editors of the time as to which values were more relevant than others, as well as on the cultural assumptions underlying those choices. The science fiction of the pulp magazines ended up betraying its own premises when, in the name of catering to their constituency by refusing to challenge the set of values this constituency held dear, it refused to utilize the scientific method to examine every aspect of a society's path to the future, including the aspect of recursive generational transfer.

The SF writers and editors of the time would not have framed their explanation for this discrepancy in quite so many words; they would have said that without magazines there would be no genre, and magazines need to sell to stay alive and publish, so there was no other way. And they had a point, too. But the fact remains that Gernsbackian SF honored its own premises more in the breach than otherwise. Gernsback's own metaphor of mixing scientific fact and entertainment in SF with a 25 percent to 75 percent ratio was more accurate than would have been convenient for him: the overwhelming predominance of charming romance over fact resulted in a warping of the latter in order to satisfy the requirements of the former, thus undermining the very thing whose growth in American society the genre was supposed to nurture.

We are now approaching the end of the voyage that lasted 600 years, and a reader may be forgiven for wishing that, after enduring centuries of unsolicited confinement inside the *Flashaway*, the aggregate of human lives that came and went in the course of its voyage could find some form of reward in the story's denouement. Since we are in a pulp environment, perhaps it will not be excessive to imagine a particularly pleasant stretch of lawn in the palace grounds of the Robinello Colony governor's estate, situated in the capital of the system's main planet, carefully landscaped and lovingly tended on a daily basis, and featuring at its center an exquisitely carved block of black marble with all the names of those who lived and died onboard the *Flashaway* written on its face. It would be nice to imagine such a tribute to those who made it possible to open humanity's first extraterrestrial colony, the overwhelming majority of whom lived out lives of pointless misery at the mercy of incomprehensible agencies and never even saw the place that represented the whole point of their existence. But to indulge our wishes also opens us up to imagining the outcomes we would not want to see happen — a derelict ship, for example, drifting in utter blackness at some unspecified point between Earth and Robinello, its hull breached and worn by a combination of natural causes and human neglect, the corpses of its last crew bobbing in the wake of tiny gravitational eddies in its frozen, airless interior. No history for these people, and no reward. Just a footnote in a textbook of the farther future about a mission that left Earth and was never heard from again. Such an outcome would be terrible enough, but at least the tribute of story would remain. The expectant citizens of America in the years beyond 2666 would be left forever waiting for news of the long-dead *Flashaway*, but the readers of *Amazing Stories* would know what happened, and they would remember the lives of those who died in seeming pointlessness. There can be mercy in the world beyond stories when there is none in the world within them.

This, however, is not one of those cases. There is no mercy at the end of Wilcox's story, neither in its fictional dynamics nor in its metafictional negotiations. There is only betrayal, for the ultimate outcome of the *Flashaway*'s voyage is the worst imaginable. After a dispirited last toast with the 2466 captain of the ship, Grimstone returns directly to his hibernation chamber. There is nothing he can do for the people of that iteration. He goes back to sleep, hoping that the generational drift he was supposed to prevent will help him by layering another century of forgetfulness over the consequences of the events of 2366. When he wakes up again in 2566, he finds out that both his hopes and his fears have become true: his status as evil legend has subsided somewhat, leaving him marginally free to walk among the ship's crew again, but on the other hand their state of degradation is so extreme that there is again very little he can do to motivate them. When he reaches the ship's command center, moreover, he discovers that the few people who still retain a measure of sentience have used it to commit the ultimate treason. They have changed course, and when Grimstone, enraged over their mutiny, demands that they immediately return to the proper heading, their reply is perfectly in keeping with what we might expect from people who have been isolated in space for 500 years: the *Flashaway* is their ship now, not Grimstone's or the USA's, and they will steer it in whichever direction they please. They had no say in the decisions made by earthmen in 2066, and therefore feel no compulsion toward obeying them (102). Paradoxically, the lessening of the crew's superstitious fear of Grimstone and his magic has made them more of a danger, not less. They have forgotten enough about his powers to be defiant instead of cowering in his presence. But all legends have a grain of truth in them, and in Grimstone's case that means he still has his old instruments of persuasion; out pops the pistol again, and when the least careful of his opponents decides to call his bluff he shoots the man, killing him instantly. After that, he thaws Lora-Louise and puts the other two men in hibernation, piloting the *Flashaway* back on its proper course. No more hibernation for either of them. They will stay awake, pilot the ship, and have children whom they will teach how to fly it, so that they will finish the last stretch of the trip to

Robinello after their parents' passing. At the beginning he and Lora-Louise have to endure alone, but in time they do achieve a measure of success in imbuing the rest of the ship's population with the original vision of an American colony on Robinello (104). The mission, in fact, could still succeed. One hundred years of continued guidance on the part of a newly formed community of civilized leaders could turn things around enough to get the ship safely to destination, at which point the prospect of finally regaining a free existence, with its far more abundant resources and a new requirement to actually increase the population as much as possible, would restore the customary, planet-bound social and cultural dynamics in the fullness of time.

It is at this point, at the very end of the trip, that the real tragedy of this story explodes. In 2600, thirty-three years after Grimstone and Lora-Louise took control, things are going as well as can be expected. They have four children, all of them married; they have the running of the *Flashaway* and the trust of its native population; and they have each other. Then, one day on that year, they receive a radio message from a point some few light years ahead: it is the American colony on Robinello, founded fifty years before. When an astonished Grimstone asks him how they all got there, he explains that new methods of propulsion, developed after the *Flashaway* had left, shortened the time to target by a factor of a hundred. Now it only takes six years to reach the planet (104). The last two paragraphs of the story end with everyone onboard the generation starship waiting to embark on the fast shuttle the colony sent out to bring them there:

> The eighty-five *Flashaway* natives are scared half to death and at the same time as eager as children going to a circus. Lora-Louise has finished packing our boxes, bless her heart. That teasing smile she just gave me was because she noticed the "Who's Who Aboard the *Flashaway*" tucked snugly under my arm [104].

Why is everybody happy? What delusion of the mind possessed these people to cheer at the news that reached them from far ahead? Their civilization, the entity in the name of whose welfare almost three dozen generations of human beings lived and died inside a steel coffin, has forgotten and betrayed them. Their trip has no meaning, and to make matters worse the colony they were supposed to found has done nothing to go look for them in the fifty years since its founding. There is no part of the story, and no sentence at the end of it, that can give us a glimmer of hope in that respect. Yes, we readers can engage in all the ex post facto speculation we want, and say that maybe they did send someone, but it was during the time the *Flashaway* was off course so they never found it; or maybe finding an object as small as a single ship[11] in the vastness of interstellar space is well nigh impossible; or again that there is a welcoming committee ready for the *Flashaway* and its crew on arrival, and the Robinello colony worships them as pioneers. All plausible explanations, certainly, but not one of them matters. They are nothing but doubletalk, justifications designed to explain things the story does not bother to address, and in the end we can truthfully say that it is not their country that betrayed the generation starship's colonists; it is the story itself. Hundreds of captive, benighted lives used up and thrown away over a period of over half a millennium, forgotten except for the ship's log, and the single event that would give them all meaning is stripped away at the last minute by the cruelest plot twist the writer of "The Voyage That Lasted 600 Years" could have concocted — or maybe it was the editor. It does not matter. A cruel fate at the end of a story is one thing; in the world outside the story, a reader will remember and empathize with the characters. However, a cruel and meaningless fate at every level in a fictional enterprise and in every realm connected to it is something else altogether. The demiurges presiding over the engine of story have looked down at the characters they created and told them that they would have to go through 550 years of hell and like it, standing at the end of the last line in the narrative wearing an inane, psychotic grin more closely resembling the frozen rictus on the face of the condemned. Gregory Grimstone is, at the end of this tale, a good man in a rigged simulation, walking the pathways of the matrix in an attempt to make good on a promise delivered to other people in the same virtual world, and it is not his fault that the only way to fulfill his function as Keeper of Traditions — breaking through the fourth wall and addressing the problem on a larger chessboard — is denied to him. Unlike Pirandello's six characters, he is not aware of his creators, and therefore cannot confront them.

Thus ends the flight of the *Flashaway*. Its human cargo and the aggregate of their lives are largely gone, except for those 85 crewmembers waiting in the hold at the end of the tale. What they might have done but could not do, and what their warden might have seen but was prevented from seeing, stands as the legacy of the very first generation starship story to address the variables of human life inside its confines. Weighing its achievements and disappointments as objectively as possible, we would still have to conclude that the story is largely a failure — but if this is the case, it is not the character's failure, displayed in bright primary colors for us to dissect and use as a tool for learning. It is the failure of the writers and editors of the SF pulps, self-assured people who arranged for this story and many others like it to trip over their own plot, a flawed simulation featuring a set of self-contradictory premises destined to be forgotten halfway through its development. We should love Gregory Grimstone, Lora-Louise, the Dickinsons, the Sperrys, and everyone else on board, even if we may not like them. They did what they could in extremely trying circumstances.

2. The Gernsback Era, 1926–1940

During the three years between the founding of *Amazing Stories* and Gernsback's loss of its editorship, the magazine sported, in the frontispiece above the table of contents, a header that read "Extravagant Fiction Today ... Cold Fact Tomorrow." When Gernsback left the caption went as well, but the editorial attitude it had been written to announce remained. Then Gernsback started editing *Wonder Stories*, which carried another tagline above the table of contents, this one reading "The Magazine of Prophetic Fiction." The choice of wording in both captions is far from casual, especially in the latter case. Today, the readers and practitioners of science fiction use the genre's name to indicate a set of goals expressive of a contemporary, post-pulp perspective on its function: SF is advocacy and emplotment, social commentary, adventurous romp through space, speculation on our increasingly future-shocked present, and so on. More than anything else it is fiction, a participant in the great literary marketplace of our culture. For Gernsback, however, it was prophecy first and foremost. Only after that was it charming romance and didactic experience, and it is exactly because we are aware of the tenor of his times that we no longer expect SF to actually forecast our future. Whatever the critics and writers of the present think of Gernsback's editorial practices and financial handlings, whatever hoodlum cunning he may have brought to the job he created, and whatever sclerosis he may have fostered in the actual practice of SF writing, we can meaningfully argue that he was sincere in the aims he had established for his brainchild, and that he honestly believed science fiction to be the guide to tomorrow — or to the next 500 million years. Indeed, critics such as Gary Westfahl have recently published studies arguing in favor this interpretation.[12] The fault, if fault it was, lay somewhere else.

David Gerrold once pointed out that: "Science fiction is not a western with ray guns and spaceships. It is a genre so demanding that few of its practitioners are more than moderately competent at it. The responsibility to be logical and scientifically accurate, while at the same time telling a good dramatic story, will continually defeat any writer who approaches the field with less than total respect for its requirements" (37). Looking back on the age of the SF pulps, it is now fairly evident that Gernsback and most of the writers and editors in the field were too literal in the application of his 75 percent charming romance–25 percent science rule to actually analyze what kind of fictional constructs they were building for publication on a monthly basis, and unfortunately the generation starship stories we saw in this chapter are no exception. For example:

- Why does the Keeper of Tradition wake up from hibernation only once in a hundred years? The interval is arbitrary, designed to artificially increase the story's dramatic impact by creating the very problem it is supposed to forestall. A far more functional choice would have been to have Grimstone wake up at the birth or early adulthood of every generation, instruct them for a year or so, and then go back to his chamber. He is 28 at the moment of departure (104), so these intervals would be spread widely enough to enable the *Flashaway* to reach Robinello before his death (he would be in his early fifties by then), while at the same time allowing him to much more effectively keep his finger on the pulse of shipboard life.

- If population control is so fundamental in a closed system like a generation ship, and if sterilization was available to the crew in 2266, why did they not use it from the beginning? Again, this is an artificial obstacle, established more for the sake of cheap dramatic tension than anything else. Every couple in every generation, irrespective of romantic maladies, starry backgrounds, or other vagaries of the reproductive instinct, could easily have been sterilized immediately after the second child — unless the ship had been underpopulated, in which case everyone could have indulged themselves until the emergency had subsided. Also, it is hard to imagine the absence of contraceptives in the 21st century, considering that the 1940s already had some rudimentary means of birth control.

- Most crucially, however, why bother sending out the *Flashaway* as a generation starship at all? If we have postulated a technology of cryogenic suspension advanced enough to sustain human life through repeated episodes of thawing and re-freezing over a period of 600 years, why go to all the trouble of filling the ship with dozens of generations' worth of live bodies? The organizers of the trip might have saved themselves and their cosmonauts a lot of trouble by simply stuffing two hundred people in hibernation chambers and letting the automatic systems of the ship take it to Robinello. Every ten years or so, a skeleton crew would wake up, perform maintenance and check the course, and then go back to sleep. Alternating the crews would give everyone on board the chance to get to Robinello with a lot of life left in them, especially if they had been picked in their twenties.

American science fiction in the Gernsback era was not a (mostly) low-level literary endeavor because its premises or dreams were somehow flawed; it was low-level because editorial practices, always conscious of what the publisher thought the public wanted, corrupted the observance of these premises in the name of satisfying a commercial demand for a certain kind of formula fiction. Even Attebery and Wollheim's consensus history of the future, the highest potential achievement of the Gernsbackian plan for SF's scientific advocacy, suffered through too many inconsistent setups, contradictory plot developments, and unexamined implications. The adherence of a science fiction narrative to the internal consistency of its technological and scientific premises is everything that stands between writing SF and writing fancy. It is comparatively easy to stick trees upside down in the ground, paint people bright orange, and make nightstands walk around on four stubby boar legs, but in this case there is no story. If we solve all our plot twists and moral dilemmas by inventing deus ex machina solutions, then there is no dramatic tension, no barrier on the way to the characters' goals, and no need to explore their inner lives. The writing of mainstream fiction in general thrives on the limitations built into our world, because those limitations give us the basic dramatic conflict of a narrative. Science fiction, on the other hand, is a genre where coming up with transcendent, larger-than-life developments is not so much possible as necessary, so that the temptation to overcome conflict with whiz-bangs becomes more difficult to resist. Such is the case, for example, of "The Living Galaxy." If Manning's story feels less riddled with contradiction and silliness than "The Voyage That Lasted 600 Years," this is only because most of the premises and plot developments that would have led to such dangers were eliminated before the narrative began, replaced by virtual omnipotence. Manning postulated the existence of a sort of lay heaven, a commonwealth of demigods. Premises of this caliber will make even the sturdiest of character conflicts vanish. That is why stories written along this pattern, with the notable exception of Stapledon's *Last and First Men* (1929) and *Star Maker* (1937), are usually fairly short. A narrative can only bear so much weight for so long.

By the time "The Voyage That Lasted 600 Years" appeared in print, the Gernsback era was coming to a close. His brand of advocacy was still alive and well, but the practices through which he and his followers were trying to implement it were not. The thematic paucity and stylistic awkwardness of most of the fiction appearing in the pulps were beginning to attract a degree of hostility superior to that usually awarded them by the public at large, and most of it was coming from within the SF field itself. A new generation of writers and editors had started developing more effective ways of advocating the future of American desire. With the benefit of hindsight, we can now say that the beginning of the end for the Gernsback era can be situated in 1937, when John W. Campbell, Jr., took over the editorship of *Astounding Stories* from F. Orlin Tremaine, renamed the magazine *Astounding Science Fiction*, and transformed it into the most influential serial SF publication of the 1940s and 1950s. The new generation of practitioners in the field had grown up reading the pulps and had loved them, but they had also seen their flaws. They took the lessons of their forebears and improved on them, creating new SF stories for a new generation of readers. Thus values were transmitted from parents to children, so to speak, and the enterprise thrived. The passage from one era in science fiction to the other was to be mirrored and refracted in the generation starship stories of the next iteration.

CHAPTER 3

The Campbell Era, 1937–1949

They were astounding years. They were *Astounding* years. They were the years of Isaac Asimov and Robert Heinlein, of psychohistory and the Sevagram, of Chesley Bonestell, Wernher Von Braun, and *The Conquest of Space*. They were also years of growth for the generation starship, but most importantly, they were the years of John W. Campbell, of the man who edited the magazine and wrote the editorials and answered the letters and hired the writers and told them — and through them told us — what science fiction really was:

> Campbell and his magazine *Astounding* stand for the second era of the sf magazines as Gernsback stands for the first. The period that begins with his editorship is often called the Golden Age of sf, and many of the best-known writers in the field first appeared in his magazine. However, part of Campbell's success was a matter of building on Gernsback's inventions, which included not only the fictional content but also the standard format: the chatty editorials, the advertising ... the letters from fans [Attebery 37].

The dreams of future advocacy of the Gernsback age, and the desires these dreams had sheltered within the heart of magazine SF, were not dead. In fact, they had never been more alive, but their practical application on the part of the original generation of science fiction writers and editors was losing traction. By the 1940s most of the SF writers of the Gernsback school had run out of meaningful things to say, and were gradually replaced by "the first generation of writers who had grown up on science fiction, had been grounded and, as it were, schooled in science fiction and hence were able to utilize this in advancing further" (Wollheim 75). When this new generation matured enough to start publishing, they found Campbell waiting for them at the helm of *Astounding Science Fiction*. He told them the narrative of the future, instructed them on how to tell the tale themselves, and once they were being published in his magazine, he integrated their voices in the ultimate resonance chamber for his brand of advocacy — an advocacy that, however different from Gernsback's in its procedures, looked almost the same in its intentions.

At the beginning of his editorial in the same issue of *Astounding* in which "Universe," the first part in Robert Heinlein's generation starship narrative, appeared, Campbell wrote that "Science-fiction novels are 'period pieces,' historical novels laid against a background of history that hasn't happened yet," and Gernsback would certainly have echoed this opinion (5). Gernsback, however, had dressed SF in the garb of a superhuman, larger-than-life clown, all pleasing entertainment peppered with science in an ultimately flighty package, while Campbell embedded the technological wonders featured in the Gernsback pulps into the everyday. In Asimov's words, "Science fiction became more than a personal battle between an all-good hero and an all-bad villain ... the irascible old scientist, the beautiful daughter of the scientist, the cardboard menace from alien worlds ... all were discarded. In their place, Campbell wanted businessmen, space-ship crewmen, young engineers, housewives, robots that were logical machines" (41–42). Campbell did not make the dream of science fiction more real than Gernsback had; he made the act of storytelling this dream more pervasive and plausible. He dressed SF in plainer clothes, gave it the face of everyday people, and made sure that it spoke its advocacy in the language of the times. This chapter is the story of those times, of the generation of writers who spoke the future of desire to the people living in them, and of the generation starships that took this future on a crawling, sometimes stuttering voyage to the distant stars.

The thirties had been good to American science fiction. The decade "began with the United States doubting itself, even questioning its own survival, and ended with an optimistic look at a future of increasing technological miracles ... even though that hope was shadowed by the beginnings of the war in Europe" (Gunn 129). In the two generations of writers and editors that coexisted during those ten years or so, SF had answers for both states of mind in the collective psyche. In times of hardship we turn to our storytellers for comfort, and at the beginning of the thirties, public anxieties about the country's socio-economic future sent millions to Broadway, to theatres, to radio shows, and to the newsstand. Not everyone was able to afford the price of a play, a musical, or a movie, but the pulps were cheap and the stories they featured were simple, outlandish, and fun.[1] To someone suffering through unemployment, poverty, and an increasing sense of entrapment inside a featureless industrial wasteland grinding slowly to a halt, the luridly colored covers of a magazine like *Wonder Stories* and the equally bright future presented in such narratives as "The Living Galaxy" must have represented a welcome outlet for their desire to escape, as well as a chance to hope that there might actually *be* a future. Indeed, the entertainment industry of the 1930s may well have had a fundamental role to play in keeping the American public sane and functional throughout the Depression.

Towards the end of the decade, as the American economy repaired itself and a more optimistic population at home turned towards darkening skies abroad, science fiction again provided an imaginative outlet for the collective psyche. The stories were essentially the same kind that had kept people entertained a few years before, but now their influence expressed itself both through advocacy for the bright American future of the Gernsback zeitgeist and through a militant commitment to enabling the United States to develop the technological and industrial power necessary to face the increasingly worsening situation in Europe. "AMERICA *must prepare* NOW," screamed the title of an editorial in the same issue of *Amazing Stories* where "The Voyage That Lasted 600 Years" appeared. The author was not Raymond Palmer, but the publisher himself, William B. Ziff of Ziff-Davis, and the tone of his piece was that of a preacher warning against the apocalypse:

> We face a combination of powerful enemies in both Europe and Asia, who control between them military establishments of the most fantastic proportions ever contemplated in this world. Hungry and predatory, they are ruled by an acknowledged dream of world conquest. Their hatred and contempt for us and our system of life is implacable and unbounded. Also, the greatest booty in the world is to be found here in the rich and unprotected United States [8].

The language Ziff employed to unfavorably compare the military preparedness of the U.S. to that of imperial Japan and Nazi Germany was pure pulp SF — hyperbolic adjectives, horrified wonder at the enemy's cutting-edge technology, fear at the aggressiveness of foreigners, and outrage at "their hatred and contempt for us and our system of life." In the power fantasy created within the emplotment of his editorial's narrative, America has become the defenseless damsel in distress of that issue's cover, Lady Liberty hijacked by the monstrous, highly technological Other while her men shoot at it with obsolete guns of negligible impact. The representation of the enemy on the cover's painting replaces the drab grey, black, or khaki of the Nazi or Japanese uniform with the bright green metal of an outlandish alien robot, but the cathartic power of the symbol remains. America was in danger, and science fiction was there to do its part.

The pulp magazines of the Gernsback generation, however, found it difficult to mirror the increasing seriousness of the international situation that had started bleeding into the burgeoning optimism in American society with a new-found sense of urgency. Born in different, altogether more relaxed times, their light-hearted tones, simple plots, and primary-color covers had been a godsend for allaying the more inchoate anxieties of Depression-era economic hardship. However, once these anxieties subsided with the gradual waning of the Depression, they were replaced by more direct physical dangers to American interests, and the Gernsback template started losing its power to convey the message of future advocacy that still remained the genre's primary goal. Its desire for the future was as strong as it had been in 1926, but something had drained out of the procedures that were supposed to transform this desire into actuality.

It is likely that the problem was further exacerbated by Gernsback's disappearance from the SF publishing scene. In 1936, in the wake of poor sales and a dwindling reader base, Gernsback sold *Wonder Stories* to Standard Magazines and left the field to which he had given birth. He would return to it briefly between 1952 and 1953 before abandoning it for good, and in the process he would contribute to that period's crop of generation starship stories. In the meantime, however, SF had lost its first voice. Gernsback's execution of his plans for the genre may have been flawed, and some of the writers who had had trouble getting him to pay them for their stories may have called him "Hugo the Rat," but he was nevertheless the father of science fiction, the man who had given it a name, a venue of publication, a sense of identity, and a direction. His departure suddenly left a substantial void, and the field was quick to fill it. In January 1930, Clayton Magazines had started publishing another SF pulp, *Astounding Stories of Super Science*. Under its first two editors, Harry Bates and F. Orlin Tremaine, the magazine had been a standard example of the Gernsbackian template, with the relevant exception of "its new word rate: two cents a word, on acceptance. That was magnificence compared to the customary half-cent a word paid by *Amazing Stories* on publication ... and by *Wonder Stories* after publication" (Gunn 129). When John W. Campbell, Jr., became editor of *Astounding* in 1937, the word rate remained, but everything else went. Campbell had a very clear idea of what he wanted from — and for — science fiction, and wasted little time in setting up the conditions necessary to achieve it:

> *Astounding* in that period certainly had a unique feel to it, and it is reasonable to conclude that it was largely because of the personality of the editor, perceived both directly, through his editorials, and indirectly, through his writers. If it should seem odd that one magazine should dominate the entire genre ... it must be remembered that sf during the 1940s ... was magazine fiction, and thus very largely short fiction [James 62–63].

Campbell's influence was not simply the result of a strong, often domineering personality (a dominance that, in later years, would devolve into a stagnating, uncompromising perspective). It was also the result of a deep knowledge of the field, both as a writer and as an editor. Born in 1910, Campbell had grown up with the science fiction magazines of the Gernsback era, and had started selling his stories to them while still in his teens. James Gunn describes him as "a prototype for the precocious youngster who turns to science fiction to make up for his own social inadequacies, who makes science fiction a career or a religion because reality is both disappointing and dull" (146), and shorn of its more romantic overtones, this picture is essentially correct. Campbell had started reading the more generic fantastic pulps like *Weird Tales* and *Argosy* before the birth of *Amazing*, and since 1926 he had been an avid reader of the genre magazines Gernsback and his peers had started publishing in rapid succession. Of the contributors to *Amazing* during Campbell's formative years, it was the galactic-empire, raygun space opera of E. E. "Doc" Smith that had a lasting influence on him. When Campbell started publishing his own SF, his early stories displayed the same focus and themes, so that "in the early 1930s JWC quickly built a reputation as ... Smith's chief rival in writing galactic epics of superscience" (Clute & Nicholls 187). Then, in the mid–1930s, Campbell entered the second—and final—phase of his writing career, when he started publishing, under the pseudonym of Don A. Stuart, a series of stories that "helped create a new kind of science fiction in which the exterior problem was only a means of getting at a deeper problem of psychology, philosophy, or sociology, mixed with personal and racial tragedy and all arranged neatly along an effective story line" (Gunn 147).

But it was not just these narratives' thematic concerns that had changed; their tone represented an equally decisive break from the stories of the Gernsback generation. Consider, for example, this passage from the first of the Don A. Stuart stories, "Twilight," published in 1934 in *Astounding Stories*. In distinctly Wellsian fashion, the time traveler in the narrative returns from seven million years in the future to tell his astonished listener about the end of the human race, a period in which mankind has lost all knowledge and drive and is living out its last remaining years tended by nearly eternal, perfect machines whose workings and function nobody remembers any longer:

> Twilight. The sun has set. The desert out beyond, in its mystic, changing colors. The great, metal city rising straight-walled to the human city broken by spires and towers and great trees with scented blossoms. The silvery-rose glow in the paradise of gardens above. And all the great city structure throbbing and humming to the steady gentle beat of perfect, deathless machines built more than three million years before—and never touched since that time by human hands. And they go on. The dead city. The men that have lived, and hoped, and built—and died to leave behind them those little men who can only wonder and look and long for a forgotten kind of companionship. They wander through the vast cities their ancestors built, knowing less of them than the machines themselves [41].

"Twilight" was published in the same year as "The Living Galaxy," and the two narratives certainly share some similarities in the hypertrophic timelines and majestic mechanical constructs peppering their landscapes, but the handling of these features varies considerably from one to the other. In his generation-starship story, Laurence Manning had used the vast stretches of time and the technological miracles enveloping the action almost purely for their direct aesthetic impact, without letting the human fallout of their existence enter the dramatic balance of the tale. We know that, over a four-million-year voyage, Bzonn and his cohorts advance every branch of human knowledge and seed the universe with the human genetic template, but we have no idea of what makes them laugh or cry, what kind of new dishes their cooks have invented during the voyage, how their scientific discoveries influenced their perception of the divine, or whether some of them were bothered by the potentially dehumanizing effects of the anti-aging treatments that made them virtually immortal. Details of this kind simply do not enter the computations affecting the drama of the story, a condition that robs the narrative of the possibility to extrapolate and reflect on the social implications of the technology it postulates and ultimately undermines much of its long-term plausibility.

Campbell, on the contrary, wrote to place the smallness of the human within the largeness of the universe. The result is still space opera, still a larger-than-life tale of distant times, but possessed of a lyrical quality and empathy for the human condition generally absent from the SF of the Gernsback generation. Equally rare in the early pulps would have been the story's pervasive sense of the causal relationship between intent and outcome, cause and consequence, all brought down to plateau at a human, not superhuman, level. In "Twilight," mankind is still enthralled by the grand space-opera dream of immortality and freedom from want, but our attempt to bring this dream into the realm of the actual crumbles to dust in our hands at the very moment of success. In a world where perfect, indestructible, eternal machines work ceaselessly to take care of our every want, the desire to know the world decreases with the disappearance of the survival-related drive to understand, invent, and innovate. In the world of Campbell's story, the first is linked to the second, and dies if the other does. As a result, there is no multi-galactic polity in the far future, no immortal, omnipotent humankind, and no mighty threat to its existence to spice up the action. There are only the grey years succeeding one another in listless monotony, while the remnants of our civilization wait out their lifespan on the way to extinction, tended by machines they no longer comprehend. Their mistake, so the time traveler tells us, was that "They didn't realize that things shouldn't go on forever" (28). No such line of thought found its way into "Doc" Smith's *The Skylark of Space* (1928),

Gernsback's *Ralph 124C 41+*, or the two generation starship narratives analyzed in Chapter 2. In the Gernsback zeitgeist the future was our birthright, but in Campbell's world the reality of our eventual circumstances may well dictate otherwise. That this story should appear in a new, high-paying magazine was the index of how different the next generation of SF narratives was going to be.

In the years between 1934 and 1937, Campbell published several stories in the same mold as "Twilight," all under the Don A. Stuart pseudonym, and even though his literary production all but ceased when he became editor of *Astounding* (a position he kept until his death in 1971), the themes and writing style he had developed informed his attitude in his new role. In keeping with the kind of science fiction he had been writing before taking on the job, Campbell had an image of the genre as a substantially less jocular, less haphazard enterprise than the Gernsback era had either conceived or practiced. Under his editorship *Astounding Stories of Super Science* changed on every level — beginning with the magazine's name, which became *Astounding Science Fiction*. Campbell would also have dropped the sensationalistic adjective from the title, but he was beaten to the punch by the publication in 1939 of another SF periodical, simply entitled *Science Fiction*. He eventually got his more appropriate label in 1960, when the magazine was renamed *Analog*.

Astounding's graphic presentation matched the seriousness of its new title. During the Gernsback years, the covers of *Amazing Stories* and *Wonder Stories*, themselves representative of the artwork featured in the SF pulps at large, suffered from "trademark eye-popping, flat colors, [which] were actually necessary because, to cut costs, Gernsback seemingly used a three color printing process rather than the normal four-color" (Holland 31). These garish hues often conspired with the choice of subjects to undermine the quality of the artwork it was supposed to bring to life, giving it a juvenile, cartoonish look strongly at odds with the intent of making the future portrayed on the magazine's cover seem plausible. Under Campbell's guidance, on the other hand, the *Astounding* covers became "sombre in colour, with slick modernistic machinery, plausible human beings, and sometimes with realistic astronomical paintings" (James 56). Underlining this change in attitude towards the visualization of the magazine's contents was Campbell's realization that SF relies on graphic illustration more heavily than other genres do. Gernsback himself had had an inkling of this situation at the beginning of his tenure with *Amazing*, when he found and hired such artists as Leo Morey, Frank R. Paul, and Virgil Finlay. In a decade or so of mostly lurid covers and toyish illustrations, their work represented what was best in the capacity of the early pulps to visualize the future. Campbell continued this trend, insisting on a basic level of quality in *Astounding*'s visual production standards that would at least guarantee a default amount of plausibility, even when the covers and the interior illustrations were not the highest examples of their kind.

And then the writers came: Isaac Asimov, Robert Heinlein, James Blish, Ray Bradbury, "Doc" Smith, A. E. Van Vogt, Jack Williamson, L. Sprague de Camp, Clifford D. Simak, Henry Kuttner, Catherine L. Moore, Theodore Sturgeon, and Lester Del Rey. They were the best their two generations had to offer — already established authors like Williamson and Simak, who had a relevant publishing record for the Gernsback pulps and now found themselves writing for the new stage in the genre's development; and newly minted writers like Blish and Asimov, the first generation to grow up within — and learn from — SF as an established literary genre. "Science fiction builds upon science fiction," wrote Donald A. Wollheim in 1971, "and in the fact that magazines had been publishing s-f [sic] under that label since 1926 lay the reason why this generation of writers reached their twenties in time to write for Campbell when he, who was also a first-generation writer raised in the same school, was waiting and looking for better stuff" (75). Campbell may have stopped writing fiction of his own, but he knew how innovative the themes and narrative strategies he had developed in it were, and now he set about teaching what he had learned:

> Campbell soon proved himself a good and ambitious editor. He forced his writers to think much harder about what they were trying to say, and clamped down on gosh-wowery.... Also, he had the fortune to take over at a good time, when the monstrous footprints of Burroughs and Gernsback had, to some extent at least, obliterated one another. The stiffening breeze from Europe also introduced a more responsible note. He worked, too, on logic — a quality his competitors had always been short of ... it led him to reject the Bug-Eyed Monsters — known in the trade as BEMs — and many of the trashy plots that went with them [Aldiss & Wingrove 234].

Like Gernsback, Campbell believed that "the business of science fiction is to predict the probable trends of the future" (qtd. in Landon 56), and again like Gernsback, he had in mind a particular set of these probable trends which he wanted his SF to advocate. However, during his formative years as a writer for the early pulps, he had realized that there can be no long-lasting advocacy without a pervasive, fully integrated, internally self-consistent vision of this possible future to be transmitted to a large audience. If the issues on the table were still belief and desire, if the goal remained what it had been for the Gernsback generation — to train the public for the onset of the future — then succeeding where they had failed required SF to take itself utterly seriously, dress for the role, and speak the language of the world to come as if it were already here. Campbell ultimately believed that the enterprise of science fiction truly had the power to change the world, as witnessed, he pointed out more than once, by the fact that there were a lot of subscribers to *Astounding* in Los Alamos during the creation of the bomb, as well as at NASA during the sixties. Thus he taught his writers how to emplot the future, argued with them, and harassed them when he thought they were not thinking hard enough or logically enough about the human consequences of the technology and science they postulated in their stories.

He almost always had things his way, too. He was a forceful personality, bordering on the domineering and often crossing that border, but he was no hidebound apologist of science and technology, at least not in his glory years. His ideas were sound, his editorial suggestions to the point, and his ability to brainstorm with his writers considerable — it gave SF its best ideas of those times. For example, there was Campbell's hand behind the writing of "Nightfall," one of Asimov's best known stories, as well as in the formulation of the latter's famous three laws of robotics. Theodore Sturgeon, one of the most consciously lyrical of the new generation of *Astounding* writers, "recounted that the editor would challenge his writers with assignments such as: 'Write me a story about a man who will die in twenty-four hours unless he can answer this question: "How do you know you're sane?"' or 'Write me a story about a creature who thinks as well as a man but not like a man'" (Landon 55).

Perhaps the most influential among the writers of the new generation, and certainly the one who most effectively embodied and expressed the Campbell ethos of SF advocacy, was Robert Heinlein. By the end of 1941, the year he had published his two-part generation starship story in *Astounding*, Heinlein had become a father figure of sorts for the younger authors whom Campbell had assembled. Born in 1907, he was older than any of them — thirteen years older than Asimov and Bradbury; fourteen years older than Blish; eleven years older than Sturgeon; and three years older than Campbell himself. In fact, had he been a science fiction writer from the beginning, he would have fit squarely into the Gernsback generation. But he was not. Before publishing his first SF story in 1939, Heinlein had graduated from Annapolis, served onboard the USS *Lexington* and USS *Roper* before being discharged from the Navy in the aftermath of a bout with tuberculosis, attended college for a while, worked such different jobs as real estate sales and silver mining, and unsuccessfully ran for the California State Assembly. When he became part of Campbell's group of writers, he brought with him a set of skills and a level of life experience unmatched in an essentially teenage and post-teenage intellectual environment. He was the only one who could go toe-to-toe with Campbell in an argument on science fiction writing and hope to win, although he often did bow down to Campbell's advice during the first year or so of his presence in *Astounding*. In the fullness of time, their relationship would cool down considerably, especially after World War II when Heinlein became the first SF writer to publish his stories outside genre magazines, but the parameters for SF writing they created together exerted an enormous influence over later generations of writers. In his 1947 paper "On the Writing of Speculative Fiction," Heinlein codified the *Astounding* approach to SF writing by identifying five basic precepts that every story in the field was expected to follow:

1. The conditions must be, in some respect, different from here-and-now, although the difference may lie only in an invention made in the course of the story.
2. The new conditions must be an essential part of the story.
3. The problem itself—the "plot"—must be a *human* problem.
4. The human problem must be one which is created by, or indispensably affected by, the new conditions.
5. And lastly, no established fact shall be violated, and, furthermore, when the story requires that a theory contrary to present accepted theory be used, the new theory should be rendered reasonably plausible and it must include and explain established facts as satisfactorily as the one the author saw fit to junk. It may be far-fetched, it may be fantastic, but it must *not* be at variance with observed facts, i.e., if you are going to assume that the human race descended from Martians, then you've *got* to explain our apparent close relationship to terrestrial anthropoid apes as well [qtd. in James 59].

SF stories, in Heinlein's formulation, should no longer be about gadgets, machines, or an individual stroke of genius. They would address, for example, the industrial infrastructure and socio-political dynamics that made it both possible and desirable to mass produce the gadgets; the changed conditions imposed upon the world of human affairs by the invention, production, and deployment of the machines; and the paradigm shifts that particular stroke of genius would bring about in our world view and in the human race's sense of its place in the universe. For both Campbell and Heinlein, scientific accuracy in SF was of paramount importance. It supported the narrative by lending it believability and legitimacy, while the fiction contributed to the science by giving it an immediate human dimension, thereby creating a feedback loop that would prompt writers to use SF's unique combination of science and literature to push the boundaries of both.

But the Heinlein/Campbell recipe did not treat rigorous extrapolation, internal consistency, logic, and the primacy of the human element simply as a set of themes to be applied in a science fiction story. They were also stylistic and linguistic expressions of a worldview, the meta-language of the inchoate future made into a shadow of actuality by a powerful act of embedding. The science fiction of the Gernsback era had spoken the language of recess in kindergarten, of children in bright costumes playing at Earthlings and Martians with fake rayguns; its language had been the language of the 1920s and 1930s with a few strange-sounding names and titles thrown in: Ralph 124C 41+, History Zeta Nine, Bzonn. No more than that was needed to make these characters pass for citizens of tomorrow, because there was precious little sense of an inside to them. They walked around playing with their almighty toys and name-dropping the wonders of the world on each other, and that was all. But Campbell, Heinlein, and the rest of the *Astounding* writers wanted real people with real existences, and to do that they needed these people to talk, walk, argue, love, and hate plausibly, something requiring the development of writing techniques that could present the future as a) exotic and strange enough to stimulate the readers' sense of wonder and b) plausible enough to avoid making their readers feel like they were looking at a papier-mâché world.

Campbell had already practiced this technique and passed it on to his writers, but Heinlein was the first and the best at developing and implementing it. He devised an alternative to the infodump lectures that were typical of the Gernsback era by narrating the story under the assumption that the estranging elements he had postulated were perfectly normal to the characters living with them—because, in fact, they really were. The characters would not find their world amazing, because they were born in it. The readers, on the other hand, would. Heinlein fundamentally changed the game of SF by playing it at a meta-narrative level. Suddenly, the burden of living in the future was shifted from the characters to the readers, who had to piece together the information they needed to understand the changed conditions by careful sifting of the clues sprinkled here and there throughout the text. It literally was, and still is today, armchair detective work. Perhaps the most classic (and certainly the most frequently mentioned) example of Heinlein's figure-it-out-as-you-go writing style can be found at the beginning of his novel *Beyond This Horizon*. First published in *Astounding* as a two-part serial in the April and May 1942 issues, and re-issued in book form in 1948, the novel is set in a future Earth that has been transformed into an economic utopia. At the beginning of the book, the protagonist is walking to a business meeting at the "Bureau of Business Statistics":

> Hamilton Felix let himself off at the thirteenth level of the Department of Finance, mounted a slideway to the left, and stepped off the strip at a door marked:
>
> BUREAU OF ECONOMIC STATISTICS
> Office of Analysis and Prediction
> Director
> PRIVATE

He punched the door with a code combination, and awaited face check. It came promptly. The door dilated, and a voice inside said, "Come in, Felix." He stepped inside, glanced at his host and remarked, "You make ninety-eight." "Ninety-eight what?" "Ninety-eight sourpusses in the last twenty minutes. It's a game. I just made it up" [5].

The scene in itself—someone walking into someone else's office and starting a conversation—is potentially as normal as any other of its kind in a mainstream novel, but there are estranging elements in the background that immediately identify it as SF. For example, Felix uses a "slideway" to reach the director's office, and once there he goes through a security check using a system comprising a lock with a digital code combination and a "face check." For a 21st-century reader, these two elements may actually not be estranging any longer; it is now commonplace to find moving walkways in stores, offices, and other public places, and security checks involving digital locks and visual recognition systems have been around for a while. In 1942, however, they were not, and a reader of those times would immediately have noticed the unusual term. If they had been experienced SF readers, and therefore already familiar with the infodump strategies of the Gernsback pulps, they would also have noticed that Heinlein was not bothering to either justify his usage of those terms or explain the technology of the artifact they indicate. They were just there. And then, of course, there is that business of the dilating door. This time nobody is familiar with that verb as applied to that particular action, not in 1942 or in the early 2000s, and again, that thing is just there. In an essay written in the late 1960s, Harlan Ellison related his reaction to reading that line when he wrote, "And no discussion. Just 'the door dilated.' I read across it, and was two lines down before I realised what the image had been, what the words had called forth. A *dilating* door. It didn't open, it *irized!* Dear God, now I knew I was in a future world" (qtd. in James 115). As do we. If *Beyond This Horizon* had been a tale written in the Gernsback mold, a lengthy, clumsy infodump-cum-lecture paragraph would have followed these small instances of estrangement, explaining their workings and extolling the virtues of the society that had created them. But this was Heinlein, these were the 1940s, and the magazine was *Astounding*, so the reader was left to contextualize the gadgets and reason through the connections—technological, scientific, social, historical—that the existence of these gadgets implied.

The same happens with the social aspects of the world portrayed in the story. Immediately after the exchange quoted above, Felix's interlocutor muses about his guest's lopsided sense of humor, and the third-person narrative voice lets us look over his shoulder when he thinks that "Hamilton's remarks often did not appear serious, frequently even seemed technically sense-free. Nor did they appear to follow the six principles of humor—Monroe-Alpha prided himself on his sense of humor" (5). From this brief passage we can infer that in the world of *Beyond This Horizon* the employment of a sense of humor is a far more regimented practice than it is today, for reasons that the book does not explain at that stage in the plot. We will have to wait for more of those tiny windows onto the social landscape of the future until, bit by bit, the piecing together of all the tiny windows creates a comprehensive mosaic, a full picture of the world. Everything in Heinlein's story moves at the pace of everyday life *in the world within the fiction*. The characters in it would not lecture each other on slideways, dilating doors and the six principles of humor, for the same reason two teenagers of today would not lecture each other on how to use an iPod. They already know, and it is neither their fault nor their problem that we do not.

The Gernsback generation had tried to overcome this narrative problem by explaining the whys and hows of one or more estranging elements through lengthy, plot-stopping infodump lectures, but the net effect of this rather blunt technique was that it pulled the readers out of the story. Suddenly hearing the professorial voice of the Author explaining this or that aspect of the future made them aware of being in a fictional world, and the contract was broken. There was no drama, no story, and no future. Heinlein's technique, on the other hand, constituted a far better solution to the problem of presenting information about the future plausibly, so that after reading a story like *Beyond This Horizon* a reader might find it easier to believe in a world inhabited by real people with real lives, people similar enough to us to look and sound like our distant descendants, but different enough from us to emanate an agreeable aura of otherness, of not coming from here and now.

At a panel discussion in the September 2007 issue of *Locus* magazine, organized on the occasion of the centenary of Heinlein's birth,[2] Graham Sleight commented on the basic attitude underlying his SF writing:

> The distinguishing thing about Heinlein is this axiom that the universe can be made sense of, that there is one set of answers to the questions we have, and someone who's smart enough and works hard enough can get somewhere by using those answers. Ultimately, this is philosophically a positivist point of view, as opposed to, say, modernism or postmodernism, in which there are no answers or multiple answers [52].

Sleight's appreciation is a fair description of everything that was constructive in Heinlein's SF — and everything that was not. On the constructive side, this outlook imbued his writing with the ethos, language, and attitude of the American middle class, both inside the fiction and outside of it — inside because the typical Heinleinian heroes are representative of this set of values, competent men who find the right answers to the right questions and use them to build the future, like for example D. D. Harriman, the visionary entrepreneur who single-handedly jump-starts the American space program in "The Man Who Sold the Moon" (1949); outside because those same values imbue the act of reading itself. Like a meta-narrative Heinleinian hero, we readers must piece together the puzzle of the future world portrayed in the story, working our way toward a fully integrated image of its peculiarities and distinctive traits. At the same time as the characters in a Heinlein story put together the pieces that give them the key to unlocking the meaning of the world, the readers on the other side of the wall of fiction must do the same to map out the action, understand the morals underlying the main dramatic conflict, and find the way to open the full image of the future in the mind's eye. As had been the case for Campbell's fiction, the future is not a birthright in Heinlein's. It must be earned by dint of hard work and the application of reason, and everyone must work at it, characters and readers alike. Otherwise, how can the public learn how to build the future from the template provided in *Astounding*?

On the less constructive side, the positivist outlook informing Heinlein's writing also fostered a cold-hearted attitude towards those characters — and, by extension, those readers — who did not agree with the single set of answers he had developed. Most narratives need an antagonist of some sort to provide the engine of story with enough fuel to run its course, and it was common for Heinlein to create characters espousing values with which he did not agree precisely so they could become the antagonist:

> In Heinlein's early story "The Roads Must Roll" (1940), the engineer hero Gaines is in charge of keeping an elaborate system of automated highways working. He faces what seems to be mechanical failure but is really an act of sabotage by disaffected workers. Heinlein deftly suggests that it is the application of Gaines's engineering knowledge to a human situation that restores order.... So long as the solution is neat and efficient, the human cost (never borne by the engineer himself) seems worthwhile. The story glorifies Gaines and his core of managers and disparages the striking workers, whose concerns are merely personal and emotional [Attebery 38–39].

It is interesting to note how a revision of science fiction's attitude that involved greater attention towards the human element in a story full of wonderful machinery could suddenly turn on this human element and swallow it whole. Heinlein's recipe for SF writing paradoxically promoted the development of believable characters so that they could be used to better glorify the world machine they themselves had created, thereby sliding back into the role of adjuncts to technology which the Gernsback generation had originally created for them. If this characteristic had been exclusively specific to Heinlein's fiction, his assumptions would have been less damaging to the development of the genre than they actually were, and Heinlein himself would be substantially less famous than he is today. But we must remember that besides being his own writer he was also the front man for the *Astounding* outlook, and in those years the magazine ruled with near-absolute sway. Charles N. Brown commented that "all modern science fiction is based on Heinlein. He's the elephant in the room. It doesn't matter if anyone's reading him now; he set the course of modern science fiction," and Gary K. Wolfe echoed this opinion: "he's the person who invented the language of modern SF.... The platform modern science fiction is built on is essentially what Heinlein gave us in the early '40s" (*Locus* 51). These comments are neither hyperbolic nor overly romanticized. For better and for worse, Campbell, Heinlein, and the rest of the *Astounding* writers made SF what it is today, and it is a lucky thing indeed that during the period between 1937 and 1949, the Golden Age of science fiction, the innovative thrust this new generation possessed transcended the limitations inherent in their essentially positivist worldview. There would be time later — during the fifties and sixties — for this worldview to sclerotize into dogma and right-wing preaching, when events in the world outside started robbing SF's Campbells and Heinleins of the real-life basis for their advocacy, and another, younger generation of writers began questioning the validity and desirability of the new world they wanted. J. D. Bernal had explained what the future of his desire was, but at the same time he had been aware of the difference between advocacy and actuality. The Campbell/Heinlein generation, on the other hand, became stuck inside their set of solutions, treating them as if they were the only set available or practicable, at which point it became only a matter of time before the future of fate overtook the future of their desire and swept it away, like it had already done with Gernsback's.

In the meantime, however, it was still the early 1940s, and science fiction's tomorrows were still brand new. *Astounding* stood at the top of the field, as did the writers publishing in it, and Campbell was carefully weaving the thread of the future around the stories featured in the magazine. Editorials, articles, advertisements — every page of *Astounding* presented a facet of the edifice Campbell was building.

By the time "Universe," the first of his two-part generation-starship narrative, appeared in the May 1941 issue of *Astounding*, Heinlein was well on his way to completing the string of 28 interconnected stories he published in SF magazines between 1938 and 1942, the year he briefly left the field to do war work at the Naval Experimental Station in Philadelphia (James 65). These stories, only four of which appeared in other magazines, constitute the bedrock of Heinlein's influence on the field, a bedrock on which he would keep building once he returned to SF at the end of World War II. By May of 1941 enough of them had seen the light of day to have reached the critical mass necessary to constitute the first actual consensus history of the future whose construction had been the leitmotif of SF since the Gernsback years. In fact, it was precisely in that May 1941 issue that Campbell announced the publication of "a graphical extract from the Heinlein 'History of Tomorrow'" (5), a chart Heinlein kept at home and on which he marked the timeline of his future history, placing the individual stories he either had already published or was on the way to publishing along its course so as to create a sense of a gradually self-assembling future. Campbell's argument for suggesting to Heinlein that he allow *Astounding* to print that chart is a more consistent, more comprehensively developed version of the argument describing SF as the history of the future which we have seen in Chapter 2. Starting from his comment that SF stories are "historical novels laid against a background of a history that hasn't happened yet," Campbell moves on to detail the similarities between writing straight historical fiction and writing its SF version. The writer of mainstream historical fiction, he says, "studies the manners of the time, the customs and the tools available, the means of travel and the social and economic conflicts in the life of a man of the time"; through all this research work, he "knows what his characters cannot — the ultimate outcome. He can see, and play up in his writing, the obscure trends of a selected era that carried hidden in them the seed of whole new histories to come" (5). The writer of science fiction can do the same thing for the multiple potential trends of tomorrow, with the relevant difference that, in the latter case, the absence of physical records for things that have not happened yet leads the writer to conducting "mental research into possible future" (5) instead of doing research into archives, libraries, and ancient texts.

The building of a mental map of the future as a sort of inverse historical process, however, will require a timeline before it needs anything else. Time's arrow may have doubled back on history within an SF environment, but even in that case a time-specific grid will be necessary to set the events detailed in the various narratives in their proper context[3] and give them meaning — hence Robert Heinlein's time chart:

> [B]y giving himself the added help of a carefully worked out history, building up in his mind a picture of a world of tomorrow that's "lived in," his stories have achieved manifold greater reality — and done it a lot more easily. The author that cooks up a special history of the future and a special world of the future for each story never attains a "lived-in" world. It's always, somehow, like an interior decorator's just-finished result. All the chairs and tables and ashtrays are there, and the lamps are lighted — but it's a stage setting, and stiff as the binding of an unread book. It needs the rug pulled a little askew, and the ash trays with a few butts in them, the cushions rumpled — to be lived in and enjoyed [5].

Thus, advocacy turns itself into evidence before the event. Campbell's description of the creation of a lived-in feel to the world within the fiction contains the implicit acknowledgement that SF is not exclusively the main participant to the crafting of a future—it is also a literature, an artistic endeavor regulated by aesthetic precepts. Certainly, most of the writers in the *Astounding* generation, Campbell included, still saw the artistic aspects of science fiction as secondary to its predictive faculties, and this short-sightedness may well have been the principal agent in the eventual crumbling of their collective voice towards the end of the fifties. However, even if the Campbell/Heinlein school may never have produced a writer of the caliber of Philip K. Dick, Ursula Le Guin, Samuel Delany, or Gene Wolfe, it did foster the development of a cadre of extremely gifted, imaginative writers who worked together to lay down the groundwork for the birth and education of those who would one day surpass their achievements. Science fiction as a whole was about a hundred and twenty years old, if we accept Aldiss's cutoff point for the first SF work at 1818, the year Mary Shelley published *Frankenstein*. But genre SF in America was very young, as was its magazine format. It was learning as it went and learning fast, and the lesson it learned with the Campbell/Heinlein generation was that it could no more avoid being plausible and internally consistent than mainstream realism or naturalism could—a less-than-obvious conclusion to reach for writers in a field whose existence was predicated on presenting its readers with the mimesis of the non-real.

It was also a matter of advocacy. If the task at hand consisted in making readers believe that the future presented in *Astounding* could become actuality, then these readers needed to imagine themselves as sharers in this future. They needed to empathize with the characters, in other words, and the characters themselves needed to be down-to-earth enough that even their cognitively overdriven world of tomorrow could not fully estrange them from the reading public—hence skewed rugs, used ashtrays, and rumpled cushions next to laser blasters, portable atomic watches, and advanced life-support systems. Also, Heinlein had begun tracing the path of his future chronology by writing stories literally set in the United Sates of tomorrow: "Life-Line," the narrative that begins his future history chart, was published in 1939 and narrated events taking place in 1940; "Let There Be Light," published in 1940, was set around 1950; "The Roads Must Roll," also published in 1940, tells a story of the year 1960 or thereabouts; and so on. Every story represented a logical link in this causal chain of events; for example, the invention and mass production of the new technology featured in "Let There Be Light," a cheap, clean, and virtually limitless source of energy in the form of proto-LED lights, is instrumental to the socio-economic developments leading to the moving roads of "The Roads Must Roll"; these, in turn, represent an evolutionary step on the way to the world portrayed in "Blow-Ups Happen" (1940); and so forth.

As the end of Campbell's editorial reveals, Heinlein's choice to begin storytelling the future at a point in time so close to the present had a few advantages:

> The Heinlein "History" starts in 1940. It might be of very real interest to you to trace in on this suggestion for the future your own life line. My own, I imagine, should extend up to about 1980 — a bit beyond the time of "Roads Must Roll" and "Blowups Happen." My children may see the days of "Logic of Empire." Where does your life line fall? Where will your children's end? [6].

This was the promise lying at the heart of the Campbell/Heinlein recipe for advocacy in science fiction: that those who were alive in 1939 would live long enough to see at least part of the future outlined in these stories, and that their children and grandchildren would be the witnesses of further advancements along the same track. By grounding the beginning of the future into his present, and thus by involving us personally in its making, Heinlein was able to present a far more compelling argument for the plausibility of his extrapolations than would otherwise have been the case. He was also very careful in presenting his innovations: "Life-Line" and "Let There Be Light," the two stories placed at the beginning of the timeline, only feature one estranging element each in an otherwise standard environment, so as not to tax our suspension of disbelief by having a fully science-fictionalized society within a decade of the present. Then, for every story positioned further along that path, the world becomes increasingly different and more estranged from our experience, as the interdependent innovations in the previous stories start exerting a cumulative influence in the narratives following them. Towards the end of the chart, in tales like "If This Goes on" (published serially in *Astounding* in 1940, and set around 2070), the future is indeed very different from today, in both its social and material aspects, but thanks to the logically worked-out development that led to it we can trace its lineage all the way back along Heinlein's timeline to the first narratives.

Today, the SF authors who write their stories using the playbook Campbell and Heinlein wrote are capable of performing this topsy-turvy act of historical analysis with a level of complexity that may have surprised their forebears. The field is replete with histories, timelines, chronologies, and complex networks of interlinked narratives working together to create the feel of a future. It would be commonplace if it were not still so much fun. But in the 1940s, this meta-narrative technique was unheard of in science fiction, and the *Astounding* readership received it with the enthusiasm of a revelation. For a decade or so, it truly felt like people would go to sleep at night in one world and wake up the next morning in another, and it was all thanks to the deft sleight-of-hand performed by the Campbells and Heinleins of that period. They persuaded their readers that the future can truly happen the way you want it to happen if you emplot it well enough, and that a vision of potential things to be can turn into actuality if it reverberates within a powerful enough resonance chamber. In the 1940s, this vision was still pliant and flexible enough to transcend its limitations, so that the fatal flaw hidden inside it did not become apparent until it was too set in its brand of advocacy to change, evolve, and survive.

"Universe" is a quintessential SF story in the Heinlein mold. New infodump strategies, future advocacy, reader participation, full integration into the future timeline; everything is there. The narrative occupies the bottom slot on Heinlein's time chart, and is therefore shifted towards the farther future. A brief excerpt at the beginning, taken from a book by a Franklin Buck entitled *The Romance of Modern Astrography* and published by Lux Transcriptions, Ltd., informs us of the fate of the Proxima Centauri Expedition, financed by the Jordan Foundation and launched in 2119 in the direction of the star systems nearer ours. It was the first such attempt and may possibly have been the last, because nobody has heard from it again (9).

There has never been such a book as *The Romance of Modern Astrography*, nor has there ever been such a publisher as Lux Transcriptions, but H. P. Lovecraft's *Necronomicon* and Asimov's *Encyclopedia Galactica* never existed either. Between the first and second generations of pulp SF writing another infodump technique was developed, and it has been practiced ever since; it consists in enhancing the lived-in feel of the fictional world by peppering the narrative with excerpts from fictitious historical or sociological textbooks, or from equally fictitious news articles. This technique, famously exemplified by the paragraphs from the *Encyclopedia Galactica* containing crucial background information about the universe of Asimov's *Foundation* trilogy, reinforces the illusion of historical development in a science fiction narrative. Also, it provides another layer of reality to its portrayal of its future society through hinting at the presence of a functional intellectual establishment comprising universities, news services, and publishing houses. In the case of "Universe," this introductory excerpt resonates both within and without the narrative; on the one hand, it clues us in on what we will have to look for within the text — the story will have something to do with this lost expedition; on the other hand, it places the incipit of the story on our future time chart, thus making it an integral part of Heinlein's structured advocacy.

So, something went wrong with the Jordan Foundation mission. It never reached Proxima Centauri, or if it did it never radioed Earth with news of its arrival. What the introductory excerpt does not show, the narrative itself will have to fill in, so we begin reading the first paragraph with a precise set of questions in mind, questions that will determine the nature of our hunt for textual clues in the pages to follow. And sure enough, it is a hunt: Hugh Hoyland, the protagonist and viewpoint character of the story, is leading a party of men on a search-and-destroy mission against enemies that, for now, are only identified as "muties." During the ensuing skirmish, when Hoyland ducks to avoid a hand-thrown projectile aimed at his head, the speed of his movements "lifted his feet from the floor plates. Before his body could settle slowly to the deck, he planted his feet against the bulkhead behind him and shoved" (9–10).

Neither "The Living Galaxy" nor "The Voyage That Lasted 600 Years" have prepared us readers for this kind of beginning. In "The Living Galaxy" we got a teacher, a classroom, and a textbook; the future may have been incredible, but the flow of information leading us to it was stately, reader-friendly, and easy to parse. In "The Voyage That Lasted 600 Years," we were treated to the hardly more taxing scene of a ticker tape parade immediately preceding the launch of the *Flashaway*, the perfect occasion for a generous helping of background information as Grimstone and the Captain explained the aims of the trip to the press and the bystanders. The beginning of "Universe," however, is something else altogether. There is no explicit connection between it and the pseudo-historical reference that precedes the action, and the characters are literally too busy to stop and give us a quiet infodump session. Therefore, we are left with nothing else to do but extract the necessary information by ourselves, and fortunately for us there is plenty of that. We are looking at an artificial structure of some sort; there are bulkheads, floor plates, a deck, and a passageway. Moreover, the flow of the action in this scene is at least partly determined by physical parameters at variance with those we would find on Earth, because the sequence of Hugh Hoyland's movements is consistent with that of an astronaut operating under conditions of reduced gravity — on the Moon, say. The speed of his crouch "had lifted his feet from the floor plates," so that his body takes a while to settle to the deck, and he goes "shooting down the passageway in a shallow dive" (10).

From the information gathered, we are led to assume that we are inside the Jordan Foundation's ship, that the people fighting are members of its crew, and that for some reason this crew is divided into at least two factions: the muties and the group to which Hugh Hoyland and his companions belong. The flow of information we receive from the text, however, does not always make immediate, easily extrapolated sense. After the fight breaks up in a bloodless stalemate, Hoyland and his hunting mates start on the trip back home, descending through several dozens of decks, their weight steadily increasing the further down they go. From their exchanges, we find out that they come from "farm country," and that their village in this region is run by scientists who, for some reason, have agency over matters of devoutness, sin, and morality. Also, these scientists represent a group apart from the rest of farm-country society, famed for the ability of its members to learn, write, and do numbering (10–11). As Hoyland and the others reach farm country, an apparently contradictory sight presents itself before their eyes: there are tended fields and vegetation enclosed by bulkheads, a farmer whom one of the hunting party hails as "shipmate," and a fairly heavily trafficked passageway featuring pushcarts, litters, and travelers on foot. In short, there are no cars or motorized trolleys, nothing equipped with an engine.

This is the point at which we have to start working actively to make sense of the world Heinlein portrays. Asking 1941 readers[4] to picture in the mind's eye a complex piece of machinery through the subtle layering of textual clues would have been straightforward enough; the simple fact of living in an industrial society enabled them to do so without undue difficulty. On the other hand, presenting them with a cognitive disconnect between the pre-industrial, bucolic landscape Hoyland negotiates on his way home and the highly technological environment enclosing it raised the stakes considerably. First of all, on Earth the natural world can be locally enclosed inside a man-made artifact—a park within a city; a garden within a mansion; a cultivated patch of land within a greenhouse. However, irrespective of how large this man-made artifact is, it will in turn find itself enclosed within another, larger natural environment—a city on a plain, a ship at sea, a plane in the Earth's atmosphere. The landscape described in the paragraph, where an entire agricultural district is bounded on every side by bulkheads, tunnels and decks and the very light growing the vegetation comes from a ceiling, represents a reversal of our accepted order of things. In order to understand the narrative, we are suddenly forced to readjust our assumptions concerning what is natural, what is artificial, and what is possible to do with both. Secondly, this cognitive disconnect also operates at the narrative level. Why are the members of a society capable of building a machine of this size and complexity living at an essentially pre-industrial stage? There are no cars or trains on the path along which Hoyland and his companions walk, and the only vehicles are a pushcart and a litter—nothing powered by an internal combustion engine.

The picture as a whole does not make sense at this stage. Here is a pre-industrial, pre-internal combustion engine society enclosed within a space clearly built through the employment of a technological, industrial, and academic establishment at least at—and probably beyond—the combustion-engine stage. Also, none of the characters we have seen so far have revealed the slightest awareness of being on a ship, if this is actually where they are, and the possibility that they have arrived at their destination vanishes the moment anyone looks up at the sky; there isn't one. There are only bulkheads and corridors, and the shifts in gravity between the higher and lower levels of the place they inhabit are inconsistent with the conditions one would find on a planet. And yet, one of Hoyland's friends asks the peasant for directions by first hailing him with the term "shipmate." What is going on?

Upon returning to his village, Hoyland attends two meetings; the first is with his community's Witness, a lawyer and accountant of sorts who performs his function following a highly ritualized routine, and the second is with Lieutenant Nelson, a scientist. In the first meeting, Hoyland comes to the Witness with questions concerning the meaning of the world, its nature, and the reason for its physical characteristics. He wants to know why there are so many levels above farm country, and why his weight decreases the further he climbs toward the last and highest of those levels (13). Hoyland is possessed of a rare characteristic among his people: he is intellectually curious, and his questions stem from his attempt to fit his experience of the physical world surrounding him into an intellectual system for understanding the meaning of this world. However the Witness, who has never been to the upper levels and has no phenomenological experience of the matters he discusses, answers him through the employment of an essentially Aristotelian line of reasoning — it is not necessary to have actually seen the world to know everything there is to know about it, including its purpose and meaning. The so-called "Lines from the Beginning," which it is the Witnesses' job to memorize and repeat when necessary, contain all the answers Hoyland requires, provided he has the capacity to subject them to enough exegesis to satisfy the interpretation of their meaning his society has decided to embrace. The Witness has his apprentice recite the lines for Hoyland, and what emerges from the boy's mouth is a myth of origin comprised of two strangely paired narratives: one is a compressed, restructured retelling of key events in the Old Testament — genesis, the creation of Man, the fall of Man, the war in Heaven, Satan's fall, the Ten Commandments, the birth and death of Christ. The other is an oddly ritualized history of the original planning and launching of the Jordan Foundation's mission, complete with hints at the outbreak of a mutiny sometime during the voyage. The two stories, however, are not separate. They exist in a continuous process of intercommunication, flowing together into a supernarrative that casts the planners of the mission as one single godlike entity (Jordan), the crew of the ship as mankind, the Regulations and the Plan containing them as the Ten Commandments, a man named Huff as the Satan figure responsible at once for the war in Heaven and the fall of Man, and the Captain as Christ. Within this creation myth, the Ship is synonymous with the universe, the Crew with mankind, and the Jordan Foundation with the creator of it all. As the apprentice's voice keeps reciting the poem, we also find out the origin of the "muties." They are the descendants of the rebels who had betrayed and brought war to their fellow men, and who now live confined in the upper levels (13).

The very existence of the muties reveals to the reader the conundrum at the heart of the Witness' "Lines from the Beginning." On the one hand, treating the history of an interstellar mission as if it were the history of God and the universe according to Christian doctrine seems contradictory, for the same reason that looking at a landscape of farms, fields, and villages enclosed by an enormous artificial structure seems wrong: the natural world, from a patch of grass to the whole cosmos, should theoretically be the province of God, whereas technological artifacts are, supposedly, inherently human constructs. The two realms should not merge. On the other hand, at least some parts of this creation myth seem supported by actual evidence. At the beginning of the story, Hoyland narrowly escapes a mutie's ambush in the far upper reaches of the "ship," which suggests that the muties actually exist, that they do live in these mysterious regions, and that there is indeed a state of war between the two populations. Also, everybody on the ship uses the names Jordan and Huff as oaths, in much the same way a 1940 reader would use the terms God or Hell to express annoyance, distress, or fear: the Witness exclaims "Jordan's name" while talking to Hoyland, and Hoyland himself uses the expression "by Jordan" after the ambush, when one of his hunting mates tries to dissuade him from pursuing one of the muties. Whatever happened to establish this connection between the names used in the Lines and the actual human beings who had originally carried them, these figures are now the lynchpins underlying the sense of cultural identity of an entire society, and they also stand at the center of a history whose unfolding, as recounted in the Witness' narrative, is supported by enough physical evidence to make it more than a simple fairy tale.

The Witness, however, does not know more than the "Lines from the Beginning" reveal, and Hoyland, who has actually seen the upper levels of the world, cannot find solace in them. He is the quintessential Heinleinian hero: intelligent, enterprising, curious, and competent. Had he been born on Earth and trained as an engineer, he would have been Gaines, the hero of "The Roads Must Roll"; had he been trained as an executive, he would have become D. D. Harriman, the protagonist of "The Man Who Sold the Moon." But in his world, where people seem content to go through their lives without asking structural questions of their frame of reality, his qualities mark him as something of a loner and misfit. As befits a science fiction hero in the Campbell age, Hoyland experiences the lack of answers from his peers first and foremost as a moral problem — not knowing the world is a fault, not understanding its workings a sin. For him, curiosity is not an urge to be satisfied by commonplace answers in the same way one satisfies one's hunger by eating; it is a fundamental psychological trait to be nurtured through deep reflection and supported by the evidence of experience. It is for this reason that Hoyland, like Gaines and Harriman, is at once the hero and the viewpoint character. We readers need to have the world of the story explained to us. We do not know it, and the rest of the characters, incurious and content with their lot, do not constitute a plausible infodump platform. We need someone who is dissatisfied enough with the status quo to want answers to the most basic questions about it, so that when he goes to those who should know and they explain things to him, we hear the explanations as well.

So far these explanations have only generated more questions, but Hoyland's second meeting, this time with Lieutenant Nelson, the scientist "in charge of the spiritual and physical welfare of the Ship's sector which included Hugh's native village" (14), finally yields some answers. Nelson calls upon Hoyland because he has plans for him; he wants to turn him into a scientist. He had noticed the younger man's curiosity, drive, and leadership skills, and had therefore stopped those who, when he was born, wanted to send him to the converter because his head was larger than average and thus suspect of being a mutation. This converter, whose functioning is never fully explained in the story, is where everybody goes when they die, a machine that converts the raw matter making up their bodies into energy. Hoyland's society refers to death as "making the Trip to the converter," or simply as "making the Trip." It is also where everybody goes when they are sentenced to death for one reason or another — because they are found to carry physical mutations at birth, because of some infraction of the Regulations, or because their behavior is at variance with the orthodox workings of Jordan's Plan. Hoyland's curiosity, Nelson explains to him, puts him at far greater risk of being sentenced to the converter than he had imagined. Other than annihilation, the only option open to Hugh is to become a scientist himself, one of the custodians of his society's lore. This way, he can be initiated into the mysteries he craves to understand within a learned framework that can police his curiosity, thereby turning him from a potential liability into an asset (15).

Nelson's casual acknowledgement of Hoyland's limited options, chilling as it is, gives a plausible explanation for the listlessness and lack of curiosity of most of the villagers, and also hints at the basic power structure underlying their society's life. The Lines from the Beginning seem to have it right: there really had been a rebellion or a civil war once, something so destructive that the survivors who emerged from its ashes created an entire system of social and cultural regulations to make sure nothing like it could happen again. This system is based on the elevation to absolute power of one social class, the scientists, who answer to the Captain and no one else. The scientists exercise their power through ownership of all means of communication and erudition, down to forbidding everyone else from learning even the most basic means of information gathering, such as reading, writing, and counting. Even the fundamental function of Witness must be performed exclusively through mnemonic recording, rote learning, and oral recitation. This draconian policing of the flow of information goes hand in hand with the punishment that awaits those who display excessive curiosity untutored by right thinking, and the punishment is always the Trip — otherwise such free thinkers could spread among the crew and disseminate the wrong ideas. The scientists need the commoners to be dull and incurious; this way they are easier to control and to monitor for heretical thoughts. When a particularly promising individual like Hoyland recommends themselves to the scientists' attention, this individual receives a smattering of learning and is kept under surveillance until such time as their fate is decided — either entrance into the ranks of the scientists or the converter. This way, orthodoxy is preserved. No form of alternative thinking can develop, and even if it could there would be no way to record and codify it for transmission to future generations or other social classes.

More answers await Hoyland, and us along with him, in the mysteries to which he is introduced as a scientist-in-training. It is during a particularly frustrating study session that Nelson comes to his aid. Hoyland is reading "Basic Modern Physics," which the older scientist describes as "one of the most valuable of the sacred writings" (16), and Hoyland is having trouble understanding its meaning. The reason why Hoyland is having trouble, Nelson explains, is that he takes their wording literally, whereas the linguistic expression of the wisdom of the ancients — who "were incurable romantics, rather than rationalists, as we are" (16) — takes a more allegorical shape. As an example, Nelson illustrates the meaning of the "Law of Gravitation":

> "Two bodies attract each other directly as the product of their masses and inversely as the square of their distance" ... was the poetical way the old ones had of expressing the rule of propinquity which governs the emotion of love. The bodies referred to are human bodies, mass is their capacity for love ... when they are thrown together, they fall in love, yet when they are separated they soon get over it [16].

The maddening thing about Nelson's spiritualized misreading of Newton's Second Law of Gravitation is that it does make a preposterous kind of sense. Everything is upside down in Nelson's worldview: the fanciful is practical, the pragmatic is romantic, and the laws of the non-human are the laws of love. That he should describe the ancients as "incurable romantics" and his society as pragmatists, and then give the above reasoning as evidence for his contention, is as comical as accusing Hoyland of indulging a flight of fancy because the latter is trying to understand the laws of gravity on their own terms. Like the Witness, but without the moral alibi that comes with the ignorance of illiteracy, Nelson believes in an essentially Aristotelian process of knowledge gathering. He needs to give no other evidence than the authority of the orthodox ruling class for his society's interpretation of basic modern physics as divinely inspired moral laws, either to himself or to Hoyland. Moreover, he is educating the younger man not only in the unquestioning acceptance of this orthodoxy, but also in the enforcement of its acceptance by the collective and in the punishment of those who will not acquiesce through execution by Converter.

Hoyland's questions are not over, however; he wants to know about the moral status of the muties (can they be considered human beings?), and there is something bothering him about the sacred texts' constant reference to a trip to a place called "far Centaurus" in which their world is supposedly engaged. Nelson's answer to his first question gives Hoyland little trouble: the muties are indeed the distant descendants of those long-ago rebels who managed to escape the Converter and went to live in the upper levels of the world, and as such they could be said to belong to the human race. However, they are also the result of long generations of mutation in the wilderness, so that they could also be described as abhumans. That is why they are called "muties": the term happily covers both interpretations of their existential status — mutineers and mutants, humans and monsters, but evil and dangerous in either case (16–17).

The answer to Hoyland's second question is substantially more problematic for him, and for us readers it represents a paradigm shift in our understanding of the nature of this future world; we finally get our answers, and they are estranging indeed. Hoyland's problem is of a philosophical nature: how can the Sacred Texts "speak of the Trip as if it were an actual *moving*" (17)? Nelson's answer once again steers his apprentice's attention towards an allegorical interpretation of the testimony contained in the writings:

> Of course, the Ship is solid, immovable in a physical sense. How can the whole universe move? Yet, it *does* move, in a spiritual sense. With every righteous act we move closer to the sublime destination of Jordan's plan.... One school invented an entire mythology of a topsy-turvy world of endless reaches of space, empty save for pin points of light and bodyless mythological monsters. They called it the heavenly world or heaven, as if to contrast it with the solid reality of the Ship... [17].

In ancient times on Earth, early astronomers had looked at the open sky and tried to measure the size of the observable cosmos through the gathering of empirical evidence. Now, in an unknown future year somewhere far away, Lieutenant Nelson and his fellow scientists stare at the windowless bulkheads enclosing everything they have ever experienced and conclude that the universe must perforce end where the rivets meet the steel plates. We do not yet know exactly what happened to the Jordan Foundation's mission that could shape it the way it has, but by now we have enough information to know where we are and what is happening. Unlike Wilcox a year before him, Heinlein has not postulated the existence of a hibernation technology that can preserve the life of a generation starship's crew for centuries, nor has he envisioned a longer lifespan for his future humans than the average expectancy of a reader of *Astounding* in the early 1940s. Therefore, the crew of the Jordan Foundation's ship had to do things the hard way, transmitting knowledge, cultural values, and a continued sense of purpose through the same means by which people here on Earth pass on to their children what they deem worth keeping among their collective experiences. There is no Keeper of Traditions on the Ship, no Gregory Grimstone to provide the thread of story linking the contingent lives of the Crew to the transcendent purpose of their millennial voyage. If the process of generational transmission failed for some reason, if an accident or a miscalculation were to interrupt the flow of information between generations and across social strata, what would be the consequences? How far into decay and barbarism would such a collective fall?

Based on the information the narrative has so far provided, we can extrapolate. The mutiny happened, engineered by Huff—a satanic antagonist in the present of the story, but just a man with a grudge or a good reason to rebel in his own time. It happened, and in the aftermath too many key crewmembers were dead, too many teachers, tutors, thinkers, and administrators were gone. Those who were left did not have the education to transmit to a new generation the skills necessary not only to fly the ship, but also to understand the physical principles underlying its construction and operation. Everyone forgot everything—gravity, thermodynamics, relativity, electromagnetism, the periodic table of elements, everything. Devolution occurred rapidly then, and reached a point beyond anything the people onboard the *Flashaway* had experienced, even at the lowest ebb of their fortunes. At least a few of the latter had retained enough knowledge to drive the ship, but Hoyland's people were not so lucky. They fell into ignorance of such proportions that they no longer remembered they were onboard a spacefaring vessel on its way to another star system. At some point, they must even have forgotten the distinction between man-made and natural, inside and outside, human and divine. It is difficult to imagine such decay, but some unknowable amount of time after their loss of sentience, the distant descendants of that long-ago generation must have opened their eyes, seen the bulkheads and the levels for the first time since the fall, and started climbing their way out of their essentially prehistoric state, replicating on a smaller scale the climb to civilization that the human race accomplished on Earth.

Somewhere along the way up from non-sentience, the Crew must have started reading again. They must have found a way to understand the writing of their ancestors, probably through the use of whatever instructional material was left intact onboard the Ship after the mutiny, and they must have understood, at a semi-conscious level, that these ancient texts were somehow fundamental for their existence. So the Crew studied, and came to formulate a theory of everything out of whatever meaningful data they could extract from these books, but the accuracy of this theory was crippled by their inability to reconstruct the original context of their sources of information. The product of their studies ended up taking the shape of myth, an emplotted view of reality cobbling together dim memories of the original crew's religious beliefs and of the events of the mutiny with the information contained in the books, contextualizing the latter through the lens of the other two. This cultural construction must have been essentially identical to the process by which the decayed descendants of the *Flashaway*'s crew of 2366 erased their memory of Grimstone as the Keeper and recast him as the Traddy Man in the wake of the violent events of that year — with one crucial difference: in the earlier story, the readers saw the effect of this mythologizing process through the eyes of its functionally immortal victim. In "Universe," they see it through the eyes of the descendants of those who operated this emplotment. The perpetrators had long been dead by then.

Like the myth of the Traddy Man in Wilcox's narrative, the legends of the Crew in Heinlein's provide us with a meaningful retelling of the real events. For example, the conflation of the Christian myths of Satan's fall from Heaven and Man's fall from grace with whatever was left of the mutiny's historical memory is basically sound. There really was a fall from an age of enlightenment to an age of barbarism, brought about by an original act of sin perpetrated through the instigation of one individual. For all its religious fervor, the section of the Lines from the Beginning that narrates the unfolding of the mutiny yields a fairly precise sense of the sequence of events as they must have happened: the outbreak was probably triggered by a sense of discontent among some members of the crew that remained quiescent until one man spoke it out loud. Once Huff— an abbreviation of the original? A distortion? We do not know at this stage — dared speak his grievance he must have found the courage to seek those among the crew he knew shared his feelings, and together they sparked a revolt during which many died, including the Captain, and in whose aftermath the survivors of those who had opposed the mutineers found themselves devoid of guidance, aim, or purpose.

Were Huff and his rebels evil? Was their grievance really the result of some kind of Miltonian sin, or was it motivated by more human-scaled impulses — homesickness, despair, the desire to alter the circumstances of the trip in the face of a now forgotten emergency? We do not know, and Hoyland's society does not want to. What is more, it probably does not matter. The inhabitants of the generation starship at this point in the future are so different from the people who started the trip that, whatever interpretation they picked to explain the events that led to their current situation, this interpretation would be less important than the means through which the collective enforced its status as absolute truth, complete with a view of creation that stopped the boundaries of the universe at the hull of the Ship and cast its voyage as a philosophical condition. Even death is described as an allegorical Trip (to the Converter). The scientists' rule is not draconian and blinkered because it believes what it believes; in the absence of any windows or portholes affording an external view, it is actually not that difficult to understand why they would reach the conclusions they did. Their rule is draconian because in their eyes it has acquired the status of dogma, a set of views so structural to the existence of that society that to defy them would be tantamount to usher in the preconditions that led to the original mutiny.

Given its characteristics as we have enumerated them so far, Hugh Hoyland's community can be equated with a fair degree of precision with the stereotypical 20th-century perception of European society on Earth during the Middle Ages: a mass of illiterate commoners ruled by an aristocracy-cum-clergy acting in the name of an individual divine principle and enforcing its orthodoxy through fear and obscurantism. This picture comes complete with Aristotelian syllogisms, a system for the acquisition of evidence based on rhetoric instead of empirical observation, and a constant preoccupation with social collapse through the spread of heretical ideas. It is, in fact, a world ready for a Galilean figure, someone curious, intelligent, impatient, and prone to base his reasoning concerning first principles not on rhetorical constructs or orthodox doctrine, but on personal experience and the evidence of his own eyes—an experimenter, in other words, a scientist in the sense the readers of *Astounding* would have understood the term.

The next stage in Hoyland's education takes place when, shortly after his interview with Lieutenant Nelson, he is captured by the muties and taken to the upper levels of the ship. Their leader, a two-headed man named Joe-Jim, takes it upon himself to educate Hoyland on the true nature of the ship and its mission, running him through a Gernsback-style infodump session aimed at restoring his cosmology to its proper shape. When the weight of years of orthodoxy prevents Hoyland from conceptualizing the idea of a space outside the hull through which the Ship is literally traveling, Joe-Jim decides to take him to the only place onboard the vessel where he can see things for himself—the control room, where all the functions of navigation, engine control, and ship management are located. The centerpiece of the control room is a virtual 3-D map of the sector of the galaxy through which the ship is traveling. When Joe-Jim turns off the lights and switches on the control for the map, and Hoyland's world becomes infinitely larger than it had been an instant before, "for the first time in his life [Hugh] knew the intolerable ecstasy of beauty unallayed. It shook him and hurt him, like the first trembling intensity of sex" (27).

Heinlein's equation of the pleasures of discovery with those of sex is not casual. In the worldview of Campbell-era science fiction, the experience of knowing the world does not stimulate the intellect alone; it also engages the body and the heart. For Hoyland, the first member of his society to see the stars after generations of collective blindness, the view is a reenactment of creation. However, the instrument of Hoyland's revelation is just another simulation, another intellectual construct designed to represent the reality of something nobody has ever seen — or rather, almost nobody. There is, it turns out, a "Captain's veranda" not far from the control room, a space provided with a large window through which the cosmos can be seen in all its actual glory. Joe-Jim has seen through it, and his word as to the existence of the veranda is enough for Hoyland. In an interesting relaxation of his customary skepticism, he lets himself be wholly persuaded by Joe-Jim, and returns to his quarters in mutie country to begin a second period of study and meditation, this time reading the books Joe-Jim has given him. The only element preventing Hoyland's seemingly contradictory behavior from damaging narrative plausibility is the sentence at the beginning of the paragraph where the authorial voice declares that the stars shining in the stellarium are the exact counterpart of the original stars out in space. That comment is not meant for the characters' ears. With it, Heinlein bypasses them and directly addresses the readers of *Astounding*, telling them that it is all right for Hoyland to believe in the authenticity of this simulacrum, because unlike the simulacrum Lieutenant Nelson gave him, this one actually illustrates the reality outside the ship.

We could certainly make a case for the plausibility of Hoyland's behavior. A lifetime of enforced orthodoxy supported by several generations' worth of rote learning is difficult to shrug off right away, even for a mind of uncommon intellectual powers, so Hoyland's ready acceptance of Joe-Jim's word about the existence of this window on the universe can be chalked off to sheer social pressure. But the problem is the delivery of the message, not its substance; if that sentence were the only survivor of Gernsback-era infodump techniques in "Universe" and its sequel, its effects would end up not amounting to much, especially since the veranda does exist and it does play a fundamental role in the events to come. However, as we shall see, there are other, more substantial Gernsbackian remnants in the structure of this story.

Hoyland's renewed studies, now based on Joe-Jim's books and helped by texts that had not been available in his native village, persuade him of the fundamental truth of all the muties told him. Moreover, they yield fundamental information about the origin and duration of the trip: originally, the voyage to "far Centaurus" was supposed to last for a mere sixty years, a lifetime in human terms but a fairly short hop in the vastness of interstellar space. However, the engineers who built the ship[5] incorporated in its design such a vast array of redundancies and advanced life-support systems that it is essentially self-maintaining and self-repairing — to the point where, had everyone onboard been killed in the mutiny, the vessel would have continued on in near-perpetuity, empty and alone and perfectly functional for eons (29–30).

It is easy enough to imagine that one or more of the texts Hoyland consults contain information on the history of the Ship's construction and functioning. He may or may not have trouble believing what he is reading, but he still has access to that information, and so do we. The Ship was never meant to be a generation starship. Sixty years — a plausible timespan for reaching the star system closest to Earth — may have been enough for the birth of one or two new generations of spacefarers, but by the time the expedition had arrived at its destination these spacefarers would have become planetary colonists, and their lives would not have taken on a fully spaceborne pattern like those of the *Flashaway*'s inhabitants. In fact, most of the original crew would probably have been still alive to see their new planet. Also, the relative proximity to Earth would have made retaining their sense of identity as members of the human race a smaller problem; communications between Far Centaurus and Earth would have been fast enough to maintain some form of intercourse between the two planets, so that the institutional memory of the emerging society on Centaurus would have been informed to a relevant extent by the sense of Earth's presence in their affairs.

Then the mutiny happened, somewhere between Earth and the Centauri system. People died, the survivors forgot, and the Ship traveled past its destination and ever onwards, the functionality of its systems preserved by the technology and science that went into their construction. Since the mission had not been designed as a generational endeavor, the social interactions between members of the crew, as well as the power structure that regulated their lives, had retained the characteristics of such non-permanent arrangements as one might find, for example, on a seafaring ship on Earth. However, once the mutiny had run its course and the Crew had reemerged from non-sentience, they had no choice but to reorganize their life around the creation of an Earth-equivalent society — which explains the survival of the old rank distinctions between crewmembers (Captain, Lieutenants, Scientists). They are part of the dim, distorted memories of the pre-mutiny years, when their usage indicated distinctions of agency and status pertaining to a different power structure. And yet, there is a resonant symbolic quality to the odd coupling of these terms with the retooled social functions they now describe, entirely in keeping with this society's penchant for allegorical interpretations of reality.

Hoyland's discoveries in mutie country further reinforce the sense of a correspondence between the population of the Ship and European society during the Middle Ages, or, perhaps more accurately, at the time of the Counter-Reformation. As the Protestant countries, vilified by the Catholic Church for their espousal of the heretical Copernican model, inhabited the northern regions of Europe, so the muties, equally detested by the crew for their ancestors' part in the mutiny, inhabit the upper reaches of the ship, literal northerners to the Crew's southern existence. Also, just like the Protestant countries of those times, they happen to favor the more scientific model of the cosmos, something for which the Crew would probably be even more hostile toward them. In the middle of this ideologically motivated struggle sits Hugh Hoyland, truly a Galileo figure in his open, ungrudging connection to both worlds as well as in his desire to help his countrymen grow closer to the Truth. Like his real-life predecessor, Hoyland is not prompted by his discovery of the truth to deny his country and let it rot in ignorance. As he explains to Joe-Jim when he announces his desire to go back to the village, he wants to talk to the scientists and the Captain, bring them to the veranda so they can see the stars, and enlist their help in unifying the crew and the muties into a single society. Once they are a single Crew again, they can learn to fly the ship and complete the voyage of planetary colonization. At this point, knowing Galileo's real-life vicissitudes, we can anticipate what happens next: Hoyland returns to the village, relates his discovery, illustrates his plan to resume the voyage, and is promptly thrown in jail for heresy, there to await execution by Converter. His last words to the Captain before he is marched off to prison are "Nevertheless — it *still* moves!" (36).

The whole point of the narrative that begins in "Universe" and ends in its sequel "Common Sense" is the depiction of the Galilean struggle for the mind of a society. All the plot developments and infodump sessions we have seen so far bear down on this moment in the narrative, the instant when Hoyland utters out loud the sentence that signals his explicit identification with his real-life counterpart. He has made the conscious choice to be a lightbringer, and as had been the case for Galileo himself, the light he brings to lead the way out of ignorance comes from a multitude of stars — and the similarities do not stop there. While the sole factual evidence of the veracity of Galileo's calculations rested within the tiny window of his telescope's lens, the somewhat larger viewing screen of the veranda also represents the only proof of the ultimate truthfulness of Hoyland's assertions; both Galileo and Hoyland base the main thrust of their argument on the unimpeachable truth of the world, pitting it against the Aristotelian line of reasoning adopted both by the Catholic church in the early 1600s and by the shipboard society of the far future; both display a certain impatience with arguments solely based on rhetoric (an annoyance for Galileo, who had no choice but to present his discoveries in the shape of his *Discourse*, and an ironic twist for Hoyland, who is after all a character in a narrative); and finally, both seem to operate under the impression that the paradigm shift they bring to their society will be greeted with a similar degree of enthusiasm to that with which they themselves embraced it.

And of course, Hoyland follows Galileo in having his hopes quickly dashed. He may be bringing a fundamental truth to his world, but his fellow countrymen are not thankful for it. It takes the help of the only two friends he has — one of whom is Lieutenant Nelson — to organize a breakout with the further assistance of the muties. On their way back to the upper levels, they capture Bill Ertz, the head of the engineers — a subordinate caste entrusted with the management of the few machines their society knows how to operate. "Universe" ends on a cliffhanger, with Hoyland and Joe-Jim leading the muties carrying the unconscious Ertz to the veranda. Once there, they will show the stars to the Chief Engineer and Alan Mahoney, Hoyland's other friend whose desire to help the heretic and the muties has now condemned him to exile or death. Then they will enlist their help to proceed with the plan.

The readers of *Astounding* had to wait until the October 1941 issue before the sequel to "Universe" appeared, and when they got to its first page Heinlein ran them over. It may have been that the necessity for a recap of the events in the previous story demanded it, or maybe the circumstances of serial publication left him no other choice; whatever the reason, the first page of "Common Sense" reprints the pseudo-bibliographical note that had appeared at the beginning of "Universe" and then hits the reader with five paragraphs of blunt, direct infodump (102). We are allowed to see the ship from outside, while Heinlein's narrative voice reveals the conditions of life onboard the vessel, the status of its inhabitants' lives, and so on through a brief retelling of Hoyland's adventures in mutie country, his education and imprisonment, the rescue mission that frees him, and their capture of Bill Ertz. If one were eager for spoilers to ruin any pleasure involved in reading this narrative, one could do a lot worse than skim through the first page of "Common Sense" first and then read the whole thing from the beginning. Heinlein's Gernsbackian lecture has given us the measure of the world; we know the shape and size of the ship, its internal arrangement, its people and their lives, and we should not. Science fiction is a literary mode that thrives on a careful mixture of cognition and mystery — the first lets us know the essentials of the world, the second keeps it receptive to our sense of wonder. Any imbalance in this mixture risks damaging the value of reading a SF story. Too much wonder and not enough cognition turns the world into an arbitrary landscape populated by absurd shapes; too much cognition and not enough wonder forces it to try mimicking the real, a situation that always leads SF to absurdity.

The point here is not that Heinlein should have withheld this information from us. On the contrary, knowing more about the environment postulated in the narrative would have increased the dramatic tension at its heart — if the delivery of this information had been handled properly. Had we continued to discover the world of "Universe" and "Common Sense" from the inside out, the narrative would have remained what it had been throughout its first part: a love song to the joy of knowing the world. After this lecture, after we have been forced to look at the ship from space and peer through is hull at the benighted lives of the people inside it, the narrative has become what it should not have let itself be: a funeral dirge to the darkness of ignorance. Instead of working our way out towards enlightenment along with Hugh Hoyland and his shipmates, we are now working our way in *from* enlightenment and towards ignorance. The difference only seems small: in the first part of the story we empathized with the people onboard the Ship, patting on the back those who discovered the world and at least understanding the plight of those who did not. In the second part, however, we have been arbitrarily placed outside the hull and told to snicker at them.

Heinlein, like a *2001: A Space Odyssey* black monolith lookalike, has decided to speed up our education, so the first page of "Common Sense" marks the change in our agency of data delivery from the characters to the authorial voice. From that moment on, we no longer receive our information through eavesdropping on Hoyland's intellectual struggles; instead, we get it directly from Heinlein himself, who time and again guides us through the geography of the ship and the history of the future in a voice essentially identical to that of Gernsback and his contemporaries. Heinlein is always there to tell us exactly how much Hoyland does not and cannot understand, how much will be forever beyond him and why. Our problem as readers, however, is that we are like Hoyland; we do not know the world any more than he does, and being plucked out of our intellectual dialogue with him, only to be thrust into a lecture situation where we have nothing to do except shut up and let Mr. Gradgrind fill us with facts facts facts, enhances our reading experience not at all. It feels a little like being removed from our seventh-grade class and rushed to college in a day or so. Now we can safely look down on our evidently dim-witted former classmates, but after listening to Heinlein going on and on about the engineering, astronomy, physics, and whatnot of the far future, the suspicion dawns on us that we may be in over our heads, and that finding stuff out for ourselves was actually more fun. We may even wish we were back in seventh grade—anything to stop Heinlein from joggling our elbows.

In any case, whatever our feelings on the matter, the truth remains that Hugh Hoyland and his shipmates are no longer able to speak with us. We can now look at the twists and turns of their maze and at the inside of their heads with a level of agency only possible in a narrative with an explicitly omniscient authorial voice, and for this reason they are not our companions anymore. They have become, like Gregory Grimstone and the crew of the *Flashaway*, guinea pigs in a cognitive experiment. It is therefore ironic that, just as we gain full probing rights into their minds, the narrative shifts its attention from reflection to action, and from science to realpolitik. The intellectual balance of the story has by now been established, and its central character has unpacked the motivations propelling his desire and channeled them into focused advocacy for the future of the world. After this moment, the dynamics of power negotiation in the society of the ship—which, we have come to learn, is called the *Vanguard*—transmogrify into political intrigue, assassination, and war.

For this reason, "Common Sense" is a substantially faster read than "Universe." Once Bill Ertz sees the stars outside the window in the captain's veranda, he becomes fully engaged in furthering Hoyland's plan to bring every person on the Ship to the veranda, show them the stars, and reeducate them in order to finally carry out the original mission. He also has bad news for the muties: the Crew has decided, for the first time in its history, to begin a systematic search-and-destroy program to get rid of them once and for all. Facing the prospect of certain annihilation, Joe-Jim goes along with Hoyland's idea. Together, Hoyland, Bill Ertz, Alan Mahoney, Joe-Jim, and the muties under the latter's authority set about triggering a paradigm shift in the worldview of the *Vanguard*'s Crew (104–09). To do that they enlist the help of Commander Phineas Narby, the crew's second in command, an intelligent, ruthless man of a distinctly Machiavellian bent who sees in Hoyland's band of rebels a chance to finally seize power for himself. And so he does: during a routine meeting of all the scientists and engineers on the Ship, a meeting over which the Captain himself presides, the muties burst into the room, kill the Captain, and install Narby in his place, with Joe-Jim as second in command. Now the muties truly are what both meanings of their name suggest— mutants because many of them are deformed, mutineers because they have reenacted the original rebellion onboard the *Vanguard*. And Hoyland, the intellectual force behind this sea change, has now become a figure uncomfortably similar to that of the original Huff (124–29).

Narby, however, has a nasty surprise awaiting his fellow conspirators. In many ways, he is Hoyland's specular opposite; he has seen the stars outside the veranda, but instead of reacting with awe and joy like Hoyland had, he responds with a cold, calculating stance. Politically as well as intellectually, his hunger for power pushes him to look constantly inward with the same intensity with which Hoyland's thirst for knowledge pushes him to look outward, so that the revelation he has just received means nothing more to him than a chance to become absolute ruler of the ship by profiting from the chaos that follows the mutiny. The two men's different natures also explain why Hoyland remains blind to the other's machinations. From the aftermath of the mutiny to the moment he betrays his former comrades-in-arms, Narby keeps preventing Hoyland from bringing members of the Crew to the veranda and then to the control room, with the excuse that such a staggering change in the Crew's worldview would undermine his rule as Captain, still in a state of flux (132–33). Narby is persuasive enough that Hoyland, Joe-Jim, and Bill Ertz go along with his idea until it is too late for them to realize that they are undermining the only social development that stands between the new Captain and absolute power. The Galileian revolution the three men had agreed to initiate depends wholly on their ability to get every man, woman and child onboard the Ship to look through the window and understand that the vessel does indeed move. Without that experience, the Crew will only read Narby's ascension to power as one more shift in shipboard politics, not as the truly world-changing development it was supposed to become.

Once things return to a condition approaching the old status quo, Narby turns against his friends. He has Joe-Jim's mutants killed, thereby eliminating the only force capable of opposing the military power of his own guards, and essentially reestablishes the rule of the old order. When Hoyland, Ertz and Joe-Jim oppose his actions and demand an explanation for his behavior, Narby answers that he has never believed in the heresy that the ship moves. To him the idea is just another, very clever simulacrum representing nothing more than a conceit just like his own. As for the veranda, it is merely a complicated stage for the performance of a drama designed to lure fools into heresy (144). Incapable of gainsaying an essentially impermeable line of reasoning, and too shocked to move, Hoyland, Joe-Jim and Ertz are ambushed by Narby's guards; in the fight that ensues the Captain runs away. At this point, hunted and sentenced to death for treason, the few remnants of Hoyland's gang fight their way topside to one of the *Vanguard*'s lifeboats, which they had discovered a few days before. Only six of them — Hoyland, Ertz, Mahoney and their wives — make it to the lifeboat, leave the Ship, and manage to land on a planet located conveniently close to the vessel at the moment they had left it. The story ends with the six men and women looking upon their new home, ready to populate it with a new offshoot of the human race (146–52).

Aside from the opening of "Common Sense," Heinlein is an economical, effective writer. He handles the nearly constant action in the second part with a deft hand and a good eye for suspense and dramatic momentum. There are many fine episodes in the narrative, none more poignant than the deaths of Joe-Jim and his cheerfully brutish servant Bobo, and none sadder than the death of Lieutenant Nelson. He had helped Hoyland escape, and for his pains he ends up being executed — by order of the newly appointed Captain — in a hollow Stalinist purge of the old order. The portrayal of Hoyland's ambivalent feelings towards the old man's murder is vivid and tasteful. Moreover, in spite of its currently blunt form the process of information gathering continues. We come to learn the name of the Ship, and also that the mythical Huff of the legend is the actual last name of the *Vanguard*'s chief metal-smith, Roy Huff— an evocative moniker for a mutineer. As Hoyland and his associates negotiate the upper levels, we receive interesting glimpses of mutie society, including the four-armed old hag who manufactures the muties' knives inside a thermodynamic laboratory whose door is labeled in a language nobody understands anymore (114).

If there is a truly improbable aspect to this fairly carefully worked out narrative, it is the ending. First of all, its technical aspects are difficult to accept, especially after all the authorial lectures on how little Hoyland can truly grasp of what he needs to know to operate a starship or a lifeboat. Heinlein's solution to the corner into which he has argued himself is to bluff his way out of it by over-emphasizing the improbability of the escape, thereby turning it into the focus of that last part of the narrative (150).[6] The list of lucky breaks and sound engineering premises goes on for three pages, at the end of which even the clever trick of advertising Hoyland's charmed life has worn thin and we have started seeing Heinlein's bluff for what it is: an ultimately implausible extrapolation from premises that were too tightly constructed to allow the writer to have his way without violating narrative sense. The idea that Hoyland and his five friends have now completed the *Vanguard*'s mission all by themselves also rests on very shaky ground. Even in 1941, at a time when genetic research was still in its infancy, it was already known that the gene-pool of a total population of three men and three women would not be enough to jump-start another offshoot of the human race. It is doubtful that they would even have made it past the fourth or fifth generation.

Secondly, the same blustering rhetorical machinery that vitiates the believability of the story's ending also taints our final assessment of the characters. When he decided on heavy-handed authorial intrusion in "Common Sense," Heinlein was already working with a set of premises for his key character. He had recreated a fictional version of Galileo Galilei, and then he had set up the narrative to use him as the catalyst for a struggle for a society's future between the forces of cultural stagnation and the forces of progress.

The social outcome of the struggle may or may not leave the reader feeling cheated of a full answer to the socio-historical variables Heinlein conjures up, but it is neither inconceivable nor implausible, especially if we consider the upheavals that accompanied the dawn of the Age of Reason in 17th-century Europe. Moreover, the idea of the few survivors of yet another mutiny exiling themselves on a planet and letting the rest of the Crew continue on their benighted path has poignancy. The problem lies elsewhere, specifically in Heinlein's handling of Hoyland's achievements in the second part of the story. If the repeated, frequent top-down lectures in "Common Sense" are somewhat embarrassing for the readers, they are downright humiliating for the characters. Yes, Hoyland does not understand a lot of what he sees, and yes, Heinlein does take pains to explain that it is not his fault he was born in a world like the one inside the Ship. However, despite all the protestations to the contrary, the net effect of hearing this constantly reiterated critical refrain is to turn Hoyland into a buffoon and a fool, an impression only reinforced by his blindness to Narby's treachery. During "Universe," the down-to-top learning process in which we were engaged along with Hoyland made him look like the smart, paradigm-shifting man Heinlein had created him to be. In the learning environment of the second part, he just looks dumb and listless to our artificially enhanced perception — it's a little like being told that Newton is dumber than Heisenberg because he never figured out quantum physics. If Hoyland is the Galileian figure for his generation, then we should respect him for that, and the problem is that at the end of the story we do not necessarily do so. He just seems an improbably lucky little man who ended up on a planet because his creator wanted to spare him a Trip to the Converter. He probably deserves better than this.

For the above reasons, the best path out of Heinlein's generation starship story does not go through the end; instead, it passes through the *Vanguard*'s ship log, the one instance of modern infodump in "Common Sense" and the one factor that saves part two from undermining the accomplishments of part one. Hoyland and Joe-Jim discover it in the lifeboat immediately before Narby's betrayal, and reading it they find many answers to a lot of as yet unanswered questions, and more importantly, a pithy, effective analysis of the situation that transformed the Ship into a generation starship. The rebellion broke out at 0431 on June 6, 2172, when Huff gathered his men around him, appointed himself captain, and started shutting off key systems in an attempt to force the loyalists to surrender. The ensuing civil war lasted for about four months, killed the great majority of the Ship's crew, and then petered out for sheer lack of manpower (138). The date of the first post-mutiny entry in the log is fixed, with a certain degree of approximation, at October 1, 2172 (138), and its author is Theodor Mawson, formerly Storekeeper Ordinary and now

Captain of the *Vanguard*. Ninety percent of the Ship's population is dead, all of them key personnel. Food and supplies are running dangerously low, and the mutineers who have not yet surrendered have started engaging in cannibalistic practices to stay alive. The crew is struggling to plant new crops, keep the converter running, maintain discipline, and fight off the rebels.

The next entry, undated, portrays a steadily worsening situation. The clocks on the ship no longer work, so nobody knows about the time and date. The converter has been restarted but there is no one able to fly the ship. Mawson has attempted to learn the principles and practice of astrogation from the relevant technical manuals, but the complex mathematics he is required to master are defeating him (138). Since the *Vanguard*'s radiation shield was irreparably damaged during the fighting, mutations have started showing up in newborn children, so he decrees that such mutations should be rooted out of the gene pool by eliminating the affected (139).

Mawson's last entry ends the log, and poignantly sums up the plight of the *Vanguard*'s Crew:

> I am growing very old and feeble and must consider the selection of my successor. I am the last member of the crew to be born on Earth, and even I have little recollection of it.... There has been a curious change in orientation in my people. Never having lived on a planet, it becomes more difficult as time passes for them to comprehend anything not connected with the ship ... [140].

It is a good thing that Mawson's voice should come to us at the end of the story. Had Hoyland found the diary early on, say at the beginning of "Universe," the chance for both the characters and the reader to learn the world from the inside out would have died a swift death. As it is, not even the clumsiness of the infodumps in "Common Sense" can completely dull the experience of understanding what happened to the people onboard the *Vanguard*, an experience that goes a long way towards putting in perspective their decisions and the reasons that prompted them. Comprehending what factors generated the inward-looking attitude that would eventually give rise to the Crew's religious beliefs will not turn Narby into a good person, any more than seeing how awful the original mutiny really was will turn Hoyland or Joe-Jim into devils. It will, however, historicize their behavior, thereby shading the color of their respective moralities a little further towards the grey.

Like the people onboard the *Flashaway*, the crew of the *Vanguard* experienced a conflict of desires, but in the latter case there was no Gregory Grimstone to mediate, however ineffectively, between the desires of the generation that issued the ship and those of the generations traveling in it. No transcendental agency kept the crew in awe of its power, and no overarching will kept the ship on its course, ready to intervene should this course be altered by those whose desires were at variance with the will of the state. Alone, deprived of perspective and history, the successive generations of the *Vanguard*'s Crew retreated inside their minds and inside their ship, turning the first into Aristotelian simulations and the second into the physical limit at once justifying and requiring these simulations. And so the worldship flew on, as it still does at the end of "Common Sense," its engines idle and its control room silent, awaiting the return of a purpose born of desire. Without that purpose, it has indeed become like Earth itself, a planetary body (albeit man-made) on a directionless path through space, carrying a population of human beings largely unaware of and unconcerned with their home's physical motion.

CHAPTER 4

The Birth of the Space Age, 1946–1957

"Common Sense" was published a scant couple of months before the Japanese attack on Pearl Harbor that brought the United States into World War II. Between then and the end of the war, the SF publishing field went into a holding pattern, consolidating their reader base but otherwise waiting for better times as many of its key authors — Heinlein among them — temporarily put their writing careers on hold and went to do war work. When they came back, something had changed.

Since its earliest days, but especially after Campbell became editor of *Astounding*, American science fiction had made the idea of space flight the cornerstone of its advocacy:

> One thing *Astounding* had which can never be recaptured. It had faith. The peculiar faith that space travel was possible and that it would come about. This belief has long ago been translated into fact. At the time, however — in the forties and fifties — it was greeted with almost universal skepticism or ignorance. To be a part of Campbell's audience was to feel oneself a member of a privileged minority who knew in their bones what was going to happen in future. Space travel was the major chord [Aldiss & Wingrove 240].

Campbell and his readers were essentially correct in feeling like a privileged minority. In the years leading up to and including the Second World War, they had represented the only voice advocating spaceflight in a country preoccupied with more earthly matters — coming out of the Great Depression at the end of the thirties, and gearing up for the looming conflict immediately after that. Also, as we have seen in Chapter 1, the United States had not been able to profit from Robert Goddard's experiments in rocketry. Goddard's fear of intellectual theft had prompted him to conduct his work in secrecy, so that the man who could have become the pre-war pioneer of an American spaceflight program spent his life in virtual obscurity, well known only in academic circles. The consequences of this lack of professional advocacy proved to be a boon for science fiction:

> The absence of any eminent U.S. scientist to serve as a spokesperson for the awakening space movement left the American wing in the hands of two groups devoutly committed to the romantic exploration vision: German expatriates and science fiction fans. Both found reinforcement for their astonishing views within newly organized rocket societies. Responding to the increasing volume of extraterrestrial narratives, both fictional and nonfictional, partisans of space flight throughout Europe and the United States founded societies devoted to the conquest of space [McCurdy 18].

In the long term, the marriage between science fiction and the two most important rocket societies, the German VFR (Verein für Raumschifart, established in 1927) and the American Interplanetary Society (founded in 1930), would help shape the birth of the space age. In the short term, it provided the burgeoning SF field with a focus and a sense of legitimacy that its humble origins alone could probably not have provided. In 1935 Willy Ley, a pupil of Hermann Oberth and one of the key figures in the VFR, expatriated to the United States with help from members of the American Rocket Society. He was fleeing a rapidly rearming Germany, whose government had noticed the largely successful efforts of the VFR and decided to make the society work for the Wehrmacht. Around the time Ley fled the country, a number of VFR members were transferred to a secret government laboratory on the island of Peneemünde to work on the military applications of rocketry. They were led by Wernher von Braun, whom Ley had inducted into the VFR and whose work for the Nazi regime would lead to the development of the V-2, the first true ICBM (McCurdy 22–23).

Upon arriving in the U.S., Ley found the lack of attention towards rocket technology dismaying, so he decided to dedicate himself to generating the interest necessary to create an American rocket program. He published a very successful study entitled *Rockets: The Future of Travel Beyond the Stratosphere* (1944), and entered into personal contact with several members of the American Rocket Society, especially its president, G. Edward Pendray. Pendray, a reporter for the *New York Herald Tribune* and SF writer, had been a regular contributor to Gernsback's *Science Wonder Stories*, the predecessor to that same *Wonder Stories* where Manning had published the first generation starship narrative in 1934. It was in his apartment that he and a group of SF writers had met in 1930 to form the American Rocket Society, and it was with him that Ley started working after 1935 to create a movement devoted to rocket-powered space flight (McCurdy 24).

It was not enough, though. The passion was there, and so were the stories — in the Gernsback-era pulps first, and in the magazines of the Campbell generation later. The portrayal of spaceflight as the carrier wave for tomorrow was as vibrant and enthusiastic as Campbell, Heinlein, and the rest of the *Astounding* writers could make it, but while they were writing of sleek machines rocketing crews of Competent Men out to the stars, American aircrews were daily making their way to the heart of the Ruhr inside heavily-laden bombers amidst a sea of flak. Elsewhere in the Pacific, more Americans were slogging through the sands of Okinawa or Iwo Jima, trying to dodge Japanese bullets as they went. The U.S. public did read SF and dream of a better future, but they used their dreams to help themselves focus on the earthbound struggles of the present, and the fact that so many SF writers had put their work for the genre magazines on the back burner to concentrate on war work was telling. The time was not right.

It became right in the aftermath of World War II. The winners of the conflict dissolved their already grudging alliance and rapidly froze the geopolitical map of the world in the shape of the Cold War. By then, Wernher von Braun was in the United States, ready to continue the work he had done for the Nazis for the profit of his newly adopted country. Once in the U.S., he wasted no time in finding his old friend Willy Ley, and together they used the American Rocket Society as the springboard for their spaceflight advocacy, supplanting Pendray as the main driving force behind the society's projects through their technical know-how. At the same time as he was designing rockets for the U.S. Army, von Braun was engaged with Ley in attracting the attention of the public towards space flight, for the development of which he asked, in a speech delivered at a symposium organized by Ley in 1952, for the creation of a specialized, separate government initiative. Thus the American Space Program was born.

What ultimately attracted the U.S. government to von Braun's idea was the deft marrying of the sense of wonder inherent in the exploration of the unknown with Cold War paranoia. Already in 1946, Pendray had written an article in the September 7 issue of *Collier's* magazine, in which he expostulated at length about the strategic advantages of building an ICBM-equipped military base on the Moon. The Moon "may be the fortress of the next conqueror of the Earth" (qtd. in McCurdy 64), Pendray concluded at the end of the article, thereby implying that if the U.S. did not get there first, the Soviet Union would. Nor was Pendray's the only voice raised on the topic. In the August 30, 1947, issue of *Collier's*, an article co-written by Heinlein and U.S. Navy Captain Caleb Laning explained "how the absence of a space corps would leave the U.S. defenseless" (McCurdy 65), and the article in the October 23, 1948, issue, entitled "Rocket Blitz from the Moon," featured a two-page set illustrating the possible outcome of the conquest of the Moon on the part of a power hostile to America. In the first page, two rockets are seen taking off from the surface of the Earth's satellite, and on the second, two mushroom clouds bloom over New York (McCurdy 65–66; Miller and Durant 72–73). The illustrator for the article was Chesley Bonestell, a frequent contributor of space-related artwork to the SF magazines of the time. Bonestell's realistic portrayal of rockets, space stations, and planetary bodies attracted the attention of both Ley and von Braun, who separately collaborated with him on two major projects of space popularization.

Ley and Bonestell's effort, published in 1949, was a book entitled *The Conquest of Space*. In its pages, Ley's plain-spoken narrative persona illustrated the principles involved in the launch of a spacecraft from Earth, the establishment of an orbit around our planet, the building of space stations, and the exploration of the solar system, all of it accompanied by Bonestell's sleek, vivid imagery, for whose creation he had studied telescopic images of the Moon and other planets (Miller and Durant 46–47, 54–62). Then, on March 22, 1952, came the result of Bonestell's collaboration with von Braun, an eight-part series of articles for *Collier's*— to be published over two years— in which von Braun explained the various stages of man's conquest of space. "Man Will Conquer Space Soon — top scientists tell how in 15 startling pages," proclaimed the blurb accompanying Bonestell's cover for that first issue: the image of a winged rocket, which von Braun had designed, detaching one of its stages in orbit over the Earth (McCurdy 38–39; Miller and Durant 75–76). Over the course of the eight installments comprising the series, von Braun and Bonestell emplotted the immediate future of the human race beyond the Earth, beginning with the blueprints for building an Earth-orbiting space station — an enterprise which, von Braun predicted, could be realized within fifteen years (McCurdy 38). Von Braun also warned the American public of the uses to which such an artifact could be put:

> There will also be another possible use for the space station — and a most terrifying one. It can be converted into a terribly effective atomic bomb carrier. Small winged rocket missiles with atomic war heads could be launched from the station in such a manner that they would strike their targets at supersonic speeds.... In view of the station's ability to pass over all inhabited regions on earth, such atom-bombing techniques would offer the satellite's builders the most important tactical and strategic advantage in military history [qtd. in McCurdy 66–67].

The article carefully neglected to give the American public an identity for the builders of the space station, thereby ensuring that its prediction could serve at once as a promise of power and as a warning of doom. If the U.S. built the station first, it would enjoy this tactical and strategic advance in the name of worldwide peace; if the Soviet Union beat the Americans to it, equally large-scale destruction would certainly ensue. This rhetorical merging of desire for a better future and fear for a destructive present became a leitmotif not only of the entire von Braun/Bonestell *Collier's* series, but also of most other articles published on the subject in those years. From *Life* to *Astounding Science Fiction*, the American press echoed and amplified these two seemingly different appeals into one single message: be prepared. Train, build, travel, explore, and colonize, both for the sake of advancing human progress and in the interest of peace and freedom.

Hollywood contributed to spreading the message as well, in movies like *Destination Moon* (1950), *When Worlds Collide* (1951), and *The War of the Worlds* (1953). All three movies were produced by George Pal, and all three featured Bonestell's contribution as technical and artistic consultant, but it was *Destination Moon* that proved to have the greater impact on the American public. The movie "saw Bonestell collaborate with writer Robert Heinlein in making the film as technically accurate as possible, even computing the correct phases of the Earth as seen from the Moon. The results of their efforts led to an Academy Award for the movie's special effects" (Holland 128). Also, their work gave the American people their first accurate approximation of what a landing site on the moon would look like, largely thanks to the numerous shots of the Moon itself, realistically portrayed by Bonestell through the use of those same telescopic pictures which he had employed to make his artwork for *The Conquest of Space* look so accurate (McCurdy 47).

By the time the *Collier's* series had run its course, von Braun and Ley had become the driving force behind the burgeoning American space program, and from the point of view of SF writers and readers alike, the living example of how the dreams of science fiction and the actuality of present circumstances were substantially closer than anyone thought. They both wrote science fiction, and their work was either published or reviewed in the major venues of the day—*Astounding*, *Galaxy*, and *The Magazine of Fantasy and Science Fiction* among others. As for Bonestell, his artwork had become the paragon for realism in the depiction of space art. Besides appearing in the mainstream press, it was prominently featured in the major SF magazines of the time—again, *Astounding* and its equivalents. Bonestell's style, "a photographic realism, showing great attention to correctness of perspective and scale in conformity with the scientific knowledge of the day" (Clute & Nicholls 143), proved intensely attractive to editors like Campbell for the same reason von Braun and Ley's writing did: both advocacies conceived space exploration as a desirable, practically achievable, and even necessary endeavor at the same time as they preserved its exotic appeal. Moreover, von Braun's main selling point for the space program—that it could be achieved within the lifetime of those reading *Collier's* in 1952—nicely dovetailed with the Campbell/Heinlein timeline of the future, as well as with all the other timelines that had been published since May 1941. For the first time since Gernsback had published that first issue of *Amazing Stories*, SF's most fundamental dream had ceased to be the exclusive province of fans and writers isolated from the wider world by the walls of genre. Now there were creditable scientists, military personnel, even politicians telling everyone that space flight was possible — no, necessary. Suddenly, science fiction found itself that much closer to realizing its advocacies.

In later years, the unexamined assumptions hidden in this technocratic desire for space as a function of national pride would come back to haunt American science fiction. In its essence the dream was a worthy one, but its underpinnings were rooted in global war, bloodshed, and genocide. Von Braun had had astonishingly few qualms about using slave labor to work on the V-2 project, and the fate of those he picked bothered him not at all. Bonestell, for his part, was as unfazed by the roots of the burgeoning space program as von Braun; when he was asked by an American scientist why he had chosen to work with a former Nazi instead of an American scientist, Bonestell replied that "he had more successful experience building rockets, and more faith in going into space, than anyone else I could find ... he was the only one who had ever sent up rockets. What did I care that they came down on London?" (qtd. in Miller & Durant 73). The technologies developed to build the rockets that would ultimately place the *Apollo 11* lander on the surface of the moon were the direct offspring of those von Braun and his colleagues had devised for the V-2s that had fallen on London by the thousands between 1944 and 1945. They were also the same technologies that were currently being employed to build the ICBMs that the U.S. government was procuring in increasingly large numbers. Indeed, it is doubtful that the U.S. space program would have received the attention and funding it did had it not been for the perceived necessity to transform the space race into a showcase for nuclear delivery system technology. As has been the case for most other major technological advances, it was the potential military applications that skyrocketed space flight to the top of the government's list of fundable priorities. In the meantime, however, it must have seemed to those working in SF that their consensus history of the future truly was a consensus now, both within and without the field. It really did look like the future of their desire coincided with the future of fate, so that the realization of their dreams would in fact correspond to the creation of the best of all possible worlds for everyone concerned.

Post-war generation starship narratives kept pace with events. The May 1946 issue of *Astounding* published "Rescue Party," an energetic romp through a doomed solar system written by Arthur C. Clarke, who five years later would contribute to raising public awareness of space flight through the publication of *The Exploration of Space*, a non-fiction work in a significantly different spirit from its near-namesake *The Conquest of Space*. In "Rescue Party," after picking up signs of tidal stresses in the Sun, a multi-racial, highly technological alien civilization enters the solar system and approaches the third planet, now wracked by worldwide volcanic eruptions. Our star is about to go nova, so the crew of the survey vessel above the Earth use the little time they have left to explore the burning cities of mankind, now deserted, in order to find survivors they can relocate to another planet. At great risk to themselves, the rescue party remains on Earth for as long as they can, but eventually they have to leave the system empty-handed. Their disappointment turns to wonder when their screens light up with multiple contact icons:

> "That is the greatest fleet of which there has ever been a record. Each of those points of light represents a ship larger than our own.... Yes, they dared to use rockets to bridge interstellar space! You realize what that means. It would take them centuries to reach the nearest star. The whole race must have embarked on this journey in the hope that its descendants would complete it, generations later" [54].

The tale ends with the survey ship speeding to meet the human fleet, initiate first contact, and spoil all the fun of generational space travel by giving humans warp drive technology. Clarke's narrative does not afford us a glimpse inside the generation starships themselves, and the promised speedy development of FTL capabilities on the part of the humans would have made the point moot in any case. From our point of view, perhaps the most relevant feature of this brief story is the momentary glimpse we receive of the two stages of space exploration in Wollheim's consensus history of the future together in the same passage, as the warp drive-equipped alien survey vessel approaches the human fleet slogging its centuries-long way to deep space in search of a home.

In 1953, after an absence of 17 years, Hugo Gernsback returned to magazine SF with a new offering, *Science Fiction Plus*. Subtitled "Preview of the Future," it was a large-size magazine printed on glossy, high-quality paper, in whose pages Gernsback "attempted to recover something of the flavour of his early pulps, including some Frank R. Paul covers" (Clute & Nicholls 1071). Unfortunately, the venture proved short-lived; only seven issues were published, the last of them on the old, cheap pulp paper, and after that Gernsback left the field forever. Before *Science Fiction Plus* folded, however, two generation-starship offerings appeared in its pages.

The first, a scientific article entitled "Interstellar Flight" and authored by Leslie R. Shepherd, then-technical director of the British Interplanetary

Society, appeared in the April 1953 issue, its subject foreshadowed by a Frank R. Paul cover painting entitled "Thousand-Year Space Ark." The image features a generation starship of whose design Konstantin Tsiolkovsky, J.D. Bernal, and Laurence Manning would have approved — a hollowed-out and fully retrofitted asteroid equipped with radar, communication systems, and telescopic domes on the surface, viewing ports around the entire circumference, and powered by seven huge engines shooting a green-tinted stream of ionized particles out into space. The bulk of the article deals with the principles necessary to transform Paul's artistic concept into reality — nuclear and ion engines for propulsion, thick layers of asteroidal rock for protection from radiation, time to target, resources, communication systems. Shepherd postulates a voyage of about a thousand years in the direction of one of the star systems nearest ours, and works out the technical details of the enterprise in considerable detail for such a highly speculative subject. His assessment of the human and environmental factors, despite being somewhat streamlined in comparison to the scientific and technological discussion, is perceptive:

> It is obvious that a vehicle carrying a colony of men to a new system should be a veritable Noah's Ark. Many other creatures beside man might be needed to colonize the other world. Similarly, a wide range of flora would need to be carried. A very careful control of population would be required, particularly in view of the large number of generations involved. This would apply alike to humankind and all creatures transported. Life would go on in the vehicle in a closed cycle. It would be a completely self-contained world. For this and many other obvious reasons the vehicle would assume huge proportions.... Clever design might make it a sufficiently varied world to make living bearable [57].

Some of the variables Shepherd indicates had been represented in generation-starship narratives before this point — for example, population control in Wilcox and agriculture in Heinlein. Others had not. Indeed, Shepherd's article is the first to address the issues of ecological control and psychological welfare since the generation starship was developed as a fully worked-out concept. Both Tsiolkovsky and Bernal had neglected to discuss psychological issues, simply assuming that far-future mankind would be developed enough that they would be taken care of automatically. Manning had followed in their footsteps, postulating another far-future polity of such power that the crew of the *Humanity* could shrug off these potential problems by concentrating on doing science and worrying about the galaxy-sized matter-eater from the fringes of creation. Wilcox and Heinlein, on the other hand, had made a token gesture in the right direction by mentioning the presence of ballrooms in their ships, while Heinlein alone had mentioned a sports center. Nevertheless, even these small nods to psychological well-being would constitute scant protection against boredom, claustrophobia, space sickness, alienation, loneliness, and all the other potential ailments inherent in having a planet-bound species attempt to spend several generations surrounded by nothing but pitch-black void in all directions.

As for the matter of managing a closed ecological system, the only writer to address it had been Tsiolkovsky. For the others it simply had not existed. The problem was not that nobody talked about farming or raising livestock; Heinlein, for one, was fairly specific on the subject. Rather, it was that nobody had yet looked at farming and raising livestock as two interconnected aspects of a whole ecological system. How did the environmental-support systems on the *Flashaway* or the *Vanguard* manage to set up the climatic and weather conditions necessary to grow crops? Where were the animals kept, and what kind of food did they eat? What kind of germs could they have carried on board, assuming equivalence between the biology of Earth animals and that of future generations of shipboard animals? How was water produced, both for the animals and for the humans? Granted, the discipline of ecology was still in its infancy when Heinlein and Wilcox wrote their stories, but at least some of its disjointed parts were not unknown, and yet were completely absent from those narratives.

Ecology and psychology, moreover, are not really separate issues. One influences the other. Human beings respond in different ways to different environments — we are wired to fear the dark, for example, and to find the presence of water and greenery, along with all the olfactory and tactile inputs they provide, relaxing. How would a human collective in a long-term space voyage behave, knowing they are completely enveloped in light-year upon light-year of utterly dark, airless void? Astronauts in orbit around the Earth are known to stare at the planet for long periods when not on duty, and if any experiments involving the growing of crops are being conducted onboard, there is a good chance they will spend as much free time as possible tending them. People crave the green of grass, the blue of sea and sky, the yellow of the Sun's rays refracted through our atmosphere, and the bright hues on the petals of flowers. Shepherd's last comment in the passage above, that the huge size of a generation starship could well be the only thing making life *bearable* onboard by allowing enough room for the presence of entire ecological niches, is a good index of how complex and difficult such an adventure could be.

SF is, by and large, a factually exact literary genre; it needs to be. Therefore, Wilcox and Heinlein's lack of consideration for these variables does constitute something of a problem. Both had sent their generational travelers out among the stars in purpose-built ships, man-made hulls constructed by using the same general principles one would employ to build a ship on Earth, but would this have been enough? At least the *Vanguard* is described as very large by any planet-referent standards of measurement — but again, would that have been enough? To wonder whether the insufficient ecological awareness implicit in the building of the *Flashaway* and the *Vanguard* might have been responsible for the collapse of their respective societies is academic. There is no ecological awareness in the structure of those two narratives themselves. Shepherd, however, is writing from a time in which environmental issues are taken more seriously — an attitude ensured less than a decade before by the threat of nuclear holocaust. His article adds a new set of variables to the representation of a generational space voyage, both in works of fiction and in non-fictional treatises.

These variables, moreover, are further complicated by the addition of a purely social element:

> The passage of perhaps thirty generations would pose major problems of a sociological nature. The control of population would be only one of many. Children could only be born according to some prearranged plan, since overpopulation or under population would be disastrous. The community would be subjected to a degree of discipline not maintained in any existing community. This isolated group would need to preserve its civilization, and hand on precious knowledge and culture from generation to generation and even add to the store of science and art, since stagnation would probably be the first step to degradation [57].

By now, an assiduous reader of generation-starship lore will probably have noticed the curious reluctance on the part of writers of fiction and non-fiction alike to discuss social issues in anything but the most professional, task-oriented terms. There seems to be no room left for recreation and simple fun. Manning had paid lip service to the sociological aspects of generational travel by reassuring his readers that art and science were well taken care of onboard the *Humanity*. Wilcox's Keeper of Traditions had kept insisting that the cure for the "romantic malady" affecting the crew — a telling label for the only recreational activity onboard the *Flashaway*— consisted in astronomical studies, blithely ignoring that such studies were precisely the origin of the problem; even his suggestions concerning the birth of a shipboard tradition of dramatic arts was delivered with the deadly seriousness of those fighting for survival. Heinlein's characters had simply displayed no desire or need whatsoever to engage in such activities, if one discounts mutie hunting and Joe-Jim's passion for chess (itself a highly cerebral game). And now we have Shepherd, who follows the path already blazed by concentrating on the serious needs and procedures of cultural production to the detriment of simple recreation. Once again, the problem does not consist in a flaw in the spirit of the message itself; indeed, science, art, and history do need to be practiced and improved in order to retain the sense of a cohesive cultural identity. But nobody can work incessantly for their entire life. Where are the provisions for an onboard recreational network? True enough, in the cutaway of the generation starship accompanying the article there are compartments in the hollowed-out asteroid reserved for an assembly hall, a recreation park, playgrounds, a swimming pool, and a few theaters, but unlike the other compartments in the cutaway, the functions they represent are not discussed in the main body of the text. They are just there, their mere presence acknowledged but their actual influence on the ship's population ignored.

Ultimately, it is difficult to lay Shepherd's unwillingness to tackle all the psychological aspects of generational travel at his door. First of all, he himself has the humility to warn the reader, at the beginning of his discussion of the human factors of interstellar travel, that since he is an engineer and a physicist he is not qualified to give meaningful answers to them — in fact, we could say that his perceptiveness in identifying and verbalizing them is already noteworthy. Secondly, if we really wanted to take Shepherd to task for not developing these issues to their full extent, then we would have to do the same for nearly everyone else in the field. Space-age advocacy in the fifties was long on science and technology and short on biology, ecology, and psychology. Not even von Braun, Ley, and Bonestell dedicated much thought to how humans would employ their time once they were in space — it was enough to declare that they should be there within a short timespan and show how the feat could be accomplished. For its part, the SF of the Campbell era limited its realistic portrayal of future humans to their higher intellectual functions, leaving these functions to administer the lower ones through the application of rational thought and common sense. The Campbell/Heinlein citizen of the future was largely a working man, happy to be working and needing not much else. Thus, Shepherd's article should probably be praised for raising issues that were not well represented in the space flight-related discourse of the time.

Also, the generation starship stories written from the time of Shepherd's article onwards started showing a growing awareness of these issues, beginning with Clifford Simak's "Spacebred Generations," which appeared in the August 1953 issue of *Science Fiction Plus*. The structure of the narrative itself is strongly reminiscent of Heinlein — another shipboard society that forgot everything, including being on a ship. As in Heinlein, a Galileian character surfaces to ask the questions no one wants to ask, find out the truth, and guide the ship through the final stages of its voyage of planetary colonization — successfully this time. Simak is a strong writer, and his characters are both believable and likable. His exposition is effective and, perhaps owing to the more tightly compressed narrative required by the short-story format, does not stutter and fizzle out quite as much as Heinlein's did. The notable features in this story, however, are not the narrative itself — whose template we have already seen — but rather the kind of shipboard existence Simak portrays.

Jon Hoff, the Galileian protagonist of the story, lives with his wife inside one of the many family units onboard the ship, clustered together to form what their society understands as a village, in the same way Hoyland's society understood their place as a village in "Universe." They are as yet childless, because population control, scrupulously observed, is not an isolated procedure of environmental husbandry. It is part of an entire system:

> For there was nothing wasted; there was nothing thrown away. That was the law.... You ate only enough food — no more, no less. You drank only enough water — no more, no less. You used the same air over and over again — literally the same air. The wastes of your body went into the converter to be changed into something that you, or someone else, would use again. Even the dead — you used the dead again. In months to come ... Joshua would be added to the dead, would give over his body to the converter for the benefit of his fellow-folk ... and would give Jon and Mary the right to have a child [5–6].

Within a closed ecological system, every shred of resource has two values: the transient value of the object or the organism itself — a pair of shoes, a cloth, an individual human being — and the permanent systemic value of its building blocks — molecules, atoms, chemical compounds, gases. In an environment that cannot replenish its resources through the renewing processes of a vast, buffered biosphere, the only way to maintain a functional relationship between production and loss of resources is to recycle and reuse as much raw material as possible — in the case of Simak's shipboard ecology, by once again feeding it to the ubiquitous converter, whose functioning still remains unexplained because even today nobody knows how such a mechanism is supposed to work. We only know what the writers of SF during those years expected it to do: break down every complex biological and non-biological construct into its component atoms, and then utilize the resulting mass to create something else — a pair of shoes, a few yards of fabric, food, water, or a new human being.

One of the key components of Simak's ecological system is the hydroponic gardens. In "Universe" and "Common Sense," Heinlein had mentioned the term a couple of times without explaining it, but for Simak it is important enough that he dedicates a rather long, very accurate footnote to his first mention of it. "Hydroponics," he explains, "is the art of growing plants in water with added chemical nutrients instead of soil.... On board a spaceship, hydroponics would be an ideal way to produce food, with the added advantage that the plant growth would aid in atmospheric engineering by absorbing carbon dioxide and releasing oxygen" (7), and thereby constantly regenerating the atmosphere onboard the vessel. As Simak himself acknowledges in the footnote, hydroponics was still at the experimental stage in 1953, but the description he gives of its functioning — including the necessity of providing the plants with lamp-derived light instead of sunlight — represents the blueprint according to whose dictates current experiments on hydroponic plants as part of life support systems for long-term space missions (the mission to Mars, for example) are being run. Also, the gardens are not simply there as a source of food. In much the same way the rest of the ecological balance onboard the generation starship informs the warp and woof of the crew's life, so do the hydroponic cultures — to the extent that the position of caretaker for them is hereditary (7).

Simak's story was the first step in the direction of presenting life onboard a generation starship as something more than just the springboard for a moral lesson on culture, memory, progress, and national pride. To be sure, these elements were worked into the fabric of the story, so that the process of remembrance on Jon Hoff's part, as well as his successful attempt to guide the ship to its destination, does conform to an adapted and updated Heinleinian model. However, for the first time the characters themselves achieved a three-dimensional life, an existence guided by a set of motivations not exclusively belonging to a superego-driven worldview. Jon Hoff, his wife, and the rest of the people onboard play, enjoy themselves, and worry about having children for the sake of the personal fulfillment these activities bring them. The generation starship narratives to follow would start negotiating their way through a balancing act between the necessities of the mission — a function of the desires of people who did not necessarily take the trip themselves — and the necessities of the individual — a function of personal desires born out of the contingent situation of the crew once the voyage is under way.

Why go? Why leave everything and everybody you have ever known to enlist for a mission to a place only your distant descendants will ever see? Also, from the point of view of the ship's builders, why fund such a mission? Why embark on an enterprise of very dubious material worth? No current corporation or government on Earth would sink large amounts of money and resources into a mission from which they could not expect any returns for centuries or millennia to come (always assuming the mission were successful), by which time those who had organized the voyage, and therefore stood to profit or lose from it, would be long dead. Both Tsiolkovsky and Bernal had originally faced the problem, eventually coming up with a few answers: in their opinion, the natural human instinct to know, understand, grow, and innovate would be reason enough to go — supplemented, in Tsiolkovsky's case, by the wondrous prospect of making contact with other galactic civilizations — but it would not be the only one. The survival of the human race would ultimately represent the main drive of such a venture, as Goddard had predicted it would in "The Last Migration." Shepherd had also gone along the same line of reasoning when he wrote that "scientific curiosity and the love of adventure for its own sake will be sufficient motives for the first exploratory voyages, [but] many who hold a more materialistic outlook may see in man's confinement to a single planet a factor reducing his probability of survival" (57).

For their part, the writers of generation starship stories had so far been a good deal less specific. In "The Living Galaxy," Manning had been able to sidestep the issue in much the same way he had sidestepped every other factor involving human motive: the crew were functionally immortal and superhumanly well-adjusted, and in any case there was a clear and present danger to worry about — for any given value of "present" over a period of four million years. In "The Voyage That Lasted 600 Years," Wilcox had blustered his way past the problem by making national prestige the single motivating factor in the decision to go ahead with the mission. Heinlein had not even bothered to give a reason for going; the *Vanguard* had just left Earth after the Jordan Foundation had built it, headed for the Centauri system on another mission of colonization, and that was that. Simak had followed in Heinlein's footsteps. Only Clarke had given a plausible reason — again, survival of the human race, this time in the face of a nova event.

The question is not an idle one. In his article, Shepherd had mentioned the necessity to make life onboard the generation starship not good, or fun, or constructive, but simply bearable. This adjective contains the implicit acknowledgement of the profoundly estranging experience of space travel for a species that so far has only known the reality of a biosphere-bound existence. Space is a merciless environment, deeply hostile to human life, and the travelers would know that. Their life would be a constant struggle to maintain the closed ecological system of the ship and repair its technological components, knowing full well that they could tap no other resources outside those already available onboard the vessel. Psychologically as well as practically, the stresses involved in such an existence would be considerable, and so far the science fiction of the time had not truly addressed the issue — Clarke's narrative only mentioned the generation starship at the end, and even then we only saw the fleet from the bridge of a warp drive-equipped ship, speeding toward the human vessels on its way to ending their generational voyage before it had even begun. So, the question remained. Who would go and why?

Since we last saw him at his editorial post at *Amazing Stories*, Ray Palmer had not been idle. In 1948 he had started a very successful occult magazine, *Fate*, to which he later added *Other Worlds* (1949) and *Imagination* (1950). In 1953, after recovering from a severe accident that had forced him to sell *Imagination* and let a colleague, Bea Mahaffey, edit *Other Worlds*, Palmer returned to the field by taking over editorship of *Universe Science Fiction* and starting a companion publication, a bimonthly magazine entitled *Science Stories*. This last he co-edited with Mahaffey (Clute & Nicholls 905).

Like Gernsback's *Science Fiction Plus*, *Science Stories* did not fare well. Only four issues were published between October 1953 and April 1954, and those under more than one publisher (Clute & Nicholls 1074). Before going out of business, however, the last issue of the magazine published Frank M. Robinson's generation starship novella, "The Oceans Are Wide." As Heinlein had done for his pseudo-bibliographical excerpt, Robinson began the narrative with an incipit from the *Dialogues of Lykos*:

> *When we talk of voyages and the planting of colonies, Junius, what interests me is not the ones that fail, for after all the oceans are wide and the Fates can frown upon you with a thousand faces. But, ah, the ones that succeed—what manner of men must lead them!* [7].

The discourse in the incipit contains in a nutshell the main themes of Robinson's story: the perils of a long voyage of colonization across uncharted regions, the workings of fate and human agency, the nature of leadership, and the price leadership exacts on those who acquire it. Unlike Wilcox, Heinlein, and Simak before him, Robinson is more interested in dramatizing the impact of these dynamics within a fully self-aware shipboard society than within a collective plagued by generational forgetfulness. Thus, everyone onboard the generation starship *Astra* knows full well where they are, why they are onboard such a vessel, and where they are going.

Mathew Kendrick is the son of the *Astra*'s Director, the chairman of a hereditary board of Executives who control all aspects of life onboard the generation starship. The position of Director is itself hereditary, and since the current incumbent is about to die, his son is scheduled to succeed him. Matty, however, is currently no Director material. Barely eleven years of age, he is a slightly built, elfin youth with an emotional demeanor and a passion for the arts—especially for playing his sound box, at which he is extremely talented. In short, he is a textbook example of those boy kings in Medieval Europe whose precarious, short-lived existences pepper the pages of history books treating the dynastic feuds of those times. And indeed, he is surrounded by enemies; the Executives, all of them Matty's family members, already have a better candidate for the Directorate in mind—one of his cousins, a family-loyal youth through whom they will be able to further consolidate their power. And so it is that, a few scant minutes after the death of his unloving father, Matty narrowly escapes a murder attempt on the part of his uncles, and then only through the help of his nurse Margaret. Margaret sends him up to the front of the ship to seek refuge with the Predict, "The immortal man whom nobody had seen—the stories went—for the last twenty-five years. And there were some who said that he didn't exist at all, that he was only a legend" (12).

The Predict, however, does exist. His name is Joseph Smith, and he has been alive for a very long time. The position of Predict is neither hereditary nor elective; it is for life—a greatly extended life. Smith has been around for as long as the *Astra* has been flying. Born on Earth centuries before Matty's time, he is kept virtually immortal by a longevity serum that Robinson has postulated for the same reason Wilcox had postulated Grimstone's hibernation chamber: to keep the memory of Earth alive and functioning until the end of the trip. Smith, who carries a deeply evocative name given his status onboard the *Astra*, is called Predict while Grimstone was called Keeper of Traditions, but they both represent the same overarching dictatorial authority. Grimstone's longevity device, however, was not efficient enough; it forced him to spend long periods of time away from the collective he was supposed to administer, with the effects we have seen. Smith's serum, on the other hand, solves every potential problem in one deft stroke. The Predict's immortality allows him to remain constantly awake, and therefore capable of managing the voyage of the *Astra* at once on a daily basis and across centuries of careful planning that the rest of the crew, with their merely human lifespans, cannot fathom. And he has plans for Matty.

The *Astra*, it turns out, has been flying for five hundred years, one of a fleet of fourteen generation starships that left a heavily irradiated, dying Earth in the aftermath of a nuclear conflict. Since then, the fates have indeed frowned on the fleet:

> "The *Astra* is the only one left. The *Star-Rover*, *Man's Hope*, the *Aldebaran*— all gone now. Tube trouble or pile blow-ups or else hulled by meteors. Any number of reasons.... Kenworthy, Tucker, Reynolds—they're all gone, too.... Out of four billion human beings five centuries ago, there's only the few thousand of us on board who remain. And all our lives depend on the man at the top—the Director. He has to be a strong man, Matty" [16].

The idea of using one or more generation starships to escape a dying Earth is not new; the reason for the Earth's death, however, is. In 1949, a SF author like George R. Stewart could still write an end-of-civilization novel like *Earth Abides* and make this end the result of a mindless, random plague. However, in the years that followed the Rise of the Berlin Wall, the Korean War, and the beginning of the Cold War, the increasingly real terror of a nuclear holocaust displaced other plausible causes for the end of life on Earth for the next two decades. Indeed, "The Oceans Are Wide" is one of the earlier SF stories to lay the cause for our planet's demise at humanity's door, instead of portraying it as the result of the actions of blind natural forces or alien civilizations. Many more narratives of this kind would follow in the years to come—among them Pat Frank's *Alas, Babylon*, Walter M. Miller's *A Canticle for Leibowitz*, Leigh Brackett's *The Long Tomorrow* (all written in 1955), Nevil Shute's *On the Beach* (1957), Poul Anderson's "Cold Victory" (1957) and *After Doomsday* (1962), and Robert Heinlein's *Farnham's Freehold* (1964).

The realization that mankind had finally acquired the power to terminally influence the Earth's environment contributed to change American science fiction. First of all, it gave its technocratic dreams a dark side—the same nuclear-powered technology that writers like Asimov had used to build civilization in stories like those comprising the *Foundation* series could now be used to end civilization forever, depending on the agency that wielded this technology. Secondly, It gave the Campbell generation its first, uneasy glimpse at the possibility that science and technology were not moral values in and of themselves, and that a Heinleinian application of engineering principles to human problem-solving might well nurture the very social cruelties SF's new approach was supposed to eliminate. Thirdly, it developed the potential for transforming the generation starship motif into a discussion not only of the skills necessary to transmit a cultural ethos from one generation to another, but also on the relative merits of this very ethos.

In "The Oceans Are Wide," this potential translates itself into the fundamental overarching question the narrative needs to answer: how much of itself should a biosphere-destroying civilization keep in order to acquire the means for long-term survival on another biosphere? The reason why Smith has taken Matty under his wing is that the young man is the best chance the people onboard have of reaching their destination intact and productive enough to begin again, to rebuild mankind from the ground up. As the Predict explains to Matty, "the ship and the colonists on it have one purpose and one purpose only. We are to colonize a planet and establish a civilization there. Everything we do must be directed towards that one end" (18). And indeed, the remainder of the narrative is essentially geared towards the portrayal of Matty's training from an artistically minded young boy into a Machiavellian ruler—a training Matty himself welcomes. When, after listening to his music and professing himself impressed by it, Smith offers him the chance to let go of the cares of command and become what his natural inclination seems to indicate, Matty replies that he wants to become Director of the *Astra* at all costs. Smith does warn him that the costs of becoming director far outweigh the advantages, and that he will have to sacrifice his life and desires to the task resting on his shoulders. However, when Matty remains unchanged in his desires, Smith acquiesces to begin training him, and his first act as the future Director's mentor is to smash his pupil's musical instrument (17).

We could say that Matty has confused his perception of the future of his desire with his appreciation of the future of his fate. He wants the Directorship, and he finally does get it, but the price the position brings with it is indeed steep—steeper, maybe, than Matty's satisfaction at confounding the plans of his relatives and proving his dead father wrong. In the following years, he has to learn how to plot, scheme, and administer the *Astra* together with those he despises, as well as sacrifice the occasional pawn to the greater good both of the ship and of himself as its ultimate authority. Also, he learns that the consequences of his mistakes do not fall exclusively on his head, but also on those of his loved ones. This lesson is brought home to him in a most painful way when he decides to indulge himself by participating in a tournament of an illegal gladiatorial game called Slith. At the time he is still incognito, growing up with an adoptive family until he is eighteen and can claim his throne, and his foster brother Sylvanus goes with him to the tournament. Unbeknownst to either of them, his relatives have set a trap for Matty that comes very close to succeeding. Bleeding and hunted, Matty barely escapes with his life, and when the Predict summons him to impart a humiliating lecture on the dangers of incautiousness, he concludes by informing him that Sylvanus is dead. Whoever wanted to kill Matty managed to at least dispose of his foster brother (29).

Things do not get easier with the progress of the years. Close to the time when he can finally step out from the shadows to claim the Directorship, Matty has to look on as Nurse Margaret is sentenced to the public strangler, allegedly for poisoning food but in actuality for helping him escape years before. The power structure onboard the *Astra* is designed so that every member of the council of Executives will run one of the ship's governing bodies or specialized departments — agriculture, technology and repairs, navigation — and the judiciary system in particular is run by Junius Schroeder, one of the Executives who is most hostile to Matty. Therefore, unable to either show his hand too early or get the Predict to intercede for Margaret, Matty has to watch impotently as the executioner completes his business and his old nurse falls dead to the floor of the courtroom (30–31).

Once he has become Director, Matty finds his resources taxed to the limit by the constant demands on his time — setting up supply lines and preparing the ship for the end of the voyage, facing emergencies, administering day-to-day business. Also, he remains subject to assassination attempts and other, less overtly violent political moves designed to unseat him from power. Even the satisfaction of having many of his relatives follow Margaret to the strangler does not ameliorate the suffering involved in seeing many of his loved ones distance themselves from him, as the weight of his Directorial authority forces him to implement unpopular, often cold-hearted policies. Particularly painful is the failure of his plan to wed the girl he loves, as the necessity to secure his power base through a political marriage becomes inescapable in the wake of an accident that costs the lives of many children onboard the *Astra*. And all along, every day of his life as Director, Matty has to confront the implacable will of the Predict, the immortal who has dedicated every shred of his energy to a five-hundred-year plan for the survival of what is left of mankind. Smith is unsympathetic and seemingly emotionless, always ready to return Matty to the reality of his life choices when the latter's basically caring nature, still alive and healthy despite the years of hard-heartedness imposed upon it, threatens to push him in a more compassionate direction than the great plan warrants.

And finally there comes the day when all the suffering and the deprivations, all the sacrifices and the planning, come to fruition. The *Astra* arrives at the planet of its destination, and it is a place more lush, welcoming, and plentiful than Earth had ever been. There are many plant and animal species, all compatible with human life, and the absence of any settlements or artifacts belonging to an intelligent civilization ensures that the crew will not have to fight an indigenous population for a share of the planet. Climatic conditions are also perfect, and the food is more plentiful and nourishing than that provided by hydroponics. The planet is very beautiful in every one of its separate biospheric niches, and the absence of any violent weather patterns makes it unnecessary to work on erecting a shelter for the colonists. As a matter of fact, no amount of work or planning is necessary, so that the crew starts falling behind schedule until, six weeks later, there is no longer a schedule to speak of (57–58). And of course, Smith is there to do something about it:

> "Civilizations usually arise in response to a challenge, either from nature or from marauding tribes. And people huddle in towns and villages for mutual protection — that's another incentive for civilization. But here there isn't any threat from nature, or from other forms of life. And people aren't huddling — they're leaving…. If we stay here, within a generation we'll have degenerated to little scattered groups of savages. Within three we'll have forgotten our science. We'll probably even have forgotten where we came from. And why" [59].

In the end, Matty goes along with Smith's suggestion: drug everybody and, with the help of the few loyal followers Matty has, put them back on the ship and fly to the planet immediately farther out from the primary — a much bleaker place, compatible with human life but far less forgiving, and populated by a primitive race of primates who will be sure to give the *Astra*'s colonists a run for their money. Also, in order to make sure nobody will think of returning to paradise, Smith has Matty and his people crash the ship on their new planet, thereby killing several dozen people in the utterly destructive impact that ensues and burning their bridges behind the survivors. The end of the story sees Matty, now the new Predict of the colony after denouncing Smith as the instigator of the move to the new planet, stick the needle containing the immortality serum in his arm. The *Astra*'s population has already started building huts and fortifications, and hunting parties are going out to secure provisions from the environment's meager food supply and make sure the natives are not in the mood to attack. Matty has paid the ultimate price of power: he is alone, an immortal among mayflies, and his Machiavellian training is now complete. He has become his teacher.

Robinson's story is well written, effective in its emplotment, and thorough in its presentation of a consistent picture of shipboard life. The colonists' daily routine onboard the *Astra*, from the gladiatorial game of Slith to the crowd's passion for life-or-death trials, merges well with the preparations for landing, the emergencies, the recreational activities, and the administrative details. Moreover, the lifestyle choices that preserving the efficiency of the ship's closed ecological system imposes upon the crew — for example, the obligatory self-euthanizing everyone is compelled to carry out upon reaching sixty years of age — are allowed to inform the politics of intrigue between Matty, the Predict, and the council of Executives, so that their plausibility and lived-in feel are enhanced by their multi-functional role. Even the biblical overtones inherent in the choice to abandon a planetary heaven for a place of struggle and suffering, all in the name of greater civilizational knowledge, are meaningfully and tastefully worked into the fabric of the narrative.

Yet, the story ultimately betrays us. Let us return for a moment to the basic premise at the heart of this narrative: mankind has been forced to embark on a generational voyage to the distant stars because of the cataclysm it brought upon its own head through nuclear war. The paramount task of the survivors, especially now that the *Astra* is the only ship left, is to build another civilization from the ashes of the old one. Now, Robinson does not actually have any of his characters go ahead and utter it out loud, but the implication of the situation is that this new civilization should possess the wisdom to avoid what happened to the old — otherwise it would remain stuck in a recursively destructive loop; it would rise to create a military-industrial complex, destroy its biosphere through nuclear war or man-made environmental collapse, flee its burning world onboard a generation starship to a new planet, and so on. Again, the fundamental question that the resolution of this narrative's main dramatic premise is supposed to answer is: how much of itself should such a civilization preserve?

Robinson's answer, issued through his mouthpieces, is that such a civilization should preserve every last thing. Matty's world has everything the old one had: Machiavellian power games, betrayal, sacrifice of innocents in the name of an abstraction, cruelty of every kind, grief, loneliness, unsatisfied desires, lack of foresight in the face of material gain. It is a long list indeed. Moreover, the Predict's argument for leaving the paradise planet at once justifies and requires this kind of behavior. It is a maddening piece of circular reasoning by whose dictates the rise of civilization requires the very germs of conflict that, once their impact has been increased by several orders of magnitude through the development of advanced technological artifacts, will destroy it. So an admittedly naïve reader, ignorant of the necessities of contemporary and future-time realpolitik, might ask how such a collective hopes to forestall its demise if it behaves in exactly the same way as the old, both within — through every imaginable abuse its members perpetrate on each other — and without — because now the new planet's original inhabitants are understandably upset at having to share it with colonialist aliens for whom the only way to progress is through (a) a healthy clash with natural forces and (b) a good scrap with the natives.

Smith's final argument in favor of leaving the paradise planet is the ultimate distillation of the Campbell generation's credo. We need to suffer and want because that is the only way to either develop or maintain our science, and therefore our technology and industry. We are fully within a Heinleinian ideological model here, where everything is subsumed to the needs of the world machine. Robinson does not treat Matty's suffering — or the suffering of others — lightly, but at the end of the day everything is justified in the name of preserving the same kind of techno-industrial collective whose earlier incarnation had caused its own demise through the very traits its heir is going to such lengths to cherish. For all the strength of its biblical metaphor, the idea that it is necessary to abandon paradise in order to mature as a collective was as bankrupt in 1954 as it is today. Would you really live here and degrade to a happy, full-bellied savagery, the Predict asks, and Matty answers no, I would not. As fruitless as ex post facto speculation may be, however, it is difficult not to wonder how the story might have turned out if his answer had been yes. In that case, the few survivors of our distant descendants might have spared themselves and the rest of the galaxy the rise of another, dangerously powerful collective of fully industrialized, murderous imperialist pests, and faded into a happy state of innocence from which no law of the universe would have tried to pluck them, except those in which the Campbell generation believed.

As the 1950s continued inching their way toward their end, Campbellian SF began to show signs of strain. The events of the present were starting to catch up with it, and its brand of advocacy was aging rapidly. In hindsight, it was inevitable that it should have turned out to be so. The great strength of American science fiction throughout the Campbell/Heinlein years — its promise of a radically different future a mere couple of decades from the present in which its advocacy was being published — was also its weakness, because it had traded short-term plausibility for long-term actuality.

Science fiction has always had a strange relationship with the futures it either advocates or fears. The more distant the future in a SF narrative, the less plausible it looks to the eyes of those who are reading it in the present.

It is not always easy to read a novel like Greg Bear's *City at the End of Time* (2008), with its multi-trillion-year-old city at the fringes of creation and, indeed, at the end of time, or James Blish's *Cities in Flight* (1970), with its spacefaring chunks of urbanized Earth plying the starlanes billions of years after our planet's demise. Narratives of this kind require the reader to place their faith in a representation of stretches of time and gulfs of space that are usually difficult to visualize in the mind's eye. Once the numerical expressions of these quantities start looking more like telephone numbers than actual figures, the mind tends to lose its capacity to understand — and therefore dramatize — them. That is one of the reasons why this kind of megayear and gigaparsec-heavy science fiction is often difficult to embrace for readers who come to it for the first time.

However, once it is accepted by the reader, this kind of SF narrative ends up retaining its long-term appeal more easily than other sub-genres, because the very size of its canvas stretches its advocacy throughout such a broad front that it is difficult to gainsay the changes it postulates. Who is to know what mankind will look like a million years from now, and where we will be? If we changed from apes to what we are today within a scant 100,000 years or so, there is no telling what might happen over stretches of time at least ten times as large. Thus, this strain of SF finds plausibility in amplitude.

On the other hand, the kind of science fiction the Campbell/Heinlein school was publishing mostly favored a much more restrained set of quantities, both in time and space,[1] because this gave its writers the chance to present a far tighter, substantially less outlandish map of the path from here and now to there and tomorrow. It was an almost realist SF mode, in the sense that, as was the case for the Heinlein timeline, the starting point for its development consisted in altering the known world only by one seemingly small element, and then building up the changes resulting from it in a crescendo of estrangement ultimately leading to colonies on the Moon, interstellar voyages, and the colonization of the solar system. This way, the changes introduced in the timeline could become as convoluted and future-shocked as the writer wanted, but they could always be traced back to their humble beginnings in a mimetic representation of our world.

Campbellian SF had made an art out of presenting this kind of future history as if it had been about to become actuality. Indeed, the readers of *Astounding* routinely entered into two different but interconnected contracts with their writers: the first consisted in the normal suspension of disbelief that has always been the necessary condition for reading a science fiction narrative; the second consisted in a contract of faith — faith that the cultural assumptions of the Campbell ethos would be proven right a few years down the line. The blunt operations of social engineering characters like William

Gaines performed on their hapless subordinates in stories like "The Roads Must Roll" may have been unpalatable on first principles,[2] but such was the plausibility of the stories' canvas that most readers of *Astounding* accepted them like they accepted many of the institutional evils in their everyday world. Both were real — or rather, some were already real, others were about to become so.

Then the fifties rolled around, and the present started to catch up with the future. "Let There Be Light," which Heinlein had published in 1940, had postulated a major scientific and technological breakthrough around 1950, a breakthrough that would enable the moving walkways that by 1960 would have changed the face of America in "The Roads Must Roll." At the closing of the 1950s, however, neither innovation had taken place, and all the other changes postulated in later stories, themselves dependent on the changes in the first two, were becoming increasingly more improbable by virtue of the domino effect thus generated. At the same time, the unraveling of the future postulated in the narratives was exposing the advocacy with which Heinlein had accompanied it, revealing it for what it actually was: desire's ultimately bankrupt gamble against the future of fate.

Fate had yet more in store for desire, however. If we look at the generation starship narratives between 1937 and the late '50s and take them to represent a meaningful cross-section of typical science fiction stories for those times, we will notice that not a single one of them features even one character with a non–English name. True, Wilcox had been the only writer to explicitly make his generational voyage an affair of national pride, while Heinlein, Simak, and Robinson had not even bothered to address the issue — but that is in itself telling. The characters in "Universe," "Common Sense," "Spacebred Generations," and "The Oceans Are Wide" all have American names, and all behave following the assumptions and mores of 1940s and 1950s America, to the extent that the very lack of self-consciousness on their part is indicative of the certainty these attitudes embodied. Magazines like *Astounding* had taken the idea of American primacy in the space race, eloquently foreshadowed and advocated by Ley, von Braun and Bonestell, and turned it into certainty through an act of fictional reiteration. If the Campbell future was about to become real, then everything it advocated was about to become real as well, which meant that the United States would be the country to colonize space and set the tone for the future of the world. In the end, as the stories written in those years implied, in the far future the term "mankind" and the term "American" would be one and the same. We only needed to wait for it to actually happen.

CHAPTER 5

The New Wave and Beyond, 1957–1979

"For me, the terror," writes Stephen King at the beginning of *Danse Macabre* (1981), "... began on an afternoon in October 1957" (15). King was in a movie theater watching the Saturday matinee, Fred F. Sears' *Earth vs. the Flying Saucers* (1956), a classic 1950s representation of American Cold War anxieties disguised as alien invasion. In the movie, a race of intergalactic plunderers attack the Earth and wreak havoc for a few reels before the hero of the story, an adventurer-scientist straight out of a Gernsback pulp, devises a hard-sf big-think raygun doodad and wipes out the entire alien fleet with it.

That October day in 1957, King and his contemporaries were in the movie theater to watch Americans repel the aliens in much the same way — so their government had told their parents and they in turn had told their children — as they would watch the U.S. Army kick out the Soviets in case of an actual Communist invasion. Three quarters of the way through the movie, however, they received an unpleasant surprise; as the aliens were about to launch their final attack on Washington DC, the movie abruptly stopped, the lights came on, and the theatre manager walked out in front of his surprised audience. In a trembling voice, he told the children that "the Russians have put a space satellite in orbit around the earth. They call it ... *spootnik*" (21). That the manager should have thought it necessary to stop the show to impart this news to a room full of pre-teens may seem unnecessary, but the children had been paying attention to what their parents and teachers had taught them, and they understood the meaning of the event: "The Russians had beaten us into space. Somewhere over our heads, beeping triumphantly, was an electronic ball which had been launched and constructed behind the Iron Curtain.... It was up there ... and they called it Spootnik" (22).

Today, in the first decade of the twenty-first century, the eyes of generations raised in the aftermath of *Apollo 11*, the space shuttle, Perestroika, the crumbling of the Berlin Wall, and the ISS, look at the golf-ball shape of *Sputnik I* and find it quaint — almost as quaint as the nationalistic rhetoric and brinksmanship that accompanied the technological achievements of the first space age. For those of us who did not have to live through those times, it is difficult to comprehend the terror and the anxiety that *Sputnik*'s launch generated among the upper political and military echelons of the government, who knew that if "the Soviets had the rocket power to launch *Sputnik* it meant that they now had the capacity to deliver the bomb on an intercontinental ballistic missile. The panic reached far beyond the relatively sane concern for tactical weaponry, however. *Sputnik I* took on a magical dimension" (Wolfe 54). Ironically, this magical dimension was not the result of Soviet propaganda, nor was it the outcome of an objective assessment of Russian technological superiority on the part of Western rocket scientists; as King explains, it was the direct offspring of the cultural climate of 1950s America within which he and his contemporaries had been reared:

> We were fertile ground for the seeds of terror, we war babies; we had been raised in a strange circus atmosphere of paranoia, patriotism, and national *hubris*. We were told that we were the greatest nation on earth and that any Iron Curtain outlaw who tried to draw down on us in that great saloon of international politics would discover who the fastest gun in the West was ... but we were also told exactly what to keep in our fallout shelters and how long we would have to stay in there after we had won the war [23].

Thus had von Braun and Ley's rhetoric of terrified triumphalism made its way into the education of the generation sired by the men and women who had won World War II. The message that the Cold War space-age discourse had prompted these parents to transmit to their children layered a bedrock of technocratic, aggressive nationalism under a vein of utopian dream-making to generate what Carl Sagan has described as "rocket potency ... a rite of national manhood; the shape of the boosters made this point readily understood without anyone actually having to explain it. The communication seemed to be transmitted from unconscious mind to unconscious mind without the higher mental faculties catching a whiff of what was going on" (209–10). In King's recollection of his years as a war baby, this techno-sexual communication spawned an oddly pre-technological mindset, harkening back to the myth of the frontier and the colonization of the American West, and the science fiction of the time contributed substantially to the development of this mindset:

> I and my fellow kids grew up secure in this knowledge of America's PIONEER SPIRIT ... what a world stretched ahead! It was all outlined in the stories of Robert A. Heinlein, Lester del Rey, Alfred Bester, Stanley Weinbaum,

5. The New Wave and Beyond, 1957–1979

and dozens of others.... Space would be more than conquered ... it would be PIONEERED! Silver needles piercing the void, followed by flaming rockets lowering huge ships onto alien worlds, followed by hardy colonies full of men and women (*American* men and women, need one add) with PIONEER SPIRIT bursting from every pore [24].

The use of science fiction narratives as cautionary tales against the lack of military preparedness — scaremongering for warmongers, we might call it — was far from new. In fact, it predated the birth of genre SF by exactly fifty-five years. The May 1871 issue of *Blackwood's Magazine* had featured an anonymous narrative entitled *The Battle of Dorking: Reminiscences of a Volunteer*. Its author, it was later discovered, was a lieutenant-colonel in the British Army, Sir George Tomkyns Chesney, and his intention was to warn the British Government against the rapidly waxing Prussian military power in the wake of its spectacular success during the freshly concluded Franco-Prussian War. In his story, which takes place fifty years in the future from the date of publication, a grandfather tells his grandchildren about the German invasion that caught an unprepared, underarmed British Empire by surprise and conquered England, dissolving its colonial holdings and turning it into a province of the German Empire. Chesney's story gained enormous success, was translated in several languages, and spawned an entire subgenre, to which even H.G. Wells contributed with his novel *The War in the Air* (1908). In later years, with the waning of British supremacy and the rise of American power, this narrative mode migrated to U.S. shores and generated another slew of cautionary tales and alarmist editorials, of which William Ziff's piece in the October 1940 issue of *Amazing Stories* was just one example.

But now it was the 1950s, and the game of scaremongering had changed. For the first time in history, the immediate solution for allaying the public's fear of invasion — building weapons in greater numbers and with greater destructive power than those of the enemy — had actually become the problem. Even in those pre-nuclear winter times, the memory of the mushroom clouds blooming over Hiroshima and Nagasaki had left the American public with few illusions as to what would happen in case of a nuclear exchange between the U.S. and the Soviet Union. Suddenly, it was no longer a matter of building more dreadnoughts to defeat the German High Seas Fleet at Jutland in 1916, or producing enough aircraft carriers to bring Japan to heel in 1942. It had become a matter of building weapons and then steadfastly declining to use them, while at the same time snarling and flexing one's muscles at an equally well-armed enemy across the Iron Curtain. The logic of war had shifted its parameters from an active policy of aggressiveness in the name of territorial gain to a carefully constructed posture of militant passivity (peppered by instances of localized war making) in the face of the zero-sum game of Mutually Assured Destruction.

In such a climate, arguing the necessity of armament acquisition as a function of fear over a dystopian future would have left the American public with no room for hope — foreign domination on one side, and an irradiated planetary wasteland on the other. Therefore, the more militant arm of science fiction had cooperated with the von Brauns and Leys of real-life politics to generate a schizophrenic, anachronistic emplotment within whose narrative the technocratic celebration of American power harkened back to the myth of a time when knee-jerk responses to threats — unholstering one's six-shooter and showing an opponent who the fastest gun in the West was — did not carry catastrophic global consequences. In the final analysis, a substantial amount of SF published during those years argued for militarism without consequences — or rather, without an acknowledgement of those consequences. For all its future-shocked advocacy of technological and scientific advancement, most Campbellian SF refused to let this advancement operate within a context where its consequences would be commensurate with its premises. Even a narrative like "The Oceans Are Wide," propelled by a premise that should have made it impossible to ignore the outcome of a nuclear conflict, ended with a militant commitment to repeating the same mistakes on the new planet, chiefly because the narrative was structured to make that kind of advocacy work when it should not have.

Then came *Sputnik*'s flight. Wernher von Braun, Willy Ley, Robert Heinlein, or John W. Campbell had not been able to either stop it or beat it into space. In the face of the Soviet Union's triumph, the rhetoric of militant technocracy that had sustained the illusion of American primacy gave way to that equally uncritical litany of fear Stephen King witnessed in that movie theater. *Danse Macabre*, King's critical history of horror from 1950 to 1980, bases its analytical apparatus on the premise that the tale of terror constitutes a cathartic exercise for the imaginative exorcism of one's own anxieties through the destruction of a monstrous, aggressive Other. This Other coalesces those anxieties in a repulsive or otherwise terrifying physical shape, thereby becoming a sort of conceptual shorthand for them — a shorthand that a given social nexus at a certain stage in its development can recognize as its own and imaginatively repel. So, following this line of reasoning, we could say that Bram Stoker's *Dracula* (1897) featured the embodiment of a certain fear of — and desire for — sexual deviancy in England at the end of the 19th century, while possessed little Regan in William Friedkin's film *The Exorcist* (1973, based upon William Peter Blatty's 1971 novel of the same name) concretized the anxieties resulting from the end-of-the-sixties generation gap that had separated 1950s parents from their 1960s children. As King himself writes, "the dream of horror is in itself an out-letting and a lancing ... and it may well be that the mass-media dream of horror can sometimes become a nationwide analyst's couch" (27).

King's point in connecting the news of *Sputnik*'s launch to the movie playing at the Stratford Theater is that this fortuitous coupling afforded him and the rest of the children the chance to exorcise their real-life fears by witnessing the destruction of the flying saucers on the screen. For those working in science fiction, however, it was not as easy as that. The horror genre lent itself well to the task of coping with 1950s anxieties over the Bomb,[1] because it replaced those fears with desire. Once the monster was dead, once the skies were clear, the story released us from the grip of anxiety, ready to wish for a different world again. But 1950s science fiction, and its Campbellian strain in particular, had not been designed that way; they had been created not to exorcise terrors, but to cheerlead a dream, and this dream required the realization of a certain set of parameters to survive. Now that one of those parameters had failed to materialize, now that the pioneering savvy of D.D. Harriman's private enterprise had been beaten to the beginning of the space age by the socialist five-year planning of the Central Committee, a rift had opened up between expectation and reality, desire and fate. The science fiction of the Campbell generation had already begun to age, but it might have been kept alive and well for a while longer if the pillar of its future advocacy — American primacy in space — had been realized as promised. As it was, the first major crack had appeared on the screen showing the picture of tomorrow, and it was only a matter of time before others showed up as well.

In the short term, however, the advocates of the space age ended up seeing the successful launch of *Sputnik* as something of a blessing in disguise. Until 1957, their clamoring for a relevant commitment of resources toward the space program on the part of the U.S. government had been largely frustrated by the Eisenhower administration, which favored a more gradual, lower-profile solution in the form of developing satellite technology. Had it not been for *Sputnik*, the American public would probably have remained largely content to buy the SF magazines of the time, dream of going into space, and then actually vote in favor other forms of public spending. Once the Russian capsule started sending its signals from low Earth orbit, however, public opinion changed, and so did the political stance toward the space race in general and going to the moon in particular. The following exchange took place in 1958 between Richard E. Horner, Air Force Assistant Secretary, and Rep Daniel J. Flood (D-Penn), on the occasion of a hearing before the Defense Appropriations Subcommittee of the House of Representatives:

> HORNER: [W]hy is it desirable from the military point of view to have a man on the moon? Partly, from the classic point of view, because it is there. Partly

because we might be afraid that the U.S.S.R. might get one there first and realize advantages which we had not anticipated existed there.

FLOOD: [I]f we gave you all the money you said was necessary, regardless of how much it was, can you in the Air Force hit the moon with something, anything, before Christmas?

HORNER: ... we feel that we can do that; yes, sir.

FLOOD: Have you asked anybody in the Air Force or the Department of Defense to give you enough money, hardware, and people, starting at midnight tonight, to chip a piece out of that ball of green cheese for a Christmas present to Uncle Sam? ... I am for giving it to them as of this minute, Mr. Chairman, with our supplemental, without waiting for somebody downtown to make up his mind and ask for it. If this man means what he says and if he knows what he is talking about — and I think he does — then this committee should not wait five minutes more today [qtd. in Sagan 210–12].

We are dealing with two narrative stereotypes here: the Can-Do Military Man Who Will Win Us Our Wars and the Crusty Old Administrator Who Speaks Plainly and Thinks Keenly. It is hard to figure out which one of the two interlocutors in this exchange is enjoying his part more, or even if either of them is aware of the level of performativity in their dialogue. We do not know whether Horner or Flood had read any Heinlein, but the resemblance between their rhetoric and that displayed by characters like William Gaines or D.D. Harriman is uncanny. Also, it indicates that the lingo of Campbellian SF and the language of Cold-War politics had penetrated each other to such an extent that, in that time of exaggerated national stress, both men were falling back on emplotted personas resulting from that odd mixture of technopotency and pioneer spirit we have seen above. That the reality of spaceflight made the prospect of "hitting the moon with something before Christmas" and "chipping out a piece of green cheese for Uncle Sam" ludicrous did not matter, nor did it matter that, as the Eisenhower administration's Science Advisory Committee had already pointed out, the moon actually made for a lousy launch platform.[2] What mattered was the dream of spaceflight as a test of national manhood, and the heady mixture of fear and desire it generated. Goaded by the scaremongers, the American public started clamoring for the development of a space initiative that would put a man on the moon before the Soviets, and their leaders obliged them. First the Kennedy and then the Johnson administrations made sure that the generous helpings of money, men, and resources for which Representative Flood had clamored in 1958 would make their way to those who needed them, although not necessarily with the same blind profligacy his words had suggested.[3] And, as we know, the United States succeeded. In July of 1969 Neil Armstrong and Buzz Aldrin became the first men to walk on the moon, and by extension the first to walk on a planetary body other than Earth. The dream of Campbellian

SF had finally become real — and it died at that very moment, forever and irrevocably.

The original formulation of the Campbell/Heinlein recipe for future advocacy had entailed not just the human venture into space, and not just the *American* human venture into space before anyone else. A certain ideology had also been expected to accompany the enterprise, an ideology that would at once justify and be justified by the enterprise's material success. Heinlein in particular had envisioned the opening of the frontier of space as a private capitalist venture, organized and jump-started by entrepreneurs who embodied at once the moneyed technocracy of the mid–20th century and the pioneer spirit of their forefathers, men who had tamed the West in the same way their descendants were going to tame the stars. He had found the perfect springboard for this mixture of ideological traits in Delos D. Harriman, the protagonist and hero of the aptly titled story "The Man Who Sold the Moon." Harriman literally sells the entire planet Earth on the idea of going to the moon and later to the outer planets of the solar system, and he does so by single-handedly managing the world's economy, using both his allies and the governments that oppose him as pawns in a game of chess he is playing on a board far too large for anyone else to understand. Once the space age has begun, a flood of human beings, all of them Competent Men straight out of the cultural template favored by Campbell-era SF, follows Harriman's blazing trail. Prosperity, can-do competence, and a vigilant *pax Americana* ensue.

But it did not happen that way. The *Apollo* lander was not a sleek, futuristic rocket like those imagined by Chesley Bonestell, Frank R. Paul, or Virgil Finlay; it was an ungainly, aesthetically awkward construct designed purely for usefulness. No businessman like Harriman had managed to sidestep the will of the state. The beginning of the space age, far from bursting open the door to a better future, had instead only underscored the painful differences between nations on Earth. Born in the fires of the Nazi hegemonic dream in the 1930s and 1940s, and fueled by the distorted logic of Cold-War détente in the 1950s, the American space program had put men on the moon bearing a plaque that read "We Come in Peace for All Mankind" at the same time as the U.S. was involved in the longest war of the twentieth century, a war motivated by the same search for a strategic advantage that had sent *Apollo 11* to our satellite. Within the borders of the United States itself, many members of the generation Stephen King calls "war babies" would not do as their country ordered them, refusing to go to Vietnam and putting flowers in the muzzles of guns. Campbellian SF would have died anyway. Too many assumptions based on gender, class, and race had riddled it with a sclerotic WASP mindset that could no more adapt to the changing conditions at the end of the 1950s than their counterparts in the wider world of American culture could. But even before that happened, it had fatally allied itself with the military-minded enterprise of the space program, which only shared SF's desire for space exploration insofar as it gave the U.S. a military and political edge against the Soviet Union. Campbellian SF, we might say, ended up dying of too much fate and too little fulfilled desire.

In 1940, Don Wilcox had sent Americans to the stars on a voyage of colonization and cultural transmission, and though their mission had failed, their motherland's initiative had not. In later years, Robert Heinlein, Clifford Simak, and Frank M. Robinson had managed, however haphazardly, to spread American values among the stars, following the blueprint for generational transfer already established by John W. Campbell in the early years of *Astounding*. Now, with the grand narrative of spaceflight dying on the wire before their eyes, the writers of generation starship stories of the sixties and seventies found themselves having to tell the tale of a voyage whose inception, aims, and procedures no longer obeyed a single overarching template.

Roughly twenty generation-starship narratives appeared in the twenty years that separated the onset of SF's so-called New Wave from the edge of the information revolution and the beginning of the genre's modern age—a more than twofold increase from the two decades encompassing the Campbell period, and a nearly tenfold increase from the fifteen or so years comprising the Gernsback era. The reasons for this sudden, explosive proliferation are rooted in the internal dynamics that were beginning to shape the coming trends in science fiction, at the same time as the events in Cold-War politics were unraveling the grand narrative of the genre's previous incarnation.

At the end of the 1940s, the appearance of other forms of SF publishing besides magazines, as well as other magazines besides *Astounding*, had started challenging the Campbell brand of advocacy—not enough to undermine it, at least not until the end of the 1950s, but enough to successfully present new alternatives to its vision of a hard-science future. In 1949, *The Magazine of Fantasy and Science Fiction* (*F&SF* for the sake of brevity) had been launched, and a year later *Galaxy* had followed it:

> [*F&SF*] established a reputation for literary quality, thanks to the high standards of its editors ... and their willingness to publish authors who would never have been seen in *Astounding*.... It attracted *Astounding* authors as well, and gave them much more liberty to write what they wanted than Campbell had ever done.... *Galaxy* was usually seen as occupying a middle ground between *Astounding* and *F&SF*: not so literary and experimental as *F&SF* ... but not so hidebound and dominated by editorial obsessions as *Astounding* was becoming in the 1950s [James 86].

Campbell had not always been that way. From the start of his tenure at *Astounding* until the beginning of the fifties, he had been flexible enough in his thinking to accept stories from writers who did not conform to the template he favored—writers like Henry Kuttner, Eric Frank Russell, and E.E. "Doc" Smith, one of the survivors of the Gernsback era who had found a way to recycle his space opera for the new age. Far from undermining the Campbell/Heinlein template, the presence of these narratives had contributed to lending credibility to it, in the same way a counterpoint supports the main refrain of a symphony. By the early 1950s, however, Campbell's "views of the genre became so rigid as to exclude exciting new writers, his view of science shaded into a troubling fascination with pseudoscience such as L. Ron Hubbard's Dianetics, and his racial views approached bigotry" (Landon 56). He had already ended his friendship with Heinlein when the latter, always looking for different publishing venues from the SF magazines of his time, "did just that, starting in 1947 with several sales to the *Saturday Evening Post* and, between 1947 and 1959, with a very popular series of 12 novels aimed at juvenile boys and published by Scribner's. At the same time ... he continued to write serialized fiction for *Astounding, Galaxy*, and the *Magazine of Fantasy and Science Fiction*" (Landon 58).

Among the many things SF owes Heinlein, one of the most important is the genre's expansion into the world of novel and anthology publication, which began in 1947 in the wake of his juveniles' financial success. In 1952, five years after the appearance of the first among Heinlein's long narratives, *Rocket Ship Galileo*, three events conspired to propel the still embryonic SF novel market toward full development: Harcourt Brace started publishing another series of novels aimed at the juvenile market, this time written by Andre Norton; Ian Ballantine created Ballantine Books, an imprint that published some of the most relevant science fiction novels of the 1950s, both in hardcover and paperback; and Donald A. Wollheim became an editor at Ace, where he began publishing SF novels in paperback format, both as singles and in the form of the now famous Ace Doubles. It is likely that Heinlein and Norton's juveniles played a relevant role in expanding science fiction's adult readership a few years down the line, besides representing a probable factor in Ace and Ballantine's determination that there was indeed a market ready to receive original SF works in long form; Wollheim's editorship, on the other hand, provided then-fledgling writers with their first chance to publish a novel-length work in a high-visibility market. Among the authors whose first novel was published as part of an Ace Double are some of the key figures of the New Wave and beyond—Samuel Delany, Ursula Le Guin, and Philip K. Dick. As for Ballantine Books, the simultaneous publication of science fiction novels in hardback and paperback, almost unheard of at the time, further stimulated the establishment of a science fiction book market, and provided other publishers like Signet and Pocket with the impetus to create their own SF lines. Among the variety of original novels published during this period, the first two generation starship narratives in long form appeared as well: Milton Lesser's *The Star Seekers* (1953), a Heinleinian coming-of-age story set against the standard background of forgetfulness and rediscovery, and E. C. Tubb's *The Space-Born* (1956), which owed its main dramatic drive — a shipboard power struggle against a tight-fisted oligarchy — more to the social dynamics presented in "The Oceans Are Wide" than to the Galilean processes informing "Universe" and "Common Sense."

Ironically for Heinlein, this expansion also contributed to a relevant challenge of the kind of advocacy he and Campbell had been championing since the early 1940s. As a result of the increased exposure, science fiction became able to support a larger market than the one exclusively constituted by the pulps, and this opening up of its horizons gave it the chance to achieve greater relevance through the publication of narratives of larger scope and reflectivity. And so the grand narrative of the future advocated by Campbellian science fiction started unraveling at the end of the fifties, eroded from outside by the events following the launch of *Sputnik* and undermined from inside by the multiplication of publishing venues for viewpoints other than its own. The most vocal supporters of those viewpoints were the British writers of the postwar generation who, like their American counterparts, had grown up reading *Astounding* (the magazine was very successful in England as well) and, again like the Americans but for different reasons, had found themselves increasingly dissatisfied by the ideology it fostered. Britain's experience of the twentieth century had been very different from that of the United States. At the end of the First World War, an exhausted British Empire had been forced to cede world leadership to the United States, and its situation only worsened with the coming of the second global conflict. Britain won the Second World War, albeit largely thanks to U.S. help, but victory had cost it every fundamental resource it possessed at the beginning of hostilities, both human and material. Already before the end of World War II, the British Army had found itself so thoroughly drained of manpower that it had been unable to raise any more levies to replace combat losses, so that the final months of the European conflict saw it take a forced backseat to American and Soviet initiative. Also, the steep costs of the U-boat onslaught between 1941 and 1944, and the financial consequences of the lend-lease act Britain had been forced to contract with the United States, had compromised its economy to the extent that rationing of some key supplies — butter, for example — was not lifted for several years. Then, in the post-war period, the Empire itself collapsed, as its colonies achieved independence one after the other.

For these reasons, 20th-century British SF featured little of the hypertrophic, technocratic optimism displayed by its American counterpart. Gernsback had reprinted a number of H.G. Wells's tales in the first few issues of *Amazing Stories* and, along with Jules Verne, had called him the father of science fiction. That assessment had been essentially correct, or at the very least meaningfully arguable, but either Gernsback had failed to perceive that the kind of SF produced by Wells in the twentieth century had a more pronounced social bent than anything published in the United States, or he thought that its lead should be followed by something different. The key general difference between American and British SF until the 1960s was that the former adopted and advocated a view of the future that we can generally place somewhere in the right-hand side of the political spectrum, whereas the latter tended toward a more left-wing, socially motivated mindset. Writers like Wells and Stapledon had emerged from the horrors of the trenches in the First World War with a sense of pessimism and loss that their American colleagues, whose country had triumphed over the Prussian and Austro-Hungarian empires with little loss of life and a substantial financial payoff, did not share. In the aftermath of World War II, the generation that had grown up interspersing its reading of *Astounding* with Wells and Stapledon's novels found itself looking at the dawn of the Cold War with a similar worldview to the one that had animated the narratives of their predecessors.

This worldview, updated and actualized by a strong focus on contemporary issues, also amounted to a feeling that "too many writers were working with the same few traditional sf themes, and both the style and content of sf were becoming generally overpredictable. Many young writers entering the field came to feel … that genre sf had become a straitjacket" (Nicholls 866). And so, spurred by their desire to bring fresh perspectives to the field, the writers of the postwar generation reacted against the influence of their forebears. The New Wave officially began within the pages of the leading British SF magazine of the times, aptly entitled *New Worlds*, when Michael Moorcock became its editor in 1964. *New Worlds*' previous editor, John Carnell, had been instrumental in shaping and managing the magazine throughout the forties and fifties to make sure that it "provided a stable domestic market for the leading UK writers and played a considerable role in the careers of Brian W. Aldiss, J.G. Ballard, John Brunner, … E.C. Tubb and James White" (Stableford and Nicholls 868). Barely a year before succeeding Carnell at the helm of *New Worlds*, Moorcock had contributed an editorial to the April 1963 issue of the magazine in which he lamented the narrowness of the ideological posture in most of the science fiction published at the time, as well as its excessive focus on telling boy's stories to the near-exclusion of everything else. Most importantly, however, he bemoaned its lack of artistic accomplishment:

It was his view that too many writers were backward-looking, trying to repeat the glories of past science fiction, and that the field catered for too many amateur writers who would never have survived in the mainstream and who had not learned or developed.... His message was that science-fiction writers needed to improve their standards, otherwise they would be overtaken by writers from the mainstream who had seen that sf was "becoming a legitimate field for serious expression again." He cited Angus Wilson and Anthony Burgess as examples [Ashley 236].

Until that point, the commonly accepted justification for the presence of science fiction narratives on the shelves of bookstores or in newsstands had been their didactic role. For both the Gernsback and Campbell generations, SF was important because it was true to its teaching and accurate in its forecasts. What did it matter if the writing was often clumsy, or if the ethos developed in most narratives was narrow and reactionary? SF, John W. Campbell had promised, was a view of the future as it was going to actually happen, so that whatever clumsiness was present in a given generic text was the clumsiness of reality — ultimately preferable to the carefully arranged artifice of wish-fulfillment. Science fiction, in the worldview of the *Astounding* generation, was often blunt and unwieldy for the same reason the world was: both were real. Moorcock's editorial, on the other hand, uttered out loud what few writers of the previous generation had thought: that science fiction was first and foremost a literature and a participant in the larger artistic life of its times. There was an art and a style to SF, and a craft; there were voices, a multiplicity of them; there was passion and feeling, and an aesthetic sense that only needed itself to justify its existence to the wider world.

The writers Moorcock attracted to his magazine were young and eager to make their mark on the genre, with as strong a set of opinions concerning SF as their predecessors had entertained a couple of decades before. They came from both shores of the Atlantic — American writers like Thomas M. Disch and John Sladek, as well as British writers like J.G. Ballard, Brian Aldiss, and Moorcock himself. Ballard in particular became a similar figure for *New Worlds* to what Robert Heinlein had been for *Astounding*. In much the same way as Heinlein had defined the role of science fiction for the forties and fifties in opposition to the outlook of the Gernsback generation, Ballard defined it for the sixties and seventies by contrasting the new age to the Campbell era. He had begun publishing in American and British SF magazines in 1956, writing in a style strongly influenced by Surrealist painting, pop art, and Jung's holistic psychology. Then, in 1962, a year before Moorcock's manifesto and at the same time as his generation starship story saw print, he wrote a guest editorial of his own in *New Worlds*, urging SF to reject its traditional tropes — space travel, galactic empires, faster-than-light drives — as the overused, exhausted relics they had become in the seventy years or so since H.G.

Wells had started introducing them into the proto-genre at the end of the 1800s.[4] Ballard lamented the absence in science fiction of "the experimental enthusiasm which has characterized painting, music, and the cinema during the last four or five decades, particularly as these have become wholeheartedly speculative," whereas written SF, the literary form that should have made speculation its greatest intellectual tool, had gradually boiled away the revolutionary potential of its early years through the constant employment of formulaic plots and inflexible ideological stances (197). His recipe for the genre's renovation, therefore, consisted in rejecting traditional themes and narrative devices and returning to an Earth-bound perspective, both in the sense of refocusing the genre's attention toward our planetary home and of beginning to use SF tropes to explore the human psyche:

> The biggest developments of the immediate future will take place, not on the Moon or Mars, but on Earth, and it is *inner* space, not outer, that needs to be explored. The only truly alien planet is Earth. In the past the scientific bias of s-f has been towards the physical sciences ... the emphasis should switch to the biological sciences. Accuracy, that last refuge of the unimaginative, doesn't matter a hoot.... I'd like to see more psycho-literary ideas, more meta-biological and meta-chemical concepts, private time-systems, synthetic psychologies and space times ... all in all a complete speculative poetry and fantasy of science [197–198].

Since the beginning of his career, Ballard had taken care to develop in his writing the aesthetic whose appearance he advocated. He did so by "fusing the low cultural energies of magazine sf with the avant-garde in the 1960s, using it to produce an extraordinary vision of alienated, science-fictionalized existence in the technologically saturated, advanced-capitalist West" (Luckhurst 13). Panoramas of alien locales and vistas of byzantine technological landscapes had always been a staple of SF narratives, both literally as actual places and figuratively as tropes for the development of a worldview, and whatever the time period, whoever the writer, they had all been designed to stimulate our sense of wonder. Even when these landscapes had featured ruined buildings, abandoned cities, and derelict spacecraft lying broken on the ground, their function within the economy of the story had not changed very greatly. They still engaged the reader's imagination by presenting them with the techno-futuristic equivalent of a view of the Parthenon, Angkor Wat, or Macchu Picchu — the archaeology of the as yet inchoate future, and frequently the springboard for a nostalgic Wellsian reflection on the passing of time and the waning of human aspirations.[5] Ballard, however, created in his fictional landscapes a world of ruins devoid of mystical power. His futures, every one of them too close to the present to look much like tomorrow, featured the often damaged hulks of strip malls, gas stations, movie theatres, airports, turnpikes, and hospitals, all quietly rusting under a dry sun while the characters populating the story come and go through their doors, unmoved by any suggestion of wonder in their architecture. For all their deserted sadness, or rather precisely because of it, the ruins of the future city in Campbell's "Twilight" were possessed of a transcendental beauty that was intended to move the heart and stimulate the imagination; they were a symbol of the marvelous at the end of human time, and as such they had value in and of themselves. Ballard's ruins, on the other hand, are the ruins of next year, and they are not the legacy of immanent cosmic forces; they are the detritus of capitalist enterprise. Ballard was an admirer of Andy Warhol's pop art, and from that he learned how to create meaning through the creation of complex systems of reference comprised of parts that were individually worthless. His narratives are haunting and hallucinatory not because what they show is transcendental in itself, but because, like Warhol's Campbell Soup and Coca-Cola paintings, they treat the cheap and tawdry in transcendental terms. The result is the further devaluation of the already cheap, and the concomitant transformation of the narrative employing it into a greater whole than the sum of its parts should plausibly have warranted.

Between them, Moorcock and Ballard's manifestos stimulated the creation of a consciously literary, artistically engaged, soft science-inspired movement that, in its various incarnations and in its different authorial approaches, did succeed in its general aim of changing the face of science fiction. "Between 1962 and 1970," Roger Luckhurst writes, "*New Worlds* became a leading London avant-garde journal and the home of New Wave sf. Ballard and Moorcock encouraged cross-fertilizations between counter-cultural literary, film, and art-worlds, and the magazine even gained an Arts Council grant to become a glossy, heavily illustrated journal" (14). Later in the decade, this sensibility reached the other side of the Atlantic, where it gave birth to a slightly different American New Wave. The U.S. version of Moorcock and Ballard's movement stayed close to its hard-science roots, refusing to abandon the usual icons of the genre but at the same time injecting them with new complexity — a previously absent awareness for the soft, human side of its large-scale dreams of transcendent hardware and exotic locales. Robert Silverberg, Harlan Ellison, and Samuel Delany became the most visible representatives of the American New Wave, and among them it was perhaps Delany who gave us what we might call the quintessential examples of this new mixture of hard and soft sciences. He was literally writing from the perspective of the alien — because in the early sixties, when his career began, this was how an African-American bisexual man was perceived, both within the comparatively small confines of the American SF community and in society at large. Delany seemed to evoke in his work everything the New Wave on both sides of the Atlantic stood for:

a continuing interest in space travel and first contact with alien civilizations, either seen from the perspective of the alien itself or otherwise perceived through the study of language, semiotics, or psychology rather than through engineering, physics, or chemistry. His narratives made frequent and pervasive use of metafictional features — for example, the narrative of *The Einstein Intersection* (1967) is interspersed with paragraphs of authorial intrusion where Delany informs us of his plans for his characters, and *Babel 17* (1967) is a space-opera romp through the galaxy in search not of an artifact or an alien civilization, but of the key to unlocking a meta-language of enormous power.

As before, the generation starship narratives for this period fully expressed the range of cultural and literary responses that the genre at large had devised to cope with its new conditions. Already in 1957 things had started changing for the slow boats to the stars, almost as if *Sputnik*'s launch had been a carefully staged outward signal for the beginning of change in SF and the generation starship one of its literary expressions. In that year, the December issue of *New Worlds*, at the time still edited by Carnell, published John Brunner's "Lungfish." In an unspecified year in the not-too-distant future, the oddly unnamed generation starship carrying its cargo toward the second planet around the star Tau Ceti is in the final weeks of its thirty-seven-year voyage, a timespan sufficient for just two generations of shipboard population: the original crewmembers, the so-called Earthborn, and their multiple sons and daughters, the Tripborn. The semantic distinction between the two groups indicates the presence of deeper differences. When Franz Yerring, the Earthborn chief of the hydroponics section and the viewpoint character in the narrative, calls one of his Tripborn senior subordinates to a meeting with the captain and the ship's council, he is unsettled by the other's response:

> Quentin Hatcher merely looked at him with the strange cold eyes that all the Tripborn seemed to share.... The rest of his team also glanced up; Franz could almost feel the chill of their gaze on his nape as he walked on. *I wonder when it first began. I wonder when we split in two* [56].

Brunner's choice to limit the generation starship's voyage to thirty-seven years, thus allowing for only one new generation before the vessel arrives at its destination, serves to dramatize the generational rift between the Earthborn and their children without cluttering it with too much time spent in transit and too many cultural, social, and historical variables. In 1940, Don Wilcox had portrayed the generational conflict in "The Voyage That Lasted 600 Years" as a function of the crew's loss of purpose in the wake of the Keeper's inability to maintain their cultural focus, and the succeeding generations onboard the *Flashaway* had experienced the progressive loss of motivation in their lives as a descent into barbarism and ignorance. In "Lungfish," however, there is no loss of skill, intelligence, or erudition on the part of the Tripborn. The lack of affect Yerring has noticed in his exchanges with them does not indicate a commensurate lack of intellectual interests, nor does it reveal the absence of caring for shipboard life — quite the opposite, in fact. Born onboard the ship, they are far more attuned to the ebb and flow of its functioning than their planet-born parents, and therefore more capable of maintaining and repairing its various components. The Earthborn are still the nominal authority in all departments — each of which, like those of the *Astra* in "The Oceans Are Wide," is presided over by a member of the ruling council — but the Tripborn now outnumber them ten to one, and the rift between the two generations is starting to affect the efficiency of the ship.

The crux of the problem, it turns out, is located not in the Tripborn's intellectual accomplishments, curiosity, or caring toward their shipmates. It is located in their loyalties and in their perception of what the desirable goals of the trip are. As soon as the Captain decides to make the approach of what everybody calls "Trip's End" official (61), the section chiefs are tasked with informing their staff. When Yerring tells his Tripborn subordinates in hydroponics about the Captain's announcement, Quentin Hatcher and another crew member confront him with a challenge to his planet-referent assumptions, and ask him to define the Earthborn's oft-reiterated definition of Tau Ceti II as a "good world." The conversation ends with Yerring walking away from the two Tripborn in anger and frustration, their difference of opinion worse than before. For someone like him, born on Earth and later confined inside a metal and polyalloy hull for thirty-seven years, the idea that someone might not want a planet-bound existence if they could have the choice is pure lunacy. Yerring's emotional responses to the others' methodical, calm line of reasoning indicate a series of unexamined assumptions in his attitude, an impression further strengthened by his failure to explain to them what he sees as obvious. In a way not overly dissimilar from what happened to Gregory Grimstone onboard the *Flashaway*, Yerring and the rest of the Earthborn cannot reach their Tripborn offspring because, at some point during the voyage, something changed in the latter's psychological makeup. None of the new generation's crewmembers have ever experienced any other life than that onboard the starship. They do not know or particularly care about the feeling of wind through their hair or the smell of wet grass after a spring rainstorm, for essentially the same reason the Earthborn can tolerate but never really like life on the ship: they do not belong there.

Brunner's story prefigures the generational rift of the 1960s, both in the world at large and in the smaller environment of science fiction, by postulating a situation in which the cultural and ideological differences between parents and children are exacerbated by the onset of biological, psychological, and environmental alterations that have transformed the children into creatures at once less and more than human in their parents' eyes. The Tripborn are far from incompetent, and far from foolish; their intellectual grasp of the procedures necessary to maintain the closed ecological system onboard the generation starship, as well as of the necessities and requirements inherent in colonizing another planetary biosphere, is perfect. What they lack is the desire to leave the ship, and that is in itself not a problem or a shortcoming, but rather a cultural trait that the changed conditions of life onboard the vessel have allowed to surface.

The crucial difference between the psychological attitudes of the two generations is that, while the Earthborn struggle in vain to understand why their offspring do not feel any sense of excitement toward the prospect of finally touching the planet's surface, the Tripborn are fully aware of their elders' inner conflicts. In fact, they know several things that the Earthborn do not, especially concerning Yoseida — the man who, back on Earth, had dreamed up, financed, and designed the mission to Tau Ceti II. To the Earthborn, he is an almost godlike figure. While poring over a set of instructions for coercing the Tripborn into colonizing the planet, instructions Yoseida himself had written in case such an eventuality should occur, Yerring is struck by the brutality of the psychological conditioning they advocate. However, once he gets to the end of the document and sees Yoseida's signature, "all the doubt he had been entertaining vanished.... He clenched his fists with determination. In that moment he was more certain than he had ever been that they would not — must not — fail!" (69). If it seems difficult to believe that Yerring could suddenly develop such a fanatical commitment to implementing the procedures he had thus far been finding morally objectionable,[6] this may be because there truly is something wrong with the grand narrative of the generational voyage that the Earthborn have so far been upholding as dogma. This grand narrative is finally exposed in the aftermath of the crew's first attempt to scout Tau Ceti II; upon opening the canopy of his scoutship, the Tripborn pilot gazes at an open sky for the first time in his life, and as a result suffers a massive agoraphobic seizure. Screaming and clawing at his own face, the man has to be returned to the ship via remote control, and as soon as he is retrieved and sent to sickbay the Tripborn take over control of the ship's functions from their parents. Then, they expose Yoseida's dream with the help of Tsien, the Earthborn psychologist. Tsien tells Yerring that, contrary to what they had always believed, none of the original crew had actually volunteered for the trip to Tau Ceti II; they were "conditioned via a posthypnotic compulsion, and one of the releasers is the sight of Yoseida's signature.... Yoseida, the idealist, the visionary dreamer, was a megalomaniac who could not be satisfied with less than a brand new planet as a tribute to his memory. And stopped at nothing to make us obey the demands he put on us" (86).

In 1946 and 1954 respectively, Arthur C. Clarke and Frank M. Robinson had solved the problem presented by the issue of crew motivation and economic viability by sidestepping it altogether. Their answer to the dilemma had consisted in postulating the destruction of the Earth, at which point building and manning a generation starship had presented no problem in plausibility. Life within a metal shell is preferable to no life at all. However, for those writers who did not wish to begin their stories with such a premise the issue persisted, and Brunner, already in 1957 looking forward to the break with Campbell's SF that he and his fellow writers of the 1960s would soon institute, provided one answer. Who would embark on a generational voyage of colonization? A group of convicts would, either the prisoners of the will of the state or the victims of someone else's desire. Who would finance the construction of such a ship and then send it out? A sociopath, someone who would have no problem at all in foisting the future of his desire on two generations of his victims — the first brainwashed, the second trapped inside a situation generated by the very crime whose successful completion required their birth.

Brunner, however, is kinder toward his fictional offspring than Wilcox and Robinson were with theirs; there is a way out. Once they have realized the full implications of what has been done to them, the Earthborn and the Tripborn begin working together for the first time since the new generation's birth. They start building a second starship, one that will take the first home while the second use the original generation starship to continue doing what they have always wanted to do: roam the stars. At the end of the story, it is Yerring that makes the implications of this development explicit:

> "This isn't the end of mankind; there are still snakes and birds and dogs on Earth, still amphibians, even, which have to return to a pond and lay their eggs. That's what I think the Tripborn have become: amphibians, who will have to return to their rock pools, their planetary bases, when they want to reproduce. But that need only be a temporary phase. The ship we are going to build here will teach the Tripborn how to breed. And after the amphibian, there will be a snake, and a bird, and a dog.... And in the end.... There will be a man" [89].

The potential for this development had always been there, ever since Tsiolkovsky and Bernal had proposed that their generation starships could become home to a race of humans adapted to space, and therefore independent of a planetary biosphere. The SF authors of the thirties, forties, and fifties, however, had declined to actualize this potential, preferring instead to treat the generation starship as just that — a tendril of the will of the state with a mission, a crew, and an ideological and cultural dependence on the life of the collective that had sent it out to the stars. Even as writers like Wilcox, Heinlein, and Simak understood the basic conundrum at the heart of this attitude and dramatized it in the form of the forgetfulness pattern we have seen in "The Voyage That Lasted 600 Years," "Universe" and "Common Sense," and "Spacebred Generations," they still pulled back from the logical conclusion of the situations they portrayed.[7]

Thus, Brunner was the first to utter the idea out loud: why does a generation starship need a mission? The Tripborn in the aptly titled "Lungfish" are about to embark on the creation of another strain of the *Homo* genus, a strain we might call, for the sake of argument, *Homo sapiens spatialis*. The circumstances of their life have changed their relationship toward their starship to the point that the vessel has now become what Earth is for Yerring and the rest of the Earthborn: home. In much the same way our planet travels around the sun, their generation starship, now a worldship in every sense of the term, can voyage in deep space with no other aim or goal than to simply move— with the added advantage that, should the crew wish it, they could steer the ship in a direction compatible with desire.

Another fundamental aspect that set "Lungfish" apart from previous generation starship narratives consisted in the psychological and professional makeup of the protagonists, as well as in their impact on their social nexus. Gregory Grimstone, Hugh Hoyland, Jon Hoff, and Mathew Kendrick had been — or, in Kendrick's case, had become — hard-science intellectuals, in terms of their thought patterns if not always in their professional bent. In accordance with the mission statement of the Gernsback/Campbell brand of SF, they existed within a network of physical laws that were permeable to cognition and penetrable by a properly trained intellect. Once penetrated, moreover, they automatically informed the social laws of the collective affected by them. Whether the protagonist succeeded or not in changing the fate of their pocket universe according to the true nature of reality, we readers always knew why the outcome of their actions had been a triumph or a disaster. Whether or not they unlocked the processes leading to the solutions to their problems, we always knew what these solutions were. Thus, independently of dramatic outcome, cognition afforded us a measure of satisfaction in the wake of the characters' decoding of the mysteries in the narrative.

Also, those early generation-starship protagonists, irrespective of the conditions foisted upon them by external forces, wanted to fit into their society. When they found themselves in the role of misfits, they always suffered it as a distressing experience, and only accepted this role because their discovery of the overarching plan everyone else seemed to have forgotten, never known to begin with, or replaced with agendas of their own, revealed to them the order of things as it had always been supposed to unfold. In other words, the misfits' defiance of their social contract was at once morally justified and cognitively supported by their awareness that they were obeying a greater, transcendental contract between their ancestors and the laws of the world. In an entry in the *Encyclopedia of Science Fiction*, Peter Nicholls describes this act of defiance as "conceptual breakthrough," citing the figures of Prometheus and Doctor Faustus as the archetypical representatives of this character pattern. Nicholls indicates that conceptual breakthrough — by which term he means the advent of a paradigm shift in a society's understanding of their universe — is by a healthy margin the most important form of knowledge gathering in modern science fiction "in terms of both the quality and the quantity of the work that dramatizes it" (254), so that generation starship narratives are by no means its only beneficiaries. However, he also points out that they are some of the preferred exemplars of this trope:

> An important subset of conceptual-breakthrough stories consists of those in which the world is not what it seems. The structure of such stories is often that of a quest in which an intellectual nonconformist questions apparent certainties. Quite a number have been stories in which the world turns out to be a generation starship, as in "Universe" (1941) by Robert A. Heinlein [255].

Thus we can say that the misfits and discontents in the generation starship narratives we have seen so far, with the relevant exception of those in Brunner's "Lungfish," represent suitably up-teched, scientifically minded incarnations of Prometheus the Firebringer, both in terms of the price they are willing to pay for their defiance and as a function of how pervasively their conceptual breakthrough will change their world. The previous chapters in this work described them as Galilean figures to indicate the same mixture of revolutionary thinking, social disconnect, and impact on humanity's mindset, but also because the kind of breakthrough of which they had become the harbingers had been largely confined to the physical sciences. Even when the Prometheus figures in question were not scientific people, as was the case for Gregory Grimstone and Mathew Kendrick, they ended up following a hard-science, quest-for-truth approach to their situations that placed them squarely in the tradition of such characters as Larry Gaines in Heinlein's "The Roads Must Roll": engineers within and without, hardware thinkers who solved social and human problems by applying to them the same principles they applied to making their machinery work.[8]

And their worlds were shaped to provide their quests with the appropriate responses. The *Vanguard* in "Universe" and "Common Sense," Jon Hoff's unnamed ship in "Spacebred Generations," and — albeit to a lesser extent — the *Astra* in "The Oceans Are Wide"[9] are playgrounds for Promethean/Galilean probings, cognitive puzzles waiting for intellectual nonconformists to come, unlock their meaning, and open wide the jaws of the universe. There is a reason why the upper levels of the *Vanguard* are devoid of weight, or why, at the beginning of "Spacebred Generations," Jon Hoff's world suddenly finds itself turned upside-down. There are reasons for the presence of a Roman-style amphitheatre onboard the *Astra*, for the existence of the starfield projector in the *Vanguard*, and for the hidden room where Jon Hoff finds the memory tapes that teach him the truth about his circumstances. Every aspect of the physical world surrounding the protagonists is there to provide them with clues on their way to conceptual breakthrough, and to reward their persistence when they find the previously undiscovered pieces of evidence that finally shift their sense of reality in the proper direction—because, and this is the most important clue of all, there really is a proper shape of the world in those stories. The generation starships within whose confines Hugh Hoyland, Jon Hoff, and Mathew Kendrick spend their lives are shaped the way they are because this is how a starship is meant to function in its physical environment. The form of the hull, the composition of the compartments, the placement of the engineering and control sections, and the variety of equipment available are there because the universe is what it is. In other words, every shape and object in those narratives acquires a meaning insofar as it corresponds to an external frame of reference that, while independent for its existence from the society that has forgotten it,[10] also has agency over this society's worldview. Therefore, the forgetfulness that overtakes the generation starship's collective cannot but send it into a tailspin: to forget the shape of the world (or, in the case of the *Astra*'s population, the voyage's true destination) is to commit a sin,[11] and the Promethean individuals who remember it are at once vehicles of conceptual breakthrough and catalysts for the attending moral upheaval.

In 1957, when Brunner published "Lungfish," the conceptual breakthrough pattern was alive and well, and it played a prominent role in the story's dramatic resolution. In the years since "Universe" and "Common Sense," however, it had undergone a transformative process that set it apart from its earlier incarnations, once again reflecting the wider changes taking place in the genre at large. "Lungfish" featured a plant biologist and a psychologist as its main characters, the first soft-science protagonists in the subgenre, and the relevance of their professional calling for the narrative's dramatic balance becomes evident when Tsien explains to Yerring that the two of them have been able to withstand Yoseida's conditioning better than the other Earth-born precisely because of their training: in his capacity as chief plant biologist on the ship, Yerring had more invested in landing and planting his crops than anyone else, while Tsien had been able to use his skills as a psychologist to understand and counteract what had been done to them (86). As for the mystery at the heart of their world, it has nothing to do with the characters' rational apprehension of the physical reality surrounding them. Their forgetfulness was rooted in the mind and confined to its workings at the level of emotional and psychological motivation, not of intellectual processing of external stimuli provided by the senses. There has been no loss of scientific knowledge among the ship's crew, Earthborn or Tripborn, and this knowledge played no part in either alleviating or worsening the impact of the social conflict at the heart of the narrative. For the first time in the history of generation starship stories, the world of human relationships and the physical environment operated independently of one another, and the plot's dramatic tension discharged itself exclusively into the human aspects of the narrative.

It may have seemed to the writers of the New Wave that they too were a lungfish of sorts, a new order of creature in the biological soup of SF publishing struggling to breathe and express itself within a new literary environment. In much the same way as Brunner had asked why a generation starship should have a mission ruling the lives of all its inhabitants, from the crew who begin the enterprise to their latest descendants at trip's end, they in turn were asking why science fiction as a whole was supposed to obey a single overarching message across multiple generations of writers and readers. As if to cement their role in the evolution of the genre, other generation starship stories in the same vein as Brunner's appeared between the end of the fifties and the late sixties, triangulating more precisely the modern age's break with the assumptions of the previous generations. And, as was the case for the wider environment of SF as a whole, this evolutionary leap was not limited to stories published in Britain. Four months before *Sputnik*'s launch and six months before the appearance of "Lungfish" in the pages of *New Worlds*, the July 1957 issue of *F&SF* published Chad Oliver's "The Wind Blows Free":

> Have you ever heard, with your ears or with your soul, the far wind that stirs the world? Have you ever felt the deep beat of the sea, the sea that is the heart of the Earth? Samuel Kingsley had never known these things. That may have been his trouble. Samuel Kingsley was born with a fever in his bones and a fire in his blood. As a baby, he was difficult … Sam screamed, fought his food, clawed at his bed. He seldom smiled, and he was not affectionate [13–14].

Like most protagonists in generation starship stories, Sam is dissatisfied with the circumstances of his life. He too is born within a world, both social and phenomenological, whose outward façade fails to placate his sense that something does not add up between appearances and the substance that lies beneath. And indeed, Oliver's omniscient third-person narrative repeatedly describes Sam's unease at what he perceives to be the fundamental wrongness of things, an unease that finds no outlet because he cannot identify the source of this wrongness.

Beyond this threshold, however, the similarities between Sam and his predecessors stop. He is not an intellectual by bent or a scientist by profession. His sense that the world does not work reaches him through dreams and intuition, not through rational apprehension, and the environment within which he is born and grows up does not provide any outward clue pointing to a contradiction between the mind and reality; no incomprehensible machinery regulates the life of the crew, and no sections of the starship feature physical characteristics unexplainable by current scientific knowledge. Sam is not a fool (otherwise, Oliver's narrative persona coolly informs us, he would not have been permitted to live), but he does not grow up to occupy a high place in his society's hierarchy like Hugh Hoyland, Franz Yerring, or Mathew Kendrick did in theirs. When we meet him at the beginning of the story he is only an infant, and as his life progresses through an undisciplined, friendless childhood and an equally turbulent adolescence, he gradually grows up to become someone whom Marlon Brando's character in *The Wild One* would probably have understood:

> By his eighteenth year, Sam had grown big and raw-boned. Even his size was against him. He stood a rangy six-foot-four, and weighed better than two hundred pounds. His hair was black and untidy, and his eyes were dark.... Sam was marked by his body. At eighteen, he was by far the biggest man on the Ship. He stood out like a pine in a forest of ferns, and he accentuated the difference by walking proudly erect, with his head thrown back [15].

Originally born in Ohio, Chad Oliver ended up spending most of his life as a professor of anthropology at the University of Texas, Austin. Taken as a whole, we could describe his science fiction work as a long, multiple-voiced love song to his profession and to the outdoors of the American Southwest where both his academic studies and the plot of most of his narratives took place. He had grown up with — and loved — the science fiction of the '30s and '40s, but it had been a strange kind of love for an intellectual of his bent. The SF landscapes of the Gernsback and Campbell generations had featured precious little of the natural world in which Oliver was deeply rooted, and plenty of the hypertrophic techno-industrial hardware from which he was, by virtue of that same rootedness, divorced. As John Clute remarked, "he wrote as though he believed that simultaneously to love the earth and to love the future was to utter two sentences with but a single heart. For a while, he acted as though his job, his art, his planet, and his species shared the same address" (*Canary* 93). So what is he doing in this book, author of a generation starship story featuring a rebel-without-a-cause protagonist who dreams of wind, sunlight, and sailing ships in the ocean breeze from inside the metal coffin that imprisons him? Even the language Oliver employs to describe Samuel Kingsley's alienness to his own people — "a pine in a forest of ferns"[12] — conspires to accentuate the differences between his desires and his actual life.

He may be the tallest tree in the world, but it is a world of metal and plastic, not of soil and air. Sam was born in the wrong society for the kind of desire he entertains, and his people sense that in him. Therefore, ostracized and disliked, he seems doomed to a life of frustrated yearning by the reality of his circumstances. "The Wind Blows Free," however, is a science fiction story. The shape of the world on page one has no contractual obligation to remain the same to the very last word — if anything, the opposite is true. By the same token, if there is a duty by which we readers should consider ourselves bound, this duty consists in refraining from assumptions, assembling the clues, and working our way to conceptual breakthrough.

Following the first three pages of backstory, Oliver's description of Sam at eighteen brings us smoothly into the present of the narrative. The choice is not casual: at that age legal adulthood begins, and everyone onboard the generation starship must undergo the local version of a rite of passage — the so-called "Show on Heritage Day" (17). On Heritage Day, the hows and whys of their world are explained to the new generations, so that they can start taking over from the old and continue the mission in its proper shape. Thus, Sam and his fellows are taken to a 3D theatre set in the middle of the main square, seated on several rows of chairs, and made to watch something that, anachronistically, could easily have come straight out of *A Clockwork Orange*: a terrifying show of hammering sense-impressions and subliminal messages, interspersed with Big-Brother narrative pieces to form an ensemble detailing in inescapable pain the death of the Earth. The story, by now, is fairly familiar: underneath their veneer of civilization, humans are beasts. We created a mighty nuclear-powered civilization only so that the tools we made could be directed by our instincts with ultimate destructiveness. Images of irradiated plains and boiling seas succeed one another as the disembodied voice tells its shell-shocked, captive audience about the abortive search for other habitable planets within our solar system, and finally about the construction of the starships. Sam and his people are in one such vessel, their mission to preserve the existence of the human race without repeating its deadly mistakes, and in order to accomplish this mission they must practice the restraint that their ancestors had been terminally unable to teach themselves:

> *You who hear my voice may be the only human beings left. Each ship follows a different course ... remember your Heritage! Remember that you are men, and what happened to men on Earth! You must begin again, you children of Earth. And you must be careful, you must be wise. If ever you find hate in your hearts, remember, remember...* [19–20].

There is no immortal Predict onboard Sam's generation starship, no implacable will of the dead state telling everyone that peace is for weaklings and real humans need conflict, industry, and better weapons. The voice of authority in "The Wind Blows Free" is alternately threatening and sad, fiery and fearful, and Predict Smith would have found its ultimate message unthinkable: beware of the beast within. Remember its deadly onslaught on Earth, and keep it in the cage.

Besides providing an inarguable explanation for the often blind obedience to obscure rules that characterizes much of shipboard life, the Heritage Day show also casts Sam in the role of villain because he proudly displays those very characteristics against whose rising the disembodied voice on the screen had warned everybody. He is violent and passionate where the others are seemingly controlled and unassuming, and he flaunts his society's rules where the others just want to fit in as quickly and painlessly as possible. Even his body, built for action rather than the tightly regimented apathy he must struggle against, betrays his fundamental alienness.

For all the turmoil of his thought processes, however, Sam is not a sociopath. In the aftermath of the show, he begins to comprehend his parents' endless entreaties for conformity, and their constant distress at his rage against the rules. Consequently, he also understands, finally, that his people "were existing in a kind of cultural suspended animation, just hanging on between disaster and a new beginning" (20). And since he is not a villain either, he chides himself for his arrogance and decides that he has been wrong all along. There are no seas to sail or prairies to roam; there is only the ship, because the species of whose attitude he seems to be the perfect incarnation destroyed everything except what it could build in the extremity of disaster. Sam Kingsley stops being a rebel and starts fitting in.

Sam, however, is not a hero in either the Gernsback or the Campbell/ Heinlein mold. His acknowledgement of the true shape of the world does not bring him the satisfaction it had bought someone like Hugh Hoyland. Irrespective of physical evidence, desire endures. Sam works hard in the hydroponic farms, the only place onboard the ship where the air feels a little like it does in his ever-present dreams, and becomes fond of them as well as very good at his job — the best onboard, in fact. And yet he never marries, he remains friendless, and the distrust his people feel toward him does not abate (21).

In fact, it increases. After all his years of hard, productive labor in the hydroponics chamber, all of Sam's contemporaries have been promoted to members of the Crew except him, and the realization that he will never leave the post he is occupying now arrives together with an unpleasant visit from one Ralph Holbrook, a newly promoted acquaintance. Drunk with alcohol and an inflated sense of his importance, Holbrook provokes Sam, and when Sam refuses to attack a member of the Crew, Holbrook slaps him in the face and walks away laughing.

That this episode should become the trigger that sends Sam on yet another quest toward an even deeper conceptual breakthrough says a lot about the narrative we are examining. Oliver may have loved the science fiction of his youth, but he had little use for its exaggerated technophilia and lack of interest in the people inhabiting its body of work. He was an anthropologist; his focus rested on the study of human relations. Therefore he created in "The Wind Blows Free" a narrative where the fundamental spurs to Promethean defiance are always emotional or social instead of intellectual. Sam returns to his former role of misfit not out of rational apprehension of an objective problem, but rather out of anger at the unfairness of Holbrook's treatment. If years of smothering his desires for the benefit of the collective have repaid him thus, if he will not be accepted even when he tries long and hard, then he might as well follow his desires. At least he'll be at peace with himself. That same evening, Sam sneaks out past curfew and opens one of the many doors on the ship whose access is barred to everyone except members of the Crew. During his rebellious childhood and adolescence he had often roamed the forbidden areas of the ship, but after Heritage Day he had stopped. The rules were there for a reason. Now, when the rules themselves have betrayed him, he returns to his former haunts.

At this point, the ship becomes, like the *Flashaway*, the *Astra*, and Jon Hoff's unnamed vessel, a cognitive whodunit. In the human skeletons lying half-hidden in the thick patina of dust on the floor, the malfunctioning spacesuits in the airlocks, and the heavily guarded accessways to the command and control centers of the vessel, the dark hallways of the restricted areas contain answers to questions that had so far remained hidden, questions that point toward the wrongness at the heart of the world. Spotted by the guards at one of the choke points and forced to run for hours to evade capture, Sam negotiates his painful way through the dust of centuries, across the testimonies of deaths unrecorded and crimes unspoken until, cornered by a hunting party including a smug Ralph Holbrook, he goes berserk, severely beating two men and killing another outright. At this stage there is nothing left for him but death, either at his own hands through an airlock door or at the hands of his own people in the main square. In a final act of resignation, Sam chooses self-annihilation, and after closing the inner airlock door in the faces of a howling mob of Crewmembers, he opens the outer hatch and plunges into the terminal blackness of space:

> Air! ... Sam opened his eyes. *Green. Yellow. Red.* Colors! A riot of colors! He had never seen such colors; they stunned his eyes. He looked up, past a tangle of green. Light! Bright, golden light. A sun.... He smelled green growing things, flowers, trees [36].

And there, in the middle of the forest and the brooks of flowing crystalline water, sits the ship, rusted and broken after centuries of exposure to the elements. The mission had ended long before Sam's birth. The ship had reached a planet, and landed on it, but the people onboard "had been too afraid to come out. They had built their little safe sterile society in their metal tube of a world, and they had been afraid to start again" (37). In a merciful plot twist, Sam also encounters a group of tall, muscular men with tanned skin and bright smiles, sitting around a fire cooking fresh meat. They must once have been misfits themselves, dreamers of sailing ships and of the wind blowing free who had survived the same kind of experience Sam had just gone through — unlike the skeletons in the dark passageways, which may once have belonged to people who had failed to get out, either through accident or termination at the hands of a hunting party. The story ends with Sam walking toward the hunters' campfire, buoyed toward his new life by welcoming smiles, the smell of roasting meat, and the sound of the wind.

There is a lot of conceptual breakthrough in this story, and it follows the usual processes, but its revelations have now shifted toward the human sphere. Technology is rust and recycled air, industry the agent of destruction, and life is in people living free in their natural habitat. There is the world and there is the flesh on the new planet, but no devil as yet except what humans brought along with them. Even "Lungfish," the other soft-science narrative we have seen,[13] had not gone quite this far in looking at the impact that the instinctual aspects of human nature can have on shipboard life. Even in the extremity of distress, Franz Yerring and the rest of the crew, Earthborn and Tripborn alike, had taken their predicament cool-headedly, setting their differences aside as soon as the actual problem had become apparent — a problem they had not created. Oliver's story, on the other hand, places the responsibility for the circumstances of the ship's inhabitants squarely on their shoulders, both as descendants of a destructive race and as the instigators of a culture of stagnation where the process of generational transfer has become a self-perpetuating loop of meaningless rituals. That they are potentially as violent and emotional as Sam himself also indicates the brokenness of their worldview, by now necessarily devoid of any measure of self-examination.

In "The Oceans Are Wide," Frank M. Robinson had tried to wrap up his narrative with a realpolitik-inspired moral lesson for the few remaining human beings in the universe, but he had crippled its message by boiling it down to a self-contradictory set of commonplaces about a faux-Darwinian struggle for global supremacy. In "The Wind Blows Free," on the other hand, Chad Oliver has crafted an altogether more complex scenario, essentially by refusing to solve the issue. Samuel Kingsley is now fulfilled because he has finally found his true people, and we are happy for him. However, the continued existence of the beast within remains an unresolved problem. For all his basic goodness, Sam does possess all the characteristics which the voice in the Show on Heritage Day had indicated as responsible for the nuclear holocaust that had destroyed the Earth. We see it clearly in the staggering display of violence onboard the ship, at the end of which Holbrook and another man lie broken and bleeding on the floor of the corridor, while a third rests dead against the bulkheads. Moreover, the story's dramatic economy fairly clearly implies that the tanned giants Sam meets at the end are just like him, and that means potential trouble. Whatever society these people formed in their new planet, it seems very similar to a nomadic hunter-gatherer tribe, the kind of social arrangement prevailing on Earth before the adoption of agriculture, the birth of stable collectives, and the slow buildup toward technology, industry, and the modern state. Beyond our potential faith in Sam's basic goodness (but what about the others?), there is no indication in Oliver's narrative that what happened on Earth will not repeat itself here as well. The descendants of the long-dead builders of the generation starships may finally have learned their lesson, or not. They may eventually come to decide that it was their strength that allowed them to prevail over a weak society, and if that were to happen, off they'd go again into the shadow of the mushroom cloud. Moreover, "The Wind Blows Free" tells the story of only one of the many generation starships that left Earth so long ago. What happened to all the others? What did the people onboard them teach *their* children? We do not know, and that is just as well. We could in fact argue that the solutions to issues of this complexity should not be stretched and sliced on the Procrustean bed of one special-case scenario, for stories are, after all, soapboxes, advocacies for a worldview born out of desire, not proof of a trend supported by physical evidence. By refusing to provide an answer to the basic dilemma at the heart of his narrative, which is also the dilemma of our world today, Oliver refuses to be drawn into a game of ad hoc argument that has no end and brings little profit, either to him or to his readers. Like the rest of us, Sam and his fellows will have to find the solutions as they go along, in the hope that they will remember.

The year 1958 saw the appearance of Brian Aldiss's generation starship novel, *Non-Stop*. A year later, a trimmed edition of the book was published in the United States with a new title, *Starship*, which self-destructively warned readers about the nature of the game before they had even made it past the front cover. Aldiss had read "Universe" and "Common Sense," and though the generation starship setup had appealed to him, he had also found himself dissatisfied with the dramatic resolution Heinlein had devised (Nicholls 480). In his novel, therefore, he set about writing a story that, though inspired by Heinlein, also departed from his template in a number of fundamental aspects.

Aldiss's borrowings become evident when we take a look at the novel's setup and plot development. The protagonist of *Non-Stop*,[14] a hunter who goes by the pleasantly resonant name of Roy Complain, is a member of the Greene tribe, a tightly knit group of nomadic families eking out a precarious living in a territory everyone calls Quarters. Besides hunting, the tribe finds sustenance and raw materials from the ubiquitous "ponics,"[15] local plants with a very rapid, aggressive life cycle — so aggressive, in fact, that we could easily describe Quarters as a fantastic version of the Amazon rain forest, complete with stifling heat, high levels of humidity, insects of all kinds, and dangers aplenty, were it not for the pervasive presence of corridors, bulkheads, abandoned rooms, and decks. Roy Complain lives in a pre-industrial hunter-gatherer society inhabiting a hellish jungle bounded on all sides by the products of high technology, and to a certain extent interpenetrated by them: foraging parties regularly break into previously sealed rooms where they find all kinds of gadgets nobody really understands, and which are, for the most part, burned because considered dangerous to the collective. The most evident exception to this rule are the dazers, advanced energy weapons one of their scouts had found in a previously unopened compartment a few generations before the story's beginning. They have given the Greene tribe a strong edge over the other groups inhabiting Quarters and competing with it for resources and lebensraum.

Complain hopes to one day become one of the Guards, the elite warriors whose duty consists in acting as security for the head of the tribe, Lieutenant Greene, and in acquiring possession of all the exotica found in the rooms they open during inspections and resettlements. His hopes come to an end, however, when he takes his woman hunting with him and she is abducted by members of a rival tribe. Since his collective is short on fertile women, Complain's infraction is serious, and the punishment — lashes for six wakes[16] and the loss of his sleeping quarters — humiliating. It is thus with little objection that he decides to accept the offer of the tribe's priest, Marapper, to follow him in a madcap jaunt through the ship. After one of the regular break-ins into a locked compartment, Marapper stole a data-slate containing a cutaway of their world, and after understanding that the world is a ship he decides to become its captain by finding the fabled Control Room and acquiring the means of directing the vessel.

The voyage is dangerous. Between Quarters and Forwards, the section that contains the Control Room, lies Deadways, a chaotic tangle of ponics and metal inhabited by mutants, altered animals, and other dangers only mentioned in whispers around a fire — dangers like the Giants, the owners of the world before Complain's people, who, some say, will one day return to reclaim what was once theirs, and the Outsiders, proxies of the Giants who infiltrate the tribes to undermine them from within and prepare them for their masters' return. Of the five people who leave Quarters one wake, only three emerge from Deadways. The rumors were true: the area is filled with mutants, shambling parodies of humans always on the verge of starvation, with evolved rats and other animals with strange powers, and with the Giants themselves.

Forwards, by contrast, is inhabited by unaltered humans and characterized by a higher level of civilization, at least in the sense that the tribes there are stable instead of nomadic and have created a centralized power structure comprising a council and a police force. Complain, Marapper, and Fermour, the third remaining member of the Quarters expedition, finally reach one of those tribes, where they are first mistaken for outsiders and almost tortured for information, and later grudgingly accepted. Complain promptly falls in love with Inspector Vyann, a fairly high-ranking member of the local police, and in the long run she reciprocates him. Along the way, they use Marapper's map to find the Control Room and look outside into space, an act that triggers a shower of revelations about the ship, the Giants and the Outsiders, the ponics, and the tribes themselves, at which point the novel reaches its conclusion.

Aldiss was neither ignorant nor contemptuous of the body of work that had preceded him. At one level, the reading of *Non-Stop* is classic science fiction in the adventure mold, an exciting romp through dangerous locales inhabited by exotic creatures on the way to finding the Clue to It All. Aldiss conveys the alienness of the compartments negotiated by Complain and his mates through slightly hallucinatory descriptions of tangles of hardware snared by growing ponics, of bulkheads warped and blackened by ancient explosions, and of the various mutations afflicting humans and non-humans alike. Of particular power, for all that their literary creation is strongly reminiscent of pulp SF, is the horrifying description of the sentient rats: they have developed intelligence, verbal communication skills, and social organization, only to turn them into the tools of a brutal collective endeavor. They capture, enslave, and keep under miserable conditions other sentient animals[17] and, as one of Roy's hapless companions finds out to his destruction, they practice torture for the purpose of extracting information — toward the end of the novel, about a hundred pages after he disappears from the narrative, we find him dying of his wounds on the floor of a compartment in Deadways, half of his face and most of his chest chewed away by his interrogators. What they want and desire nobody knows, and we never get to find out; perhaps it is enough to follow the story's implicit suggestion that they simply want to thrive in their mutated environment. Another distinctly pulpish twist, and one carried out with elegance on Aldiss's part, is Roy's discovery that his brother Gregg, who years before had left the Greene tribe in contempt, is still alive and now the leader of a gang of Deadways outlaws. Gregg is also the carrier wave of a fundamental part of the story's infodump, which, in the time-honored Heinleinian tradition, is represented by the personal log of the ship's last captain before the disaster overtook it. Instead of destroying it like most of the Giants' hardware, Roy's brother has kept the log because, as he discovered when he found it, the captain was one Gregory Complain, their ancestor.

If the above were all we could say about *Non-Stop*, it would already be no slight compliment to Aldiss. Not many writers get to come up with a first novel like this, and one could argue that being an exciting, ably written fictional romp through strange places would already be reason enough to get picked up at the bookstore. However, this is not all one can say about *Non-Stop*. At another level, the novel acquires an unprecedented status among generation starship stories for its treatment of the complexities underlying social and interpersonal relations onboard the ship, as well as for its reflections on space flight, fate and desire, and the human quest for meaning.

Like many decayed societies in generation starship narratives, Roy Complain's tribe polices the intercourse between its individual members and their observance of public functions through what they call the Teaching, a pseudo-religious set of beliefs that, again like previous versions of the same phenomenon, recontextualizes standard human lore and history through the eyes of the new social order. The differences between the Teaching in Aldiss and, say, the Lines from the Beginning in Heinlein, consist in (a) the target of the Teaching's dictates and (b) the kind of texts that constitute the original source of those dictates. In Heinlein, the sources of the distorted information Hoyland's society has concocted belong to the fields of history (the warped memories of the mutiny), engineering, and physics (the tomes Hugh studies with Lieutenant Nelson and with Joe-Jim). Because of their nature, the regulations gleaned from these disciplines are thrust outward in the direction of that collective's external circumstances, not inward in the direction of its social life— because in most of the SF of that time, as we have seen, the first always informed the second. Roy Complain's tribe, on the other hand, obeys an altogether different belief system:

> The Teaching warned [them] that [their] mind was a foul place. The holy trinity, Froyd, Yung and Bassit, had gone alone through the terrible barriers of sleep, death's brother; there they found ... grottoes and subterranean labyrinths full of ghouls and evil treasure.... Man stood revealed to himself: a creature of infinite complexity and horror. It was the aim of the Teaching to let as much of this miasmic stuff out to the surface as possible [88].

However debased its present form, however warped the original meaning of the knowledge from which this present belief system springs, the Greene tribe finds its moral compass according to an amalgam of various psychoanalytic theories, lightly sprinkled with a measure of Christian lore. In fact, the Teaching dictates the shape of collective and personal mores to the point that every socially relevant action, from hunting to fighting to having a family, takes place within a complex system of rituals designed to, indeed, purge the psyche of the bad stuff. There is a ritual of rage, in which a person in the grip of a powerful anger externalizes it through a screaming, spitting, livid-faced pantomime, thereby avoiding dangerous psychological buildups (22–23); a ritual of prostration, designed to deal with the frequent violent deaths that are the lot of life in Quarters (47–48); and a ritual of fear, necessary to exorcise this emotion before it lodges itself in the heart and becomes uncontrollable (126). Also, there is a prayer to Consciousness, which the Greene tribe equates with life itself (126) whereas death is often referred to as "the Great Subconscious" (132), and a variety of everyday expressions (the equivalent of "by Huff" in Heinlein) that in their commonplace occurrence reveal how pervasively the Teaching has penetrated every facet of life — for example, the greeting "expansion to your ego," to which one is supposed to reply "at your expense." At that point, the first speaker completes the ritual by uttering "and turmoil in my id" (26). This web of social rituals constitutes the visible part of a deeper belief system, according to which everyone in the world is the offspring of cowards and criminals (43), in a curious switch from psychological lore to a Christian sense of original sin. By constantly acknowledging their baser natures, the members of the Greene tribe perform a sort of lopsided therapy session, at the end of which they feel purged of them and can therefore "live in psychosomatic purity" (99).

Lest we start thinking of Roy Complain and his people as blind simpletons, automatons following a broken creed and passively lying in wait for the reading of the Captain's log, the following exchange between Complain and Marapper should provide us with an idea of the sophistication that the Teaching can inject into social intercourse. Marapper has just finished explaining his plan to go through Deadways and Forwards in search of the Control Room, and when Roy replies that crossing all that territory will require courage, Marapper responds "If we went, we should be ... evading the responsibilities of grown men in society.... It will be the old back-to-nature act, boy, a fruitless attempt to return to the ancestral womb. Why, it would be the very depth and abysm of cowardice to leave here" (43). And of course Complain goes with Marapper, because the priest's line of reasoning is essentially correct. After the kidnapping of his woman and his loss of status, it is easier for a trained hunter like him to go into the ponics and never come back than stay and endure the scorn of his peers. The attention that the Greene tribe (and by implication the population of Quarters as a whole) lavishes on the Teaching does not imply a wholly enlightened world view. They are not a collective of Rousseauian wise savages, budding Freuds and Jungs leisurely walking through the ponics reflecting on the Big Answers and the innate badness of human nature. The Teaching does provide — and require — a degree of philosophical musing, in keeping with the source material from whose intellectual framework it had been born, but in the end it serves more as a salve for the conscience than as an instrument of self-examination. Roy and his people care about each other, but their world is an inherently savage one, and thus both they and their social order display the whole range of destructive traits in human nature, from violence and cruelty to greed and cowardice and so on. The Teaching, however, allows them an outlet for guilt and psychological residues from negative events, thereby giving their lives a comparatively carefree cast — a precious asset in the kind of environment they have to inhabit. The figure of Henry Marapper perfectly embodies the ethos of his society: as the tribe's priest, and therefore the sanctioned conduit of the Teaching, he is a combination of clergyman, sociologist, and psychiatrist — or rather, that is what he should be instead of entertaining dreams of ownership in whose name he is more than happy to lie, cheat, misdirect, and work against the interests of the tribe. Marapper is possibly the most energetic character to emerge from *Non-Stop*, a cheerfully untroubled con artist who always manages to survive and ingratiate himself with those in power. He is cowardly and selfish, but also intelligent, cunning, and quick on the uptake, and his deep knowledge of the Teaching allows him an utterly untroubled conscience toward everything he does.

Roy, however, is not like that. If Marapper is the most energetic character, Roy is the most adaptable, and certainly the one who grows up more than anyone else. Since he is the hero and viewpoint character, moreover, he also becomes the carrier wave for the readers' questions about his world and its nature, and thus he is the one most given to philosophical musings. Immediately after his woman is kidnapped in the ponics forest, he lies down on the deck and reflects *"Only if I stay alive can I find the something missed, the big something.... Perhaps it does not exist. But when something so big has non-existence, that in itself is existence. A hole. A wall. As the priest says, there's been a calamity"* (20). There has certainly been a calamity, but that is not the point, nor is Roy's language indicative of a "big something" out among the ponics, a hidden trove of material treasures that, once found, will fix the world and make him happy. Rather, it highlights a psychological need emanating from inside him, an emotion or experience independent of the physical circumstances prevailing in his environment — for those physical circumstances do not really seem to matter very much. In fact, the reader finds out about the ship, the voyage, and the catastrophe almost immediately, and the first time we hear the whole line of reasoning uttered out loud — we are not even a quarter of the way through the novel — is when Marapper fully explains his plan to his still hesitant recruits on the day they escape from the Greene tribe. Roy and his companions accept it readily enough, because what worries them is not that this is the true shape of their world, but rather that they have been left alone onboard a dead ship, adrift through space. Throughout the narrative, various characters take turns asking "so what?" to Marapper's excited explanations: so what if they are onboard a ship traveling through an airless void instead of, say, on a world or in heaven or hell? Their lives are still the same, and the Teaching, whose dictates are independent of the world, tells them that they are creatures of the mind, not of the body — or rather, that the effect of the inside on the outside is more powerful and lasting than the outside's influence on the inside. To underscore the point even further, their big revelation about the ship ultimately proves hollow: when Roy's band of adventurers gets to Forwards and Marapper triumphantly produces the pilfered data-slate to the people there, they respond by scoffing and telling him that they have known all along. Only ignorant savages from Quarters would still waste their time wondering about that.

Moreover, the ship itself becomes a participant in this game of inside and outside. In their book *Apertures* (1984), David Wingrove and Brian Griffin point out that Aldiss's design of his generation starship is meant to represent something more than a locale for adventure:

> This image of the starship ... is also like the human brain.... As Fermour says, "It is constructed of layers and layers." It can be divided into Quarters (the basic hunting drives on which the tribe subsists, the unquestioning acceptance of sense-data); Deadways (the dark and perilous regions of the subconscious, where ghosts, Giants and Outsiders lurk, phantoms of the inaccessible past); and Forwards, the frontal lobe of the brain, concerned with Adlerian power-drives and conscious control [13].

If we superimpose this interpretive lens on the basic narrative scaffold of *Non-Stop*, we will find that, before being anything else, Roy Complain's generation starship is a theatre of the mind and for the mind — a damaged theatre, whose corridors, blocked by tangles of ponics or ancient explosions, loop in on themselves like schizophrenic thought processes, and which, again like the thoughts of a schizophrenic, are constantly invaded by alien entities — the Giants, the Outsiders, the rats — who use secret corridors honeycombing the vessel on the other side of the bulkheads. Thus every interpretive model with which its inhabitants come up in order to explain the origin of their predicament clashes against a reality opaque to direct probing, and ends up being refracted into a multiplicity of voices, none more intelligible or meaningful than the others.

When the real conceptual breakthrough arrives, it is almost an anticlimax, so prepared have we become for a revelation of this nature. The captain's log, which Vyann reads to Complain[18] in the privacy of her quarters before they show it to anyone else in Forwards, details the onslaught of a ship-wide plague the crew calls the nine-day ague. The ague breaks out among the crew after their ship disembarks thousands of colonists onto the fifth planet orbiting around the star Procyon. Before leaving Procyon V, immediately renamed New Earth by the colonists, the ship replenishes its reserves of water and food from the human-compatible local biosphere in preparation for the six generation-long trip back to Earth, and it is through the water — of a slightly but crucially different chemical composition than the water on Earth — that the ague infects every living creature onboard: humans, animals, and the hydroponic cultures.[19] Those it does not kill after its nine-day incubation period find themselves with their bodies substantially reduced in size and their metabolic speed quadrupled. These survivors move in a jerky, unnatural fashion in the eyes of the few uncontaminated people left onboard at the end of Gregory Complain's narrative, and they lead lives four times shorter than the standard human average. In the meantime a member of the crew, a bird scientist by the name of Bassitt, uses old psychology textbooks to create a hodgepodge religion that, in the course of events, takes root among the crew. Readers will recognize his name (*sans* that final t) from the holy trinity of the Teaching. Bassitt is the Huff figure in *Non-Stop*, but unlike Roy Huff in Heinlein, he is neither a revolutionary leader nor the agent of destruction; he is simply someone who, in the absence of Earth or any other planet with which to communicate,[20] is forced to construct a private system of belief to cope with events beyond his control. The survivors of the ague and their distant descendants have carried on the legacy of Bassitt's pseudo-religion in the form of the Teaching. Roy Complain, Vyann, Fermour, and Marapper are all short-lived humans, heirs to the post-ague world (161–172).

Thus the catastrophe that overtook the ship long ago is, almost literally, an illness of the mind, a seemingly irreversible change in the life cycle — and therefore in the worldview — of those affected. Among them, if we decide to adopt Griffin and Wingrove's psychoanalytic reading, we should include the generation starship itself, sick from a virus that attacked its main function: to serve as haven and home for the living creatures within its hull. But the story and its world are not done yet. The Forwards society that first imprisons and then accepts the three survivors from Quarters is seemingly more civilized than the Greene tribe; apart from the already mentioned institutions regulating its public life and the logistical infrastructure allowing it to maintain a stable border, it already knows about the ship and the voyage and does not believe in the Teaching, which it finds barbaric and benighted. Were we in a Heinleinian scenario, this would represent the hub of a budding civilization, all industry and superego against the instinctual responses of collectives like Roy's. But this is not Heinlein, and underneath the veneer lays the beast.

Inspector Vyann's superior, a man named Scoyt, is the chief of police in Forwards, a Joe McCarthy analog obsessed with the Outsiders' and the Giants' constant intrusions into his tribe's territory. With the blessings of the council, a substantially paler entity than his powerful para-military organization, Scoyt has already organized a number of witch hunts in the hopes of finding Outsiders and getting them to talk. Many have died under torture, unable or unwilling to confess anything, and the lack of positive feedback only incenses the chief of police, who grows more paranoid with every page. Had he believed in the Teaching, he would have gone through the ritual of rage and retained a degree of control over his neuroses ("May my neuroses not offend" is a common form of apology in Quarters), but he does not, and therefore he rationalizes his brutality as a requirement of the circumstances, spreading a constantly increasing amount of misery as events progress. This gradual peeling away of the violence at the heart of the Forwards collective, a violence far in excess of anything in Quarters because it has been systematized and rationalized as necessary through the will of the state, reveals an implicit commentary on the supposedly self-evident benefits of civilization in the sense the term had for the SF of the Campbell persuasion.

When the truth about the Giants and the Outsiders finally comes out, moreover, it is not Scoyt who finds it. It is Complain and Marapper, the cunning savages who know how to eavesdrop without guilt because the Teaching absolves them of it. One of the council members, Zac Deight, is a Giant, and Complain overhears him talking to another Giant onboard the ship. After Complain has stunned Deight with his dazer and left him unconscious, Marapper happens upon the scene, and after realizing Deight's identity on his own he gets the Giant to talk in the time-honored fashion practiced by essentially everyone on board — torture. After that, he, Complain, and Vyann find a badly hurt Fermour, previously revealed as an Outsider and "softened" by Scoyt's lackeys in preparation for interrogation. The story that emerges from the mouths of both men constitutes a further layer of conceptual breakthrough: the voyage of the generation starship "Big Dog" — this is the vessel's name — is over. It rests in orbit around the Earth, after returning as planned under the guidance of its automated systems. Upon reaching it, Earth's relief ships found it in its post-ague state, overrun with ponics, altered humans, and warped animals of all kinds, and established a minimum-interference pattern of watch and study in order to reverse the effects of the ague. Twenty-three generations of hyper-metabolized humans have succeeded one another onboard the "Big Dog" since the breakout, and the Giants (normal-sized humans seen from the diminutive perspective of Roy's people) have been trying to help all along, sometimes being forced to adopt harsh measures against one or two locals — whom the giants call dizzies, after their speeded-up metabolic processes—who strayed too far and found their hideout onboard the ship. As for the Outsiders, they are normal humans as well, only short enough to pass for dizzies. They are infiltrators whose task consists in altering the dizzy worldview from within, slowly reversing the more detrimental effects of the Teaching and getting the locals used to what really happened to them. The problem, however, is that no matter how beneficent the intentions of the Giants, the people onboard the "Big Dog" are the victims of a monstrous joke, inmates of a crumbling insane asylum under observation immediately above a planet to which they would be able to return if their wardens let them (238–239).[21]

The inmates are tired of their lives, and sick of their techno-tropical wasteland. While the discussions involving Deight, Fermour, Complain, Marapper, Vyann, and Gregg are going on, Scoyt has not been idle. After discovering the Giants' system of secret walkways (again thanks to Marapper's resourcefulness) and realizing that it completely interpenetrates every corridor in the ship, the chief of police finally gives his paranoia *carte blanche*. He organizes wrecking crews by recruiting every able-bodied man in Forwards, and puts them to work searching for the Giants and their hideout. In their frenzy, goaded on by an equally raging Scoyt, the dizzies start tearing the ship apart until, too damaged to maintain its structural cohesion, the "Big Dog" literally goes to pieces in a spectacular space-opera analogue to a mental breakdown: the various compartments seal themselves off from one another, detach from the ship's chassis, and then gently descend toward Earth. The brain is dead, the dizzies have after all achieved trip's end, and when we see Complain and Vyann for the last time they are together in one of the compartments, looking through the window at the slowly growing planet underneath. They have achieved a measure of happiness together, and as for Roy, his big something turned out to be a seemingly simple thing. Not long before the end, while they are looking out into space for the first time, he realizes that "It was just to see Laur's [Vyann's] face — by sunlight" (202). It is testament to Aldiss's vision for his novel, and to his control over the material at hand, that the sentence above does not close the narrative in a somewhat saccharine happy ending. It simply closes one of the last chapters, about forty pages from the end, before the last instance of conceptual breakthrough sweeps everyone onward to a new, unimaginable life. It is also testament to Aldiss's skills as a writer that the dramatic resolution of *Non-Stop*, like that of "The Wind Blows Free," refrains from passing judgment on the characters or crafting a moral lesson in order to easily put their lives away on the shelf. The ending of the novel neither rewards nor punishes its people, in much the same way as its development had neither condemned nor praised them for their actions, chiefly because, at the meta-narrative level, Aldiss's authorial voice performs a ritual not dissimilar from the Greene tribe's act of rage: it describes Roy, Marapper, or Vyann at their worst in a deadpan tone of stark realism, thereby exorcising our outrage over their actions and preparing the reader for the moments when they are at their best. And these moments are as numerous as the bad ones, because in this story the psychological complexity of the basic narrative premises informs the makeup of the characters to the extent that even the rats are awarded an objective assessment.

If there is a topic on which *Non-Stop* may be said to adopt a definite stance, that would be the grand narrative itself—space flight and planetary colonization. At the end of his log, a bereaved Gregory Complain writes:

> Only now, when the long journey means no more than a retreat into darkness, do I begin to question the sanity behind the whole conception of inter-stellar travel.... Nothing but the full flowering of a technological age ... could have launched this miraculous ship; yet the miracle is sterile, cruel. Only a technological age could condemn unborn generations to exist in it.... At the beginning of the technological age ... stands the memory of Auschwitz-Berkenau; what can we do but hope that this more protracted agony stands at its end [171–172].

So the "Big Dog" did not really become a grotesque theatre of the mind; it had always been one. The ship is the end result of a fatal psychological flaw in the desires that had prompted its construction, and the chance that the offspring of insane parents will somehow escape their fate is very small. As much in the expression of the captain's thoughts as in the long-desired return home at the end, *Non-Stop* brings the ethos propping up the burgeoning space age back to its roots, and exposes those roots for what they are: a monstrosity nursed on bloodshed. Like Oliver before him and Ballard and Moorcock a few years down the line, Aldiss has little time for the twisted reasoning of the Campbell/von Braun school of thought, or for the logical traps into which many SF writers of the '40s and '50s tricked their readers in the interest of nurturing a conceit. Writing from the threshold of oblivion, Gregory Complain becomes a Cassandra figure of sorts, one voice from the dead past warning a future it can neither anticipate nor imagine that dreams built on top of buried nightmares turn deadly. Like the ghouls hiding in the subconscious, unacknowledged sin is either exorcised through an act of contrition or it grows inside until it is strong enough to come back—and we should listen to the Teaching, because the dizzies are, after all, us:

> We identify in a number of ways with the dizzies. We, like them, are trapped in a spaceship (called Earth), the latest of countless generations doomed to take an inconceivably long, non-stop voyage to nowhere. There is something manifestly, horribly wrong with Spaceship Earth: far away in the past some primal catastrophe, some primordial sin, must have occurred.... The nation-states constituting our so-called civilization presumably meant something at one time; but they

5. The New Wave and Beyond, 1957–1979

have degenerated into something farcical and ignoble, like the Greene tribe in Quarters.... Like the dizzies, we are encapsulated in a world of gadgets gone totally out of our control; or, as C. S. Lewis put it, we are trapped inside the archetype of the Machine [Griffin and Wingrove 12].

Seven years after *Non-Stop* had first seen print, on July 9, 1965, Adlai Stevenson gave a speech before the UN in which he described our planet as a fragile spaceship depending on equally fragile, easily expended resources for the survival of everyone onboard. A year later, the economist Barbara Ward published a book entitled *Spaceship Earth*, and also in 1966, Kenneth E. Boulding wrote an essay entitled "The Economics of the Coming Spaceship Earth," in which he argued the necessity of switching to a global economic stance that treated the Earth as a spaceship requiring care and maintenance, because its resources were no more limitless than its ecological balance was indestructible. Then, in 1969, Buckminster Fuller published *Operating Manual for Spaceship Earth*, and in the early '70s James Lovelock proposed his now famous Gaia hypothesis. While it would be far too much of a stretch to suggest that *Non-Stop*— or even the whole generation starship body of work — were directly responsible for the slow growth of our still-struggling environmental awareness, we can at least consider the possibility that the subgenre, featuring as it must a variety of concerns intimately tied to careful ecological management and resource husbanding, contributed in its small way to those developments. Certainly, Stevenson's words before the UN would have resonated powerfully with the crew of the "Big Dog," had it been possible for them to attend the session.

If *Non-Stop* metafictionally invited us to conceive Earth as a giant generation starship, the short story that follows puts a new, unsettling twist on this idea. "Thirteen to Centaurus," J. G. Ballard's generation starship narrative, appeared in April 1962 in the pages of *Amazing Stories*. Dr. Roger Francis is mission psychologist onboard a generation starship on its hundred-year voyage to Centaurus, the fourteenth and last member of the tiny shipboard community. At the beginning of the story, we find him instructing sixteen-year-old Abel, the child of the Granger clan, because the youth is starting to have doubts concerning the nature of his world. The children onboard the ship are initially led to believe they live on a space station, and only when they approach adulthood is the psychological conditioning that makes the lie possible lifted from their minds — unless the subject is particularly intelligent, like Abel, in which case they start connecting various pieces of contradictory evidence and, against the false input of their conditioning, begin to realize the truth. Dr. Francis has seen the development of Abel's thinking over a period of months, and has finally decided that the time has come to tell him about the world. After a by now familiar infodump session, during which Francis gives Abel the information necessary to break his artificially induced forgetfulness pattern, the young man goes to the infirmary, where the last of his mental blocks will be removed. After his departure, Francis goes to his sleeping unit, locks himself within it, and triggers a mechanism hidden behind its ventilation grille. Another door opens and he walks out into bright sunlight, surrounded by the sounds of trucks and maintenance teams servicing the grounded spacecraft.

"Thirteen to Centaurus" is a portrayal of space travel as a place of psychological entrapment. The generation starship never left Earth. For fifty years now, the original volunteers and their descendants — the volunteers had been fully aware of the lie — have been running around like rats in a maze, an experiment in human adaptability to conditions of prolonged confinement designed to provide useful feedback for the real mission to Centaurus, slated to leave Earth after the experiment has ended and the data processed. Since the only way to acquire reliable information was to let the rats run in their maze for as long as it would take the real generation starship to reach the Centaurus system, the original volunteers had condemned themselves and their descendants to remain onboard for a hundred years. Now, fifty years on, Francis is the only human being on Earth allowed to directly interact with those inside, and he is on site for two main reasons: first of all, to administer the subliminal suggestions and mental blocks necessary to prevent the crew from realizing they never left, and secondly to take care of whatever is left of their mental stability, already compromised by their fundamentally warped existence. The pantomime at the beginning of the story was part of a further layer of deception, designed so that, when this inner layer is lifted, the subject will believe they are in the real world.

Toward the end of *Non-Stop*, Gregory Complain had commented that only a technological civilization, psychotically in love with its machines at the expense of the individuals who built them, could have forced unborn generations to live within the confines of his starship — and the "Big Dog," if we extrapolate the size of the two spacecraft from the descriptions provided in their respective narratives, is far larger than Dr. Francis's immobile ship. If that is true, then what should we say about a society that creates this kind of scenario? At least Complain, Vyann, and their people have the satisfaction, grim as it may be, of knowing that their ship did go somewhere, and that what happened to them at least carried the full purpose of their race's desire, warped as that may have proven itself at the end. Those onboard the fake starship do not even have that. They are trapped on a stage without a curtain, a Kafkaesque farce for monsters at the expense of the helpless, and there are no excuses for this piece of theatre: if we were to justify the experiment in the name of the real mission's success, we would end up on the bottom side of the slippery slope leading to the same argument the Nazi doctors devised for their experiments on human subjects, or more to the point, to the line of reasoning von Braun employed to justify his days at Peenemünde. If, on the other hand, we tried to excuse the experiment on the grounds that the original crew embarked on this endeavor of their own will, we would find ourselves right back among the pages of Gregory Complain's log. The original crew may have made the choice, but children like Abel and Zenna — the girl slated to become Abel's wife a few years down the line — have not.

Monsters as they may be, however, some of the soldiers servicing and repairing the starship have a surprising perspective on the life going on inside its bulkheads. When Francis complains to a maintenance sergeant that one of his men had briefly cast a shadow against the supposedly empty starry backdrop of the stage, thus exposing the crew to a potential mental breakdown, the man replies that "Some people here think they have it all ways. Quiet and warm in there, nothing to do except sit back and listen to those hypno-drills.... We're the boys back here on Mother Earth who do the work, out in this Godforsaken dump. If you need any more spacecadets, Doctor, remember me" (100). The sergeant's despondency is all the more worrying to Francis because it echoes the steady loss of motivation that life inside the mockup is causing in the thirteen crewmembers. Many of them do not go out of their quarters and do not socialize, preferring to do their jobs in solitude and spending their spare time with their immediate clan members. The only exceptions are Old Peters, the ship's current captain, and Abel, whose mental readiness has allowed him to begin questioning the second layer of illusion, pointing out inconsistencies in the generation starship setup that, if not checked, may threaten the experiment. When Francis tries to deflect the young man's attention from this line of reasoning, Abel dodges his observations by suggesting that they "test the effects of continued isolation. We could select a small group, subject them to artificial stimuli, even seal them off from the rest of the crew and condition them to believe they were back on Earth. It could be a really valuable experiment, Doctor" (106).

Besides the problems he is encountering with the crew's psychological responses and Abel's growing unmanageability, more bad news meets the Doctor, this time from the outside world. In the fifty years since the beginning of the experiment, administrations have come and gone, and their budgets, especially in the wake of the failure of the two colonies on the Moon and on Mars, have slashed the funding for space settlement as the political necessities of the immediate present ended up trumping the scientific variables of the distant future. Moreover, the American public and their representatives in Washington have started questioning the morality of the endeavor, now that interrupting the experiment would actually do more psychological harm to the crew than simply letting them go on, as Francis tries to explain to the General newly appointed to close down the experiment (102, 107–108). General Short,[22] however, is not a cruel man, and the orders he has received place the mental health of the crew before any other consideration — provided he still closes down the project, that is. Thus, he establishes a deadline of fifteen years from the present for the end of the experiment and the opening of the hatches. During this time, Short and the rest of the scientific team believe that they can implement gradual alterations in the crew's psychological conditioning to slowly wean them off their metal womb, so that in the fullness of time they will be able to leave the mockup ship without losing their sanity.

The only one who disagrees is Francis himself, and that is not enough to keep the experiment on its original track. So he does the only thing he can to alleviate his charges' suffering: he returns to the ship, locks himself inside, and refuses to come out. When one of the officers tries to make him see that he is trapping himself into an artificial situation leading to nowhere, Francis replies: "Not nowhere, Colonel: Alpha Centauri" (111). Now he truly is the fourteenth member of the crew, both in his eyes and in theirs, and he will use his knowledge of the true state of affairs to ease the others into the gradual end of their lives. As soon as the doctor fully shares their existence, however, he starts falling prey to the same malady of listlessness and apathy that has gripped them, and the daily shipboard routine becomes maddening in his eyes. He finds his sessions with Abel particularly irritating, since the young man has put him on a regime of mind-numbing mathematical exercises aimed at either proving or disproving one theory or another. As he slowly grows resentful toward Abel, Francis also notices that his erstwhile charge is now paying regular visits to a seemingly unremarkable corner of the ship's hull, and decides to investigate the spot:

> Francis ... located a loosened panel that had rusted off its rivets. About ten inches by six, it slid off easily. Beyond it was the outer wall of the dome, a hand's breadth away. Here too was a loose plate, held in position by a crudely fashioned hook. Francis hesitated, then lifted the hook and drew back the panel. *He was looking straight down into the hangar!* [114].

Old Peters, the captain and the only other member of the crew who does not suffer shipboard listlessness, has known for a long time that the mission is a sham. He has nevertheless decided to go along with the pretense, "perhaps realizing that the truth would destroy the others, or preferring to be captain of an artificial ship rather than a self-exposed curiosity in the world outside." He then passes on the knowledge "to the one other lively mind, one who would keep the secret and make the most of it. For his own reasons he too had decided to stay in the dome, realizing that he would soon be the effective captain, free to pursue his experiments in applied psychology" (115).

Seemingly shocked at its own resolution, the story ends a few lines from the passage above with the same two words that had started it: "*Abel knew!*" (115). At the beginning, this exclamation had indicated a sham, a smokescreen in front of our eyes, whereas now it reveals the true extent of the game of inside and outside being played at the location of the fake starship. In the generation starship stories preceding "Thirteen to Centaurus," the reality of space travel had always regulated the value placed on the difference between inside and outside. Whether the crew found their vessel a prison or a womb, a maze of death or a source of life, their choices had had consequence because they were in space. Without space flight, the distinction loses its original meaning and acquires a significance directly related to Earth-bound lifestyle choices devoid of transcendence — hence the status of the sergeant's comment about the cozy life onboard the ship as one of the key moral coordinates in the story. And as for those who actually believe they are in space, transcendence is denied them as well: in the world of the narrative, the human adventure into space is a disaster — the Moon and Mars colonies were real enough, but they still failed. The ignorant crew on their pretend way to Centaurus find no enthusiasm in the idea of being part of such an adventure, lapse into apathy, and become easy prey for Abel's inside-out experiments.

"Thirteen to Centaurus" came out in the same year as Ballard's manifesto for the New Wave, the document in which he had invited readers and writers of science fiction to turn their backs on outer space and focus their attention on inner space, and the story efficiently embodies his intentions. At its beginning, the sergeant's comment reads more like a verbal jab aimed at goading Francis than a considered point focused on clarifying the issue. By the time the narrative reaches its conclusion, however, at least three of its characters have consciously acted on the implications of that comment: Old Peters, Abel, and Francis.[23] Old Peters may have decided to stay on board out of concern for his fellow prisoners, though the possibility that he chose the ship out of a desire to be ruler rather than guinea pig resonates more closely with the sergeant's comment. Abel's motives, on the other hand, are less opaque; he has built himself an ant farm, knowing he can play with it on the condition that he does not leave the ship, and the condition suits him fine. He is the one true master of psychological manipulation in the story, detached and calculating where Francis, the actual psychologist, makes the mistake of identifying with his patients to the point of becoming one of them. The study in crew isolation that Abel proposes to Francis is unsettling on two levels: first of all, it reveals a lack of affect toward his own community. Secondly, it highlights the fuzziness of the distinction between outer and inner space, because the multiplicity of mind games in operation at the same time throughout the story creates a landscape of cages, each one either overlapping or fully containing the others, and of all the characters it is Abel who oversees their opening and closing. Born inside a double lie, his ability to peel away all the layers of deception on his own makes him a supremely gifted student of the mind — one devoid of scruples, moreover, because the one thing he has learned better than any other is that there is no decency in his world, either inside or outside. His ancestors from inside have condemned him to life in prison, and those outside have simply stood back and looked at the cage for half a century. Thus, Abel makes everyone in both worlds a test subject in an experiment of mental isolation of his devising: while he observes the crew of the false starship go through their apathetic motions, he also observes the behavior of the world outside the ship — a world susceptible to experiment because their ignorance of Old Peters and Abel's awareness puts them into a mental cage of their own, a cage whose key is not in their possession. Abel owns it, and the only man who knows about it is now trapped in the ship with him.

There is an old joke that goes something like this: the inmate of an asylum for the insane breaks out of his room, crosses the lawn separating the main building from the wall, and climbs on top of it. Once he can see the street beyond, he attracts the attention of the nearest passerby and, when the man approaches, the inmate asks him "How many of you live in there?" Walls imply two sides — in fact, it is the building of the walls themselves that creates the sides. Someone conceptualized the separation first and made it into actuality later. Thus, which one of them is inside or outside largely depends on the perspective of the individual issuing the decision — and on their power to force that decision onto others. Abel is the most powerful individual in the story, after usurping Francis's role as mission psychologist and making him an inmate. The Doctor has crucially misunderstood the nature of life in the rat's maze he and his fellows have created for the crew, and when he becomes one of them he is unprepared for the role Abel has devised for him — as is everyone else in the world.

As the '60s wore on and the New Wave hit its multi-headed, multi-voiced stride, generation starship narratives kept coming out of the pens of SF authors, old and new alike. One in particular is of interest: in 1965, Samuel Delany published *The Ballad of Beta-2*, a novel where the role of the captain's log as an instrument of conceptual breakthrough is taken over by a poem, the ballad of the title. In the not-so-distant future, humanity has developed faster-than-light technology, so that interstellar travel, safe and fast, has become a matter of routine. The warp drive has come too late, however, to save the crews of a dozen or so generation starships and their many descendants — the

5. The New Wave and Beyond, 1957–1979

first wave of colonization, à la Wilcox — the trouble of spending their entire lives in transit. Unlike the Robinello colony in "The Voyage That Lasted 600 Years," the newly formed interstellar commonwealth immediately starts looking for their long-gone kinsfolk, but when they finally find them the generation starships are in shambles, corroded and broken by unknown phenomena that enveloped them in the void between stars. Many of the vessels failed to survive outright, and their hollowed-out husks lie together with their less unlucky brethren in orbit around one of the planetary colonies. The only clue as to what happened, where most of the crewmembers went, and why the ships are in such a parlous state, lies in a poem found onboard one of them, a ballad describing seemingly impossible events in an apparently highly allegorical language. In 1941, Heinlein had made the Lines from the Beginning the first part of the process of conceptual breakthrough Hugh Hoyland undergoes, but in Delany the poem is the only document necessary for understanding the world. It is, we could say, the story of the story, which is why *Ballad* features as protagonist a Ph.D. student of literature on his way to finish his dissertation, who travels by ftl ship to the generation starship graveyard, boards the vessel where the ballad had been found, and goes about the business of deciphering the poem, aided in his efforts by a strange child who seems to be able to appear and disappear at will. At the end, when he finally does decipher the meaning of the work, he discovers the story of humanity's first encounter with alien entities of godlike powers, of a starship captain's transcendental sexual encounter, and of the birth of a new, hybrid human/alien race.

The multiplicity of themes and linguistic experiments fostered by the New Wave, both in the UK and in the United States, exploded the subject matter of science fiction at the same time as it transformed its language, propelling it into the 1970s. Until the end of the 1950s there had been one main narrative for the genre, one way of doing things, and one advocacy for the future. Also, there had been one main template for the typical writer of science fiction: a white, middle-class, heterosexual American male. Now, however, the certainty of one future started branching out into the possibility of a multiple set of tomorrows, variously advocated or warned against by an increasingly diversified range of writers — some men and some women; some white and some not; some American, some British, and some from altogether different places; some straight and some gay. As the '60s gave way to the '70s, science fiction entered a period of reflection and consolidation, merging the chorus of voices the previous decade had given it into a heteroglossia of narrative modes. Indeed, it was during this time that the various sub-genres we know today — hard SF, space opera, feminist SF, science fantasy, and so on — were born. By 1970, the New Wave had fully expressed its influence on the genre and was starting to fade into the background, but it was not dying. Like the wall of the asylum from whose top the supposedly mad guy asks how many of us live in here, the distinction between the Campbell strain of SF and the New Wave had not been necessary until Ballard and Moorcock established it. Before the late '50s/early '60s, Robert Heinlein, Arthur C. Clarke, or Isaac Asimov had not needed to describe their stories as hard SF, space opera, Campbellian SF, or anything else. It was simply science fiction, and it was all there was — it, that is, plus a few people like Simak, Cordwainer Smith, Oliver, and Bradbury doing their still vaguely science fictional, but really rather indefinable, thing. Then the market expanded during the early '50s, the voices became many, and by the beginning of the following decade people like Moorcock and Ballard were telling everyone they were building a wall inside the genre, putting themselves and a few others on one side, and pointedly asking the old guard to please conduct a census of the inmates on *their* side.

Besides being a period of consolidation and restructuring for written science fiction, the '70s were also the decade in which the genre fully broke through the barrier of its original medium, specifically into television and movies. There had been plenty of SF movies during the preceding decades, both on TV and on the big screen, but the state of the art of special effects had made it difficult and very expensive to visually portray the wonders of literary science fiction with the same power an author could muster with a typewriter. Now, after the end of the '60s had proved, with *Star Trek* on TV and *2001: A Space Odyssey* in movie theatres, that effective SF in cinematic form was feasible and had an audience ready to watch it, the '70s saw the genre definitively enter the two realms. *Space: 1999* (1975–1977) and *Battlestar Galactica* (1978) were two of the many TV series that saw the light of day during the decade, while the big screen featured such box-office hits as *Star Wars: A New Hope* (1977), *Star Trek: The Motion Picture*, and *Alien* (both 1979). In the meantime, the newly born narrative form of role-playing games, created in 1973 when Gary Gygax and Dave Arneson published the first edition rules of *Dungeons & Dragons*, had quickly turned its attention to SF with *Traveller* (1st edition 1977) and *Gamma World* (1st edition 1978).

The generation starship narratives of the 1970s did what they had done for every other stage in the development of science fiction: they reflected their time. The two most relevant examples, Poul Anderson's *Tau Zero* (1970) and Arthur C. Clarke's *Rendezvous with Rama* (1974) hearken back to the SF of the Campbell era, now identified under the label hard SF, but both present an altogether more sophisticated portrayal of the human issues surrounding their big-think premises. *Tau Zero* is literally a romp through the whole of space-time, both in our universe and on the other side of creation. The generation starship in the story suffers an engine failure that, instead of stopping it dead in space, makes it impossible for it to stop. The vessel keeps accelerating, creeping ever closer to the fabled "tau zero" (light-speed) without actually reaching it. The time dilation effects postulated by Einsteinian physics duly take place, so that subjectively the crew experiences the entire history of the universe and its heat-death within their lifetime. They marry, separate, have babies, fight, and love one another until the very end, when the protagonist of the narrative, the dour-faced and supremely competent senior security officer, proves himself an expert enough pilot to navigate the ship through the maelstrom at the end of that cycle of creation and into the beginning of the new one. The last pages of the novel see the crew finally able to slow down enough to make planetfall on a virgin biosphere, a scant few billions of years after the new universe's big bang. They have survived the death of their reality, and made a home for themselves in another. Campbell, who would die a scant year after the publication of *Tau Zero*, could have done much worse in the way of homage to his influence.

Rendezvous with Rama is a story of first contact with a deserted alien generation starship, as the vessel comes hurtling through the solar system on its way to somewhere else. The crew of the Earth ship *Endeavour* is the only one within reach of the giant artifact — which receives the name *Rama* upon discovery — because its speed is such that they only have one week to explore it. They see incredible things: a fully functioning biosphere within the vessel's hull, the generation of energies beyond anything mankind has ever possessed, as well as alien artifacts and mechanical constructs beyond number or description. And at the end of the novel, when the time comes for them to leave before *Rama* gets too close to the sun at the beginning of its journey out of the solar system, they still have understood nothing of what they have seen,[24] which brings us to a logical question: if *Rama* remains opaque to human probing throughout the novel, how do we know it is a generation starship?

At the beginning of the novel, shortly after the *Endeavor* has landed on the artifact, the specially appointed "Rama Committee," an ad hoc group of scientists and ambassadors from the various planets of the solar system's Commonwealth, receives the first images of its interior. After looking at the footage and listening to the descriptions given by the *Endeavor*'s captain, the chairman asks for comments, and one Dr. Carlisle Pereira obligingly gets up:

> Yes, Mr. Ambassador, I think I have some information of interest. What we have here is undoubtedly a "Space Ark." It's an old idea in the astronautical literature; I've been able to trace it back to the British physicist J. D. Bernal, who proposed this method of interstellar colonization in a book published in 1929 — yes, two hundred years ago. And the great Russian pioneer Tsiolkovski put forward somewhat similar proposals even earlier [43].

And so on, through all the steps necessary to explain the basics of generational space travel to the rest of the committee. Clarke loved his lectures, and he was an expert enough writer to disguise them as necessary background elements rather than arbitrary infodump à la Gernsback. Moreover, he had a certain facility for weaving true historical information into his fictional situations, thereby making them seem all the more plausible. The potted history of the generation starship concept Pereira gives his audience probably qualifies as one of the more effective instances of this narrative ploy in Clarke's fiction. Also, we might argue that, in its recap of Tsiolkovsky and Bernal's original concepts, it constitutes a watershed of sorts — the moment when a writer adding his novel to the generation starship body of work felt it useful to provide a substantial historical background to the action, thereby making the sub-genre openly self-aware.

However, the unknown remains: Pereira's entirely plausible lecture notwithstanding, we do not know that *Rama* truly is a generation starship. In fact, we know nothing about it except that it is very old (something like a few hundreds of thousands of years), and Clarke himself is perfectly aware of the situation. That is why *Rendezvous* reads both as a fascinating — albeit frustrating — hard SF romp and as a complex Rorschach test. The alien artifact speeding through the solar system is not here to talk to us, or for that matter acknowledge our existence in any way. We are not important. So when the various planetary governments of the commonwealth, in their role as the representative bodies of billions of deeply egocentric human beings, react to its presence in a variety of ways, from fear to fascination to joy, none of the actions they take has anything to do with *Rama* itself, and none of them have the power to affect its course — including the Mercury Government's attempt to blow it up with nukes. In the event, it is the crew of the *Endeavor* that disarms the missiles, for they are afraid they may do damage, but whatever indication the novel provides that their warheads would even have dented *Rama's* surface comes exclusively from human reckoning, and again, we know nothing. The alien artifact has traveled for eons through thousands of light-years, probably traversing areas of space fraught with danger, and it is still intact. The notion that we could do anything to it at all stands an excellent chance of being nothing more than an empty conceit, and once again, the narrative displays full awareness of this: at the end of the story, the giant artifact sails serenely out of human reach, leaving the actors of the brief drama to stare at each other across the void between the sun and the inner planets, their behavior in the crisis the only known quantity in the entire equation.

In 1973, Harlan Ellison wrote the script for the pilot episode of *The Starlost*, a Canadian television series set onboard a gigantic generation starship called "The Ark" that has veered off course. In keeping with the most commonly practiced pattern in the sub-genre, the descendants of the original crew do not know that they are in a ship. In the wake of several production problems, Ellison grew dissatisfied with the series and abandoned it, also forcing the producers to change his name in the pilot's credits to "Cordwainer Bird," the moniker he always used to indicate a project that had betrayed his hopes. The series ran for sixteen episodes, while Ellison's script for the pilot went on to win a Writers' Guild of America Award for best original screenplay. The script's novelization, which Ellison wrote with Edward Bryant, came out in 1975 as *Phoenix Without Ashes*, the title he had unsuccessfully tried to give to the pilot.

Then, in 1976, TSR produced the world's first SF role-playing game, a supplement for *Dungeons & Dragons* entitled *Metamorphosis Alpha*. Originally created by James M. Ward, the game requires players to step into the role of the inhabitants of the *Warden*, an enormous generation starship struck by an unknown cataclysm in the distant past. Most of the original crew die in the cataclysm, and as a result their descendants do not know that they are onboard a ship. The setting features humans, both mutated and unaltered, mutated plants, and mutated animals of all kinds,[25] a series of borrowings that, as Ward himself openly acknowledged, makes Aldiss's *Non-Stop* the direct inspiration for the game. Over the years, *Metamorphosis Alpha* has gone through several editions, but unfortunately the generation starship setting was gradually lost, leaving the *Warden* simply as a mega-technological environment for adventure. Still, the birth of the idea itself was an achievement, and gave the ending of the 1970s the sense that, as far as the sub-genre was concerned, further inventiveness was on the way.

The beginning of the following decade, however, seemed to put the lie to those expectations. In 1966, Vernor Vinge had published a short story entitled "Bookworm, Run!" that promised the coming of something different — it prominently featured the word "information" within its pages. The word was not new in itself, but Vinge had been using it in new ways. Later on, as the seventies were coming to a close and the world seemed to be on the cusp of further change, the faint stirrings of something that looked like it wanted to be a movement could be detected at the fringes of SF, and new writers were beginning to make some room for themselves within the magazines of the time. Then, in 1981, Vinge published another work, a novella called "True Names," and within a year or so two more writers, William Gibson and Bruce Sterling, had joined him in expressing the sense of an upcoming conceptual breakthrough. Apart from them and a few intellectuals working mostly outside science fiction, however, nobody had yet foreseen what was to come, and how different the world would be after it had arrived.

Chapter 6

The Information Age, 1980–2001

Shortly after the release on DVD of James Cameron's *Terminator 2: Judgment Day* (1991; DVD 1997), TriStar Pictures produced a special edition of the movie, a director's cut that added several scenes to the original version. One of these previously absent scenes features the character of Miles Dyson, the man responsible for the creation of the microchip technology that will ultimately lead to Skynet, World War III, and the rise of the machines "out of the ashes of the nuclear fire," as the narrative exposition in the first *Terminator* (1984) had declared. Sometime during the years between the events of the two movies, the corporation Dyson works for, Cyberdyne Systems, found the damaged microchip from the original terminator. Now Dyson, blissfully ignorant of the eventual consequences of his studies, is working on replicating in the present the unit the terminator had brought inside its head from the future.[1]

Despite being the foremost figure in the field of information technology, Dyson is, at heart, a throwback to an earlier era — a utopian dreamer in the Gernsback tradition. In that scene, he sets his wife on his lap and, in front of the computer where lines of code illustrate his latest work on the microchip, paints for her a picture of the bright future to which his work will lead them all as if he could see it on the screen. He talks about "a jet airliner with a pilot who never gets tired, never makes mistakes, and never shows up to work with a hangover," all thanks to the breakthrough he is working on. His invention will eliminate the human element from the equation, allowing cars, aircraft, ships, and trains to drive themselves, thus freeing people from the risk of damage and death. And all the time he is talking, unseen in the sunlight of a California morning, the shadow of nuclear holocaust looms, and after that the blasted rubble of Earth's cities, wastelands of gutted buildings where carpets of human skulls are crushed under the treads of Skynet's hunter-killers.

James Cameron knew his science fiction history well. His insertion of a figure like Miles Dyson in a movie like *Terminator 2*, where the dream of a better life through technological advancement is revealed from the very beginning as an adumbration of hell, can be taken as a symbol for the struggle of 1980s science fiction to make up for its own tardiness in prefiguring the basic shape of the future, as well as its eventual success in this struggle during the 1990s. "Not for us the giant steam-snorting wonders of the past: the Hoover Dam, the Empire State Building, the nuclear power plant," wrote Bruce Sterling in the cyberpunk manifesto with which he prefaced the anthology *Mirrorshades* (1986); "Eighties tech sticks to the skin, responds to the touch: the personal computer, the Sony walkman, the portable telephone, the soft contact lens" (xiii). If, truthfully enough, eighties tech stuck to the skin, the tech narrated by the few 1980s SF writers with their finger on the pulse of the age wormed its way inside: prosthetic implants, nanoware enhancements, skin grafts, LSD-based psychedelic drugs, and wetwired cyberspace ports for jacking into the matrix like the character Case in William Gibson's *Neuromancer* (1984). Again, the machines from the first two *Terminator* movies stand as effective symbols of this sea-change. In imagining the original terminator, Cameron had transformed the ungainly green alien robot from the cover of the October 1941 issue of *Amazing Stories* into the quintessential machine of eighties SF: the cyborg, a combination of interdependent biological and technological parts controlled by a microchip capable of learning and adapting to changing conditions. The real source of the terminator's power, the nearly self-aware information-gathering protocols inside the microchip, operate from within the machine's skull under layers of gleaming steel-like metal, itself covered over by human tissue, skin, and blood. The Gernsback robot has literally gotten under our skin, and it is now us. When it looks in the mirror at itself, as the terminator does halfway through the first movie, the viewers see a human face, not a pair of yellow lenses on top of a metal grille, and we have to peel away the skin to reveal the monster beneath — but then again, the same can be said of people.

The creature Miles Dyson thinks he is building with his microchip never existed. It is a thing not of the future, but of the future according to the past, outmoded and surpassed by the simple birth of the present. When Sterling wrote in his preface to *Mirrorshades* that the "careless technophilia" of the Gernsback brand of SF "belongs to a vanished, sluggish era, when authority still had a comfortable margin of control" (xiii), he could well have been speaking of Dyson and of the fear-maddened military brass who, at the end of things and on the brink of destruction, realize too late what Skynet has become and unsuccessfully try to pull the plug. The missiles fly, the world ends, and the future begins in dystopia, crawling across a changed landscape of data intercourse on the way to a hope, not necessarily forlorn, that it can turn itself into something better. Much like science fiction itself.

To begin tracing this landscape, we can follow John Clute's lead. In the article he contributed to the *Cambridge Companion to Science Fiction* (2003), Clute identified the threads of change, both internal and external, which transformed SF during that time. These threads altered the world around the genre, quickly making the bulk of its pre–1980 body of work obsolete, and then forced it to upgrade itself — not unlike the computer software whose advent it had failed to foresee — to survive its radically altered environment. From his overall argument, we can isolate four main avenues along which these changes expressed themselves:

- The exponential increase in the number of science fiction users, concomitant with — and linked to — the decline in primacy of written SF. Starting in the early eighties, the majority of those who frequented science fictional environments did so through movies, television, computer games, and tabletop role-playing/board games, without feeling either the need or the desire to approach a Heinlein novel or an issue of *F&SF* (64).

- The passing away of what Clute calls "the biological model of sf," by which term he means a way of looking at the history of the genre "as a kind of 'organism' whose origins could be accessed through human memory, and whose phases were the phases of a human life" (65). By the beginning of the twenty-first century, the founding figures of the genre were dead,[2] so that the memory of SF's birth and development had now become history, and therefore only available through the use of written records and the interpretation of texts whose authors were no longer around to comment on them. Though inevitable, it was a stressful turn of events for a fictional mode that had always thought of itself as inherently forward-thrusting.

- The end of the Campbell/Heinlein template of future advocacy as a usable science fictional form. "Classic sf," Clute writes, "was deeply tied to a vision of the future whose fabric — the tools, the weapons, the technologies, the means, the armies, the emperors, the flows of capital, the waves of culture — could be seen in the mind's eye," and therefore it "ignored the transistor, described computers in terms of bulk rather than invisible intricacies, [and] failed to anticipate the nanoware-driven world we may now be entering" (66–67). When this vision was suddenly overtaken by a present of unprecedented complexity, when the inert metal skull of the Gernsback robot gave way to the microchip querying the world from inside the gleaming polyalloy shell of the cyborg's brain, classic SF stopped being able to tell the future, and became frustrated prophecy. Had the enthusiasm of the days before the moon landings remained alive, had the space program prospered through a second age of economic prosperity and commensurately greater challenges, the SF that had given the voice of desire to its earlier incarnation might have found a new lease on life in this rewritten agenda. As things turned out, however, the space program foundered in the aftermath of the cancellation of the *Apollo* program, while the lack of a clear mission statement for the post-moon years, together with the attendant loss of funds, left NASA largely directionless during the eighties and nineties. There were great achievements, no doubt, but they were mostly related to unmanned probes and astronomical observatories such as *Mariner*, *Voyager*, *Galileo*, and the Hubble Space Telescope, while the human presence in space exclusively took place in Earth orbit, a territory that *Sputnik* had negotiated thirty years before. Then, on January 28, 1986, the space shuttle *Challenger* exploded in a spectacular fireball less than two minutes after takeoff, killing all seven crewmembers and causing the entire remaining fleet to be grounded for almost three years. That day, interplanetary and interstellar human spaceflight seemed further away than it had during the 1950s, and the space conquest narratives typical of classic SF looked jejune in their assumption of a human manifest destiny among the stars.

- The growth of a new cadre of writers who could repair the damage caused by the obsolescence of classic SF. As citizens of the information revolution, these authors were able to successfully take on the task of thrusting the genre past its dead prophecies and, through re-learning the present, once again put it on the rim of the curve of change.

The last two points are particularly important. The 1980s were not the first time the grand narrative of classic SF had been challenged: the New Wave had already done that. It was the first time, however, that classic SF became, in Clute's expression, "*outmoded* ... blindsided by the future" (67). Throughout the sixties and seventies, Campbellian SF had continued to relevantly advocate its futures. It had been opposed and critiqued by those who felt there was more than one way to look at tomorrow, certainly, but it had not been made obsolete. Heinlein in particular had enjoyed undiminished exposure, largely thanks to the publication of two of his best-known works, *Stranger in a Strange Land* (1961) and *The Moon Is a Harsh Mistress* (1966). The earlier book was especially relevant in securing his reputation during that time, because as the sixties wore on and the youth counterculture of the end of the decade developed its agenda, Valentine Michael Smith's message of free love struck a chord, and *Stranger* became, together with *The Lord of the Rings*, one of its manifestos. As for Asimov, he was still as prolific as ever, and unlike Heinlein, who was by and large content to write fiction and leave the essaying to others,[3] he made himself into a household name for the publication of anthologies, themed collections of short stories, and articles on astronomy, SF, history, physics, and literature.[4] Other writers of classic SF, from A. E. Van Vogt and Poul Anderson to Arthur C. Clarke and Jack Vance, kept writing their stories, kept classic SF going, and kept pace with the other voices in the genre. In the 1960s, the science fiction of the Campbell age may no longer have been *the* voice of the future, but it was still *a* voice, expressing a set of advocacies with which one may not have agreed, but which one nevertheless could not ignore.

Then, along came the eighties, and kids in theaters were watching a young Matthew Broderick in *Wargames* (1983) use the game of tic-tac-toe to teach a Skynet analogue that global thermonuclear war is a zero-sum game. Broderick's character is not a can-do Competent Man in a future of giant starships, or a psychohistorian from a galactic empire spanning millions of light-years; he is here and now, in the present, awash in the rich information flow of the day, and the world around him belongs to his audience as well. The pretend futures of classic SF had little to offer to those kids, little that could match the potency of the experience of watching the W.O.P.R.[5] hum its way through thousands of alternate scenarios, the LEDs on the readout screens blinking alternately in random patterns while the data streams whose paths they indicate course through its circuits. And all the time as it goes through its light-speed calculations, the W.O.P.R. maneuvers the hardware of cold-war technological know-how like pawns in a game of chess, sending planes on wild goose chases while the military brass inside Cheyenne Mountain look at the screens in dismay and try to figure out the movements of Soviet units that are not there, because the machine trapped them in a simulation they cannot see.

Thus, as the eighties wore on, the great writers of classic science fiction found themselves no longer able to emplot futures that could mean anything truly relevant to their readership, while at the same time having become, by virtue of that very obsolescence, household names in the Asimov mold — that Asimov, as David Langford once put it, "who's famous and knows it, the man whose mere name on the cover could sell three hundred blank pages" (74). The result of this amalgam of outmoded mindsets and commercial viability was a slew of poorly written, often arrogantly argued revisionist works that attempted to reconfigure for the new age the glory narratives of the forties and fifties — Heinlein's history of space exploration, Asimov's *Robots* and *Foundation* series, Clarke's *Childhood's End*— and failed. However, while Asimov and Clarke largely contented themselves with staining the memory of the works of their prime, Heinlein in particular seemed to become more painful to read with every book he wrote during the last ten years or so of his life.[6] In fact, it got bad enough that in early 1988 a younger Clute, still mired in the thick chaotic soup of the struggle years from which he had described the writers of classic SF as "dinosaurs ... relics of sf's long history as a relatively closed genre (until *Sputnik* blew the walls down)," articulated the legacy of Heinlein's later work in the following terms:

> These novels are in fact nightmares of a most desperate solitude ... the worlds they inhabit ... are skillful travesties of sf worlds created by Heinlein (and others) before *Sputnik*, and their merciless disparagement in book after book bespeaks an enormity of disgust and rage on the author's part, seemingly directed at a genre grown monstrous. But in the end the disgust and the rage turn insatiably inwards [*Evidence* 20].

By the time Clute wrote these words, Heinlein was already dead, leaving behind a memory of his final years as a period of bitter polemic against a present that had betrayed his expectations. Thus the science fiction of the Campbell era entered twilight, waiting for writers who, sifting through the ashes of SF's spent tropes, could inject new life into their subject matter.

These writers, the authors who made SF what it is today, are numerous, and the enthusiasm of their collective responses to the challenges of the times, as well as the variety of forms these responses adopted, is astonishing. It would be impossible to do them all justice, so this chapter will only briefly touch on the key figures of those two decades. The first who need mentioning are the authors connected to the cyberpunk movement, the only sub-genre in SF that truly grappled with the present during the early eighties. Originally coined by Bruce Bethke for a story he published in the November 1983 issue of *Amazing Science Fiction*, the term quickly became the referent "for any slightly edgy artistic or cultural practice concerned with computers and/or the relationships between technology and the body" (Bould 217), but when Gardner Dozois co-opted it in a *Washington Post* article he wrote in 1984, it was to indicate the body of work produced in those years by a loosely connected group of writers comprising, among others, William Gibson, Bruce Sterling, and Greg Bear. In its literary form, cyberpunk fiction practiced an uneasy, conflict-ridden marriage between the two realities hinted at in its composite name: cybernetics, "a term coined in 1948 by Norbert Wiener to describe a new science devoted to the study of communication and control systems in animals and machines" (Bould 218), and punk, originally meant as the rock movement of the 1970s but later expanded to include the various moral and attitudinal characteristics typical of a generally termed punk world view: behavior deemed criminal by bourgeois society, alternate sexualities, distrust of governments, random violence, and rage against the world machine. The first part of its name gave cyberpunk the technology: implants, cyberspace decks, the matrix, software, computer viruses, drugs, and sense enhancements. The second gave it its environment, a benighted worldwide landscape of balkanized nations, giant corporations, endemic crime, and polluted mega-cities where, from the dizzying arcological heights of privately owned skyscrapers, the affluent look down on filth-chocked streets where a teeming criminal underclass conducts its nightly transactions. There are shades of Philip K. Dick's paranoid surveillance visions in cyberpunk, of J.G. Ballard's dilapidated capital-scapes, of *Blade Runner*'s perpetually rain-drenched streets, and of Raymond Chandler's desperate human relationships, all merged together and presented to the reader through a sensual, logo-conscious narrative style "in which one does not switch on a computer but jacks into an Ono-Sendai Cyberspace 7" (Bould 220–221).

Surrounding this entropic near future, existing above and beyond and beneath its visible planes, is the glittering waltz of data intercourse, the only form of truly valuable currency this world knows. Most of this waltz is conducted in cyberspace, a hard-SF retrofit of Ballard's inner space in the form of a virtual locale where the neurons in the human brain interface and communicate with pure data, "A consensual hallucination experienced daily by billions of legitimate operators, in every nation, by children being taught mathematical concepts.... A graphic representation of data abstracted from the banks of every computer in the human system. Unthinkable complexity. Lines of light ranged in the nonspace of the mind, clusters and constellations of data. Like city lights, receding" (51). This oft-quoted passage from William Gibson's *Neuromancer* (1984), the novel commonly thought to have officially begun cyberpunk, constitutes a good example of the kind of writing practiced by those authors who, with varying degrees of comfort, identified themselves as belonging to the movement. Cyberpunk as a whole was not particularly invested in extrapolating the social impact of contemporary software-based technology in order to craft a new way of talking to the world of tomorrow. Rather, it "o'erleaped the sheer vast mundanity of the information explosion, in order to create a *noir* megalopolis of inner space, imaginatively dense but clearly not directed towards explicating or illuminating the revolutions in the routines of individual and corporate life.... Cyberpunk did not domesticate the future. It treated the future as a god" (Clute, *Scores* 67–68). Ultimately, the gift of cyberpunk to science fiction consisted in the creation of the language necessary to talk technology in the information age, an electrically charged info-lingo with a new syntax, a new terminology, a new form of sentence structure, and newly configured semiotic connections to the meanings of the future. The writers in the movement may not have set out to expressly save SF from itself, but they did provide a fundamental contribution. They found a genre-derived channel for expressing their desires, and used it until cyberpunk, like the New Wave that had influenced it, merged with science fiction as a whole to became yet another of its many voices, new mulch for the growth of new stories. After cyberpunk's breakaway stance gradually changed throughout the 1980s to become dialogue, other writers, more directly tied to older concerns but at the same time able to express them through the lens of the new language of the world, created a body of work that propelled SF into the 1990s and, subsequently, the 21st century.

One of these writers is Vernor Vinge. A computer scientist by profession (until 2000, when he retired, he was professor of mathematics and computer science at San Diego State University), Vinge had published in 1981 a novella entitled *True Names*, one of the very first prefigurations of cyberspace and computer networks. At the time of publication, the story had not received any particular amount of attention, but after the advent of cyberpunk — which had absorbed from it a number of tropes and concerns — and the birth of the World Wide Web, it steadily increased in recognition until, in 2007, it received the Prometheus Hall of Fame Award for the foresight of its central themes. Vinge, not a dedicated language stylist or pop culture enthusiast like the majority of the cyberpunks, had called cyberspace "the other plane," while the cyberspace cowboys of Gibson and Sterling's novels were simply called "wizards." While his terminology was far from hokey or poorly chosen, it also lacked the sensuality and logo-heavy gleam of the cyberpunks' nomenclature, and therefore did not initially impact the genre with nearly the same power. Vinge, however, kept writing, and during the eighties published two linked novels, *The Peace War* (1984) and *Marooned in Realtime* (1986), which together constitute the first attempt in his maturity as a writer[7] to work his ideas on the information-based advances of the next century into the fabric of science fiction.

Then, in 1992, came *A Fire Upon the Deep*, the novel that propelled Vinge to the forefront of hard-SF speculation and almost single-handedly rejuvenated the sub-genre of space opera, which many had considered defunct in the wake of the information revolution. Arguably, *Fire*'s greatest achievement is in its setup. In the world Vinge created as a playground for his story, the Milky Way is divided into four main zones, each characterized by the different limitations it imposes on the laws of physics. The inner zone, comprising the center of the galaxy and most of its stellar mass, is so weighed down by the clasp of gravity that neither ftl travel nor complex technologies are possible. Wrapped around this area — aptly called the Unthinking Depths — is the Slow Zone, a realm of galactic space where stellar mass, and therefore its gravitational attraction, are less cloying. Thus, while the speed of light is still an absolute, some lower forms of artificial intelligence and other complex technologies can be achieved:

Surrounding in turn the Slow Zone ... is the Beyond, which is far greater in compass than the inner zones but includes far fewer stars. Here the speed of light is not an absolute, and can be exceeded. Here it is possible for higher machineries and sentiences to be manufactured and to take cognizance of their tasks, for in the Beyond it is possible for genuinely significant amounts of information to be gathered, compacted, conveyed, assimilated. Finally, surrounding the Beyond, is the Transcend, where the Universe is permitted to know itself through the self-explorations of Powers, who reside there in an intolerable access of clarity. They represent the natural state of self-knowledge of the universe as an information system [Clute, *Evidence* 365–366].

The plausibility of a physical model of the galaxy with such special limiting conditions is at best shaky, but since Ballard's pithy assessment of the value of accuracy in SF, the stigma placed upon self-declared science fictional material that does not conform to its rules has lost much of its power. Besides Vinge, by and large a far more accurate SF writer than most, knew perfectly well what kind of world he had created, and thus worked this awareness into the fabric of the story. The galaxy of *A Fire Upon the Deep* is inherently story-friendly, a place for narratives to thrive, because just like them it is built around a scaffold made of pure information. The novel thrusts the dense, data-rich semiotics of works like *Neuromancer* toward a new way of describing the descendants of those "steam-snorting wonders of the past" that Bruce Sterling had disparaged in his cyberpunk manifesto, thus enabling the classic hard SF/Space Opera environment to keep playing with its almighty toys while at the same time functionally grappling with the cogencies of data interaction. Later on, in 1998, Vinge wrote a prequel to *Fire*. Entitled *A Deepness in the Sky*, the story once again utilizes a space opera–derived plot to reflect on the nature of pure information and on the exchanges taking place between its bodily carriers, only this time doing so not from the rarefied heights of the beyond, but from the treacle-thick depths of the slow zone.

Vinge's renovation of the hard SF/Space Opera sub-genres was accompanied by the works of writers who had started their careers between the late seventies and the mid–'80s, writers like Greg Bear, Kim Stanley Robinson, and Iain M. Banks, who in their respective bodies of work engaged the information revolution in a discourse similar to Vinge's, but filtered through their specific sensibilities. They would have been comparative rarities in classic science fiction, writers with a background in literature and the social sciences who nevertheless have published many of the most relevant works of hard SF of the past thirty years: Bear's *Blood Music* and *Eon* (both 1985), Robinson's *Mars* trilogy (1992–1996), and Banks's *Culture* series (1987–present). Taken together, their work displays the full retrofit of classic SF themes with the extrapolation in dramatic form of the actualities of life in the industrialized West during the last quarter of the twentieth century: information-based technologies, environmental husbanding, pollution and global warming, the energy crisis, democracy and economic imperialism, the arms race, utopian desires, and dystopian realities. To them we should add William Gibson and Bruce Sterling, who evolved the affiliation with cyberpunk of their early years into a more direct relationship with the near-future worlds their SF had begun to anticipate at the beginning of the nineties. Of the two, Sterling is the more relevant for the purposes of this work because of his novella *Taklamakan* (1998), an intelligent reworking of the generation starship concept for the information age.

Only seven generation starship narratives appeared between 1980 and 2000, a substantial drop from the previous era. Moreover, a look at their chronological distribution will quickly reveal an anomaly: the first story, Damien Broderick's *The Dreaming Dragons*, was published in 1980, while the second, Thomas Hubschman's *Space Ark*, appeared in 1981, the year of *True Names* and of William Gibson's first professional magazine sale, "The Gernsback Continuum." Then nothing until 1990, when Robert J. Sawyer's *Golden Fleece* saw print, and after that the remaining stories in 1991, 1993–96, 1998, and 2000. In other words, the science fiction of the period between the birth of cyberpunk and the beginning of what we might call the contemporary era was largely devoid of generation starship narratives, while the last decade of the twentieth century slowly witnessed the return of the sub-genre. After fifty years of steady growth, both in the numbers of stories published and in the overall quality of these stories, the presence of generation starships on the bookshelves had suddenly grown sparse. Why?

We can speculate. As we have seen in the previous chapters, the number of generation starship stories started out very small and gradually increased until, during the twenty-two years comprising the advent of the New Wave and the gradual restructuring of the genre (1957–1979), almost two dozen narratives appeared, double the frequency of the Campbell era and about ten times that of the Gernsback age. Explaining this sharp spike by pointing to the growth of the publishing market during the fifties (as the overall number of science fiction narratives increased, the argument would go, so did the number of stories in the generation starship sub-genre) would only work if this trend had continued between 1980 and 2000. Instead, there was no marked loss of publication venues for SF during the last twenty years of the century, certainly nothing that could explain an almost fourfold decrease in the appearance of generation starship stories, so any explanations for this state of affairs must lie elsewhere.

It may be possible to find such an explanation if we examine the differences between the debate that had opposed the writers of classic SF with those of the New Wave and the struggle that later pitted the writers of the eighties against the Great Old Ones from the dawn of genre. On the one hand, the birth and development of the New Wave had not been an isolated phenomenon, something exclusively internal to the prevailing dynamics of science fiction at the time. It had been part of the much wider social upheavals that had involved the industrialized West in a painful critique of the world order it had helped to establish at the end of World War II, and of the Cold War mindset it had created to justify and sustain the basic structure of that order. This critique had quickly taken the form of a rift separating the postwar generation — those Stephen King had called "war babies" in his recollections of October 1957 — from their parents, who had fought and won the war only to find themselves in a worldwide political landscape constantly overshadowed by the specter of nuclear annihilation. Painting with a very broad brush, we could say that the cultural climate of the 1960s had been characterized by the refusal of the postwar generation to follow the mission statement their parents had bequeathed them — the objective of the mission was questionable, the destination would probably be an irradiated wasteland, and the means to get there were the products of a carefully glossed-over retrofit of the same Nazi power-lust that had triggered the whole mess to begin with. Outside science fiction, the generational rift had taken various forms of social and political protest, according to the shape of events as they had unfolded and the kind of triggers that had stimulated the responses. Within SF, as we have seen, the rift had shaped itself as the opposition between the representatives of classic (or Campbellian) SF and those supporting the New Wave's break with tradition, and at this point we can advance the hypothesis that the proliferation of generation starship narratives during this period had depended on the subgenre's specific characteristics, which had made it uniquely suited to provide a dramatic representation of this opposition. Looking at "Lungfish," "The Wind Blows Free," *Non-Stop*, "Thirteen to Centaurus," and indeed at the majority of generation starship stories that appeared during the sixties and seventies, it is clear that most of them shared one common trait: they were family dramas writ large, parables of generational fracture in which the wishes of the parents proved pernicious to the well-being of their children. Previous narratives of this kind had cast those wishes as the story of origin to be regained, not as the great mistake to be repaired: Gregory Grimstone, Hugh Hoyland, Jon Hoff, Mathew Kendrick, and John Smith had all been agents of generational continuity, there to ensure that the thread of memory was either kept unbroken or, if broken, re-knit. The Tripborn, Samuel Kingsley, and Roy Complain were, on the other hand, embodiments of the yearning for a break, for a recasting of the trip's priorities in the wake of changed circumstances. Therefore, the narratives they inhabited became territories of struggle between the future of desire and the future of fate, the one embodied by the parents and the other by the children, who in turn had their own future of desire by whose dictates to steer the ship, either in the direction of a voyage home or toward greater star-strewn horizons. This interpretation may also account for the high number of key writers of that time — Ballard, Delany, Harrison, Brunner, and Aldiss among many others — who had contributed stories to the sub-genre.

By contrast, the fundamental changes operating within the SF of the eighties did not channel their impact along the axis of a generational rift, because the trigger of the crisis was itself independent of human agency. While the New Wave had embodied a set of decisions originating from human agents for artistic and cultural reasons, and therefore indicative of a generational rift, the information revolution happened to everyone, young and old. Thus, the genre found its entire body of assumptions challenged, not just those of a select viewpoint within it. Moreover, the onset of the new era cast some relevant doubts on the very nature of advocacy for the future, and once again that advocacy was something common to everyone. For all its revolutionary charge and antiauthoritarian streak, the New Wave had expressed just as strong a sense of direction for SF as the Campbellian school of thought had nurtured a generation before. Both attitudes featured an overarching body of beliefs as to what the future should be, where it should go, and how science fiction was supposed to express it. Now, in the wake of an exponential growth in the number of decentralized — and therefore opaque to grand narratives — sources of information, science fictional advocacy was becoming a function of personal desire, not of the desire of a collective entity like a magazine, a publisher, or a school of thought. There were too many voices now, and too many plausible, desirable, or simply relevant futures for advocacy to exert the pervasive kind of control it had been able to bring to bear in the past. The information revolution kept desire contained, made it less boorishly sure of itself than before, and in a strangely positive contradictory development, enhanced its effectiveness, because now it was no longer necessary to rationalize its presence as the requirement of a didactic function.

Since the new axis of change was independent of generational struggles, and since the generation starship sub-genre was chiefly concerned with presenting dramatic extrapolations of the possibilities inherent in a specific form of space travel, the eighties found themselves having little use for the lens through which it viewed the future. The focus was simply somewhere else. In the nineties, however, as Vernor Vinge and others gave spacefaring SF a new voice with which to articulate tomorrow, things started changing for the better. Although still very few in comparison to the recent past, generation starship narratives made a comeback in the form of three stories of substantial quality from three writers of substantial skill.

In 1991, Frank M. Robinson returned to generation starship stories with *The Dark Beyond the Stars*, a novel-length reflection on classic SF's grand narrative of space flight that openly displayed its debt to "The Oceans Are Wide." The generation starship *Astron* has been in space for two thousand years. Originally sent out in search of life outside Earth, the vessel, traveling at an appreciable fraction of the speed of light, has scoured the sectors of space nearest the solar system without success. Now Earth itself is a dim memory, an uncertain destination for those among the crew who feel that their mission has become hollow and that they should return home, but no less uncertain than the territory awaiting the ship should those who want to keep going have their way: the Dark, an enormous gulf of utterly starless space that would take the *Astron* a thousand generations to cross. The choice between returning to an Earth nobody among the crew has ever seen and attempting a twenty-thousand-year trek across yawning nothingness, already difficult in and of itself, is further complicated by the state of the ship. Carefully crafted holographic projections, designed to show the inside of the vessel as it looked when it was new, hide dark, malfunctioning corridors and gradually failing machinery. The air smells stale and heavy, and the environmental control systems are no longer able to cope with the task of maintaining stable climatic conditions throughout the inhabited areas. As a result of this parlous state of repair, the path the crew of the *Astron* will decide to take, whatever the risks involved in the decision, will be a path of no return. Either the ship leaves near-Earth space forever, or it returns to Earth forever.

The Dark Beyond the Stars is narrated in the first person by seventeen-year-old Sparrow. At the beginning of the story, Sparrow has a near-death experience on the latest planet visited by the *Astron*, and upon awakening in the ship's sick bay, he finds out that the accident has deprived him of every memory preceding planetfall. As he slowly begins to reacquaint himself with the circumstances of his life and of the *Astron*'s mission, Sparrow must relearn the complex network of customs regulating the small, closed shipboard community. These customs, developed over the centuries out of the necessity to make the fairly limited confines of the *Astron* livable without excessive strife, have shaped the crew into a deeply caring community. There are still plenty of enmities and fights, but thanks to a powerful taboo against taking someone's life, the end results of these incidents are far less deadly and traumatic than they were, for example, onboard the *Astra* in "The Oceans Are Wide." Also, at the same time as the crew developed their taboo against killing, they also lifted many of the taboos concerning sex, which has gradually become the great outlet for pent-up emotions. Ship's custom dictates that "nobody onboard the *Astron* ever turns anybody down the first time. Nobody. And nobody asks the second time unless they've been assured it's mutual" (99).

Besides reinforcing the bond uniting the crew, the mixture of deep familiarity and fundamental respect for one's wishes resulting from this arrangement has the added effect of making rape as unthinkable as murder.

Despite the basically caring nature of shipboard life, however, Sparrow gradually becomes aware of the increasing tension between the pro–Dark and pro–Earth factions in the crew. As the Dark looms ahead and the time for the final decision regarding the continuation of the *Astron*'s mission approaches, the friction pitting the two sides against one another turns into an openly acknowledged mutiny, and only the social dictates against excessive violence prevent the situation from spiraling out of control. The pro–Dark faction has the advantage, because Michael Kusaka, the ship's captain, is by far the staunchest supporter of this choice. Possessed of a magnetic personality and the ability to inspire the utmost devotion, Kusaka has so far been able to shape the *Astron*'s course according to his desires, and for a while he convinces Sparrow as well when, in their first meeting after the accident, he brings the full force of his personality to bear on the young man's imagination. "There's no event in human history as important to the race as the task of this ship," Kusaka tells Sparrow before proceeding to give him a view of mankind's manifest destiny in space that would have pleased John W. Campbell:

> "It's vast beyond imagining, Sparrow — a galaxy teeming with billions of stars and millions of planets and hundreds of thousands of civilizations and untold numbers of creatures that crawl or swim or fly or live out their lives in the muck." There was a note of exaltation in his voice, and I stared at him with awe. His head was silhouetted against the vast field of stars, his face backlit by the faint glow from the plotting globe behind us, his mouth open, his eyes glittering in the semidarkness. "Do you ever wonder what we'll discover, Sparrow? ... Most of those civilizations will be friendly. Some of them won't. Whatever the case, we'll be the first to take back word that we're not alone, that the same God that guides our destinies guides theirs as well" [49].

Kusaka is a Campbellian true believer of the first order. After two thousand years of nothing at all, of dashed hopes and frustrated expectations, he is still convinced beyond the dimmest shadow of a doubt not only that the galaxy is full of life, but also that it is mankind's destiny to go find that life and return to Earth with the news — the part of mankind, that is, which comprises the *Astron* and its crew. As he tells Sparrow at the end of his speech, "Your name will go down in history.... So will mine and that of everybody else on board" (49). But Kusaka is something more than simply an inspirational leader with a silver tongue and a flair for the dramatic: he is also functionally immortal, the only one among the crew to have undergone a series of medical treatments resulting in a greatly increased lifespan — an advantage that gives the captain the same kind of perspective over the lives of his crew that Predict

Smith had enjoyed onboard the *Astra* in "The Oceans Are Wide." Moreover, he is the only one with direct access to the *Astron*'s computer system, through which he controls everything from navigation and propulsion to hydroponics and life support. This power of life and death over everyone onboard is the one factor that has enabled Kusaka and his faction to retain control for as long as they have. Numerically inferior to the part of the crew that wants to return, they would otherwise have already lost command of the ship.

For the time being, however, the captain has things his way. Noah, one of the leaders of the pro–Earth faction, does not have the power to successfully oppose him, and Kusaka's oratorical skills are developed enough to allow him to make a strong case for his view of the *Astron*'s destination. The effectiveness of his emplotment is such that, at the end of their interview, Sparrow leaves the captain's cabin fully persuaded of the need to go on regardless of risk or cost. However, with the passing of the days he realizes that, noble as Kusaka's desires for the future may be, they fly in the face of the reality of their circumstances. As the novel progresses and the evidence mounts, it becomes clear beyond reasonable doubt that, were the *Astron* to attempt to negotiate the Dark, there would be nobody alive to explore the star systems on the other side. Moreover, Sparrow's slowly returning memory carries with it recollections of events that took place more than seventeen years before. He has flashes of himself as someone other than Sparrow in several previous lives, and Noah keeps telling him that the number of these lives goes much further back than he currently remembers — all the way back, in fact, to the beginning of the generation starship's flight. "You're of immense value to the *Astron*," Noah tells Sparrow, and this very value is the reason why some crewmembers unthinkably want him dead: "they're afraid of what's buried in your memories" (179). Indeed, Sparrow finds out that, for reasons as yet unknown, his lifespan is as long as Kusaka's — every twenty years or so, by order of the captain himself, his memory is flatlined and a new accident manufactured to explain the loss. He becomes another crewmember with another name, and the cycle goes on and on. When he confronts Ophelia, the ship's doctor who performed the latest mind-wipe, she explains that the lives of the people onboard the *Astron* "are exactly like the lives of the generation before us. They're very structured, limited lives. They can't be anything else. They're the result of two thousand years of ship culture. But you lived your life back on Earth. You're very ... unstructured. You're very human. Watching you reminds us of what it's like" (166). Thus, while Kusaka embodies in his person the physical powers of the Predict from "The Oceans Are Wide," Sparrow embodies the Predict's psychological value. He is the living instinctual memory of Earth, the last exemplar of a behavioral model that no longer exists onboard the *Astron*, and the captain cannot fulfill this role because, having been constantly awake for two thousand years, he has become too much like the rest of the crew. That Ophelia, a doctor in a community like the *Astron*'s, would even think about doing something like this to another human being is explainable in terms of the crew's partial loss of their institutional memory; as Ophelia herself tells Sparrow, "centuries ago you must have volunteered for it! You knew what it was all about back then — you're the feedback loop that keeps us all human" (165–166). Sparrow may not remember it yet, but the person he had been at the very beginning had seemingly made that decision for all his future selves.

Meanwhile, Kusaka's attitude gradually shifts from inspirational to dictatorial. When his entreaties and starry-eyed speeches start failing to persuade the growing number of crewmembers who believe that crossing the Dark would be suicide, when he finds his desires threatened, he breaks the taboo against killing by executing the leaders of the mutiny, and accuses Sparrow of being part of it. In fact, he is more correct than he knows: instead of simply being one of the mutineers, Sparrow becomes their leader in the wake of a traumatic return of memory, when the recollections of all his lives come flooding back and he remembers his original identity, the one that has made him the decisive factor in the struggle for control of the *Astron*: "My name was Raymond Stone. I was thirty years old. I was the return captain of the *Astronomy* and it was long past time to take her home" (363). The *Astronomy* had never been intended to run for two thousand years — only for forty. It had also never been intended as a generation starship. Sparrow/Stone, the other long-lived human onboard, was slated to take over from Kusaka at the end of the ship's patrol period and take it back to Earth, but Kusaka had refused to yield command. At that point, part of the crew had mutinied against him, choosing Stone as their leader. They had lost, and Kusaka had begun his long reign as captain of a generation starship, knowing full well that the *Astronomy*'s redundancies could keep it flying a lot longer than forty years, and that the crew constituted a ready source of new generations that could continue the trip. He had killed the rest of the return crew and forced the others to breed generation after generation of descendants, but had kept Stone alive in case something happened to him — even in mutiny, Kusaka's obsession toward the mission had overridden the pragmatism that would otherwise have prompted him to simply have Stone killed. He had ordered the crew's doctors to regularly wipe his mind clean of memories, each time inventing an accident that could explain away both his mental state and his continued youthfulness, and kept on exploring. In time, Kusaka had remained the only one onboard able to directly remember the mutiny and the *Astronomy*'s original name. Everyone else was long gone, their descendants had seemingly forgotten, and Stone's mind was locked away in its prison of artificially constructed multiple lives.

But the crew had not forgotten — not entirely, at least. However dimly, they had retained a certain awareness of how the events leading to their present circumstances had come to pass, and that somehow the near-immortal crewmember who had originally been Raymond Stone was crucial to their hopes of returning to Earth one day. That knowledge had slowly become corrupted, so that Ophelia's description of Sparrow/Stone's role as the link to Earth had remained the only explanation for his repeated forgetfulness cycles, but it had not died away entirely. Noah and the other leaders of the mutiny had known that the key to going home lay in Stone's mind; if their generation no longer remembered quite why he was so fundamental, he did, in some hidden nook of his multi-chambered memory. They — and their ancestors before them — had waited patiently across centuries in the void for Stone to recover that one moment in time and, once in full possession of his identity, confront the captain with their desire to return to Earth. Now the wait is over, and Stone meets Kusaka in the captain's cabin. During their exchange, before Stone kills him in single combat, Kusaka reveals that the *Astronomy* had been the only survivor of the space program's death throes: the lunar and planetary colonies in the solar system had all failed, and the *Astronomy*'s successor, a larger and more capable ship originally intended to fulfill the same function as its predecessor, had been scrapped before the hull was completed. This disheartening string of failures had only incensed the Ahab-like Kusaka, making him all the more committed to continuing their mission until some form of life somewhere had been found.

Now, however, two thousand years of failures leer at the *Astronomy* and its crew, while a suicidal twenty-thousand-year jaunt awaits them all on the other side of home. Stone kills Kusaka, takes control of the computer using his privileges as the return captain, and plots a course that will take them back home, finally fulfilling the role that should have been his centuries before. As the decades pass in the long trip back, every one of his friends, lovers, and enemies passes away, leaving their descendants to continue the voyage, and Stone experiences part of what Kusaka had gone through as the only immortal onboard a ship of ephemerals. Finally, however, the *Astronomy* reaches Earth, now seemingly uninhabited or at least devoid of any sign of industrialized settlements. There, at the end of the trip and on the last page of the novel, a surprise awaits the crew when they find that "Sweeping into view, thrusting out from the terminator that gradually crept over the world below, was the outline of a huge, alien ship. Something from Outside had beat us home" (408).

Thus the voyage of the *Astronomy* ends in long-delayed success, as the plot of *The Dark Beyond the Stars* slingshots us into yet another future. Although we would be doing Robinson a considerable disservice if we thought of his novel simply as a way to make up for the inconsistencies in the ideological resolution of "The Oceans Are Wide" (as if, disappointed by his own thinking in 1954, he had decided to finally do it right), it would also be inaccurate not to acknowledge the parallels the two stories share. The most important is arguably the relationship between Kusaka and Sparrow/Stone, which is an almost exact counterpart of the relationship between Predict Smith and Mathew Kendrick in the earlier narrative. Both stories begin with the figure of Smith/Kusaka as the transcendental power presiding over the lives of their starship's crew, while the ancillary figure of Kendrick/Stone begins in the role of young ward — a ward who, moreover, has just survived a very close brush with death. Each story develops as a sort of Bildungsroman in space, in which the ward figure meets the Predict figure for the first time, is informed of the reason why the ship exists and where it is going, and subsequently starts learning the hows and whys of the world around him.

However, here the two narratives diverge: while Smith is following the original plan laid out for his generation starship, Kusaka has betrayed his duty. The *Astra* is on course, the *Astronomy* is not. Therefore, while Matty Kendrick's role is to obediently learn the lessons Smith teaches him and follow to the letter the Predict's instructions, the learning path upon which Sparrow/Stone embarks must necessarily lead him toward rebellion against Kusaka. Kendrick and Stone are agents of the status quo, even in defiance: when Kendrick unseats Smith as Predict and injects himself with the immortality serum, he is still following the other's plan. Tired and weary after five hundred years of iron-fisted rule over the people of the *Astra*, Smith wants to be free of the burden, so he creates the conditions necessary for an uprising and then lets events take the course he knows they will. Kusaka, on the other hand, has done the exact opposite: he has created an artificial situation in which he will not have to relinquish his power past the time allotted to him, so Sparrow/Stone's rebellion takes the classical form of an upsetting of the ruling power's schemes.

Ultimately, however, *The Dark Beyond the Stars* is a narrative of the 1990s, not a throwback to an earlier era. That Robinson's two generation starship narratives are outwardly alike only serves to highlight their deeper, more fundamental differences as stories written in — and for — two different stages in the development of science fiction. First of all, the perennial preoccupation of generation starship narratives, the retention or recovery of memory, is here played within a post-cyberpunk context on two interconnected levels: Sparrow/Stone's struggle to regain his memory and sense of identity against the scaffold of false lives with which Kusaka has burdened him, and his society's struggle to regain their memory as the crew of the *Astronomy* against the artificial set of conditions grafted onto their existence, again through Kusaka's agency. Since the passing of the generations has eroded the crew's recollections beyond the point of full recovery, and since Kusaka erased all traces of the first mutiny from the computer's memory banks, the second level is dependent on the first to completely succeed. Therefore, the overarching narrative thrust of *The Dark Beyond the Stars* utilizes Sparrow/Stone's struggle for recovery as a microcosm of the larger drama, and the participation in it of everyone onboard serves to efficiently dramatize the dynamics of hope and despair as they play themselves out among the crew, following Stone's alternating fortunes on their way to a final resolution.

Secondly, despite its respect for the proper chain of command and for the wishes of the motherland, the novel also exposes the Campbellian vision of a universe ripe for human colonization as a conceit. The speech Kusaka gives Sparrow at the beginning of the novel is not only the product of an obsessive psyche trying to turn the evidence of failure into the certainty of success; it is also the result of a willful act of denial. As the captain already knows perfectly well, the classic SF emplotment on which his case depends had died before the first mutiny: in a Ballardian plot twist, the planetary colonies had failed, the *Astronomy*'s sister ship had been scrapped, and Earth had turned its back on the two first steps in Wollheim's consensus history of the Campbellian future — colonization of the solar system and discovery of alien races. Moreover, the narrative's dramatic resolution can be read as irony of a particularly cruel bent: all those centuries in the void, all those lives gobbled up by hungry light-years of fruitless search, all the suffering endured in the name of a seemingly bankrupt idea, and the aliens have decided to pay us a visit at home. The end of the long trip seems to make the lives of everyone onboard the *Astronomy* pointless in the face of a cosmic joke. Gregory Grimstone would probably have sympathized.

However, an alternate reading is possible as well. The third — and probably most important — line of divergence between *The Dark Beyond the Stars* and "The Oceans Are Wide" consists in the gradual evolution of the *Astronomy*'s crew into its own social reality, with its own mores and values developed as a direct result of their specific environmental conditions. In this respect, the collective of *The Dark* could not be more different than the monolithic society of the *Astra* in Robinson's previous narrative, essentially kept unchanged over five hundred years of isolated flight by the implacable will of the Predict. So implacable, indeed, that when the ship finds a paradise planet where its crew would have the chance to truly develop along an independent line from that of their ancestors, Smith exerts his power to irreparably strand everyone on a hellhole world where they will be forced to replicate the evolution of humans on Earth, with all the implications that decision entails. The *Astronomy*'s crew, on the other hand, has created its own social reality over the centuries, partly reacting to their situation and, curiously enough, partly responding to the same kind of dictatorial will that had kept the lives of their literary counterparts static. More importantly, the collective that emerges as a result of those pressures corresponds in several aspects to the kind of more mature society whose development Predict Smith should have encouraged onboard the *Astra*. They are basically caring, nonviolent people, and the violence that does break out as a result of Kusaka's attempts to frustrate their desires is experienced as a deeply traumatic event, something to be ended as quickly as possible and never repeated again. If considered within the context of the crew's social progress, even that seemingly negative twist at the end becomes something more than just a slap in the face: the behavior of the *Astra*'s collective, virtually identical to the pathologically aggressive model that had spelled the doom of their ancestors, would have followed the Predict's instructions in their dealings with the aliens, and those instruction would probably have entailed an aggressive, muscular stance based on Smith's faux-Darwinian notions of life as an inevitable struggle. In other words, they would probably have turned first contact into the first interstellar war. Now, at the end of a long period of painfully learned lessons, the crew of the *Astronomy* has the chance to craft a more complex response to the presence of another sentient race, irrespective of whether the aliens themselves are friendly or otherwise. Reading "The Oceans Are Wide" and *The Dark Beyond the Stars* one after the other is an instructive experience. It provides us with a clearly written, cogently argued case study of the changes that have taken place both in generation starship narratives and in science fiction as a whole between the Campbell era and the end of the century, when the long light-years stopped being susceptible to constant trimming on the Procrustean bed of advocacy and became a more neutral territory for the exploration of a multiplicity of possible futures.

Taklamakan — or rather, the Taklamakan — is an actual place. It is the world's 17th largest desert, situated in the Xinjiang Uyghur Autonomous Region of the People's Republic of China, and its name is a borrowing from the Arabic *tark*, "to leave alone/behind," and *makan*, "place." Thus, a rough and admittedly self-serving translation of the name into English would mean something like "the place where you get left behind." Not a particularly auspicious meaning for the people inhabiting the generation starships in Bruce Sterling's 1998 novella *Taklamakan*.

Spider Pete and Katrinko are "urban intrusion freaks" (858), rock-and-wall-climbing, thieving, data-hoarding infiltration specialists from the stick-to-the-skin technology havens of the North America of the year 2052. They are the literary children of the street samurais from the flashpoint years of cyberpunk, with their digital camouflage suits out of *Neuromancer*'s Panther

Moderns, their data-heavy postindustrial lingo, the physical skills to match the talk, and biotechnological mission gear out of Apple's wildest miniaturization fantasies: silicone anti-evaporant, gelbrain cameras, pre-programmed neural tissue, gelcam drills running on sugar enzymes, Fremen stillsuit analogues to recycle bodily water, and subcutaneous lumps of fat to survive without food. If the cyberspace cowboys of the eighties used their neural interfaces to crack the ICE (Intrusion Countermeasures Electronics) defending the valuable data banks of corporations or national agencies, the urban intruders of Sterling's novella use their biotech to interface with the otherwise information-deaf skin of the Taklamakan, surviving on it, absorbing data, and scanning the landscape for telltale traces of their mission objective, an enormous Chinese rocket base buried somewhere under the desert surface.

When Pete and Katrinko find the smashed landing pod containing the pulped remains of the Lieutenant Colonel who was supposed to take command of their mission, they decide to go on alone. They find the entrance to the underground complex, and inside it the mummified bodies of three men who had climbed and hacked their way out from below, only to die of exhaustion and hunger in front of the final wall separating them from the surface. After tracing the escapees' path back to its beginning, slithering and rappelling past the lenses of long-dead surveillance and alarm systems, Pete and Katrinko finally break through the wall of the underground complex into an impossibly vast cavern. Its ceiling is painted black and festooned with artificial lights made to replicate the constellations, and in the middle of the enormous space "were three great glowing lozenges, three vertical cylinders the size of urban high rises. They seemed to be suspended in midair. 'Starships,' Pete muttered. 'Starships,' Katrinko agreed" (864).

In 1962, J. G. Ballard had written a generation starship narrative that cast the idea of the human adventure in space as a claustrophobic experiment in the dynamics of isolation, the stage for a mind game whose state of profound psychological entrapment belied the multiple exits it possessed in the physical world. Now, almost forty years later and in another country, the game of generational entrapment is still on, but the scale of the project and the reasons for its undertaking have changed. The three starships in front of Pete and Katrinko's eyes are enormous, and contain entire populations of undesirables, ethnic separatists who would not change the way they live, would not let the twenty-first century absorb them like the rest of the Sphere (or Asian Cooperation Sphere, 2052's name for the political entity of which today's China is the controlling member), and would fight constantly to retain their identity. Accordingly, their motherland had seen fit to eliminate them without compromising deniability: no pogroms, no camps, and no shanty towns in appallingly unsanitary conditions — in other words, nothing that could have caused outrage in other countries. Just a relocation program at the end of which the undesirables were gone without leaving the slightest trace, either on the light-sensitive camera lenses of a spy sat or on the conscience of the world's public opinion. "Means, motive, and opportunity," Spider Pete tells an incredulous Katrinko when she[8] points out the craziness of the idea (875). And indeed, the people onboard the three immobile generation starships seem to have been abandoned to their fate; the surveillance and alarm equipment is dead, and the camera eyes placed here and there in the caverns and inside the vessels have either been destroyed by the inmates or ceased functioning because of neglect. Apart from its prisoners, the place has been devoid of human presence for years.

But there are other presences. The Sphere executives who had devised the complex and the ships had also decided to provide a measure of security without having to tie up valuable human resources. The bottom of the cave is "an unearthly drowned maze of shattered cracks and chemical deposition, all turned to simmering tidepools of mechanical self-assemblage" that regularly give birth to strange biomechanical robots (870). The robots are dumb machines with elementary brains, programmed to fulfill one overriding task: to keep the undesirables inside the ships. To that effect, they tirelessly patrol the cave and the surface of the vessels in their thousands, sniffing and probing the air and the rock with their feelers, suckers, antennas, and other protuberances of incomprehensible origin. When they find something extraneous to the materials they have been programmed to consider standard — for example a gelcam, a rappel, or a whole human infiltrator — they destroy it, break it down into its component parts, and then bring it back to the digestion pools of protein-rich goo, where the semi-sentient, decentralized intelligence at work making the robots will study their biochemical composition and use it to make new machines with previously unknown abilities. Pete and Katrinko find this out at their expense when, on their way down to look inside the starships, they run afoul of a group of robots. Bruised and wounded, they manage to escape, but not before the robots eat almost all their gear.

Even without most of their equipment, Pete and Katrinko are still infiltration specialists, and breaking into the ships is not overly difficult for them. In the three giant vessels under the desert, Sterling has created a sort of pocket compendium of generation starship populations, a small metafictional showcase for the different social arrangements in previous narratives in the subgenre. The first ship they visit is populated by a society that could also have come out of "Universe/Common Sense," "Spacebred Generations," and "The Wind Blows Free":

> The Crew of the starship were preindustrial, tribal, Asian peasants. Men, women, old folks, little kids. [They] rose every single morning, as their hot

networks of wiring came alive in the ceiling. They would milk their goats. They would feed their sheep…. They tended melon vines and grew plums and hemp [873].

Besides taking care of fields and animals, the locals also spend a considerable amount of time and resources writing down everything they remember from outside, every scrap of information they have about the world they think they left behind. In a trick of reversal of forgetfulness similar to the one "Thirteen to Centaurus" had performed on the hapless crew of Abel's ship, the pre-industrial Asian society inside the first vessel Pete and Katrinko explore exists in a mind game that will never end; theirs are quiet lives, spent in seemingly contented resignation to their fate.

The second generation starship is an altogether different place. The hull is pitted and pockmarked by old explosions, its surface blistered by the hasty plug jobs the robots have had to carry out as a result. The inhabitants of this ship are, like Roy Complain's tribes in *Non-Stop*, a sort of nomadic warrior culture, and again like Roy's people, they are fully aware of living in a cage. The poor conditions of the hull are a direct outcome of their continued attempts to escape using crude but evidently effective battering rams. Every time they open a breach the robots swarm them, beat them back after a bitter skirmish, and then plug the hole again. As Pete and Katrinko infiltrate the second ship, another of these attempts is in progress, and they decide to help it along. Spooks they may be, all high-tech gear and *realpolitik* morals, but their literary DNA has been carefully engineered through years of refinement in the bionarrative labs of the cyberpunk movement, and they have more than their fair share of cyberspace cowboy, street samurai, and razorgirl traits in their personality. When the inmates of starship two hit the hull with their ram, a staggering explosion blows a huge hole in it, and the whole population of the vessel rushes out to engage the robot swarm in an almighty — albeit ultimately futile — battle for freedom. During the clash, the escapees manage to blow a hole in the third starship, at which point Pete and Katrinko enter it and find out that the vessel is a stinking tomb of scorched flesh. Everyone is dead, victims of a huge fire that, years before, had quickly enveloped their prison — an accident hinting at one of the possible fates of those generation starships in "The Oceans Are Wide" or "The Wind Blows Free" that had either come to grief or simply disappeared into the void, never to be heard from again. Katrinko dies as well, overcome by a combination of a bullet hit, the noxious air inside the ship, and the wounds she had suffered in their encounter with the robot patrol.

Spider Pete is now alone, both as a human being and as a professional. As a human being, he has nothing in common with those trapped inside the cavern. In fact, thanks to his camo suit they do not know he exists, and any attempt at communication on his part would be like initiating first contact with an alien race. As a professional, Pete's situation is even more complicated. Without the rest of his equipment there is little hope for him of making it through the Taklamakan desert, provided he could somehow escape the cavern, and even if he made it home, the documentary evidence he carries of the biomechanical self-assemblage pools could prove deadly. He and Katrinko had been sent to help another spy discover a superpower's military secret, a rocket base hidden somewhere in the Taklamakan, but what they actually stumbled upon "was an entire new means of industrial production ... tech of this level of revolutionary weirdness was not a spy thing, a sports thing, or a soldier thing. This was a big, big *money* thing. He might survive discovering it. He'd never get away with revealing it" (871). And the technological aspects of the secret, huge as they may be, are dwarfed by the political and social implications of the three giant ships which the biotech pools have been designed to guard:

> There just weren't that many people cooped up down here. Maybe fifteen thousand of them, tops. The Asian Sphere must have had tens of thousands of unassimilated tribal people.... And why stop at that point? This wasn't just an Asian problem. It was a very general problem. Ethnic, breakaway people who just plain couldn't, or wouldn't, play the twenty-first century's games [880].

At this point, the slightly paranoid mindset *Taklamakan* inherited from its cyberpunk roots migrates from Spider Pete's mind into our own, and starts working on the imagination. If one superpower could, why not the others? Suddenly our mind's eye is made to look along with Pete's, and see a planet Earth honeycombed with gigantic caverns, each one containing a small portion of the aggregate of our world's problematic ethnicities — the Zulus, maybe, or the Australian aborigines; or possibly gypsies, Native Americans, Basque separatists. All gone, all forgotten. Pete himself has become a political prisoner: like the people onboard the two remaining generation starships, he is now *persona non grata* in the world for whose benefit he had penetrated the cavern in the first place. Therefore, prompted as much by curiosity as by the desire to avoid succumbing to despair, he returns to starship one, and for a while amuses himself by exploiting the locals' superstitions to play a fundamentally innocent game of haunt-the-village. He steals small things, every now and then goes "boo" in front of the odd native, and haunts the local temple, politely refraining from taking advantage of the pretty young priestess in front of whom he manifests himself— when she goes into a religious rapture and duly offers her body for defilement, Pete simply tries to talk to her.

We will never know whether, given enough time, his attempts would have been successful. When Pete suddenly notices that something is draining power from the fake stars in the cavern ceiling, he realizes he is free. We readers have probably forgotten the bag of climbing and intelligence gear he and Katrinko had lost to the robots, but Sterling has not. In the wake of the nearly successful breakout of starship two's inmates, the biomechanical vats had gone into production overdrive to replenish their robots' depleted ranks with new, more evolved models. These new models did succeed in beating the humans back, once again sealing them inside their prison, but once their task was complete they did not return to their usual activities. Instead, as Pete looks on in awe, they "were migrating up the rocky walls, bounding, creeping, lurching, rappelling on a web of gooey ropes.... His equipment had fallen among them, been absorbed, and kicked open new doors of evolution ... with generations of focused human genius, and it was all about one concept: UP. Going up. Up and *out*" (882). The same nonsentient biomechanical tidepools that had previously designed generations of unquestioning jailers have now utilized the same processes to create, out of Pete and Katrinko's gear, a vast army of robot urban infiltrators, and now this army has broken through to the surface of the Taklamakan. As Pete emerges into the open air on the heels of the machine exodus, he sees lances of radiant energy from the Sphere's satellite weapons break open the sky in a belated, doomed attempt to keep the robots contained. Vast swaths of desert are fried in an instant and hundreds of machines tossed into the air like broken dolls, but thousands remain, and they are soon beyond their creators' wrath. The story ends with Spider Pete looking at one of the robots that had not made it: the machine is damaged but not dead, and it is not a Sphere robot either. It is an "ultramodern, European network drone," and it has spotted Pete, who has now become the human interest story at the core of the robot revolution. As the machine "lifted a multipronged limb, and ceremonially spat out every marvel it had witnessed ... out into the seething depths of the global web" (883), he adjusts his camo suit and gets ready to meet the world. The secret is out.

One of the few general-purpose functions of SF that nearly everybody seems to accept without too many *yes, but*s is that works in the genre tend to operate by displacing the contemporary, actual-world targets of their attention into a cognitively extrapolated elsewhere and/or elsewhen, from whose vantage point the context of the here and now can be recast into an unexpected light. Thus we can say that the near-future of "The Roads Must Roll" reflects on the problem of resource depletion by positing a world in which cars have been eliminated in favor of much less wasteful motorized walkways. Or we can look at Frank Herbert's *Dune* and see in it a funhouse-mirror commentary on the power of religious fervor, while Philip K. Dick's *The Man in the High Castle* (1965) displaces its musings on democracy and fascism, freedom and dictatorship by setting them in an alternate-history Earth where the Axis powers have won World War II. Now, if we narrow the focus of this interpretive lens from science fiction at large to the generation starship subgenre, we will see that irrespective of publication date, socio-political bent, editorial fiat, or authorial agency, the narratives comprising it collectively reiterate the displacement of the same set of tropes: the persistence or loss of memory, both social and personal; the transmission of knowledge, values, ethical principles, and goals from one generation to the next; and the effects of prolonged isolation inside a man-made container of limited size — a prison, in other words. From Wilcox to Robinson, Heinlein to Ballard, Oliver to Sterling, generation starship narratives have created a context-specific, fully isolated, easily contained locale within which the variables listed above can develop according to patterns that reflect back on their analogues here on Earth, today. Individual authors have then shaped the development of those patterns following their own artistic bent: while Don Wilcox and Clifford Simak placed the emphasis of "The Voyage That Lasted 600 Years" and "Spacebred Generations" on memory and generational transfer, Frank Robinson and John Brunner focused the dramatic premise of "The Oceans Are Wide" and "Lungfish" on the tension between the value of a generation starship as home (or even as symbolic womb) and its reality as prison — which brings us back to *Taklamakan*.

In 1958, Brian Aldiss had asked through Gregory Complain's voice what kind of people would doom children to be born, live, and die onboard a metallic coffin lost in the void. In 1962 J. G. Ballard had used the manifold viewpoints in "Thirteen to Centaurus" to posit the follow-up question: who would do those people one better, and trap one hundred years' worth of generations inside a can-sized cage that had never even left Earth? In 1998, Bruce Sterling provides in *Taklamakan* a possible answer to both questions: those who can. Those who, in Spider Pete's words, have the motive, the means, and the opportunity, and since Pete has already articulated the story's fundamental dilemma for the world of 2052, let us do the same for the year 2010, here on the other side of the fourth wall. How many people? How many tribes, nations, and communities? How many ethnic or religious minorities are there in this world, eking out a difficult living in landscapes blasted by war and revolution or slowly eroded by the simple neglect of those who cannot be bothered? We seem to know their names, here in the patronizingly self-appointed First World, but they may be half-forgotten, as unpleasant to the ear as the places where their tragedies slowly unravel over a period of generations — the Gaza Strip and Beirut; Darfur; Kosovo; Afghanistan and Pakistan; Cambodia; Haiti. It is a long list.

Both *Non-Stop* and "Thirteen to Centaurus" look at the idea of generational entrapment from a point of view guiltily sympathetic to the prisoners, and their narrative tone is accordingly heavy with the moral sickness of those who find themselves loathing a set of circumstances they themselves helped create. *Taklamakan*, on the other hand, looks at the problem through the eyes of a relatively innocent third party who serendipitously stumbled upon the situation and quickly became one of its victims. There is no spite in Pete and Katrinko's attitude toward the prisoners inside the starships, and they do try to help, even at the expense of their last remaining gear. There are only two of them, however, and they are operating against the gravitational pull of a superpower's collective will. Their moral attitudes, moreover, are the product of a mixture of twenty-first century *realpolitik*, a cyberpunk/hard SF worldview, and a very Philip K. Dick–like suspicion of everything governments do — an implicitly schizophrenic reaction from a pair of government-employed spooks. Their world is just the way it is, and wishing it were otherwise serves little purpose other than getting one killed. It is more useful to employ one's time working out the implications of the revolutionary semi-sentient froth inside the biotech pools, and of the idea of generational entrapment not as a crime against humanity, but as a practical expedient for getting rid of unwanted ethnicities.

The distinction between *Taklamakan* and a story like "The Roads Must Roll" is subtle but crucial: in the earlier narrative, Heinlein had rigged the dramatic premise so as to be able to utilize engineering-based solutions to social problems and make them look OK when they really were not. That is one of the reasons why Gaines, the story's hero, is an administrator and a powerful political figure — he is the springboard for a top-down view of social relations, an owner's perspective on the complaints of the owned. In *Taklamakan*, on the other hand, Sterling has created a wholly different scenario: the two urban infiltrators, by definition characters who are owned, have been sent by their owners to uncover a hard-SF military installation, only to find themselves among the victims of an operation of social engineering wholly analogous to the one Heinlein has Gates perform in "Roads."

There is little discussion between Spider Pete and Katrinko concerning the moral wrongness of trapping fifteen thousand people inside a giant cavern for eternity; they know it is wrong, but this is the way the world goes. What can they do about it? When Pete comments "means, motive, and opportunity," he is not sympathizing with the owners; he is simply interpreting the thinking of criminals. The reasons why neither he nor Katrinko display an excessive amount of outrage over the situation they have discovered may well be the same reasons why we are mostly unconcerned about the actual situations of generational entrapment existing on Earth nowadays. Certainly, we in the First World never built a gigantic vessel supposedly bound for space and then put a bunch of undesirables inside it — that is the job of a science fiction narrative: to displace in order to comment. What we have done, for example, was put the Native Americans on deserted patches of land nobody wanted, or corral the Australian Aborigines into hardly more desirable pieces of real estate. We have done similar things to the Māori and the Native Hawaiians, to the Inuit, the Polynesians, and the few survivors of the South American civilizations the Conquistadores could not be bothered to finish wiping out. All of them are "uncivilized" people — communities, tribes, and nations who would not play the game of progress the way we were playing it, and paid for it with confinement into miserable corners of Starship Earth, where succeeding generations of the unwanted have transmitted to one another the only message of import we have been willing to send them: that they are, indeed, unwanted. And when something terrible happens, when a genocidal civil war breaks out in one of the generational prisons because the inmates just can't take anymore, we have the residual decency to feel bad about ourselves, but there is always a desire for escape in our gaze, always a sense of revulsion at the misery for whose existence we are co-responsible.

It is therefore not surprising that those lacking in social consciousness wonder why they don't all just go away. This is not their world anymore. It was once, but bad people took it away from them, and it's not our fault those bad people were our fathers, or that we stood to gain from theft, rapine, and murder. It is also unfair that we should feel guilty over all this. We didn't actually *do* anything. Like Pete and Katrinko, we stumbled upon the problem on the way to looking for something else, and we have done what we can — helped a breakout here, behaved nicely to the natives over there, and politely refused to rape the priestess. So it's OK if we just escape with the robots and leave everyone down in the cave, because we have done our best. Right?

There is mercy in the ending of *Taklamakan*. Yes, Spider Pete has escaped alone, unable to open the other inmates' cages, and yes, he has made his peace with his decision not to report the discovery of the generational prison. However, the ray of hope at the end of the story — that in some way the robot onslaught will be traced back to its point of origin and the three starships discovered — exists largely thanks to his presence in the cave. "Eighties tech sticks to the skin," Sterling had written twelve years before *Taklamakan*, and so does the implied worldview of those who created it. One cannot utilize an iPhone without taking on at least a baseline quantity of its designers' belief in communication-based technologies, and the biotech pools in that cavern have absorbed far more than that. They have studied the tools, understood their use, and inevitably developed the mindset for whose desires those tools had been created in the first place. If there were a lesson we should take away from our reading of *Taklamakan*, it might be that the flow of data cannot really be stopped. It may be temporarily bottlenecked, or diverted into an informational cul-de-sac, but in the long run it will find a crack in the wall or a backdoor in the system, or simply subvert the programming of the guards. By its very nature it is dialectic and limitedly self-aware, so that to interface with it in any way — including the way of violence — is to be altered by the inescapable exchange of information resulting from the contact. Spies become prisoners, jailers become escape artists, and secrets become public knowledge, so that even those of us who wish the uncomfortable truths would just go away are destined to be visited by them again and again, until we do something to change things — or at least to have some peace and quiet. Before the web, the cell phone, the PC, and the dance of data, we had peace and quiet because we were too far away to hear the screams. Now the voices cannot really be dimmed anymore — from Haiti and Darfur, from Gaza and Cambodia, and from the rest of those immobile generational prisons inside which we have put those we did not want to acknowledge. There is mercy in *Taklamakan*, and the hope that the somewhat optimistic resolution of the nightmare of fictional peoples can one day be matched by an equally happy conclusion to the grief-laden stories of actual human beings alive today.

Of the three generation-starship stories under discussion, Gene Wolfe's is by far the most complex. At the beginning of *Shadows of the New Sun* (2007), Peter Wright comments on the difficulties literary critics often experience when they approach Gene Wolfe's work:

> The complexity of Wolfe's fiction discourages critics and scholars from discussing the subject at length. Indeed, to read Gene Wolfe — and especially to write about him — is not without risk. It is an autobiographical activity, a confession, an admission of puzzlement or wonder or even vainglorious revelation. Yet the sophistication of his work, its varied subject matter, its stylistic range and its collective effect upon the reader all invite greater understanding [1–2].

Wright highlights a conundrum here. On the one hand, critics have both the duty and the urge to engage Wolfe's opus in critical dialogue, but on the other hand duty and desire are always accompanied by a certain anxiety of inadequacy — the awareness that, no matter how carefully one peels away and explicates the manifold layers of Wolfe's writing, one will never really do it justice. Indeed, Wolfe has been left out of the general synopsis of 1980s and 1990s science fiction — a sin by all accounts — precisely out of a sense that to tackle his figure piecemeal, one part here and the other there in a chapter so heavily marked by his literary footprint, is to risk trivializing his work.

And there is a lot to display in Wolfe's fiction, even before we reach his *Book of the Long Sun* (1993–1996), the four-part sequence that can meaningfully be said to constitute the crowning achievement in generation starship narratives. As an entry point into the subject, we can elaborate on John Clute's assessment that if "we wish to understand the uses of sf, and of its hugely intricate, icon-choked history, as *literature*; if we wish to understand how the whole long told story of sf, which has occupied most of this century, can be used as an engine of pure imagination during the endtimes, then we must attempt to understand the gift of Wolfe's contemplative reshaping of our past" (*Scores* 141). Clute's words point to the main factor in Wolfe's importance for the history of latter-day science fiction: his deep knowledge of it and his ability to use this knowledge to create fictional constructs that, while immediately identifiable as SF, also threaten to burst open the walls of genre by their very acknowledgement of its many components, even the seemingly humblest. In fact, a blunt list of events and characters in a "typical" Wolfe narrative would read very much like a casting call for pulp SF tropes — monsters and rayguns, dying worlds and birthing stars, wars and robots, ruined starships serving as gothic castles, commoners with hidden kingly fathers, vampiric aliens and lost siblings, swords and ESP. In their unadulterated form, these tropes have become the ashes of science fiction's urchin youth, of the time when the future was something you could own if you were the right color or gender, and today their unqualified use in any story reeks of dead years. However, in Wolfe's hands they become symbols in the secret language we all have been practicing since 1926, almost without knowing. They are the hieroglyphs inscribed on the monuments of SF, and thus susceptible to new readings precisely because their antiquity, when rediscovered and uttered in that exact formulation, reconstructs our present in the same way the present images the future.

Even a cursory examination of Wolfe's writing style would probably be enough to reveal the source of our difficulties in pinning down precisely what he wants to say, or what we think he wants to say. Joan Gordon observes that it is often easy to detect the feel of fantasy hanging about his narratives because of his style, "Highly allusive, metaphorical, symbolic, and ambiguous," heavily limned with a body of lore that includes "mythology, ancient history, geography, Gnosticism, and medieval allegory" and expressed through the use of an "arcane vocabulary and bodies of information" (245–246). This style charges the objects in Wolfe's stories with overlapping layers of meaning, rendering them at once translucent in the mind's eye — as if they were the shadows of their ideal forms on the wall of Plato's cave — and utterly solid to our senses, like marble slabs under crisp sunlight. And the description of physical objects is not the only aspect of Wolfe's writing to be so enriched by the Hydra-faced thrust of his sentences: characters and their speech patterns, ideas, feelings, concepts, even everyday landscapes such as a walled garden or a clump of trees. Consider, for example, this long passage from the beginning of *Nightside the Long Sun* (1993), the first installment in the *Book of the Long Sun*:

> Enlightenment came to Patera Silk on the ball court; nothing could ever be the same after that.... The bigger boys had scored again, Patera Silk recalled, and Horn was reaching for an easy catch when those voices began and all that had been hidden was displayed. Few of these hidden things made sense, nor did they wait upon one another. He, young Patera Silk (that absurd clockwork figure), watched outside a clockwork show whose works had stopped — tall Horn reaching for the ball, his flashing grin frozen in forever [7].

And so on, through a series of near-painterly snapshots of people, buildings, and events both in the past and in the present of Viron, the city where Silk lives and performs his role as the Patera (priest) of his quarter's "'manteion'— a combination church and school" (Clute, *Scores* 143). Wolfe's prose weaves the sensual and psychological circumstances of Silk's enlightenment in precise strokes, hyper-dense with compressed information and their use of multi-functional terms, each referring to different events taking place within the story. For example, the description of Silk as a clockwork figure within a stopped clockwork show functions at once as a description of the momentary halting of time in Silk's frame of reference — during which instant his consciousness literally expands to encompass everything that happened or is happening onboard the generation starship he and his people inhabit — and as a warning of the fundamental wrongness at the heart of things. On the very first page of the first book in Wolfe's generation starship narrative, we already find ourselves in a conceptual breakthrough scenario — and the second page immediately kicks us out of it, because Silk has received in a single instant the enlightenment that had taken characters like Hugh Hoyland, Roy Complain, or Sam Kingsley the better part of their stories and all of their lives to work out for themselves. The Outsider, the godlike figure responsible for Silk's epiphany, shows him the nature of the world and the nature of the problem "so that he might know it for what it was, spread for him so that he might know how precious it was, though its shining clockwork had gone some trifle awry and must be set right by him; for this he had been born" (8). The remaining 1600 pages in the *Long Sun* sequence are dedicated to Wolfe's rendition of a theme very dear to generation starship stories: the explication of "the nature and decipherment of memory," because Silk must now "unpack, after its implantation, the inhumanly concentrated 'enlightenment' into the kind of memories or knowledge which make it possible for him to understand the meaning of the world" (Clute, *Scores* 143). In 1934, Laurence Manning had compressed hundreds of millions of years of human history into eight thin *Wonder Stories* pages. Now, on the cusp of the 21st century and sixty years after the beginning of the generation starship's voyages, Wolfe has done the exact opposite, stretching the deployment of an instant's epiphany across 1600 pages, four novels, and ten days or so of story time.

As is the case for the rest of Wolfe's body of work, the bare synopsis of the action in *The Book of the Long Sun*—despite its complex unraveling—tells the whole story in miserly succinctness, largely devoid of the complexity revealed by its actual reading. Patera Silk, his friends and enemies, the people of Viron, and those of the other cities splayed across the inner surface of the cylindrical hull, are the so-called Cargo of the generation starship *Whorl*, launched from a distant-future Earth three hundred years before in the direction of a solar system containing two inhabitable planets, named Blue and Green after their predominant colors. For the first time in the history of generation starship narratives, the implications inherent in the creation of a self-sufficient pocket world are worked out to their full extent: the *Whorl* is enormous, a true planet analogue in the hazy extension of its horizon to distances that make the ends of the cylinder impossible to see. There are snow-capped mountain ranges, lakes, forests, cultivated fields, cities and towns, roads; there is a sky, bright blue and threaded with clouds; different climates and ecological niches; weather patterns; seasons; and there is a sun, a glowing strip of incandescent plasma (the Long Sun of the title) extending from one end of the cylinder to the other. At one of those ends also lies Mainframe, a great golden city/main computer from which those comprising the *Whorl*'s Crew steer it and maintain its ecological balance. Inside Mainframe's memory banks reside the starship's presiding powers, a family of nine virtual personalities downloaded from once flesh-and-blood individuals. They have now become the gods worshiped by the population of the *Whorl*, and during the three centuries of travel from Earth to Blue/Green, they have occasionally manifested themselves to the Cargo in a series of theophanies through the medium of public-access computer screens, which their worshipers call Sacred Windows. During a theophany, the stored personality appearing in the Window can communicate their desires to their people, and occasionally download themselves—or parts of themselves—into a human being. In order to propitiate a theophany, augurs offer animal sacrifices in front of their manteions' Sacred Windows, and then interpret the will of the gods by reading their victims' entrails.

Silk is one such augur, and his manteion on Sun Street is the hub of religious life in Viron's poorest quarter. Only twenty-three years old, Silk has been the augur of the Sun Street manteion for about a year at the time of his enlightenment. His predecessor, now-dead Patera Pike, had spent the long hours of his last few months praying to the Outsider—a supposedly minor god who does not belong to the family of the Nine—for help in saving the manteion. A man named Blood, a rich speculator with ties to the criminal underworld, bought the edifice from the Chapter only to close it, thus threatening to strand the children learning there on the street. So Patera Pike prayed for help, until death silenced his voice.

The Outsider, however, has listened. As Silk explains to Blood during their first encounter, "when you pray for his help, to the Outsider, he sends it.... But not always — no, not often — of the sort we want or expect. Patera Pike, that good old man, prayed devoutly. And I'm the help" (20). So Silk's role is actually double: on the one hand he is the Outsider's answer to Patera Pike's prayers, the savior of the Sun Street manteion, and on the other he is the Outsider's solution to the stoppage afflicting the gears of the world, the agent of conceptual breakthrough for the population of the generation starship. The plot of *Long Sun* tightly weaves the twin strands of Silk's mission into the warp and woof of life in Viron, where most of the action takes place, so that saving the manteion's people becomes the microcosmic task inside the macrocosmic endeavor of saving the *Whorl*'s Cargo. The two constitute endpoints in the path that takes Silk — and us along with him — from his enlightenment at the beginning of the story to the successful completion of his duties at its end. By this time, the former augur of the Sun Street manteion has become Viron's new Caldé, a mayor/king figure whose previous incumbent had died after nominating his successor without actually revealing his identity. In one of Wolfe's many tributes to the mulch of pulp SF out of which his materials grew, Silk is eventually revealed as the defunct Caldé's long-lost successor, his foster son grown from a frozen embryo.

Wolfe's sense of dramatic development combines with his writing style to infuse this overly tired plot device with new energy. For instance, Silk really needs the influence that the position of Caldé confers him, because the wrench in the machine revealed to him by the Outsider involves all the powers in the world, and those powers are hostile to conceptual breakthrough. It is here that Wolfe's knowledge of science fiction in general and generation starship stories in particular becomes apparent. In an authorial nod to Oliver and "The Wind Blows Free," Silk gradually remembers that part of the Outsider's enlightenment contains the end of the *Whorl*'s voyage: the vessel is already in orbit around the Blue/Green system — in fact, it had arrived thirty years before the beginning of the story. Pas, the father of the Nine and the originator of the flight, had created the *Whorl* to function for a timespan not far beyond the three hundred years it would take it to reach destination. Once arrived, the Cargo and the Crew were all supposed to board the landers lying near the cylinder's circumference, leave the ship, and settle the two planets.

But human beings die, memory fades, and tyrants scheme. In time-honored generation-starship fashion, the people comprising the Cargo believe that the cylindrical universe bounding their lives is all there is, and that the Long Sun is the only star in existence. Scraps of dialogue unobtrusively placed here and there across the narrative hint that the robotic people making up part of the *Whorl*'s population — they are called "chems" — still carry dim recollections of Earth, where they were created, but these recollections are fading daily as their software, and with it every other piece of advanced machinery in the *Whorl*, gradually breaks down for lack of maintenance. In numerous passages reminiscent of "Universe," "Common Sense," and *Non-Stop*, the reader witnesses the uneasy coexistence of chems, floaters, beam weapons, powered dirigibles, and sentient combat robots with pack animals, swords, wax tablets, beast-borne litters, and the rest of the accoutrements of a middle-age/renaissance level of technological advancement. Once again, the decay of the Cargo's cognitive apprehension of the world is accompanied by the steady degradation of higher forms of technology, a situation that gives Wolfe the chance to plausibly portray these forms in that language of fantasy Joan Gordon has indicated as a crucial characteristic of his prose. Tools, robots, vehicles, and weapons have become magical artifacts or works of art, symbols of a mythical age of gods possessed of powers largely incomprehensible to the present. A few members of the Cargo still know how to build or repair them, but they are mostly seen as wizards of sorts, and their numbers are dwindling. As in previous generation-starship narratives in the forgetfulness pattern, tantalizing words of nearly forgotten meaning pepper the *Book of the Long Sun*, waypoint indicators that the world is not what we believe: Viron's roads and buildings are made of a material everyone calls shiprock. When people die, their souls are believed to ascend to Mainframe along the Aureate Path, the road of fire constituted by the Long Sun itself. The only form of currency in use in Viron are the so-called cards, thin wafers of gold-etched metal that in reality constitute the components of the shuttles' memory banks.[9] The cities, lakes, mountains, and fields on the sides of the Whorl's cylinder, and therefore on Viron's curved ceiling, are called skylands; when night falls in Viron — thanks to a shutter system alternately closing off various parts of the Long Sun's surface — they shine brightly in the city's night sky. And, perhaps most importantly, the word the Cargo uncomprehendingly use to interchangeably refer to the world and the universe is "whorl," a term clearly connected to the vessel's name. Thus, the *Whorl* is the whorl is the world. And like the unnamed starship in "The Wind Blows Free" or the "Big Dog" in *Non-Stop*, the *Whorl* is also a place of secrets: there are hidden chambers near the hull where members of the Cargo have been kept in a state of suspended animation since the ship left Earth, and who therefore retain full memory of their circumstances[10]; there are forgotten windows open to space, and a computer screen inside one of the landers from whose depths a desperate face keeps asking "Is it time?" (*Lake* 474); there is a submarine, trawling the depths of Viron's lake Limna, which the city's rulers have turned into their secret base; there are tunnels under the skin of the whorl, once part of the ship's water recycling system but now crumbling and clogged with detritus, another remainder of the disrepair into which everything has fallen.

However, the *Book of the Long Sun* carries the implications of ship-wide technological decay further than Heinlein, Oliver, or Aldiss have. It is a narrative of the 1990s, and Wolfe's knowledge of the subgenre allows him to marry the Starship-Earth developments of its previous thirty years to such end-of-the-century ecological concerns as global warming and resource depletion. Indeed, the visible signs of equipment breakdown are only the surface indicators of deeper failures in the *Whorl*'s life-support systems: the closed ecology of the generation starship has reached its design limitations, and the needs of the increasingly numerous Cargo push them to consume primary resources faster than Mainframe's machinery can replenish them. Also, the heat from the Long Sun's incandescent plasma string is gradually overcoming the climate systems' ability to create alternating seasons — the day Silk receives his enlightenment is only one among many in the longest summer the whorl has ever seen. There is no more rain, lakes and seas are drying up, crops are dying, and still the blazing heat continues well into the fall months, before a stuttering winter manages to worm its way into the *Whorl*'s sky. As one of the Crew[11] warns Silk late in the narrative, this may well be the last. Mainframe has little or nothing left to give the world.

The *Whorl*, however, also comes under the sway of the gods of Mainframe. They are false gods, and their transcendence is largely a pixel trick on the screens of the Sacred Windows, but their agency is nevertheless substantial, and the Crew obey their instructions. So where are they, and what are they doing for the whorl and its precarious ecology? In an overarching development that carries serious implications both for Silk's quests and for his faith, we gradually discover that at the time of the generation starship's arrival in the Blue/Green system, Pas's consort, Echidna, had led some elements among the Nine in an operation of digital assassination, deleting her husband's consciousness from Mainframe's data-banks. Over the course of the trip's three centuries, she and her cohorts had grown too accustomed to being worshiped as gods to let go of their position. They had killed the creator of the *Whorl*, quietly withdrawn from the universe outside, and trapped the Cargo into another mindgame. If the Nine had represented a cyberspace update of the Predict's role from "The Oceans Are Wide," legitimately appointed immortals carrying to the stars the uncorrupted memory of Earth and of the mission, the assassins could now be described as the *Long Sun*'s equivalent to Michael Kusaka from *The Dark Beyond the Stars* — mutineers giving in to power lust against the interests of their charges and the physical evidence of their kingdom's decay. Like the *Astronomy*, the *Whorl* had not been built to function indefinitely, and Echidna's coup put the ship and its inhabitants in a situation essentially identical to the one created by Kusaka after the mutiny.

Moreover, the macrocosmic power struggle among the gods of Mainframe is mirrored at the microcosmic level by the equally unlawful takeover engineered by the Ayuntamiento, Viron's city council. At the death of the last Caldé, and after conducting a murderous but ultimately fruitless search for his heir, the members of the Ayuntamiento took the reins of power, using the situation of political paralysis as cover for their schemes.[12] In yet another correspondence between the situation in Viron and the circumstances prevailing within Mainframe, the councilmen transferred their bodies to specially prepared stasis beds from which their minds could control virtually indestructible robots identical in appearance to their flesh-and-blood selves. They now rule Viron as the same malady of stasis that afflicts the whole whorl from the slowly sclerotizing data-banks of Mainframe. Both the microcosm of Silk's city and the macrocosm of the generation starship are in the hands of usurpers, while Crew and Cargo have become mirror images of each other as the impotent subjects of maddened leaders.

And Patera Silk, in quixotic holy-fool fashion, picks them all up, victims and perpetrators alike, on his way to do the Outsider's bidding — downloaded personalities, robot councilmen, thieves, soldiers, sentient machines, crime lords and their henchmen, foreign dignitaries and military personnel, members of the Crew, prostitutes, friends, enemies, lovers, pets, chems, and the void between the stars — they all accompany him; they all participate in his quest to do right by the world. In a 1998 interview with Gene Wolfe, Lawrence Person described Silk as "one of the most wholly good, in the sense of being truly moral, characters in recent science fiction," and Wolfe himself commented thus on his creation:

> The idea of the clergyman hero was very popular back around the 1900s, and has gone completely out of style except for a few clergyman detectives ... and I thought to do something with that idea again. We were talking about war in my most recent panel, how easy is and how dramatic it is. The same thing can be said about evil. A lot of people have the notion that evil is interesting and basically fun, and that good is dull and no fun, and I don't think that's true. If anything, the reverse is true, and I wanted to have a shot at proving that I was right [167].

Patera Silk is a good man in a personal situation that would normally make goodness a signally difficult achievement. The gods he worships at the beginning of the *Book of the Long Sun* are murderous downloads with an ant farm — J. G. Ballard's Abel writ large — and everything in which he had been instructed to believe is false to its core. Even the solace connected to the presence in his mind of the Outsider, whom Silk knows to be the only truly transcendental power in the whorl, is tempered by the god's essentially cool-hearted embrace. There is appreciation and a certain detached sense of approval in the Outsider's gaze, but no clearly experienced emotion of all-encompassing love, and the burden of the tasks with which Silk has been entrusted weighs more than the comparatively frigid joys his conceptual breakthrough has brought him as compensation for a life spent serving frauds.

What Silk really has is himself, his many friends, and his faith in the existence of a code of behavior adaptable enough to changing circumstances — and solid enough in the face of those same changes — to be called truly moral. In his interview with Lawrence Person, Wolfe himself underscored the nature of his character's beliefs when he said that yes, Silk does begin "by considering Pas and Echidna and the other false gods of the Long Sun world as genuinely divine, and they are not. But his ideas of what divinity *means* or what divinity consists of, I think are fairly sound" (168). The revelation that the Nine are essentially ghosts in the machine brings him considerable pain, as well as a sense of existential up-rootedness that almost pushes him beyond the brink of suicide at the end of the last book, but Silk always returns from the depths. He repeatedly draws strength and purpose from the Outsider, from the love he finds among his fellow humans, chems, and talking pets, and from the moral core at the center of his mind that allows him to serve a concept of good — good done for and to others; good done for and to the world — existing independently of its faulty avatars and flexibly within a relativistic frame of reference. In the course of his adventures, Silk finds himself forced to break into houses and secret underground bases, make pacts with criminals and usurpers, and kill both chems and humans, but he never lies about his actions or the reasons he took them, and he always attempts to solve matters otherwise before doing the irreparable. He faces both the world and his own fallibility with the utter honesty of one compelled by his faith to perform the indispensable action for the success of conceptual breakthrough: to find out the truth of the world and broadcast it. He does so even after the lynchpins of this faith have been revealed as lies, and ultimately it is this basic honesty that allows him to accomplish his missions.

And Silk does accomplish them, against the odds and in the face of their enormity. He becomes the savior of his manteion and the savior of the whorl, although not in the way he had expected. He is, after all, the Outsider's mortal agent, and when the Outsider gives us help, it is "not always ... of the sort we want or expect." Also, the fate of those chosen as the God's instruments does not necessarily conform to a meritocratic view of relations between deities and mortals — indeed, there is a whiff of the Old Testament in the story's resolution: when the process of colonization begins at the conclusion of the fourth novel, germanely entitled *Exodus from the Long Sun* (1996), Silk remains behind on the *Whorl*, a Moses figure watching the first lander take off into the void. The last anyone sees of him is when he vanishes in the chilly mist shrouding Viron, and as the shuttles fly and the story ends, he is seemingly lost to us forever.

Not quite lost, in fact, and in any case not forever. Silk may be merely human, and therefore subject to the same pain and death as his fellow mortals, but he is also an avatar of the divine, created specifically as a vessel of revelations no one else could bear. There is transcendence in store for him and the world, a transcendence we do not glimpse at the end of *Exodus from the Long Sun* because its apotheosis thrusts through the hull of the *Whorl*, the fabric of time, and the walls of story to embrace a total of three narrative cycles, twelve novels, and twenty-one years of genre history. The *Book of the Long Sun* constitutes the middle series in a long sequence that began in 1980 with the first novel of *The Book of the New Sun* (1980–1983) and ended in 2001 with the last novel in *The Book of the Short Sun* (1999–2001).[13] Wolfe's generation-starship tetralogy is linked both to the earlier and to the later installments through their shared universe and the agency of common characters, although in typical Wolfeian fashion the clues indicating their presence in the narrative are unobtrusive to the point of obscurity, and the timeline anchoring the whole apparatus to its constituent parts turns in on itself with byzantine glee.

The first cycle, the *Book of the New Sun*, is set on the same distant-future Earth from which the *Whorl* has taken off. Now known as Urth, our planet is "So densely impacted with millions of year of human life ... that even commercial mines, dug however deep into the ransacked planet, produce only bone and brick and artifact and icon, layer upon layer of human meaning.... But Urth is dying. The sun is red; stars are visible in the dark sky of midday (Clute, *Strokes* 150). Severian, the first-person narrator and protagonist of *New Sun*, is an apprentice journeyman in the Guild of Torturers, and the whole sequence is his account, written years after the fact, of his rise to god-like power from the depths of disgrace. Cast out of the Guild for providing a woman with whom he had fallen in love with the means to kill herself, Severian, armed with his black executioner's sword *Terminus Est*, embarks on a number of darkly picaresque, transcendental adventures across space and time at the end of which he has become Autarch, the supernatural king figure who rules the Urth nation known as the Commonwealth from the heights of the so-called House Absolute. As Peter Wright has observed (*Daedalus* 199–205), there are strong similarities between Severian and Silk: both "are raised in a monastic environment and wear black robes; both follow rigid traditions and rites" (199); both live on dying worlds, and ascend to power in order to avert that death (Severian, in *The Urth of the New Sun*, returns our planet to life by igniting a white hole in the sun's core); both are executioners (in Silk's case because his order instructs him to sacrifice animals); both are lame, although Silk's condition is only temporary; and, both their narratives are deeply involved in the retention, retrieval, and exercise of memory. Severian, however, is a substantially less reassuring protagonist than Silk. "It is my nature, my joy, and my curse, to forget nothing" (11), he tells us at the beginning of *Shadow of the Torturer* (1980), but a few pages further down "I realized for the first time that I am in some degree insane.... I could no longer be sure my own mind was not lying to me; all my falsehoods were recoiling on me, and I who remembered everything could not be certain those memories were not my own dreams" (27). In spite of his attempts to tell the truth, then, Severian could well be a dissembler, and knowing that he may not entirely be responsible for his lies gives us readers little room for trust.[14] He writes his account after the fact, and he is in possession of every nuance of memory concerning them, which means that, independent of its narrator's intentions, the account of his rise to power is by definition a fiction within another fiction, "a tunnel which we, as readers, navigate under the aegis of his cold, recursive, peremptory gaze" (Clute, *Scores* 141).

Ultimately, Severian's narrative finds corroboration — at least in its general outline — through the same instrument that eventually grants us knowledge of Silk's fate: its relation to the other two series in Wolfe's long sequence. As we have seen, the traits shared by Severian and Silk are too deeply rooted in their story of origin to be merely the result of happenstance. Rather, we should say that Silk's life represents a thematic confirmation of the reality of Severian's existence: while the former Torturer's narrative is a shifting first-person account of problematic veracity, the former augur's story is told in the third person by Horn, the oldest among the pupils of the Sun Street manteion.[15] Thus, while Severian's story is an autobiography, Silk's is a biography, and this crucial difference provides *Long Sun* with an objectivity that, combined with the many fundamental commonalities between Silk and Severian, lends the earlier sequence a level of trustworthiness it would not otherwise possess. Severian may have embellished his account; he may have made himself out to be better — or worse — than he actually was, and he may have decided to change or delete many facts stored in his all-encompassing memory. However, we now have circumstantial evidence that the overall shape of his life story might be trusted.

This circumstantial evidence is further supported by more solid proof. Both the *New Sun* and *Long Sun* books contain characters that resurface in later sequences, and in the case of *New Sun* one of them turns out to be the maker of the whorl. Toward the end of *Lake of the Long Sun* (1994), the head of the fraudulent Ayuntamiento tells Silk about origins of the whorl, its gods, and its people:

"A certain ruler, a man who had the strength to rule alone and so called himself the monarch, built our whorl.... The monarch's doctors tinkered with the minds of the men and women he put into the whorl ... erasing as much as they dared of their patients' personal lives.... The surgeons found, however, that their patients' memories of their ruler, his family, and some of his officials were too deeply entrenched to be eliminated altogether. To obscure the record, they renamed them. Their ruler ... became Pas, the shrew he had married Echidna, and so on" [500–501].

The character the whorl knows as Pas originally appeared in Severian's narrative, specifically in chapters 25 and 26 of *The Claw of the Conciliator* (1982) and in Chapter 29 of the stand-alone sequel, *The Urth of the New Sun* (1987). He was known as Typhon, "a 'two-headed' man, the last monarch of Urth [who] dreamed of a Second Empire to rival or surpass the fallen First Empire" (Driussi 352).[16] His dream had failed, however, and he had died a thousand years before Severian found him and resuscitated him with a magical artifact (the title's Claw of the Conciliator). At this point, the revelation that the Pas of the *Long Sun* was originally Typhon from the *New Sun* becomes important to the generation starship's fate. During their meeting in *Sword of the Lictor*, Typhon reveals to Severian information that, again typically for Wolfe, had previously been foreshadowed in a couple of seemingly unimportant episodes[17]: the red, swollen sun is not dying of natural causes. A black hole at its center is eating it from the inside out, and Typhon had been apprised of the situation by his astronomers, who erroneously "had told me that this sun's activity would decay slowly. Far too slowly, in fact, for the change to be noticeable in a human lifetime. They were wrong. The heat of the world declined by nearly two parts in a thousand over a few years, then stabilized. Crops failed, and there were famines and riots" (140). Thus, the condition of Urth in *New Sun* and that of the *Whorl* in *Long Sun* are essentially analogous: both are decaying worlds, one natural and one man-made, one dying of heat loss and the other of overheating, and their decay has reached the point where its progress can no longer remain hidden from the failing machinery of generational transfer. Now the changes take place within a human lifetime, people are getting scared, and the agency of transcendental powers introduces savior figures into the world in the same way an immune system produces white blood cells. Typhon had not been one of those figures, but he had been the one to create a generation starship, put people in it with carefully edited memories (there are shades of "Lungfish" and "Thirteen to Centaurus" in this plot twist), and install a version of himself and his family as virtual rulers before powering away into deep space. Now, none of the books comprising the *New Sun*, *Long Sun*, and *Short Sun* sequences contain any hint that Typhon had initiated generational travel as a reaction to the cancer burrowing into the core of the sun.[18] However, we can extrapolate this possibility from textual and contextual evidence; after Clarke's "Rescue Party," "The Oceans Are Wide," and "The Wind Blows Free," such a motivating trigger does come back to us as something of an old acquaintance, and Wolfe may well have left it to the readers to draw such an inference on their own.

Moreover, the timelines of the first two sequences find an important elucidation in the revelation of Pas's true identity. If Typhon/Pas was the originator of the *Whorl*'s trip, then the generation starship must have left Earth about a thousand years before Severian's birth. Subtracting from this figure the three hundred years of travel and the thirty spent in-system, we should necessarily conclude that Silk's narrative predates Severian's by almost seven hundred years. However, "the principle of time dilation neatly resolves the two figures: 300 ship years make 1000 years on Urth. Severian and Silk, therefore, are contemporaries. And Severian has almost certainly become something like a god by the time Silk hears the voice of the Outsider" (Clute, *Scores* 142). Thus, Severian's healing of the world happens in near-synchronicity with Silk's saving of the *Whorl*, and the intertextual and metatextual indications that Severian himself (or one of his aspects) may be the source of the conceptual breakthrough that sets in motion the events in the later cycle create the sense of a unified dramatic thrust, the result of myriad plot strands speeding toward a common crux in a sort of metanarrative space-time.

Wolfe's last sequence, the *Book of the Short Sun*, explores this crux. Beginning in *On Blue's Waters* (1999), the trilogy is set twenty years after the events in *Exodus from the Long Sun*, and it constitutes Horn's mostly autobiographical account of his recent — and, so he tells us in a number of asides, failed — attempt to bring Patera Silk back from his self-imposed exile. Humanity has colonized Blue and Green, but a substantial part of the Cargo, including Silk, is still onboard the increasingly unstable *Whorl*, and those who managed to land are not doing well either. The city of New Viron, Blue's capital, is rife with disorder, and the authorities fear that it will irreversibly spread to the other settlements unless Silk returns to once again lead his people out of the darkness. Thus, they charge Horn to travel to the city of Pajarocu, whose inhabitants claim to have a still functioning lander, travel to the *Whorl*, find Silk, and bring him to Blue.

Right from the start, however, Horn's narrative becomes as convoluted as Severian's. Told two years after the events it recounts have transpired, *Short Sun* combines the first-person narrative of *New Sun* and the third-person biographical storytelling of *Long Sun* into a mysterious, baroque hodgepodge of voices. Horn's own voice "indulges in flashbacks, introduces comparisons based on happenings still in the narrative future, sticks in belated afterthoughts, and even has a second go at scenes that he finds unsatisfyingly or dishonestly written" (Langford 241), all the while blaming itself for failing to deliver the same kind of honest account it had construed Silk as providing in *Long Sun*. To this substantial interpretive incertitude we must add a shift in narrative mode when, during a detour to Green in the second *Short Sun* book, a particularly difficult series of experiences push Horn away from his first-person account into the comparative psychological safety of a third-person voice. When the story returns to first person, the "I" that comes back to us is not the same "I" that had left us — as we have known for a while, sort of, because by now Horn has already dropped enough hints that the man who began the quest on Blue and the man who returned to Blue at its end are not the same. In fact, as we gradually glimpse in the interstices revealed by the narrative's contortions, Horn had died on Green, and immediately thereafter had been numinously teleported onboard the *Whorl*. There, his consciousness had been merged to that of Silk's — now another personality download inside Mainframe — through one of the Sacred Windows.

So now Horn is both himself and Silk; thus the original indication that his quest had been unsuccessful acquires an ironic twist. Also, given the many traits Silk had in common with Severian, there is some cause to believe that Horn acquired something of the latter's characteristics as well — a belief supported by the evidence of his new powers, which include the ability to transport his spirit self through space while sleeping.[19] In this guise he visits Urth, where he returns us all to the "locked and rusted gate ... with wisps of river fog threading its spikes like the mountain paths" whose image had begun the first chapter of *Shadow of the Torturer* (Wolfe, *Shadow* 9). In other words, Horn is bringing us back full circle to the very beginning of the entire cycle, a feat he repeats in *Return to the Whorl* (2001), the final novel of the *Short Sun* trilogy, when he comes back to Urth at the time a young Severian finds his pet Triskele.[20] *Return to the Whorl* brings us back to the generation starship where many among the Cargo still reside, including a number of characters from the previous sequence. The interior of the vessel is in darkness, as the Long Sun has seemingly failed again, but we later discover that it has been turned off by its inhabitants, who are trying to repair the *Whorl*'s climate systems. Horn, now fully transfigured as Horn/Silk, visits the key loci of *Long Sun*'s action in his strangely quixotic quest: the villa of the speculator Blood, where Silk's attempt at a daring robbery had left him temporarily lame; the manteion on Sun Street; and the palace of the Caldé, where Silk had resided in the later stages of the previous narrative sequence. The quest is interrupted when the authorities of Old Viron, feeling threatened by the reappearance of Horn/Silk, have him transported back to Blue, where after a series of adventures he returns home to a family who understandably has some trouble recognizing him. The story's end, penned in turn by Horn's several children and relatives, sees him return to the *Whorl* with his wife and a few characters from *Long Sun*. The generation starship, its environmental control systems now repaired, powers out of the Blue/Green system into deep space, without a specific destination because, just like a planet, it does not need one.

Of all the writers who preceded Wolfe in steering the generation starship through its conceptual path, the ones most closely resembling him would probably have to be Tsiolkovsky and Bernal, because all three utilize the concept as part of a greater view of the world and of humanity's place in it. For Tsiolkovsky and Bernal, generational travel was the final step on humanity's march to transcendence, the outward sign that our species had reached spiritual maturity. For Wolfe, it is one of the stepping stones laid along the path toward a comprehensive aesthetic statement about science fiction, literature, and their fruition on the part of human beings, which is why his work, like Tsiolkovsy's and Bernal's had done in the 1920s, slingshots us into a future of human space travel where the generation starship stops being a starship and starts becoming a worldship. Or rather, we should say a whorlship, because the purposefully confusing nomenclature that in *Long Sun* equates ship with world, whorl with word, and word with Wolfe functions as a semiotic signifier: that which was created as one thing may — and should, or maybe has no choice but to — become something else as the perception of its Cargo shifts and turns across the light-years. As is customary for Wolfe, the most crucial differences between his stories and those of most other writers are also the subtlest, and in the case of his generation starship sequence one of these differences is the complete lack of condescension or pity toward the lives Silk and the rest of his people have been forced to live. As Silk finds out that the principles he serves have value beyond the authenticity of their faulty bodily carriers, so do we readers understand that the lives of the *Whorl*'s Cargo are worth what they are worth, irrespective of where they have been spent or of whose rules they putatively serve. If we feel contempt for them, like we are invited to do in some of the generation starship stories we have seen, then we might as well be contemptuous of people who lived in the middle ages. It's not just that none of this is their fault (who gets to ask to be born in a place and time of their preference?); it's also that their lives have value in and of themselves, and we readers cherish them simply because those are the circumstances of their existence, and they are rich on their own terms — something Silk understands well, and which gives him the strength to love the world and the whorl, without exception.

In much the same way as it is not possible to talk about Tsiolkovsky and Bernal's ideas on generational travel without addressing their spiritual and intellectual beliefs, it is also impossible to discuss the *Long Sun* sequence without connecting it to its author's twelve-book opus on everything and SF.

Wolfe's knowledge of—and control over—his materials is encyclopedic, and his ability to imbue the tired tropes of pulp science fiction with new energy is akin in degree to Severian's revivification of the sun. If the whole cycle of three *Books* and twelve novels constitutes a compendium of science fiction writing between the 1920s and the 1990s, then the *Book of the Long Sun* is its microcosm, in that it contains within its pages the entire history of the generation starship subgenre: Heinlein and Manning, Robinson and Ballard, Oliver, Simak and Clarke.[21] They are all there, and Wilcox is as well, because in *The Urth of the New Sun*, written six years before the first book in the *Long Sun* sequence, Silk begins his quest for the salvation of our planet by boarding Tzadkiel's ship, a vessel capable of travel through a hyperspace analogue called Yesod.[22] In other words, by the time the *Whorl* reaches the Blue/Green system, Severian has already had access to a form of faster-than-light travel—which would make the *Whorl* obsolete, except that unlike the *Flashaway*, the whorl cannot be made obsolete, because it is at once ship and world. Like Horn, Silk, and (probably, possibly) Severian, they are one. Their existences converge at that crux in narrative space-time where everything happens, which is the book, and whose complexities readers negotiate not too differently from how we negotiate the complexities of life. This is why, when the exegeses of Wolfe's work are over, something has always been left out. There is always something else to discuss, or a way to discuss it better, so that it would not be ludicrous to believe that the only way to do justice to a work of the imagination of this complexity is to turn oneself into Borges' Pierre Menard, and reinvent it the way Menard rewrote the *Quixote*. That is to say, the only way to talk about Gene Wolfe is to write him.

The *Book of the New Sun* was the major SF cycle published in the final years of what Eric Hobsbawm, in his 1994 book *The Age of Extremes*, calls the short twentieth century. Writing from the first few years of the post–Cold War period, Hobsbawm places the century's beginning at the start of World War I—the event whose consequences ended up snowballing into World War II, the end of the old colonial empires, and the beginning of nuclear détente—and its end in 1991, the year in which the final product of 1914's fallout, the Soviet Union, collapsed. "It is not the purpose of this book to tell the story of the period which is it subject...." Hobsbawm writes in the introduction; "My object is to understand and explain *why* things turned out the way they did, and how they hang together" (3). Thus, *The Age of Extremes* constitutes its author's account, often peppered with first-person recollections, of the industrialized world's largely failed attempt to predict the future of fate through the lens of the future of desire, a failure of which Hobsbawm himself is all too aware:

There can be no serious doubt that in the late 1980s and early 1990s an era in world history ended and a new one began. That is the essential information for the historians of the century, for though they can speculate about the future in the light of their understanding of the past, their business is not that of the racing tipster.... In any case, the record of forecasters in the past thirty or forty years, whatever their professional qualification as prophets, has been so spectacularly bad that only governments and economic research institutes still have, or pretend to have, much confidence in it. It is even possible that it has gotten worse since the Second World War [5-6].

J. D. Bernal would have understood this line of reasoning, especially concerning the business of futurology. In fact, the whole book is characterized by a constant tension between the matter treated in each chapter and the epigraphs from politicians, intellectuals, writers, and philosophers at the chapter's beginning. In their entirety, these epigraphs serve as an ironic, often tragic commentary on the fallibility of human aspirations in the face of their actual unraveling, as evidenced, for example, by part of Calvin Coolidge's December 4, 1928 address to Congress, a message of optimism for the economic future of the country that opens *Age of Extremes'* Chapter 3, aptly entitled "Into the Economic Abyss" (85). Hobsbawm, arguably one of the best historians to emerge out of the roiling upheaval of the short twentieth century, effectively elucidates its unfolding, and his thinking gains depth and authenticity through the acknowledgement of his own fallibility. Like Bernal before him, he is fully aware of being as mired in the myopia of present circumstances as the great players of twentieth-century history whose aspirations he scrutinizes, and he therefore limits his own attempts at forecasting to cautious, general predictions that hint at relevant trends for the future without expecting to fix their constant state of flux into artificial, inevitably inaccurate patterns. In particular, Hobsbawm carefully indicates as one of the major trends "the democratization or privatization of the means of destruction," which had created a world where it "was now possible for quite small groups of political or other dissidents to disrupt and destroy anywhere, as the mainland activities of the IRA in Britain and the attempt to blow up the World Trade Center in New York (1993) showed" (560).

His caution was well justified. Today, our view of the world's immediate past, shaped by the events of the sixteen or so years since the publication of *Age of Extremes*, seems to have retained the perception of that period as a short century begun in 1914, while at the same time slightly extending its duration. Now we place its official end in 1989, the year the Berlin Wall came down, and think of the twelve years separating its fall from the fall of the towers on September 11, 2001, as its soft expiring, the long Indian summer between the end of the old world order and the birth of ... something else. Those twelve years, rife with conflict and turmoil as they were, now exist in the mind as a time of comparative order, a breathing space in which the enemies faced by the countries that had owned the world since the age of discovery — and that had created, among many other things, the genre of science fiction to propagate the narrative of their rise to power — still looked a little like the old ones: standing armies, navies, and air forces; easily located command posts; eminently destructible hardware and equally perishable human assets; embassies with addresses in the yellow pages. The fall of the Berlin Wall marked the end of an old terror, a world order born out of desire and eventually erased by fate, and in that twelve-year interregnum it may have seemed to us that we could keep playing in the usual ways with the usual toys without incurring retribution.

But there were new terrors around the corner, and we had failed to foresee their growth because, in a different and less virulent form, they had been with us for a while. Thus we thought we had the measure of them: throughout the eighties and nineties, audiences exorcised the anxieties of actuality by gathering in movie theaters to watch Chuck Norris kill countless Middle Eastern terrorists in *Delta Force* (1986), laugh as James Cameron and Arnold Schwarzenegger turned them into stumbling buffoons in *True Lies* (1995), and nod appreciatively as George Clooney told one of them[23] that their disagreements were not America's problem in *The Peacemaker* (1997). The industrialized West could be attacked and wounded, this we had known for a while, but we also knew that its primacy could not be challenged. The mind's eye construed terrorists as poor, ignorant, easily duped fools without the intelligence or the courage to stand up to the trained multitudes of our armies or the technological might of our F-22s. We were, by and large, safe.

We might have known better. Vietnam and Afghanistan had shown us what can happen to a technologically advanced war machine fighting against a far smaller, essentially guerrilla-style force, as well as the consequences of entering into the wrong kind of alliance. In 1988, Sylvester Stallone had gone to Afghanistan to fight the Soviets alongside the Mujahideen in *Rambo III*. Back then, we in the West called them freedom fighters. We saw them as our friends of convenience, but they were also the same people who, that morning on September 11, extinguished the twentieth century and ushered in the twenty-first in the space of five minutes — by that day, we had long been calling them drug lords, criminals, and terrorists. There were desire and fate in the four airliners that slammed into the Twin Towers, the Pentagon, and that field near Shanksville, Pennsylvania — desire for change obtained through violent action, and the fate that spun desire into the actual shape of the world to come. The people who died inside those airliners, victims and executioners alike, had neither a greater nor a lesser grasp of the rift between intent and outcome than those who had trained the terrorists — or, for that matter, than those who would soon invade the Middle East in the name of freedom and vengeance. The twentieth century, which had gradually been dying since the fall of the Wall, suddenly expired with the collapse of the Towers, and by the time the dust had cleared the future had begun.

CONCLUSION

Trip's End?

In his review of Max Page's *The City's End* (2008), a work of literary criticism focused on fictional treatments of New York's destruction, John Clute writes:

> New York — or, rather, Manhattan — is a storyteller's dream, a dream to be dwelt within. Not simply is it an *island*, and therefore bounded, with an inside and an out: it is an island whose shape is inherently ... storyable: a great ship of rock pointing into wider waters, a cigar, a sword, a City in Space. You cannot imaginarily destroy a metropolis (or a world) until you can imagine how to do it. Manhattan can be destroyed because it can be *seen* to be destroyed [*Canary* 382].

And we did see it destroyed, time and again in novels, short stories, movies, magazine covers, videogames, and songs.[1] The written word featured its fair share of such scenes — from Ignatius Donnelly's *Caesar's Column* (1890) and H.G. Wells's *The War in the Air* (1908) to George R. Stewart's *Earth Abides* (1949) and J.G. Ballard's *Hello America* (1981) — but it was primarily through the agency of visuals that The Fall of New York became what it is today: a shorthand for the collapse of human civilization or for the death of the Earth. Starting with the Gernsback pulps, a vast number of SF magazine covers have featured either New York's ruined cityscape or one of its more recognizable icons — the Empire State Building, the Statue of Liberty — set against a backdrop suggestive of some vast cataclysm in our future-now-past. Half-buried in sand or entombed under geological layers of earth, the city and its icons are visited by distant-future humans or aliens, all gazing at them with the same sense of wonder or scientific curiosity we display today when we look at the pyramids, the Temple of Tikal, or Stonehenge. These images represent the visual equivalent of the lyrical feel transmitted by a story like Campbell's "Twilight," a snapshot reflection on the failure of human ambition and the vanishing of our legacy against the rolling of the eons. And because of the characteristics Clute indicated in his review, as well as the iconic pervasiveness of its presence in Western culture, New York is, today as yesterday, the city that represents the planet entire. When it falls, the rest of the world has fallen as well, because it becomes ludicrous in the mind's eye to consider that any other human artifact could be left standing after the great colossus has gone down. Indeed, the narratives in any medium that portray the collapse of New York alone are visibly outnumbered by those that use its destruction as the symbolic curtain call for humanity or the planet in their entirety. For every story like John Carpenter's *Escape from New York* (1981), in which the city has become a rotting prison for America's booming criminal population, there are many like *Independence Day* (1996), *Deep Impact* (1998), *A.I.: Artificial Intelligence* (2000), or *Final Fantasy* (2000), where New York's condition becomes exemplary of our entire infrastructure, and the plight of its inhabitants evocative of the whole of mankind's suffering. Whether or not one likes the idea, and whether or not the intensity of our cultural perceptions do an injustice to the many other realities, urbanized or otherwise, that explicate the varied aspects of the human condition for our times, New York City has come to describe the nature of life in the industrialized world between the twentieth and the twenty-first centuries. For good and for ill, its skyline remains the most powerful single visual statement about the civilization we have built, which may help explain why someone other than science fiction writers marked it for destruction.

Looking at the aftermath of 9/11 from outside the genre, there is no reason to give science fiction a privileged or special position as a witness to the times. From within the genre, however, the images of the airliners slamming into the towers of the World Trade Center almost feel like something we had once read or written, during what we are increasingly coming to think of as less complicated times. As the great billows of dust following the collapse of the Twin Towers settled, and the awful emptiness in the heart of the New York skyline gaped from the rubble for the first time, the old images returned to us. Science fiction's cultural iconoclasm had always served before — as, in truth, it still does today — as an exhortation to pause and reflect, a reality check (perhaps a strange word to use in this context) against our presumptions that the steelglass fortresses of the post-industrial era are destined to survive the jaws of Chronos. Also, it functioned as a salve against the anxiety of history, "a fear that the engines that we made to turn the world might shake us off, that we were both responsible for that engine, and usurped by it, that progress was ... a Dark Twin grinning at us out of tomorrow" (Clute, *Scores* 409). There is a certain cathartic pleasure in the contemplation of New York as Old Earth Excavation Site #1 in the year 4286 (or numbers to that effect), because the horror of collapse is long gone, and in any case we never experienced it in the first place. And even when we do see the rubble, even when we look at Chesley Bonestell's paintings of Manhattan ravaged by Soviet nuclear warheads from a Red Moon, the cautionary prediction of a dystopian tomorrow remains just that — a warning against potential outcomes in the future of someone's desire rather than a dirge to the print left by the hand of fate.

Now, however, those warnings — and the catharsis they brought — are almost beside the point. Before September 11, the images of a drowning New York from Spielberg's *A.I.: Artificial Intelligence* adumbrated a debatable, maybe improbable future, but not an impossible one. The 1997 advocated in 1981 by Carpenter's *Escape from New York* may not have come to pass, but the possibility existed that something similar might happen at some other juncture further down the line. The tidal wave that engulfed the city toward the end of *Deep Impact* did not reflect the actuality of the present, but it did constitute a meaningful hint at a possible tomorrow — meaningful, that is, until that day in September. The image of the New York skyline in *A.I.* included the drenched, crumbling towers of the World Trade Center; in *Escape from New York*, Snake Plissken infiltrated the prison-city by landing his glider on the roof of the WTC's north tower; in *Deep Impact*, the Twin Towers were among the buildings ravaged by the tsunami. In similar fashion to how the moon landing of July 1969 made Campbellian advocacy obsolete, or how the advent of the information age trampled into dust most of SF's early visions of the future, the horror of September 11, 2001, transformed forty years of science fictional scenarios of New York's (and, by extension, of the world's) destruction into lies — or more to the point, into fantasy, for fantasy is the literature of worlds that never happened, while SF is the literature of worlds that might.

Ultimately, however, part of the problem with our visions of the days of futures past has been rejection of ownership. We were not responsible for our predictions, because we thought that our desire and the fate that would meet it somewhere down the line would inevitably become one and the same. All too often, we tried to ease the deep-seated anxiety that the great world engine would shake us off through Campbellian bluster, through the categorical certainties of the insecure who told us the world while refusing authorship of the telling. But we were answerable for our words, yesterday as we are today, and we might well argue that the history of SF's growth is also the history of its acknowledgement of the responsibility of advocacy. By the time the towers fell, the genre had indeed been embracing this responsibility for a good many years, but the events of that day provided us all with a reminder of truly awful import:

> In September 2001, it seems very terrible to think that the sentences we write ... shape the world we write about, that what we write seems to be something

like that which terrorists do, for sf novelists and terrorists have always treated the world as a story to be told.... We would never literally create an act of terrorism, but the World Trade Center is the kind of sentence we write [Clute, *Scores* 410].

So this is the world we have written. We bear ownership of it, and of the past blindness that occluded our understanding of the gap between wish and actuality. If today the word truly does make the world, if the ultimate legacy of the information age is the power to alter the case of our lives by uttering it, then we dare not expose ourselves to the dangers of blind advocacy. We may not survive the experience. Like every other form of human action that attempts to recast the bare happening of events into patterns heavy with meaning, science fiction and everything it says are now bound, more tightly than ever before, to the spider's web of causality that turns words into acts. That is to say, they are linked to an interpretive lens that reads the world as a conglomerate of information made flesh, a territory of interconnected data transactions whose overall interplay alters the course of events like a massive body warps space-time around itself. Arguably, the many SF writers who have imaginatively reknit the weave of history in the aftermath of 9/11 have honored this bond, and thus contributed to our collective act of retelling the world in the light of its new circumstances.

Looking at the landscape of science fiction publishing in the last ten years or so, one may well receive the impression of a rich, vital, chaotic dance of imaginations at work. The simple enumeration of the movies, television series, games (both tabletop and computer), comics, and literary works comprising the genre's realm in the twenty-first century would fill an entire chapter, and still leave something out. Even confining the discussion to literary science fiction would leave precious little room for analysis. Now that SF has become, in its icons if not necessarily in the spirit of its aims, fully embedded in the cultural life of the planet entire, the proliferation and diversification of its voices have become impossible to encompass in the mind's eye, or at least far less susceptible to reduction than the largely monolithic landscape of the Campbell era. Advocacy is not dead — nor should we wish it to vanish — and works of science fiction are still published that attempt to bury the evidence of seventy years of progress and return their readers to the voice of the genre's original owners, but they are strangled, twisted narratives of dry regurgitation without much faith in their own brief. The other kinds of story, those that attempt to tell the future by grappling with the texture of the present, have exploded advocacy into myriad hues of individual convictions and personal beliefs that unreservedly advertise themselves as such, thus gaining paradoxical strength from the very acknowledgement of their biases. And ensconced into the warp and woof of each of these narratives, nestling at the core of their engines of plot, there always lies the embracing knowledge of the world as data, and of life in it as a rich, vigorous exchange of information.

Over a dozen generation starship narratives have appeared since 2001, a substantial increase in publication that, should it continue along these lines (as it seem to be destined to do), would make this decade or so the richest yet for the subgenre. After the scarcity of the eighties and the slow return to publication of the nineties, the science fiction of the early twenty-first century seems to have a newfound use for the slow boats, and for the themes they bring to the table. Once again, a degree of speculation is open to us: in an age where the exponential acceleration of data exchanges across the globe seems to have commensurately speeded up the pace at which generations succeed one another, the variables portrayed in generation starship narratives — transfer of information and values from parents to children, retention or loss of cultural identity — have perhaps become more important than they have ever been before. This reality, coupled with the balkanization and individualization of advocacy, may have prompted a heightening of focus toward the subgenre, which continues to pursue its brief in the infinitely refracted light of this new world culture. Also, because SF is a literature, and therefore animated by a desire to reexamine the endeavors of its past, generation starship narratives have been revisiting their previous haunts, reconfiguring Manning, Wilcox, Heinlein, Aldiss, and others into new fictional shapes — at once bridges to yesterday and reworkings of the matter of tomorrow, like Richard Paul Russo's *Ship of Fools* (2001), Stephen Baxter's *Mayflower II* (2004), and Joe Haldeman's *Old Twentieth* (2005).

Perhaps the most complex and fully historicized among the stories that have appeared over the last few years is Ken MacLeod's *Learning the World* (2005). The title, a clear homage to conceptual breakthrough, also refers to the name of the blog (short for "biolog") written by one of the protagonists of the story. We meet her at the beginning of Chapter 1, interestingly titled "The Ship Generation," when she begins the first page of the blog by telling us that the "world is four thousand years old. I was eight years old when I found that out for myself. My name is Atomic Discourse Gale..." (17). The world to which Atomic refers is the one she was born in — the "*Sunliner* But the Sky, My Lady! The Sky! *Forged this day 6 February 10 358 AG*" (22).[2] We are in a fairly distant future, about fourteen thousand years after the beginning of the human Diaspora into interstellar space. Mankind is spreading through the galaxy in enormous generation starships, similar in size and flight pattern to Bzonn's *Humanity* from "The Living Galaxy." In fact, *Learning the World* recasts the superhuman polity in Laurence Manning's story for the twenty-first century, this time looking at it from within the hull of the generation starship and from the viewpoint of the people traveling in it. Like the *Human-*

ity, the Sunliners — thus named because of the Long Sun–analogue providing light and heat to their interior — breed a generation of colonists every once in a while to settle a newly discovered solar system, remain in-system for a few years to replenish their store of reaction mass, and then fly onward again in the direction of other promising regions of space, ready to repeat the pattern should other systems prove habitable. Like the citizens of Bzonn's galactic Commonwealth, our descendants in *Learning the World* are virtually immortal, their genetic makeup and sensorium greatly enhanced by generous helpings of near-posthuman tech, and their society has also advanced past the stage of their ancestors' most glaring evils. MacLeod, however, is not Manning, and 2005 is not 1934. Both the galactic polity of the novel and the inhabitants of the *Sky* are flawed people seen from the vantage point of their often equally defective peers, not demigods dimly perceived between the lines of a history book. The entire enterprise of space travel and planetary colonization is sustained through the auspices of a complex, time-lagged economy that depends on its various components' constant expansionist push for its health. This expansionist push is saved from becoming the engine driving yet another colonialist empire by a) the absence of complex non-human life-forms anywhere in known space, and b) the enhanced control our descendants are able to exert on their impulses. Like all the generation starships plying the skein of space-time, the *Sky* is an elective democracy based on the distribution of power among its three constituent populations: the ship generation, to which Atomic belongs; the crew; and the founders.

The ship generation constitutes the starship's colonization complement. Born onboard the *Sky*, they are its youngest inhabitants, raised, educated, and to a certain extent genetically optimized for planetary settlement and the creation of an industrial infrastructure. The crew, on the other hand, are permanent spacefarers, adapted to life onboard the ship. By and large, these two populations interact but do not mix; the crew train the ship generation in the skills necessary to employ the technologies for settlement, while the future planetary colonists become, by virtue of that training, the lynchpin of the ship's economic and financial markets. And then there is the founder generation, the financers of the current expedition, born in the solar system settled immediately before the new one. They are all hundreds of years old at least, and constitute the first and most influential ruling body onboard every generation starship. They are caretakers, administrators, parents, and figures of transcendental authority to both crew and settlers — especially the latter, since the ship generation is always the youngest of the three, born only twenty years or so before their vessel is scheduled to arrive at its destination.

Shipboard life is thus regulated by the interaction between generations, by trade between specialized professional groups, and by an almost ungraspably complex network of legal clauses protecting the enterprise of planetary settlement. Progressively updated through fourteen thousand years of constant expansion, the ship's social contract represents a near-flawless interface with the outside universe, capable of addressing all contingencies except the ones nobody has encountered before — which brings us to the solar system around the Destiny star, as the inhabitants of the *Sky* have dubbed the sun they are now approaching. When the ship's remotes start beaming images of the various planets back to their parent vessel, those onboard witness, for the first time in the history of our race, the presence of a non-human civilization on the surface of the planet they have called Destiny II. Its inhabitants, a race of oxygen breathers whose similarity to giant bats would be too pulpish to accept if MacLeod did not carry the description with gusto and an absolute lack of shame, simply call it Ground. The various nation-states on Ground "are in the early stages of a technological civilization, with theories of evolution just being formulated and imaging technology just arriving at the 'kinematograph.'" When the two bat-people protagonists of *Learning the World* discover the *Sky* on their telescope, "it's only a matter of time before the two cultures meet and come into potential conflict" (Wolfe 56).

Onboard the now-detected *Sky*,[3] Atomic and everyone else have started worrying about that upcoming meeting in an enlightened, prime directive-conscious sort of way. They are developing a set of procedures for impacting the lives of their fellow sentients without ripping their civilization apart, and wondering about the deeper implications of their circumstances. This passage in Atomic's blog encapsulates the magnitude of the change:

> Yesterday we were in a universe that included us *and lots of cool stuff*: stars, galaxies, plasmas, cometary bodies, planets, and cows and giraffes and AIs and blue-green algae and lichen and microorganisms. Today we are in a universe that contains us and lots of cool stuff *and alien space bats*.... We are not living in the universe we thought we lived in yesterday. We have to start learning the world all over again [99–100].

The inhabitants of the generation starship are not under the sway of distorted worldviews or decayed social compacts. Their perception of the universe outside the vessel's hull is as enlightened as fourteen millennia of scientific and technological advancement have been able to make it, and the bat-people have nothing to offer them in that respect. Therefore, their brand of conceptual breakthrough is a reversal of the usual practices: instead of an act of intellectual apprehension directed outward from the prison of the mind, it is now a process of internalization of external inputs with a wholly psychological, social, and cultural significance. Starting from this upside-down premise, conceptual breakthrough spreads throughout the story, informing the learning of the world on the part of the *Sky*'s population as a whole, of the bat-people (who now have to share *their* universe with cool stuff and scary aliens in moon-sized starships), and of Atomic's generation (who are, after all, twenty-somethings still in training, thus learning the world twice over).

By the end of the novel, the learning process has yielded surprising results. Far from sending the bat-people into a tailspin, like the human eminences onboard the *Sky* had feared, the potential threat represented by the generation starship approaching their planet has instead prompted their nation-states to set aside their hostilities, thus creating the beginnings of something approaching a peaceful world government. The inhabitants of the *Sky*, on the other hand, have ended up performing embarrassingly poorly. After thousands of years of untested, unexamined assumptions concerning the encounter with other developed species, a series of egregious first-contact blunders[4] culminate in a bloodless, robot-controlled, ship-wide war between factions among the founders and the crew over the moral choices necessary to improve the lot of the bat-people. This war engulfs the ship generation as well, spreading to the asteroids they have already colonized, and despite the lack of casualties it remains an embarrassing piece of evidence of human misdemeanor once the two species have successfully—and peacefully—made contact. "Like a fight in front of the children," Atomic Discourse Gale writes in her biolog's last entry before asking the crucial question: "who are the children here? We were so certain that the aliens were about to plunge into conflict.... Our arguments were over whether and how to step in and sort it out. Yet as soon as they became aware of us and thought we were a threat to them all, they united.... In a sense, it's we who are learning from them" (299). For all the embarrassment in Atomic's narrative voice, however, we might argue that there is a certain optimism to be drawn from the novel's dramatic resolution. It gives us a universe more complex and merciful than we thought would be the case—complex because it keeps defeating our unexamined assumptions, and merciful because it lets us learn our lessons about those assumptions without the wholesale destruction that would otherwise have prevailed in the course of things.

This book is over, but the voyage is not. In 2009, Stephen Baxter published *Flood* and *Ark*, the first two novels in a series where generational space travel once again becomes the escape hatch for the human race, this time from a drowning Earth. Other books will follow in the years to come.

In 2008 and 2010, Elizabeth Bear published *Dust* and *Chill*, the first two parts of her *Jacob's Ladder* trilogy. *Jacob's Ladder* is the name of a ruined generation starship orbiting a star about to go nova, while its teeming posthuman crew, divided into two factions, wage war on each other. The third novel, *Grail*, is forthcoming.

Conclusion. Trip's End?

In his review of Terry Pratchett's *Thud* (2005), John Clute wrote that "I'd be very surprised if I were the only *Discworld* reader who thinks that the planet increasingly resembles a Generation Starship ... and that this World Ship is heading somewhere, in a direction. And that maybe the journey is coming to a climax" (*Canary* 192). If Clute's reading of what is probably the single most sustained fantastic series in the world — by now numbering over thirty titles — turns out to be correct, if the subgenre can claim for itself Great A'Tuin the World Turtle and its cargo, then this book will need a companion volume before too long.

As Spaceship Earth turns, and the generations succeeding one another on its surface weave stories to make sense of this turning, the slow boats to the stars remain in our industrialized, data-drenched, haphazardly globalized society as theaters of memory and loci for the dramatic exploration of the relationship between parents and children, ancestors and descendants. Their voyages, begun in defiance of a despairing reality of bondage, have become part of our history — a tiny part, no doubt, but a part nonetheless. They have faithfully reflected in the mirror of their plots the upheavals of the short twentieth century of science fiction, and have now begun to map out the opening years of the twenty-first. And how many generations have passed since Konstantin Tsiolkovsky and J. D. Bernal formulated the concept for the first time? Five or Six? Seven, maybe? This is not nearly enough time for it to be over. Many more people and many more stories will have to be born before we can even start thinking about trip's end — and what if Tsiolkovsky was right, and the trip never ends because this is the world, and the world is a voyage unto itself? We may have only just begun.

APPENDIX

The Generation Starship: A Chronological Bibliography

The following list, arranged chronologically, collects the aggregate of all the narratives and scientific articles I found on the generation starship. Where appropriate, I have indicated the magazine or journal of publication, complete with month and year. As for those works published either as novels or in short-story collections, I have provided the bibliographical information of the original edition.

Since this book narrates developments specific to the generation starship subgenre, the periods into which I have divided this chronology do not always match the accepted cutoff points for the various transitions SF has undergone in the eighty-odd years since its birth as a genre. For example, I start the part dedicated to the Gernsback years at 1934 instead of 1926, which would be the correct date for SF as a whole. On the other hand, it makes sense to begin the New Wave period at 1957, the year *Sputnik* started unraveling the grand narrative of Campbellian advocacy.

I have little doubt that this list is incomplete. I have done my best to account for every relevant story and article within the domain of science fiction publishing, but to imply that I somehow managed to find every last one of them would be to suggest the absurd. Instead, I have endeavored to present the largest possible sample for a meaningful analysis of my subject matter.

Genesis (1918–1929)

Konstantin Tsiolkovsky. "Budushchee Zemli i Chelovechestvo" ("Earth's Future and Mankind"). Kaluga, Russia: Izd. Avtora, 1928.
J.D. Bernal. *The World, the Flesh and the Devil*. London: Kegan Paul, 1929.

The Gernsback Age (1934–1940)

Laurence Manning. "The Living Galaxy." *Wonder Stories*, September 1934.
Don Wilcox. "The Voyage That Lasted 600 Years." *Amazing Stories*, October 1940.

Astounding Science Fiction and the Golden Age of SF (1941–1957)

Robert A. Heinlein. "Universe." *Astounding Science Fiction*, May 1941.
_____. "Common Sense." *Astounding Science Fiction*, October 1941.
Arthur C. Clarke. "Rescue Party." *Astounding Science Fiction*, May 1946.
Arthur Selling. "A Start in Life." *Galaxy Science Fiction*, September 1954.
Leslie R. Shepherd. "Interstellar Flight." *Science-Fiction Plus*, April 1953.
Clifford D. Simak. "Spacebred Generations." *Science-Fiction Plus*, August 1953.
Milton Lesser. *The Star Seekers*. Philadelphia, PA: John C. Winston Co., 1953.
Frank M. Robinson. "The Oceans Are Wide." *Science Stories*, April 1954.
E.C. Tubb. *The Space-Born*. In *The Man Who Japed/The Space-Born*. New York: Ace, 1956.

From the New Wave to the Edge of Cyberpunk (1957–1979)

John Brunner. "Lungfish." *Science Fantasy*, December 1957.
Chad Oliver. "The Wind Blows Free." *The Magazine of Fantasy and Science Fiction*, July 1957.
Brian W. Aldiss. *Non-Stop*. London: Faber and Faber, 1958.
Judith Merril. "Wish upon a Star." *The Magazine of Fantasy and Science Fiction*, December 1958.
Edmund Cooper. *Seed of Light*. New York: Ballantine, 1959.
J.T. McIntosh. *200 Years to Christmas. Science Fantasy* 12, no. 35, June 1959.
David Rome. "Bliss." *Science Adventures*, January 1962.
J.G. Ballard. "Thirteen to Centaurus." *Amazing Stories*, April 1962.
A.E. Van Vogt. *Rogue Ship*. New York: Doubleday, 1965.
Samuel R. Delany. *The Ballad of Beta-2*. In *Alpha Yes, Terra No!/The Ballad of Beta-2*. New York: Ace, 1965.
Poul Anderson. *Tau Zero*. New York: Doubleday, 1970. Fixup "To Outlive Eternity." *Galaxy Magazine*, June/August 1967.
James White. *All Judgment Fled*. *If*, December 1967–February 1968.
Alexei Panshin. *Rite of Passage*. New York: Ace, 1968.
Fritz Leiber. "Ship of Shadows." *The Magazine of Fantasy and Science Fiction*, July 1969.
Harry Harrison. *Captive Universe*. New York: G. P. Putnam's Sons, 1969.

Roger Dixon. *Noah II*. New York: Ace, 1970.
Ben Bova. *Exiled from Earth. Galaxy Magazine*, January/February 1971.
_____. *Flight of Exiles*. New York: E. P. Dutton, 1972.
_____. *End of Exile*. New York: E. P. Dutton, 1975.
Arthur C. Clarke. *Rendezvous with Rama*. London: Gollancz, 1973.
Harlan Ellison and Edward Bryant. *Phoenix Without Ashes*. New York: Fawcett Gold Medal, 1975.
James M. Ward. *Metamorphosis Alpha*. Lake Geneva: TSR, 1976.
Kevin O'Donnell, Jr. *Mayflies*. New York: Berkley, 1979.
George Zebrowski. *Macrolife*. New York: Harper & Row, 1979.

The Information Revolution and Beyond (1980–2010)

Damien Broderick. *The Dreaming Dragons*. Melbourne: Norstrilia Press, 1980.
Thomas Hubschman. *Space Ark*. New York: Tower Books, 1981.
Robert J. Sawyer. *Golden Fleece*. New York: Warner Books, 1990.
Frank M. Robinson. *The Dark Beyond the Stars*. New York: Tor, 1991.
Gene Wolfe. *Nightside the Long Sun*. New York: Tor, 1993.
_____. *Lake of the Long Sun*. New York: Tor, 1994.
_____. *Caldé of the Long Sun*. New York: Tor, 1994.
_____. *Exodus from the Long Sun*. New York: Tor, 1996.
Bruce Sterling. "Taklamakan." *Asimov's Science Fiction*, October/November 1998.
Rob Grant, *Colony*. London: Viking UK, 2000.
Richard Paul Russo. *Ship of Fools*. New York: Ace, 2001.
Alastair Reynolds. *Chasm City*. London: Gollancz/Orion, 2001.
John Clute. *Appleseed*. London: Orbit, 2001.
Ursula K. LeGuin. "Paradises Lost." *The Birthday of the World and Other Stories*. New York: HarperCollins, 2002.
Y. Kondo, F.C. Bruhweiler, J. Moore, C. Sheffield (Eds.). *Interstellar Travel and Multi-Generation Space Ships*. Burlington, Ont.: Apogee, 2003.
Stephen Baxter. *Mayflower II*. Hornsea, UK: PS Publishing, 2004.
Ken MacLeod. *Learning the World*. London: Orbit, 2005.
Joe Haldeman. *Old Twentieth*. New York: Ace, 2005.
Alastair Reynolds. *Pushing Ice*. London: Gollancz/Orion, 2006.
Stephen Baxter. *Flood*. London: Gollancz, 2008.
_____. *Ark*. London: Gollancz, 2009.
Elizabeth Bear. *Dust*. New York: Bantam Spectra, 2008.
_____. *Chill*. New York: Spectra/Ballantine Books, 2010.

Chapter Notes

Introduction

1. The light-year represents the distance light travels in a solar year (slightly less than ten trillion kilometers). Any distance expressed in light-years or their fractions (-months, -hours, -minutes, -seconds) indicates the time it will take the light emanated from any event occurring at that point in space-time to reach an observer on Earth. The sun, for example, is eight light-minutes away from us, which means that every time we look at it we see it as it was eight minutes ago. Alpha Centauri, the nearest star system, is 4.3 light-years away.

2. The gravity assist is a maneuver through which a spacecraft can alter its speed and direction by using the gravity well of a planet. In *Pale Blue Dot*, Carl Sagan illustrates the principle by imagining someone jumping on a merry-go-round and staying on for a few laps before letting go, speeding away in their intended direction at a relevantly higher speed. Sagan's example suggests that, irrespective of the means used, the wisdom of actually attempting a gravity assist here on Earth is questionable. Outside, however, it allows spacecraft to greatly increase their speed at no cost in fuel whatsoever.

3. The parsec is "the distance from which 1.0 AU appears to subtend one arc second of angle [1 degree = 3600 arc sec.], the equivalent of 3.26 light years" (Mallove & Matloff 8). The acronym AU stands for Astronomical Unit, the average distance between the Earth and the Sun.

Chapter 1

1. The titles provided in the text are translations of the originals.

2. Perhaps the most famous among Fyodorov's charges was a young writer by the name of Fyodor Mikhailovich Dostoyevsky.

3. Darra Goldstein relates a possibly apocryphal anecdote, according to which Fyodorov himself set Tsiolkovsky on his path to the stars. While he was explaining to his pupil his theory of resurrection, Tsiolkovsky asked him: "but how are all these people going to be squeezed onto Earth?" Fyodorov replied that there are many, many stars out there. This answer, apparently, was enough to trigger the young man's interest in rocketry (Goldstein 134).

4. As oblivious to the larger political issues of his time as he had been during the previous government's tenure, Tsiolkovsky wrote Stalin a letter of thanks, complimenting him on "[bringing] recognition to the work of self-taught persons" (Crouch 30).

5. To this day, the writers of the several *Star Trek* series have declined, perhaps wisely, to do anything more than sketch this socio-economic utopia in anything but the scantiest detail.

6. Edward Teller (1908–2003), commonly known as "the father of the hydrogen bomb," was a theoretical physicist of Hungarian origin who collaborated on the Manhattan project. During the 1950s, he became a staunch supporter of nuclear deterrence, as well as of the constant build-up and upgrade of nuclear arsenals. Trofim Denisovich Lysenko (1898–1976) was a Soviet geneticist who, rejecting Mendelian genetics, argued that it was environment, not genetic hereditary traits, that generated evolutionary change.

7. In particular, it is worth mentioning Carl Sagan's analysis in *Pale Blue Dot* of how the first images of the Earth as seen from space contributed to the development of ecological awareness. For the first time in human history, we saw our planet as it actually is, as opposed to how we wanted it to be: a comparatively tiny globe, lost in the utter blackness of space, the only home we have ever known and the only place so far where we can possibly exist.

Chapter 2

1. Even before its birth as genre literature, science fiction loved its puns. The title of Gernsback's novel, spelled out phonetically, reads "Ralph one-to-fore-see-for-one." Advocacy for the future seems to have been in his mind from the beginning.

2. *Galaxies Like Grains of Sand* is the title of a book Aldiss wrote in 1960, comprising a series of interconnected short stories à la *Dubliners*. Taken together, these stories map out the history of human civilization over a period of millions of years and billions of light years. Despite the evident similarities in the description of both Aldiss's book and Manning's short story, the narrative tone of the former could not be further from that of the latter.

3. Ralph 124 C 41+, History Zeta Nine, Bzonn — there is little point in trying to gloss over the awkwardness of these names. One is a play in words and numbers, one is more a classification than an actual first name, and the last sounds like the noise of a raygun being fired. Like everything else in the pretend futures of SF, the names of people far removed from anything we might consider standard need to convey a sense of alienness and estrangement, while at the same time sounding plausible. Not an easy balancing act to accomplish, and the annals of science fiction are replete with choices in this matter which, cool though they may have sounded at the time of writing, have long since worn out their appeal.

4. In Fermi's case, however, this speculation served to make a completely different point. During a lunch break at Los Alamos, where they were all working on The Bomb, Fermi was arguing about the existence of complex life outside the solar system with his friends Robert Oppenheimer and Leo Szilard. In typical fashion for him, Fermi had begun the argument by bluntly asking "Where are they?" Spacefaring aliens, Fermi maintained, could not possibly exist — otherwise, given the age of the universe and the speed at which an industrial civilization like ours developed from its animal beginnings, they would already have visited us. "Fermi's Paradox," as his argument is known today, still constitutes a stimulating invitation to speculate about life in the universe and alien contact. Two recent takes on the subject are Alastair Reynolds' *Pushing Ice* and Charles Stross's *Accelerando* (both written in 2005).

5. The reader will probably have noticed that the dates of Grimstone's awakenings do not match the planned pattern. A century spent in hibernation and a year spent in action would actually result in a 101-year cycle, so that the dates of his returns to "warm" life

should advance by one-year increments: 2167, 2268, 2369, and so forth. However, Wilcox is never particularly clear as to the exact duration of Grimstone's live intervals, or for that matter as to that of his sleeping periods. Ninety-nine years is a figure well within the ballpark of what we would describe as "a century." In the end, the narrative strikes the right balance: the count of years is kept precise enough to solidly anchor us to the timeline, while at the same time being fuzzy enough to allow Wilcox his choice of a nicely resonant set of recursive dates.

6. In his 1998 book *Guns, Germs, and Steel*.

7. It turns out that the long-dead engineers who built the *Flashaway* had included a second hibernation chamber, on the grounds that, should one chamber fail for whatever reason, the Keeper would still have the other.

8. A rather schizophrenic attitude in a magazine of narratives about nonexistent places and extravagant acts of derring-do entitled *Amazing Stories*.

9. In fact, we could plausibly argue that lack of isolation is precisely the nature of the problem for a lot of these collectives.

10. Undoubtedly, this is a highly compressed reading of a very complex situation, and it is not meant to do anything more than illustrate a general point pertaining to other, distantly related circumstances.

11. How large is it, anyway? The story does not say with precision, but textual inference and the spatial awareness displayed by the people onboard the *Flashaway* seem to indicate proportions not far in excess of those of a modern day ocean liner, maybe twice or three times its size — minuscule indeed, if we consider that it represents the expanse of their entire universe for the better part of a millennium.

12. Westfahl's own book, *Hugo Gernsback and the Century of Science Fiction*, published by McFarland in 2007, is perhaps the most cogently argued defense of Gernsback's legacy to have appeared so far. Another important work in this respect is Mike Ashley and Robert A. W. Lowndes' *The Gernsback Days* (Wildside Press, 2004).

Chapter 3

1. SF was not the only genre represented in the pulps, of course, and different people had different tastes when the time came to sink some money into their entertainment. Western, noir, romance, horror, science fiction — every genre was represented in those magazines, and every one of them had something to offer to readers looking for a few hours' worth of escape.

2. The discussion had originally taken place during Readercon 2007, on July 6 and 7, and was then reprinted in the September issue of *Locus* along with memorials, tributes from several writers in the field, and critical appreciations.

3. For any given value of "proper context," depending on the intentions and desires of the author.

4. We should make a distinction between the reading experience of "Universe" when it was originally written and its reading experience today. Since the procedures through which science fiction builds its worlds have been substantially influenced by Heinlein's writing, reading him in our times is a considerably less surprising endeavor than it once was. We simply know his narrative strategies too well. At the time this and the other stories were written, however, the reading public had had no previous encounter with this cognitively charged kind of SF, and since this is a history of the genre as much as it is a history of one of its sub-genres, it makes sense to approach "Universe" from the point of view of those who read it when it was brand new.

5. The ship was built in orbit around the moon, because, so the narrative informs us,

it was far too large to be constructed on earth and then launched into space without enormous expenditures in fuel and resources.

6. In his essay on the generation starship concept (2003), Palmer hints at the problematic ending Heinlein comes up with in "Common Sense." In that case, however, Palmer simply mentions it in one sentence, without going into it at greater length.

7. There is a truly harrowing aspect to the rebellion onboard the *Vanguard*. If we compare the date of departure with that of the mutiny, we will find out that it happened a scant seven years before the ship was due to arrive at Centaurus.

Chapter 4

1. There were exceptions, of course, the most notable being, once again, Asimov's *Foundation* series. However, we should also keep in mind that, in stories like these, the writers usually refused to quantify the passage of the years and the parsecs with any exactitude. Therefore, the impression was that of a time and place a long way from the here and now, but the actual moment of calibration was left to the readers themselves.

2. Although many readers happily accepted them without question.

Chapter 5

1. This is one of the reasons why horror literature and movies did extremely well during that decade. The threats they featured often came in the guise of a science fictional premise — mutated insects or reptiles, aliens, strange phenomena from other dimensions — but like the gnarled alien trees in *Earth vs. the Flying Saucers*, they rightly belonged to the realm of night terrors and bogeymen.

2. Part of the committee's report read: "A satellite cannot simply drop a bomb. An object released from a satellite does not fall. So there is no special advantage in being over the target. Indeed, the only way to "drop" a bomb directly down from a satellite is to carry out aboard the satellite a rocket launching of the magnitude required for an intercontinental missile" (qtd. in McCurdy 68). For this reason, the moon as a launch platform would have presented considerable logistical and technical problems, while at the same time being less effective and more expensive than a missile silo on earth.

3. In fact, NASA's budget, even at the height of the *Apollo* program, never exceeded 5 percent of the total Federal Budget.

4. "Great writer though he was," Ballard comments, "H. G. Wells has had a disastrous influence on the subsequent course of science fiction" (197). This attribution seems overly harsh, however. Surely we do not have the right to lay the excesses of the Gernsback and Campbell generations at Wells' door? He used his fantastic inventions and otherworldly locales as stages for the human drama, not simply as vehicles for a power fantasy. Is it his fault that his self-styled pupils often paid little more than lip service to the spirit of his achievements?

5. Apart from *The Time Machine* itself (1895), we can cite as examples of this perspective works like Olaf Stapledon's *Last and First Men* (1930), John W. Campbell's already discussed "Twilight," and Arthur C. Clarke's *The City and the Stars* (1956).

6. The message suggests that psychological conditioning, subliminal suggestion, psychotropic drugs, and even shock treatment should be used to engender in the Tripborn a loathing for the environment of the ship, thereby forcing them to colonize Tau Ceti II. In that respect, Yoseida can be said to embody a Campbellian, pre–World War II ethos according to which the end always justifies the means.

7. Heinlein came closer to it than anyone else when he had the vast majority of the Crew continue the trip onboard the *Vanguard*. In that case, however, the continuation of the voyage had not been the result of human agency, but of human ignorance.

8. The definitive example of this mindset in the stories we have seen so far is probably the moment in "The Oceans Are Wide" when Matty Kendrick, confronted with the choice between remaining a musician and becoming captain of the *Astra*, immediately picks the captaincy, and simply watches as the Predict smashes his musical instrument to pieces.

9. The *Humanity* in Manning's "The Living Galaxy" and the *Flashaway* in Wilcox's "The Voyage That Lasted 600 Years" have been left out of this shortlist because their narrative setup and viewpoint characters prevented the emergence of the circumstances necessary for conceptual breakthrough. In the case of "The Living Galaxy," the thrust of History Zeta Nine's narrative is the same as that found in a history book — in other words, a straight academic infodump designed to *not* contain any mystery. Similarly, Wilcox's story features a first-person narrator whose role as historian and function within the plot give him — and by extension us — virtual omniscience. The origin of the ship, its flight and destination, and its relationship to the physical medium through which it is traveling are all a known quantity by the time the story begins, so that the cognitive puzzles present in the other generation starship tales simply do not exist..

10. Or, in the case of Robinson's story, mostly chosen not to remember.

11. From this perspective, for example, the pseudo–Christian myth of the Lines from the Beginning in "Universe" carries a certain metatextual resonance, despite its status as superstitious cant within the narrative itself.

12. There is also a certain tongue-in-cheek whiff of the American Southwest worldview built into Sam's character. Apart from the decidedly Texan difference in proportions between him and everyone else onboard the ship, his psychological makeup is also the quintessential embodiment of a Wild West sense of boundlessness, the yearning for a lack of frontiers that cannot but clash with the pent-up confines of his vessel.

13. We could also see Simak's "Spacebred Generations" as part of this trend. As John Clute rightly points out, Simak is one of the only two writers of the '40s and '50s (the other is Ray Bradbury) who shared Oliver's artistic bent (93), and indeed Jon Hoff's peregrinations display substantial amounts of attention to the human dynamics onboard his generation starship. On the other hand, the story also reads as a standard forgetfulness-and-rediscovery scenario, complete with an outside-referent conceptual breakthrough supported by physical clues pointing toward the disconnect between the social worldview and its correspondent reality. Those readers who, like this writer, have developed an appreciation for graceful cop-outs, should consider calling this story "transitional."

14. Aldiss dedicated the novel to Ted Carnell, "Editor of *New Worlds* and *Science Fantasy* and starter of *Non-Stop*."

15. "Spacebred Generations," "Lungfish," "The Wind Blows Free," and *Non-Stop* all feature one or more types of hydroponic plants. The idea had evidently become commonplace, and not just in generation starship stories.

16. Time periods roughly equivalent to days.

17. Like, for example, a telepathic rabbit, whom they force to briefly interrogate Complain during a particularly tense plot turn.

18. The play on words is probably not casual. Once Vyann finds out what actually happened, she really does read to complain.

19. At one point toward the end of the log, Gregory Complain finds a moment to mourn Procyon V's colonists, who are certainly going through the same experience.

20. By the time the ague manifests itself, the ship is beyond even communicating with the colony, and it would literally take years for the crew to turn it around at the speed at which they are moving.

21. It turns out that the Giants have kidnapped a number of dizzy children to test their bodies' ability to survive on Earth. Those tests were successful.

22. A significant last name, given his function.

23. Again, it is difficult not to see resonances in the two names. Abel, the man named after Cain's saintly, murdered brother, is gradually revealed as a manipulator. On the other hand Francis, who carries the name of the saint who loved all creatures great and small, grows tired of the people he is trying to save as soon as he truly comes into contact with them.

24. Not for long, however. In the 1980s, Clarke and his co-writer, Gentry Lee, transformed *Rama* into a series, exploding the mystery and bringing it into the light of a Campbellian day.

25. Players could choose to interpret any of these characters.

Chapter 6

1. In much the same way John Connor had ensured his birth by sending his own father into the past, Skynet had sent the first terminator after Kyle Reese to ensure its own birth as well. The two pairs constituted by John Connor/Skynet and Kyle Reese/terminator are essentially specular opposites in the timeline of the first two movies.

2. With the notable exceptions of Jack Williamson, who kept writing almost up to his death in 2006, and Arthur C. Clarke, who, though semi-retired, published a few collaborations (especially with Stephen Baxter) until his passing in 2009.

3. That is mostly because Heinlein's fiction very often served as the springboard for his political and social views. More often than not, reading a Heinlein narrative entails the careful negotiation of a maze of advocacy and proselytizing half-hidden among the honest, truthful lie.

4. At the time of his death in 1991, his body of work included an edited compendium of Shakespeare's collected works.

5. War Operation Plan Response. As with many other acronyms in fiction, there is a tongue-in-cheek aspect to the name ("whopper"), of which the computer's operators and military authorities are hilariously unaware. Steven Falken, the scientist who had originally created the artificial intelligence and understands it for what it really is, calls it Joshua, after his defunct son.

6. With the exception of his 1982 novel *Friday*. Even that, however, failed to recapture the energy of the early years, when computers were just boxes that did stuff and the future was new. Langford briskly summed up the novel's substance when he wrote that "*Friday* is not bad at all; on the other hand it isn't startlingly good, and comes nowhere near Heinlein's one-time peaks" (47).

7. Before the eighties, Vinge had published two other novels, *Grimm's World* (1969; revised in 1987 with the title *Tatja Grimm's World*) and *The Witling* (1976), in which his concerns with information theory and with the runaway technological progress he saw coming in the near future appear in embryonic form.

8. Although Spider Pete thinks of Katrinko as a woman, he is also aware that his choice is prompted by nothing more than a mixture of appearances and semantic convenience. Katrinko is a neuter, a fully degendered human who has traded its sexual organs for, as we learn in the story, an eight percent increase in its metabolic processes — a considerable advantage in its line of work (868).

9. Thus the cards are at once data and money, the physical embodiment of our age's perception of information as currency.

10. In *Lake of the Long Sun*, Silk revives one of them. Her name is Mamelta, and she is the first to openly tell him that their world is actually the "starcrosser *Whorl*" (460).

11. Unlike the Cargo, who people the whorl and the narrative from the beginning to the end, we do not get to see much at all of the Crew in the *Long Sun* sequence. We meet a few "fliers," airborne maintenance and repair crews who, under Mainframe's guidance, ceaselessly fight a losing battle against the dying of the *Whorl*'s systems, and the manifestations of the Nine through the Sacred Windows. For the rest, the inner workings and social life of Mainframe remain largely shrouded in mystery.

12. Even worse, one of the numerous minor characters in the *Long Sun* cycle — albeit not one of the most trustworthy — tells Silk that the Caldé was actually murdered by the Ayuntamiento.

13. At this stage, and in the interest of clarity, it is useful to give the full sequence. *The Book of the New Sun* includes *The Shadow of the Torturer* (1980), *The Claw of the Conciliator* (1981), *The Sword of the Lictor* (1982), *The Citadel of the Autarch* (1983), and a coda, *The Urth of the New Sun* (1987). *The Book of the Long Sun* comprises *Nightside the Long Sun* (1993), *Lake of the Long Sun*, *Caldé of the Long Sun* (both 1994), and *Exodus from the Long Sun* (1996). Finally, *The Book of the Short Sun* is a trilogy constituted by *On Blue's Waters* (1999), *In Green's Jungles* (2000), and *Return to the Whorl* (2001). Over the years, the *New Sun* and *Short Sun* tetralogies have also been collected in omnibus editions: the first tetralogy became *Shadow & Claw* and *Sword & Citadel* (both 1994), while the second became *Litany of the Long Sun* and *Epiphany of the Long Sun* (both 2000). The quotes and page references in this chapter are taken from the omnibus editions.

14. But then again, how do we know his acknowledgement of insanity is not itself a lie?

15. Horn had originally planned to call his narrative *The Book of Silk*, as he himself tells Silk at the end of *Exodus from the Long Sun*.

16. A characteristic shared by Typhon's personality download, whom the people of the whorl also know as "Two-Headed Pas."

17. Specifically, in *Claw of the Conciliator*, chapters 4 (p. 234) and 24 (p. 360).

18. Or rather, I was not able to find any. This does not necessarily constitute evidence that such hints are actually present, but it is nevertheless useful, when reading anything written by Wolfe, to pepper one's critical analysis with these handy disclaimers.

19. "He is *probably not* Severian," John Clute writes with commendable caution before reminding us that, during one of his spiritual trips to Urth, Horn is nevertheless "mistaken for a torturer from the Matachin Tower where Severian grew up, because of his mien, his clothing, and the black sword he conjures out of thin air to replace the staff he has left behind on Blue, where his real body sleeps" (251). With Wolfe, one never knows.

20. In *Shadow of the Torturer*, Severian's finding of Triskele takes place in chapter 4.

21. Like the *Whorl*, *Rama* is cylindrical, and many of its workings remain mysterious.

22. Our Einsteinian universe, where Urth resides, carries the name of Briah.

23. In fact, the terrorists in *Peacemaker* come from several different countries, including Pakistan and Eastern Europe, and they receive help from a disaffected Red Army colonel.

Conclusion

1. One of these songs is Billy Joel's "Miami 2017 (Seen the Lights Go Out on Broadway)," which closed his 1976 album *Turnstiles*. Its lyrics constitute an unnamed man's first-person recollections of New York's last night sometime in the early 21st century (as the title implies, he now lives in Miami in the year 2017), when he and thousands of people gathered at an unauthorized concert in Brooklyn "*to watch the island bridges blow.*" Originally written as a science-fictional commentary on the city's near-bankruptcy in the early 1970s, the song acquired a particularly painful poignancy exactly twenty-five years later,

when the 9/11 attacks literally realized some of the images Joel had created for its lyrics ("*I watched the mighty skyline fall*"). At the October 20, 2001, concert for New York, Joel played "Miami 2017," and at its end said: "I wrote that song 25 years ago. I thought it was going to be a science fiction song; I never thought it would happen. But unlike the end of that song, we ain't going anywhere!" As he went right into "New York State of Mind," the roar of the crowd's standing ovation almost drowned out the first few notes of that second piece (http://www.youtube.com/watch?v=2Xl558k0QAo).

2. We have come a long way from the names in the pulps, and yet a whiff of them remains in the knowing playfulness of such monikers as Atomic Discourse Gale, Horrocks Mathematical, or Synchronic Narrative Storm (the last two are both members of the generation starship's population). As for the ship itself, Gary K. Wolfe remarks that with a name like *But the Sky, My Lady! The Sky!* it sounds like something coming "from the used-ship lot of Iain Banks' Culture" (55), a comment referring to Banks' habit of giving his starships outrageous, winkingly funny names, often indicative of a peculiar trait in the personality of the vessel's AI. Some, like the Torturer-class Rapid Offensive Unit *Killing Time* in *Excession* (1996), or the General Contact Unit *Arbitrary* in "The State of the Art" (1989), are relatively uncomplicated. Others, like the General Systems Vehicle *Anticipation of a New Lover's Arrival, The*— again from *Excession*— are enough to make unwary readers feel put upon.

3. There may be a play on words here between Ground and *Sky*, and if so, then the novel is the place where the sky meets the ground, both literally in the encounter between the two species and figuratively in the connection between the wanderlust of flying (both species can) and the rootedness of a planet-referential mindset (which both species need).

4. Remotes are discovered by the bat-people, who proceed to reverse-engineer them into jumpstarting a scientific and technological evolution almost overnight; bug-ridden software automatically responds to what it interprets as crude hails with an unauthorized transmission from the ship to Ground; the AIs overseeing the creation of the remotes use them to "infect" the brain of the planet's slave caste, the so-called "trudges," who suddenly develop the power of speech.

Bibliography

Aldiss, Brian. *Non-Stop*. London: Gollancz, 2000.
_____, and David Wingrove. *Trillion Year Spree*. 2nd ed. London: House of Stratus, 2001.
Anderson, Poul. *Tau Zero*. London: Gollancz, 2006.
Ashley, Mike. *Transformations: The Story of the Science Fiction Magazines from 1950 to 1970*. Liverpool: Liverpool University Press, 2005.
Asimov, Isaac. "Social Science Fiction." *Turning Points: Essays on the Art of Science Fiction*. Ed. Damon Knight. New York: Harper, 1977. 29–61.
_____, Martin Harry Greenberg, and Charles G. Waugh, eds. *Starships*. New York: Ballantine, 1983.
Attebery, Brian. "The Magazine Era: 1926–1960." James and Mendlesohn 32–47.
Ballard, J.G. "Thirteen to Centaurus." *The Voices of Time*. 2nd ed. London: Orion 2001. 92–115.
_____. "Which Way to Inner Space?" *A User's Guide to the Millennium*. New York: Picador USA, 1996. 195–198.
Bernal, J. D. *The World, the Flesh, and the Devil: An Enquiry into the Future of the Three Enemies of the Rational Soul*. Bloomington: Indiana University Press, 1969.
Bould, Mark. "Cyberpunk." *A Companion to Science Fiction*. Ed. David Seed. Malden, MA: Blackwell, 2008. 217–247.
_____, et al., eds. *Fifty Key Figures in Science Fiction*. London: Routledge, 2010.
Brown, Charles N., John Clute, Graham Sleight, and Gary K. Wolfe. "Heinlein at 100." *Locus*. Sept. 2007: 51–54.
Brunner, John. "Lungfish." *Entry to Elsewhen*. New York: DAW, 1972. 53–89.
Burrows, William E. *This New Ocean: The Story of the First Space Age*. London: Random, 1998.
Campbell, John W. "Twilight." *The Science Fiction Hall of Fame: Volume One, 1929–1964*. Ed. Robert Silverberg. 2nd ed. New York: Orb, 1998. 24–41.
_____. "History to Come." *Astounding Science Fiction*. May 1941: 5–6.
Clarke, Arthur C. *Rendezvous with Rama*. London: Gollancz, 2006.
_____. "Rescue Party." *Arthur C. Clarke: The Collected Stories*. London: Gollancz 2001. 35–55.
Clary, David A. *Rocket Man: Robert H. Goddard and the Birth of the Space Age*. New York: Hyperion, 2003.
Clute, John. *Canary Fever: Reviews*. Harold Wood, UK: Beccon, 2009.
_____. *Look at the Evidence: Essays and Reviews*. New York: Serconia Press, 1995.
_____. "Science Fiction from 1980 to the Present." James and Mendlesohn 64–78.

_____. *Scores: Reviews 1993–2003*. Harold Wood, UK: Beccon, 2003.
_____, and Peter Nicholls, eds. *The Encyclopedia of Science Fiction*. London: Orbit, 1993.
Conklin, Groff, ed. *The Science Fiction Galaxy*. New York: Permabooks, 1950.
Crouch, Tom D. *Aiming for the Stars: The Dreamers and Doers of the Space Age*. Washington: Smithsonian, 1999.
Dickinson, Terence. *The Universe and Beyond*. 4th ed. New York: Firefly, 2004.
Driussi, Michael Andre. *Lexicon Urthus: A Dictionary for the Urth Cycle*. 2nd ed. Albany, CA: Sirius Fiction, 2008.
Edwards, Malcolm J. "Gernsback, Hugo." Clute and Nicholls 490–491.
_____, and John Clute. "Palmer, Raymond A(rthur)." Clute and Nicholls 905.
_____, and _____. "Campbell, John W(ood) Jr." Clute and Nicholls 187–188.
Freeman, Chris. "The Social Function of Science." Swann and Apprahamian. London: 101–131.
Gerrold, David. *The World of Star Trek*. 3rd ed. London: Virgin, 1996.
Gibson, William. *Burning Chrome*. 2nd ed. New York: Eos, 2003.
Goldstein, Darra. *Nikolai Zabolotsky: Play for Mortal Stakes*. Cambridge: Cambridge University Press, 1993.
Gordon, Joan. "Gene [Rodman] Wolfe." Bould et al. 245–250.
Griffin, Brian, and David Wingrove. *Apertures: A Study of the Writings of Brian W. Aldiss*. Westport, CT: Greenwood Press, 1984.
Gunn, James. *Alternate Worlds: The Illustrated History of Science Fiction*. Englewood Cliffs, NJ: Prentice-Hall, 1975.
Gustafson, John, and Peter Nicholls. "Bonestell, Chesley." Clute and Nicholls 143.
Hagerty, Jack, and John C. Rogers. *Spaceship Handbook*. Livermore, CA: ARA, 2001.
Haldeman, Joe. "Colonizing Other Worlds." Kondo et al. 62–68.
Harrison, Albert A. *Spacefaring: The Human Dimension*. Berkeley: University of California Press, 2001.
Harrison, Harry. *Captive Universe*. New York: Berkley, 1969.
Heinlein, Robert. *Beyond This Horizon*. New York: New American, 1948.
_____. "Common Sense." *Astounding Science Fiction*. Oct 1941: 102–154.
_____. "Universe." *Astounding Science Fiction*. May 1941: 9–42.
Herbert, Frank. *Dune*. New York: Ace, 1999.
Hobsbawm, Eric. *The Age of Extremes: A History of the World, 1914–1991*. New York: Vintage, 1996.
Holland, Steve. *Sci-Fi Art: A Graphic History*. New York: Collins, 2009.
James, Edward. *Science Fiction in the 20th Century*. Oxford: Oxford University Press, 1994.
_____, and Farah Mendlesohn, eds. *The Cambridge Companion to Science Fiction*. Cambridge, UK: Cambridge University Press, 2003.
King, Stephen. *Danse Macabre*. London: Warner, 1993.
Kondo, Yoji, et al., eds. *Interstellar Travel and Multi-Generation Space Ships*. Burlington, Ont.: Apogee, 2003.
Landon, Brooks. *Science Fiction after 1900: From the Steam Man to the Stars*. New York: Routledge, 1995.
Langford, David. *Up Through an Empty House of Stars: Reviews and Essays, 1980–2002*. Holicong, PA: Cosmos Press, 2003.
Lovecraft, H. P. "The Call of Cthulhu." *The Dunwich Horror and Others*. Corrected 10th ed. Sauk City, WI: Arkham, 1989. 125–54.
Luckhurst, Roger. "J[ames] G[raham] Ballard." Bould, Butler, Roberts and Vint 12–17.
MacLeod, Ken. *Learning the World: A Scientific Romance*. New York: Tor, 2005.
Mallove, Eugene, and Gregory Matloff. *The Starflight Handbook: A Pioneer's Guide to Interstellar Travel*. New York: John Wiley, 1989.

Manning, Laurence. "The Living Galaxy." *Wonder Stories*. Sept. 1934: 437–44.
Matloff, Gregory L., Les Johnson, and C. Bangs. *Living off the Land in Space: Green Roads to the Cosmos*. New York: Springer, 2007.
McCurdy, Howard E. *Space and the American Imagination*. Washington: Smithsonian, 1997.
Miller, Ron. *The Dream Machines: A Pictorial History of the Spaceship in Art, Science and Literature*. Malabar, Florida: Krieger, 1993.
_____, and Frederick C. Durant III. *The Art of Chesley Bonestell*. London: Paper Tiger, 2001.
Nicholls, Peter. "Conceptual Breakthrough." Clute and Nicholls 254–257.
_____. "Generation Starships." Clute and Nicholls 480–481.
_____. "New Wave." Clute and Nicholls 865–867.
Oliver, Chad. "The Wind Blows Free." *A Sea of Space*. Ed. William F. Nolan. New York: Bantam, 1970. 13–39.
Osman, Tony. *Space History*. New York: St. Martin's, 1983.
Palmer, Christopher. "Generation Starships and After: 'Never Anywhere to Go but In?'" *Extrapolation* 44 (2003): 311–330.
Parnell, Frank H., and Peter Nicholls. "Science Stories." Clute and Nicholls 1074.
Person, Lawrence. "Suns New, Long, and Short: An Interview with Gene Wolfe." Wright 167–176.
Prantzos, Nikos. *Our Cosmic Future: Humanity's Fate in the Universe*. Cambridge: Cambridge University Press, 2000.
Regis, Edward, Jr. "The Moral Status of Multigenerational Interstellar Exploration." *Interstellar Migration and the Human Experience*. Ed. Ben Finney and Eric M. Jones. Berkeley: University of California Press, 1985. 248–59.
Robinson, Frank M. *The Dark Beyond the Stars*. New York: Tor, 1998.
_____. "The Oceans Are Wide." *Science Stories* Apr. 1954: 6–70.
Russo, Richard Paul. *Ship of Fools*. New York: Ace, 2001.
Rynin, N.A., ed. *K.E. Tsiolkovskii: Life, Writings, and Rockets*. Jerusalem: Israel Program for Scientific Translations, 1971.
Sagan, Carl. *Pale Blue Dot: A Vision of the Human Future in Space*. London: Headline, 1995.
Sheffield, Charles. "Fly Me to the Stars: Interstellar Travel in Fact and Fiction." Kondo et al. 20–28.
Shepherd, Leslie R. "Interstellar Flight." *Science Fiction Plus*. Apr. 1953: 56–60.
Simak, Clifford D. "Spacebred Generations." *Science Fiction Plus*. Aug. 1953: 4–21.
Stableford, Brian, and Peter Nicholls. "Science Fiction Plus." Clute and Nicholls 1071.
_____. "New Worlds." Clute and Nicholls 867–868.
Sterling, Bruce. "Preface." *Mirrorshades: The Cyberpunk Anthology*. Ed. Bruce Sterling. New York: Ace, 1988. ix-xvi.
_____. "*Taklamakan*." *The Hard SF Renaissance*. Ed. David G. Hartwell and Kathryn Cramer. New York: Tor, 2003. 856–883.
Steward, Fred. "Political Formation." Swann and Apprahamian 37–77.
Swann, Brenda, and Francis Apprahamian. *J. D. Bernal: A Life in Science and Politics*. London: Verso, 1999.
Synge, Ann. "Early Years and Influences." Swann and Apprahamian 1–16.
Tsiolkovsky, Konstantin Eduardovich. "Budushchee Zemli i Chelovechestvo." Kaluga, Russia: Izd. Avtora, 1928.
_____. "Exploration of the Universe with Reaction Machines." *Collected Works of K.E. Tsiolkovskiy, Volume 2: Reactive Flying Machines*. Ed. A.A. Blagonravov. Washington, D.C.: NASA Technical Translations, 1965. 212–349.

Vinge, Vernor. "Bookworm, Run!" *The Collected Stories of Vernor Vinge*. New York: Orb, 2002. 16–44.

———. *A Deepness in the Sky*. New York: Tor, 2000.

———. *A Fire upon the Deep*. New York: Tor, 1993.

Wilcox, Don. "The Voyage That Lasted 600 Years." *Amazing Stories*. Oct. 1940: 82–104.

Wolfe, Gary K. "Learning the World." *Locus*. November 2005: 55–56.

Wolfe, Gene. *Caldé of the Long Sun*. *Epiphany of the Long Sun*. New York: Orb, 2000. 9–315.

———. *The Citadel of the Autarch*. *Sword & Citadel*. New York: Orb, 1994. 205–411.

———. *The Claw of the Conciliator*. *Shadow & Claw*. New York: Orb, 1994. 217–413.

———. *Exodus from the Long Sun*. *Epiphany of the Long Sun*. New York: Orb, 2000. 319–718.

———. *In Green's Jungles*. New York: Tor, 2000.

———. *Lake of the Long Sun*. *Litany of the Long Sun*. New York: Orb, 2000. 267–543.

———. *Nightside the Long Sun*. *Litany of the Long Sun*. New York: Orb, 2000. 7–264.

———. *On Blue's Waters*. New York: Tor, 2000.

———. *Return to the Whorl*. New York: Tor, 2001.

———. *The Shadow of the Torturer*. *Shadow & Claw*. New York: Orb, 1994. 9–211.

———. *The Sword of the Lictor*. *Sword & Citadel*. New York: Orb, 1994. 9–202.

———. *The Urth of the New Sun*. New York: Orb, 1987.

Wolfe, Tom. *The Right Stuff*. New York: Bantam, 2001.

Wollheim, Donald A. *The Universe Makers: Science Fiction Today*. New York: Harper, 1971.

Wright, Peter. *Attending Daedalus: Gene Wolfe, Artifice, and the Reader*. Liverpool: Liverpool University Press, 2003.

———, ed. *Shadows of the New Sun: Wolfe on Writing/Writers on Wolfe*. Liverpool: Liverpool University Press, 2007.

Ziff, William B. "AMERICA *Must Prepare* NOW!" *Amazing Stories* Oct. 1940: 8–9.

Zubrin, Robert. *The Case for Mars: The Plan to Settle the Red Planet and Why We Must*. New York: Simon & Schuster, 1996.

Index

The Age of Extremes (Hobsbawm) 235–238
A.I.: Artificial Intelligence (film) 240–241
Aldiss, Brian 2–3, 14, 43, 96, 153, 154, 217, 226, 254*n*, 257*n*
Amazing Stories 41, 45–46, 55, 63, 67, 77, 82, 83, 86, 133, 145, 153, 181, 254*n*
"AMERICA *Must Prepare* NOW!" 82
Anderson, Poul 3, 196
Apertures (Wingrove and Griffin) 176
Apollo 11 149
Ark (Baxter) 246
Ashley, Mike 255*n*
Asimov, Isaac 7–8, 14, 37, 39, 66, 87, 98, 136, 188
Astounding Science Fiction 63, 79, 80–81, 83, 86, 88, 90, 94, 95, 97, 106, 108, 109, 112, 120, 124, 125, 141–142, 150–153, 154
Attebery, Brian 41, 44, 53, 78

The Ballad of Beta-2 (Delany) 3, 186–187
Ballard, J.G. 2–3, 153, 154–157, 180, 188, 200, 212, 217, 227, 235, 256*n*
Banks, Iain M. 1, 200–201, 259*n*
The Battle of Dorking (Chesney) 145
Bear, Greg 200–201
Bernal, J.D. 4, 11, 19, 30–38, 40, 44–45, 47, 52, 54, 94, 127, 132, 160, 190, 234, 236, 247
Bethke, Bruce 197
Beyond This Horizon (Heinlein) 90–92
"Blow-Ups Happen" (Heinlein) 97
Bonestell, Chesley 39, 123–125, 130, 142, 149
The Book of the Long Sun (Wolfe) 3, 220–238, 258*n*
The Book of the New Sun (Wolfe) 229–238, 258*n*
The Book of the Short Sun (Wolfe) 229, 232–238, 258*n*

"Bookworm, Run!" (Vinge) 191
Brown, Charles N. 94
Brunner, John 3, 153, 164

"The Call of Cthulhu" (Lovecraft) 9
Campbell, John W. 3, 14, 39, 48, 63, 79, 80–81, 83–89, 90, 94, 95–98, 109, 120, 140–141, 146, 147, 149–152, 154, 167, 178, 180, 189, 194, 201, 205, 241–242
Carnell, John 153, 157, 257*n*
Challenger disaster 195
Childhood's End (Clarke) 196
Chill (Elizabeth Bear) 246
The City and the Stars (Clarke) 256*n*
The City's End (Page) 239
Clarke, Arthur C. 3, 133, 160, 188, 196, 235, 257*n*
Clute, John 2, 9, 165, 194–197, 220–221, 239–242, 256*n*, 258*n*
Collier's 122–123
Collier's series (Bonestell and Von Braun) 39, 123–124
"Common Sense" (Heinlein) 2–3, 12, 14–15, 111–119, 120, 131, 142, 152, 161, 162, 163, 213, 225
conceptual breakthrough (Nicholls) 162–164, 169, 191, 243
Conklin, Groff 47
The Conquest of Space (Ley and Bonestell) 39, 123, 124, 126

Danse Macabre (King) 143–147
The Dark Beyond the Stars (Robinson) 2–3, 204–211, 226
Deep Impact (film) 240–241
A Deepness in the Sky (Vinge) 200
Delany, Samuel R. 3, 96, 151, 156–157
Delta Force (film) 237

Destination Moon (film) 124
Diamond, Jared 61
Discworld series (Pratchett) 246–247
Dozois, Gardner 197
The Dreaming Dragons (Broderick) 201
Dune (Herbert) 66, 216
Dust (Elizabeth Bear) 246

Earth Abides (Stewart) 135
Earth vs. the Flying Saucers (film) 143, 147, 255n
Edwards, Malcolm J. 43
Ellison, Harlan 3, 91, 156
Escape from New York (film) 240–241
Excession (Banks) 1
The Exorcist (film) 146
The Exploration of Space (Clarke) 126

Fermi, Enrico 53, 254n
Final Fantasy (film) 240
A Fire Upon the Deep (Vinge) 1, 199–200
Flood (Baxter) 246
forgetfulness pattern 15–17, 161
Foundation series (Asimov) 66, 136, 255n
Freeman, Chris
"The Future of Earth and Mankind" (Tsiolkovsky) 11, 27–29, 54
Fyodorov, Nikolai 25–27

Galaxy 124, 150, 151
Galileian revolution 108, 111–112, 116–117, 162–163
Gernsback, Hugo 3, 14, 39, 41–47, 48, 52, 55, 63, 73, 77–78, 82–83, 86, 87, 89–90, 108, 109, 121, 126, 153, 167, 190, 192, 201
"The Gernsback Continuum" (Gibson) 40, 201
Gerrold, David 77
Gibson, William 39–40, 191, 197–199
Goddard, Robert 4, 19, 20–25, 28–30, 32–33, 35–38, 44–45, 50, 55, 120–121, 132
Golden Fleece (Sawyer) 201
Goldstein, Darra 253n
Gordon, Joan 221
Grail (Elizabeth Bear) 246
Gunn, James 43, 45

Haldeman, Joe 5, 17
Harrison, Albert A.
Heinlein, Robert 2–3, 12, 14, 39, 40, 87, 88–98, 122, 127, 128, 129, 133, 134, 140–141, 146, 149, 150, 151–152, 154, 167, 170, 173, 177, 187, 188, 194–197, 226, 235, 256n, 257n
Herbert, Frank 66

"History of Tomorrow" (Campbell) 95–98
Hubble, Edwin 7, 50–51
hydroponics 131–132

"If This Goes On" (Heinlein) 97
Independence Day (film) 240
"Interstellar Flight" (Shepherd) 3, 126–130, 132–133

King, Stephen 202

Landon, Brooks 42–43
Langford, David 196
Last and First Men (Stapledon) 256n
Learning the World (MacLeod) 2, 4, 243–246
"Let There Be Light" (Heinlein) 96–97, 142
Ley, Willy 30, 39, 121–125, 130, 142, 144, 146
"Life-Line" (Heinlein) 96–97
"The Living Galaxy" (Manning) 3, 11, 46–55, 59, 79, 82, 99, 133, 243–245, 256n
Locus magazine 92, 255n
Lovecraft, H.P. 9, 51, 98
Lowndes, Robert A.W. 255n
Luckhurst, Roger 156
"Lungfish" (Brunner) 3, 157–164, 169, 202, 217, 231, 257n
Lysenko, Trofim Denisovich 253–254n

MacLeod, Ken 2, 4
The Magazine of Fantasy and Science Fiction 124, 150, 151
The Man in the High Castle (Dick) 216
"The Man Who Sold the Moon" (Heinlein) 93, 102, 149
Manning, Laurence 2–3, 11, 46, 59, 79, 127, 129, 222, 235
Marooned in Realtime (Vinge) 199
Mayflower II (Baxter) 243
Metamorphosis Alpha (Ward) 3, 191
"Miami 2017 (Seen the Lights Go Out on Broadway)" (Joel) 258–259n
The Moon Is a Harsh Mistress (Heinlein) 195
Moorcock, Michael 153–157, 180, 188

Neuromancer (Gibson) 198, 200
New Worlds 153–157, 164
Nicholls, Peter 2, 162
Non-Stop (Aldiss) 2–3, 14, 170–181, 182, 202, 214, 217, 225, 257n

Oberth, Hermann 24, 28–29, 121
"The Oceans Are Wide" (Robinson) 3, 40, 134–140, 142, 146, 152, 158, 162, 169,

204, 206, 209–211, 214, 217, 226, 232, 256n
Old Twentieth (Haldeman) 243
Oliver, Chad 3, 180, 188, 226, 235
"On the Electrodynamics of Moving Bodies" (Einstein) 6

Pale Blue Dot (Sagan) 1, 253n, 254n
Palmer, Christopher 14–18, 255n
Palmer, Raymond A. 55, 67, 69–72, 133
The Peace War (Vinge) 199
The Peacemaker (film) 237, 258n
Pendray, G. Edward 121, 122
Person, Lawrence 227
Phoenix Without Ashes (Ellison and Bryant) 191
Poe, Edgar Allan 41

Ralph 124C 41+ (Gernsback) 41, 48, 86, 254n
Rambo III (film) 237
Rendezvous with Rama (Clarke) 3, 188–190
"Rescue Party" (Clarke) 3, 125–126, 232
Return to the Whorl (Wolfe) 3
"The Roads Must Roll" (Heinlein) 93, 96, 102, 142, 162, 216, 218
Robinson, Frank M. 2–3, 40, 150, 160, 235
Robinson, Kim Stanley 200–201
Rocket Ship Galileo (Heinlein) 151
Rockets: The Future of Travel Beyond the Stratosphere (Ley) 121
Roddenberry, Gene 31
Ross, Andrew 44–45
Russo, Richard Paul 2

Sagan, Carl 1, 144
Science Fiction Plus 126–127, 130, 134
Science Stories 133–134
September 11 237–238, 239–242
Sheffield, Charles 6, 9–11
Shepherd, Leslie R. 3
Ship of Fools (Russo) 2, 243
Simak, Clifford D. 3, 87, 133, 134, 150, 188, 235
Sleight, Graham 92
Space Ark (Hubschman) 201
The Space-Born (Tubb) 152
"Spacebred Generations" (Simak) 3, 130–132, 142, 161, 162, 163, 213, 217, 256n, 257n
Spacefaring: the Human Dimension (Harrison) 12
spaceship Earth concept 181
Sputnik 3, 39, 143–150, 152, 157, 164, 195, 197
Stapledon, Olaf 79, 153

The Star Seekers (Lesser) 152
The Starlost (Ellison) 3, 190–191
Sterling, Bruce 3, 191, 193, 197–199, 200
Stranger in a Strange Land (Heinlein) 195–196
Sturgeon, Theodore 88

Taklamakan (Sterling) 3, 211–220
Tau Zero (Anderson) 3, 188–189
Teller, Edward 253n
Terminator movies (Cameron) 192–194
"Thirteen to Centaurus" (Ballard) 2–3, 181–186, 202, 217, 231
Tiresias 36–37
True Lies (film) 237
True Names (Vinge) 191, 199
Tsiolkovsky, Konstantin 2, 4, 11, 14, 19, 23–30, 32–33, 35–38, 40, 44–45, 47, 52, 54, 127, 128, 132, 160, 190, 234, 247, 253n
"Twilight" (Campbell) 84–86, 156, 239, 256n

"Universe" (Heinlein) 2–3, 12, 14–15, 40, 94, 98–119, 131, 142, 152, 161, 162, 163, 213, 225, 255n, 256n

Verne, Jules 21, 24–25, 41, 153
Vinge, Vernor 1, 199–200, 203, 257–258n
Von Braun, Wernher 28, 30, 39, 121–125, 130, 142, 144, 146, 180, 183
"The Voyage That Lasted 600 Years" (Wilcox) 3, 11, 14, 55–76, 79, 99, 133, 157, 161, 187, 217, 256n

Ward, James M. 3
Wargames (film) 196
Wells, H.G. 21, 41, 62, 153, 155, 256n
Westfahl, Gary 77, 255n
White, Hayden 68
Wilcox, Don 2–3, 11, 14, 55, 107, 127, 128, 129, 134, 150, 160
"The Wind Blows Free" (Oliver) 3, 164–170, 179, 202, 213, 214, 224, 225, 232, 257n
Wolfe, Gary K. 94, 259n
Wolfe, Gene 3, 96, 227–228
Wollheim, Donald 40, 78, 87, 126, 151–152
Wonder Stories 46, 55, 77, 81, 83, 86, 121, 222
The World, the Flesh, and the Devil (Bernal) 11, 19, 32–36, 46, 54
Wright, Peter 220, 229–230

Ziff, William B. 82, 145
Zubrin, Robert 9

www.ingramcontent.com/pod-product-compliance
Ingram Content Group UK Ltd.
Pitfield, Milton Keynes, MK11 3LW, UK
UKHW041931140426
5217IPUK00014B/426